Se

MW00881067

Joe Nobody
&
P.A. Troit

Copyright © 2014

Kemah Bay Marketing, LLC

All rights reserved.

Edited by:
E. T. Ivester
D. Allen

www.joenobodybooks.com

Other Books by Joe Nobody:

Holding Your Ground: Preparing for Defense if it All Falls Apart
The TEOTWAWKI Tuxedo: Formal Survival Attire
Without Rule of Law: Advanced Skills to Help You Survive
Holding Their Own: A Story of Survival
Holding Their Own II: The Independents
Holding Their Own III: Pedestals of Ash
Holding Their Own IV: The Ascent
Holding Their Own V: The Alpha Chronicles
Holding Their Own VI: Bishop's Song
Holding Their Own VII: Phoenix Star
The Home Schooled Shootist: Training to Fight with a Carbine
Apocalypse Drift
The Little River Otter
The Olympus Device: Book One
The Olympus Device: Book Two

Forward from Joe Nobody

I am a man with simple needs and a simple life. I write a lot, shoot a little, and devote a respectable amount of time to research.

Every once in a while, something unusual crosses my desk that changes my daily priorities. This past summer, a close friend demanded I read P.A. Troit's manuscript, and I was instantly motivated to work with her on this project.

Aside from a similar writing style, I felt a kindred spirit in the message and delivery of *Secession.*
Patricia and I soon became friends, her strong commitment to professionalism and tireless work ethic making the project enjoyable.

We discovered that both of us shared a core belief that none of the answers we seek as a nation are as simple as pure conservative versus liberal "solutions." Life, liberty, and the pursuit of happiness can never be defined in a single dimension. It is our hope that this work respects our complexity and differences as a people. For readers who may expect a rant justifying a hard-right political perspective, *Secession* isn't it. The same can be said for those of a more progressive nature – you won't find this work a testament to pure left-wing politics.

The weapons, tactics, and capabilities described in this work are real. They exist today, and are commercially available. We changed some product names so as not to infringe.

Formulas and designs of explosive materials and incendiary devices were modified or left intentionally vague. The authors have no wish to promote illegal activities or contribute to delinquency.

The economic statements, figures, and estimates stated herein are accurate to the best of our ability. It is impossible to be 100% precise, given that different sources often tout conflicting numbers. We exercised reasonable diligence to base this tale on real-world facts and certain historical events.

And finally, while we were wrapping up the editorial process, Scotland held its historic vote on whether or not to separate from the United Kingdom. While *Secession* was essentially a completed work before that referendum, we couldn't help but reopen the manuscript and apply a few perspectives garnered from that event. I believe that additional insight gives the story even more credibility.

Enjoy,

Joe

Chapter 1 – The Brewing Storm

One quick glance was all Zach needed to understand why everybody called the man "Tusk." Local gossip alleged the contorted ridge expanding one side of the fellow's forehead was the result of an adolescent brawl. Other lore attributed the sharp, prominent crest of bone to a direct lineage from Satan. While it was doubtful anyone had broached the subject with him directly, discreet whispers around town speculated that he might be an evolutionary anomaly, the "missing link" between humankind and the underworld.

No way this guy is a candidate for the Mount Rushmore of Criminal Masterminds, the Texas Ranger thought. *What an ugly dude.*

Evidently, Tusk was proud of his malformation. A charcoal black tattoo had been applied to accent the protrusion, highlighting the irregularity's depth and ferocity. Similar ink also adorned the opposite side of the man's skull, a low-rent attempt to construct a pair of devilish horns either as a psychological advantage against his foes... or a year-round Halloween costume. Zach assumed the former.

Despite his reputation of being a first-class badass, Zach noticed the fugitive's hand was shaking, the barrel of his pistol trembling against the woman's temple. *He's scared*; the lawman observed. *Good. He should be.*

"Put the weapon down, and let her go," Zach said firmly. "You know how this is going to end."

"Fuck you!" came the reply. "Put *your* gun down, and I might not kill both of you."

Tusk was sweating, the layer of perspiration making the cranial distortion even more apparent. His hostage was glistening as well; her wide eyes scanning right and left in panic, her open mouth inhaling small, desperate puffs of breath.

Zach didn't know the woman's name. Clearly, she was Latino, and most likely a prostitute working one of the small, home-based bars that dotted the border slums of El Paso. The colonias were known as a place where a man could purchase cheap tequila and even cheaper female companionship. Questions were rarely asked, even if things got a little out of hand. *She has no idea how rough things were going to get once he was done with her*, Zach mused.

He'd gotten word of Tusk's crossing over from Mexico last night. An informant's message indicated the Gulf Cartel had lost the latest turf skirmish, the organization's foot soldiers retreating to the safety of the United States to regroup, liquor-up their courage, and perhaps entertain a señorita or two.

Tusk's real name was Antonio Luis Chavez, a nefarious individual who neither country claimed as an upstanding member of its citizenry. Zach's interest in the man stemmed from a bank robbery four weeks ago in Van Horn, two of the financial institution's employees shot execution-style during the heist.

Enjoying quite the reputation as a cartel enforcer, Tusk's claim to fame was his sickening expertise with a machete. The New Mexico authorities had encountered a mélange of hacked-up bodies over the last five years. Most witnesses credited the carnage to a deranged, semi-mystical figure rumored to be part diablo, part man - Tusk.

A stolen pickup, a missing bargirl, and a rancher's report of some asshole crashing through his fences led Zach to a 20-year old, dilapidated house trailer outside Study Butte. Tusk was alert, ferretted inside the modular home, hiding behind the topless woman, using her body as a shield.

"Put it down, or she dies," Tusk reminded his nemesis. "Do it now!"

"I'm going to give you to the count of three to let the woman go and drop that cap gun, Tusk," Zach replied coldly. "If ya don't, I'm going to de-horn that thick skull of yours with 230 grains of lead."

"One," the ranger muttered, his eye calculating how much of Tusk's face was visible behind the hostage's disheveled hair.

"Two," he continued, deciding he didn't have enough margin.

The ranger started tapping his toe, the steady rhythm causing Tusk to raise his head just slightly for a look, exposing a bit more of himself over the terrified woman's shoulder. *This is going to be close*, the Texan judged.

The lawman thought about giving the third count but decided against it. *He probably can't count anyway*, he decided, squeezing the trigger. The .45 ACP roared like a thunderbolt inside the confined space. Tusk's head jerked backwards, his body following suit, the gun wavering around his hostage's temple.

Before the spent brass hit the floor, the ranger re-centered the front post, and fired again.

Both woman and thug went down, Zach stepping closer as they fell. The ranger's eyes remained fixated on Tusk's pistol hand, which he found empty. A swift scrape of his boot sent the criminal's weapon scooting across the linoleum floor.

A glance at Tusk's skull left no doubt the county just incurred a $300 burial fee for the cartel henchman. "Ladies and gentlemen, our tax dollars at work," the lawman grumbled. A moan from the hostage drew his attention to the prone woman, a stream of blood curving down her exposed shoulder and chest.

"Damn," Zach whispered, eyeing the bullet wound just above her collarbone. "That *was* a little tight."

He examined her injury closely, quickly determining she'd live. His first shot had carved a trench through the flesh on her shoulder, the bullet missing the carotid artery by less than an inch. When the damage mended, she'd sport a ropey-looking scar to show her gentlemen's club patrons, but apparently suffered no other long-term, physical consequences.

He spotted her thin, cotton camisole next to the bed. Folding it over a few times, he pushed the square of material against the wound. It took a few moments before the woman's shock subsided and she could manage the dressing on her own. "Press," Zach repeatedly reminded her, "Press hard."

The town of Study Butte, Texas didn't house a hospital or clinic. Five minutes away, there was a 4-star resort in Terlingua, offering a variety of services and entertainment from its "pamper yourself silly" spa treatments or Texas-sized golf course, to the horseback mesa tours or Old West shootout town. But he doubted there was a physician on staff, and a masseuse just wasn't going to cut it. Alpine, just over an hour north, was the surest bet for the kind of medical care she required.

At his insistence, the rescued hostage attempted to stand. Between the shock of the encounter and her loss of blood, Zach ruled her legs too unsteady to reliably support her own weight, much less shuffle to his pickup. After wrapping her in a sheet from the bed, he scooped her up and headed for his truck. He'd call the Brewster County Sheriff's office as soon as his cell phone registered a signal, probably 40 miles closer to Alpine.

After placing the victim in the backseat of the crew cab, Zach opened a bottle of water and handed it to the wide-eyed woman. He tried to explain to her in broken Spanish that she wasn't being kidnapped or arrested, but doubted the message got through.

He flashed his badge and credentials, hoping to settle down the skittish señorita, but the act had the opposite effect on her demeanor. With an expression of pure terror, she stared at the silver star in his hand, her mouth rattling off a stream of words, a tear rolling down her cheek as she begged for mercy.

"I'm not here to deport you," Zach replied in perfect textbook Spanish... but the ranger's assurances didn't seem to comfort the girl at all. Zach's metered, conversational tone was no match for the fast-forward rambling of the native speaker. It was times like this when he wished he had paid a little more attention to his Spanish professor instead of flirting so much with that Chi Omega hottie. Still more fluid than most, his command of the Spanish language was no match for the speed of the Latina's rant.

"Oh, for gawd's sake, chill out," he snarled, exasperated at the failed attempt to communicate thus far. The victim paused, taking in his words as she took in air.

He pivoted, intending to minimally process the crime scene before transporting the victim to the emergency room. In a flash, the girl bolted in hope of escape. Zach barely caught her wrist as she made a last ditch effort at freedom. Concerned for the former hostage's injury, the lawman took more than a couple of minutes to contain the thrashing ball of flailing arms and kicking legs back inside the truck.

Words, English or Spanish, seemed to have no lasting impact on her desperation. Sighing, he finally handcuffed her to the door.

Zach straightened his hat and reentered the trailer, still mumbling about her reaction. "I should have anticipated that," he whispered, "but it never ceases to amaze me. She didn't struggle very hard when Tusk was about to blow her head off… but the thought of deportation… that's enough to turn her into a wildcat."

His first act after surveying the crime scene was to snap a few pictures with his cell phone. He had a much better camera out in the pickup, but it wasn't warranted here. Besides, he had a problem handcuffed to his truck, and high definition pictures might further complicate his current situation.

Mentally rehashing the morning's drama, Zach envisioned some "Oilcan Harry" attorney getting a hold of the woman and making a federal issue over his bullet's grazing wound. He'd run into some real scumbags before, many of the so-called lawyers worse than the criminals he encountered. "So much for my promising career in law enforcement," the ranger scowled.

Zach realized that these ambulance chasers frequently represented lobbyist organizations in East Texas. Immigration reform was an up and coming political darling there, the Latino communities hiring the greasiest of attorneys they could manage. Given the Texas Rangers' history of accumulating Mexican blood on their boots, lawmen like Zach were prime targets for those seeking to make a name for themselves in both Austin and Washington. *"Wonder if they are still looking for a security guard at the apartment complex,"* he thought. *"At least I would get to drive one of those little golf carts. Maybe I could negotiate for priority parking."*

A whirlwind of negative thoughts continued to spin through Zach's brain. Could his career survive the media circus of a lawsuit? How would he repay the $25,000 he owed in student loans if he were not gainfully employed? But then, an idea occurred to Zach, a small indiscretion that might make life simpler. Leaning over to retrieve Tusk's pistol, he hefted the revolver while recreating the encounter in his mind.

Finally coming to a decision, he carefully dipped the barrel in the woman's blood and fired the old .38 Special at just the right angle. If anybody made a fuss, it would appear that the criminal's shot had injured the hostage - not his. *After all,* he rationed, *my life shouldn't become more complicated when I am the white hat.*

Zach turned to leave when the green and white logo emblazoned across a gym bag on a nearby table commanded his attention. The emblem on the outside proudly read, "The Jets," and Zach recognized the design sported by the New York football team. Zach hesitated for a moment, considering the small number of folks he knew who cheered for out of state teams – something certainly not commonplace in remote West Texas. Electing to investigate further, he tugged the zipper to see what might be inside. Halfway expecting to be greeted with sweat laden gym shorts and rancid athletic socks, he was only mildly surprised to discover a bag filled with Franklins – somewhere between twenty and thirty thousand dollars in hundred dollar bills secured in rubber banded bundles.

"Tusk, you old devil, you were planning on some serious partying, my man. Even an ugly fuck like you can arrange a good time with that much cash," the ranger commented to the dead man at his feet.

A hint of white in the sea of green drew Zach's attention. Being careful not to leave any prints on the bag or money, he gingerly fished out a piece of copy paper, complete with a photograph.

Zach inhaled sharply when he flipped the sheet over. The image confronting the ranger was that of his superior, Major Alcorn, the man in charge of Company E.

"The boss isn't going to like this," Zach whispered to the carcass lying next to his boot. "But then again, what man *would* appreciate having a contract out on his life?"

Five minutes later, after snapping a few more pictures of Tusk's body, Ranger Bass was leaving a trail of dust in the air as his truck sped north.

After driving 30 minutes across featureless desert and then through the northwest corner of Big Bend National Park, Zach had to slow for the Border Patrol Inspection Station on Highway 118.

The change in the truck's momentum prompted the woman to glance up. When she spied the familiar green and white color scheme of several parked official vehicles, she nearly stroked out. Zach ignored her desperate pleas and whines, flashing his badge to the bored agents manning the remote outpost and then passing through.

The traveler in the backseat calmed instantly, now studying Zachariah with a shrewd expression.

Movement in the rear of the crew cab caught Zach's attention in the mirror. His passenger had removed the bed sheet, exposing her breasts. She had also shimmied out of her already skimpy skirt, baring her lower body. Realizing she had his attention, she seductively caressed her thighs beginning just above her knees and ending at her bikini line. Her smile was suggestive as she gestured toward her panties. A clear outline of her lady-charms was visible through the thin material, her intent even clearer.

Zach almost broke out laughing, the woman's underwear printed with a confetti background decorated with several strategically placed, brightly hued balloons. "No doubt there's a party going on down there," he chuckled under his breath.

The prisoner mistook his reaction. "The hombre won't be disappointed in my skills," she said in a sultry string of broken English. "I understand what is expected for taking me past the green men (Border Patrol). I know how to express my gratitude... especially for such a strong, handsome gringo."

"Save it, cupcake, not interested," Zach responded. "You want to express your gratitude? Then tell the truth about what happened back at the trailer."

She stuck out her bottom lip in a pout and then covered herself with the bed linen.

Twenty minutes later, the ranger picked up his smart phone and confirmed he had signal.

He dialed the Brewster County Sheriff's office, advised them of his estimated arrival, and asked the dispatcher to give the local hospital warning that he was inbound with a gunshot victim. "She's not critical," he informed the woman on the other end. "As a matter of fact, I thought that skinny gal was going to kick my ass for a minute back there. We had a failure to communicate."

"So you think I should let Barb know to expect a walking freebie?"

Zach understood the inquiry and its implication. The local clinics and hospitals along the border were inundated with undocumented patients, most without insurance or money. Yet, the law said they couldn't turn anyone away. For a small town operation, like the one in Alpine, it was a crushing rock pushing them against an unmoving, hard place. And the rock kept getting bigger.

"The state might pick this one up; I'm not sure. She's a material witness and a victim as well. Hell, the feds might even want to talk to her given the company she was keeping."

As soon as he disconnected that call, his next priority was to update his superior, Major Alcorn. "Sir, the suspect was somewhat less than cooperative with the investigation," the ranger began. A response buzzed in his ear, his boss demanding clarification. "Well, sir, as it turns out, Tusk is dead. He's nearly decapitated, lying in a house trailer just off Highway 170, two miles east of Study Butte. I have the GPS coordinates."

"He committed suicide, Zach?"

Ranger Bass knew what his boss was implying, and it had nothing to do with Tusk ending his own life. Within Company E, headquartered in El Paso, pointing a firearm at a ranger was considered "suicidal."

"Yes, sir."

"Witnesses?"

"Yes, sir, an unknown Latino female who was also wounded in the exchange - not critically though. I was unable to communicate my intent because of the language barrier, so she is handcuffed in my backseat. I'm driving her into Alpine for medical treatment. And sir, there is something else I think you should know. I found a gym bag stuffed full of cash... and your picture was inside with the money."

"Really? That's odd. I'm not sure what to make of that," Alcorn replied, his tone carrying more puzzlement than concern.

"My read is that the cartel may have put a price on your head, sir. I think Tusk received his down payment, and then probably visited our area, planning to look you up as soon as he had satisfied his needs."

"Interesting theory," the lawman's supervisor answered, seemingly dismissing Zach's hypothesis. "So, how far out are you, Bass?"

"Less than 30 minutes, sir," Zach replied, wondering why his location and estimated time of arrival took precedence over an apparent contract killer.

"I see," Alcorn responded flatly. There was a long pause, the major apparently considering his options. Finally, "I've had another assignment come up, and I'm going to give it to you. I'm afraid it can't wait until you've completed your paperwork on this cartel enforcer," the supervisor explained, hesitating to switch gears and gather his thoughts. "I'm sure you have been watching this storm in the Gulf and probably know that this hurricane is kicking our Louisiana neighbors' butts. Now that the levees in New Orleans have been breached and most of the city is under water, they've been bussing thousands of survivors into Houston. Bottom line... Company A is overwhelmed and undermanned. It seems our friends over in the Crescent City are gifting us their prisoners... cleaning out their jails and shipping their felons over here. The governor has ordered all of our units to send supplemental manpower to shore up our efforts. I'm sending you to visit H-Town."

Damn it, Zach promptly thought, but he said nothing. "Yes, sir. When and where do I report?"

As his boss detailed the contact information, Zach barely managed to keep his disappointment in check. He was pulling into the Alpine hospital by the time the call ended.

Jane Doe-Garcia walked into the emergency area, her bloody shoulder and sheet-blanket advancing her position forward as a triage priority. After watching her being shown to an examination room, Zach turned to find a Department of Public Safety uniformed officer standing behind him.

"Hey, Hinton, what's up?" Zach greeted.

"You suck, Ranger Bass," the officer grinned. "That's what's up. I just got a call to show up here and take over this case for your sorry, privileged ass."

"Ahhh," the ranger replied sarcastically, "I'm so sorry you have to do a little work for a change, Trooper Hinton."

The two lawman strolled outside, Hinton more curious than angry. "So what gives, Zach? I know you ranger-types are all-important, all-busy keepers of the peace, but this is the first time I've ever been asked to clean up behind one of your cases."

"Sorry, Hinton. Not my doing, I swear. There's some emergency down in Houston, and Austin has issued orders. Believe me; the last place in the world I want to be is back east."

Hinton nodded, understanding his co-worker's position thoroughly. "Back east" meant population density, oversized, bureaucratic police departments, and morally-challenged defense attorneys. It was an entirely different world to an officer of the law.

Zach handed the money over to the state trooper and then made sure the wounded woman hadn't left anything in the back seat of his truck.

Peering inside the gym bag, Hinton let out a whistle, "Damn, that's a lot of cash, even for one of the cartel guys. You would have thought he could have afforded a little higher class female companionship with this much moola."

Zach shrugged, "No kidding. Did you notice that little 'Kodak moment' inside? I talked to the old man. Told him about the cash and the picture. I hope he watches his backside. He's pissed somebody off – real good."

"That tough, old bird? Alcorn?" the trooper replied, shaking his head. "They better send somebody a little more skilled if they want to take down that decrepit bastard."

"I wish I could hang around and see the fireworks, but I've got to head east. Make sure the boss takes care of himself, would you, Hinton?"

"Will do. Sorry you've got to take a bite of the shit sandwich, Zach... especially after a nice takedown like this one. Give the boys back in Houston my regrets."

Zach knew exactly what was meant. The ranger's role in Texas law enforcement had transitioned over the years. The small group of men sworn into the organization now numbered fewer than 200 individuals. Long gone were the days when the agency was the forefront of peacekeeping, at times more closely resembling a paramilitary organization than a group of policemen.

In modern times, the rangers were called upon to supplement local, rural law enforcement, and they utilized their scientific skills more than their firearms. Forensics, cyber investigations, audit, and financial examinations dominated the caseload.

Only in West Texas was there still a high demand for rugged, sturdy men who used their weapons more than their keyboards. And that legacy was being eroded over time. The gentlemen back in Houston were little more than forensic Boy Fridays, at the beck and call of the city's cops or working unwanted cases from the surrounding counties.

When Zach had been accepted into the ranks a few years prior, he'd been thrilled with his assignment to Company E out of El Paso. Even as a newcomer, he understood the nuances. Back east, different rules, complex roles, tainted scrutiny, and unclear boundaries overrode what he believed was real, authentic, community service.

The rangers were still on the frontline of justice in West Texas, and that suited Zachariah Bass just fine.

"Dad's in trouble, and we have to go," Charlie declared.

Abe didn't meet his brother's gaze, instead choosing to keep his eyes on the unfathonable news video streaming from New Orleans. "You're right, of course. We have to pull the old man out. I wish he'd listened to us and evacuated before the storm hit."

Charlie waved him off, "You know that stubborn old goat won't leave his house. Hell, it's like pulling wisdom teeth just to get him to come to holiday celebrations and graduations. No way is a little, old hurricane going to make him retreat."

The television flashed to images of a submerged stop sign, only the top few inches of the white letters visible above the muddy waters. "Yeah, a hurricane might not do it, but I bet a flood will. That doesn't look good, brother."

"I'll hook my bass boat up to the 4-wheel drive. We can be down there in six hours... maybe seven if the cops have the main roads blocked," Charlie replied.

The older brother didn't respond for a minute, the parade of rain-swollen landscapes governing the TV coverage now usurped by the first reports of gunfire, looting, and vandalism coming out of the Crescent City.

Abe ruminated over his brother's estimated travel schedule. The hurricane had weakened by the time it had reached their northeastern Louisiana homes, the electricity only out for a few hours after the worst of the storm had passed. For once, he was glad to be living away from the coast.

"We'll have to deal with *that*," Abe said, nodding toward a still image of a young man exiting a jewelry store, heavy-duty shotgun in one hand, a fistful of gold chains dangling from the other.

Charlie's words projected bravado, but his tone carried doubt. "Dad's got his duck guns. He can take care of himself."

"Maybe. And he can go upstairs to escape the rising flood. But he's not going to last long up there without food and water. We better get packing."

Charlie was on his feet and moving for the back door. "We're going to need extra gas, flashlights, some emergency food, and water. I can do all that if you can pack the guns and bring along some cash."

"Cash?"

"We might need to bribe our way in, or buy something along the way. Hell, I don't know.... Isn't cash always king?"

Abe nodded, shooing his brother out the door. "I guess. I'll pull together some supplies while you get the truck ready. Then I'll come over in a bit and help you hook up the boat."

Abe flipped off the television, his own personal hurricane of thought whirling through his brain. In his mind-storm, the logistics of the rescue was like the wind, changing direction and speed at a moment's notice. The risk associated with entering an area already experiencing violence was as steady as the rain. He snickered when he realized that the storm surge, always the most dangerous part, was going to be explaining the plan to his wife.

He found Kara in the living room, calculator, bank statements, and the checkbook scattered across her lap and the coffee table. "Any word on your father?" she asked, peering up with concerned eyes.

"No, not specifically. But things have deteriorated badly. The levees have breached, and the city is flooding. Charlie and I are going to drive down and pull dad out."

"You're what? No, you're not...," Kara stopped mid-sentence, desperately not wanting to come across like the stereotypical nagging, demanding mate. Perhaps a more tempered response would be met with less resistance. "What I mean is... Abe, that sounds like a dangerous idea," she continued, more carefully choosing her words. "Besides, aren't the authorities already responding? Won't the police and fire departments be better equipped to rescue people?"

My beautiful, sweet Kara, Abe thought. *Your vision of the world is so naïve... so orderly and proper. I dread the day when reality strikes close to home.*

"The squall has caused more damage than was expected, and it looks like the emergency responders are completely overwhelmed. The streets are choked with rushing floodwaters; one report claiming it was over 10 feet deep in spots. Electrical power is out all over the city, no fresh drinking water and no working phone system either."

"When was the last time you talked to Edward? Is his cell working at all? How do you know that you can get to him anyway?" Kara fired the questions in rapid succession as her mind grasped the apparent seriousness of the situation, the escalating apprehension apparent in her voice.

"We haven't been able to get dad on the phone all day. Charlie and I are just going to drive as far as the road will take us safely, then launch his little boat and go get dad. We'll be back in a day or two, three at the outside."

Kara stood, concern etched across her face. "You know how the media is. Maybe the news crews are making more of this storm than it really is. And even if the reports are accurate, surely the federal government is sending in massive amounts of assistance," she stated. "Those TV crews are always out for the ratings instead of the truth. And if the situation truly is catastrophic, I doubt Uncle Sam needs your help. What makes you think this risk is necessary?" his mate queried, hoping more than believing that the situation had been blown out of proportion.

"You have had your nose in those bank statements for way too long, sweetie. Why don't you put your work aside and watch cable news for a few minutes while I gather my things? Just five minutes ago, the screen was inundated with footage of families scampering onto their rooftops to evade the storm waters. It was surreal… as if the ocean were reclaiming the city. Check it out, honey. If you still feel like Charlie and I are misreading the situation, then we can talk about it some more, but from what I saw, he and I need to get to New Orleans right away."

Kara nodded, rising from the couch and padding toward the den.

Abe watched her go, shaking his head after she'd rounded the corner. They'd had this conversation so many times; he should have anticipated her reaction.

The first time had been just over a year after they had been married. Their household income had finally reached a level that enabled the purchase of a modest first home.

Unshackled by the space constraints associated with their initial tiny apartment, Abe had arrived at the new hacienda with a pickup bed full of personal effects he'd kept stored in his parents' basement. A stuffed and mounted shark, three hunting rifles, and a .45 caliber pistol were among the treasures retrieved.

"I didn't realize you owned a handgun," Kara had commented. "I knew you liked to hunt now and then, but why do you need a pistol?"

"Home protection," came the response. "Dad always had one in the nightstand drawer, just in case. I kind of like being able to defend my castle."

The young Mrs. Hendricks reacted with crossed arms and a tilted head. "Doesn't our tax money pay for police protection? We don't exactly live on the brink of civilization here in suburbia, ya know?" she continued, barely pausing to take a breath in the middle of her outburst. "I am sure we have 9-1-1 services in our neighborhood. I do *not* see the need for a gun."

And her position had never shifted.

Their marriage endured because of love, mutual respect, and great sex. They preferred the same food, wine, vacations, and music – but political bliss was never a resident in the Hendricks's household. Kara was on the left; Abe on the right, and it was never going to change. Both realized the subject was best left unmentioned and almost always kept their opinions private. Almost.

Both of them soon realized that domestic happiness far outweighed political perspective. Love conquered all as the Hendricks's marriage matured.

Abe unlocked his gun safe, choosing his lightest Remington 700 hunting rifle as well as a Mossberg 12-gauge pump. He grabbed a few boxes of shells for each and stuffed the weapons and ammo into a couple of cases.

He then selected two handguns from the safe's upper compartment, choosing a bullnose .357 Magnum revolver and a 1911 model .45 ACP. Two boxes of shells for each weapon were stashed into the small range bag lying nearby.

He located the flashlights in the kitchen drawer, quickly replacing the batteries in each – just to be safe.

Ten minutes later, he'd pulled $1,000 in cash from his underwear drawer, tossed three days' worth of clothes into a gym bag, and laced up his best hunting boots.

Kara met him at their bedroom door, a look of dread on her face, the manifestation of fear apparent in her voice. She pulled him close in a tight embrace, an attempt to refocus his attention and consider her verbal appeal. "I know it's not my father over there... but I really, really don't want you to go. I don't mean to sound cruel... I just think this is a crazy idea. It looks like a warzone from what I saw on the news."

"That's why I want to get my father out of there," he replied sternly. "Charlie and I know every inch of that town. We grew up fishing and hunting on those bayous and channels. We'll be fine."

"Please let the authorities handle this. I can't shake this terrible feeling about your going on this trip."

"I have to go, Kara. I can't leave my father alone in that mess. I'd feel the same way if it were your parents. It's part of why I am who I am…. Family means everything to me."

She didn't mount any additional protest, choosing instead to withdraw from an argument she had no hope of winning. "Be careful. Call me as soon as you can, and remember that I love you," her only parting words as she spun away from him in an attempt to conceal the single, hot tear streaming down her cheek.

Abe watched her return to the living room, wishing he could make her understand. Moments later, he was out the door, lugging his gear and wondering how they would make peace when he returned.

Zach hastily secured a bath towel around his waist, pat-dried his hair and headed toward the bedroom. In a single motion, he tossed some clothes into the open backpack on his bed and turned toward the kitchen. *Better grab a bite here. Probably no jambalaya or red beans and rice on this trip,* he mused. As he pulled open the refrigerator door, he scooted the tub of furry strawberries out of the way and examined the remnants of the leftover cold cuts. Quickly sniffing the meat to verify its lack of toxicity, he assembled a sandwich and swallowed it while he cleaned his sidearm. Packing a little emergency cash out of the gun safe rounded out his pre-travel preparations. He was on the road to Houston less than two hours after receiving the new assignment.

Seven hours later, he reported into the local ranger company's headquarters. Road tired and truck-stiff, his attitude was further depleted by discovering what could only be described as absolute bedlam.

Officers, civilian employees, federal agents, and even the cleaning crew were running around as if their heads were on fire, and their asses were catching. The receptionist couldn't find the local major or either of his subordinate captains. Sensing her overwhelming anxiety, Zach leaned over the counter and flashed a charming smile that the older woman could not resist. Double-checking her records, she informed the Texan that she had no advance notice of his arrival or orders for him to execute. No temporary housing was available, hurricane evacuees occupying every available hotel room for over 200 miles. It seemed Zach would never advance past the gatekeeper.

After an hour of waiting, asking, calling, and generally building a mountain of internal frustration, Zach finally recognized a familiar face.

Ranger Putnam had visited West Texas not a month before, enlisting the native company's help to run down a suspected real estate scam artist who was hiding in a remote cabin in the Davis Mountains. The criminal had brought along two AK47s and 5,000 rounds of ammo for companionship.

Putnam looked up as he scrambled past, pausing for just a moment to shake Zach's hand. "What brings you out to our neck of the woods, Ranger?"

When Zach explained his predicament, Putnam waved him past the reception area and into the inner workings of the Houston-based Company.

"Everybody's down at the Astrodome," Putnam explained. "One of the local Houston detectives recognized a convicted pedophile he'd put away just last year. The guy had been extradited to New Orleans and was standing trial in Louisiana for a molestation charge. All of a sudden, this pervert is sauntering off an evacuation bus – right here in our peaceful city. It set off the alarm bells."

"Was it an isolated incident?"

"No, unfortunately not," Putnam replied, shaking his head in disgust. "From what we're hearing, most of the city and parish lock-ups over there were either intentionally emptied out or opened automatically when the power went down and the backups failed. We started running background checks on the new arrivals, and so far, we've found hundreds of people who should be guests of the state. The problem is we can only check the incoming that still possess identification. There's a horde of those refugees who barely got out with the shirts on their backs - no ID, no papers, just their names and addresses. I don't mean to sound cynical, but we both know how easy it would be to tell the smiling volunteer at the registration desk a story of lost ID. Even the dumbest crooks could lie their way through that checkpoint and onto our streets."

Zach nodded, understanding the predicament. "So what can I do to help?"

Putnam's face painted with an expression the younger ranger had grown to hate. It was a snide grin, always a harbinger of the new guy receiving bad news. "You, Ranger Bass, are slated to become a diplomat for the great State of Texas. Scuttlebutt has it that you're going to New Orleans to deliver a message from the governor. 'Stop sending us your felons, and give us the return address so we can ship back the ones who are already here.'"

"I wonder if the FBI is still hiring," mumbled Zach.

Chapter 2 – Like Father, Like Son

Abe and Charlie's drive through Louisiana was like a scene out of a disaster movie. The effects of the storm grew more evident as they approached the southern portion of the state – downed trees, standing water, and thousands upon thousands of cars streaming in the opposite direction.

They ventured off the main highway, choosing instead to travel surface roads as they zigzagged closer to New Orleans. Fifty miles north of Lake Pontchartrain, evidence of Katrina's wrath began dictating the passing landscape.

The sparse foliage left standing was completely stripped of all greenery, leaving odd forests of utility poles. More than once, they had utilized the road clearance of Charlie's massive truck, pushing their way through high water, flowing tributaries of mud, and downed power lines.

Even the remote, secondary traffic arteries were busy with refugees heading north. Every gas station's lot was jammed with motorists waiting in line, praying the electricity would come on soon so they could pump fuel into their empty tanks.

When the rescuers finally did stop to refill the truck, Abe made sure Charlie pulled off the road in a relatively hidden spot, worried their cache of fuel cans lining the bed would make them a target. The faces they saw troubled them, portraits of desperation and despair in every car and window. He stood guard with the 30-06 while his brother emptied three five-gallon cans into the thirsty pickup's fill.

Four times, they'd had to backtrack. One egress was due to a washed out bridge, another necessary when they encountered standing water whose murky depths had been too daunting for even the 4-wheel drive. The third, and most troubling, had been the police roadblock.

Abe didn't recognize what type of cops they were, and it didn't matter. Pulling up to the barricade of four patrol cars, Charlie had rolled down his window prepared to explain their intent. He never got the chance.

"Turn this truck around, right now. No one is allowed south of here."

"But… but we're on our way to…"

"I don't give a fuck what you're doing. I said get this truck out of here – right now. Do it! Do it now, or I'll have both of your asses in handcuffs."

Abe was glad his brother decided it wasn't a good time to debate the police officer. Apparently, the screaming deputy was stressed and not in the mood for a conversation. Charlie replied with a quick, "Yes, sir," and put the pickup in reverse.

"I think we should stop driving and start floating as soon as possible," Charlie announced. "The cops don't seem to want any tourists in the French Quarter right now."

"You can't blame them," the older Hendricks replied. "Besides, these guys are just following orders. How about the old Gibson Fish Camp? That place is pretty remote, and we could put the boat in there and motor down to the city."

Forty minutes later, they were winching Charlie's johnboat off the trailer and into the coal black water of some unnamed bayou.

Charlie guided the small craft through the narrow waterway, the banks lined with the gnarled roots of ancient cypress and fields of waist-high cattails. As they progressed closer, debris began to clutter the surface, Katrina's destruction evident even in this remote location.

Maneuvering the nimble vessel around a bobbing refrigerator, the carcass of a horse, deciduous tree limbs, and even the floating door of a car, the two brothers continued their trek south.

Dusk was claiming the day by the time they could identify the shadowy skyline of New Orleans in the distance. It was dark before they finally scrambled up the side of an earthen levee and gazed across a suburban landscape that seemed foreign and destitute.

Moonlight illuminated the indistinct, shadowy outlines of hundreds of homes. Not a single, incandescent flicker was visible for as far as the brothers' elevated perch allowed a vantage. Many of the streets were filled with the glimmer of an amber lunar glow - a reflection on the standing water.

Charlie pointed to the south, indicating the section of the city where their father lived. "Looks like we might be in luck," he whispered. "The flooding doesn't seem so bad over there."

Abe nodded, wondering if they'd made the treacherous journey without cause. "Let's go see. Maybe the old man has cold beer in the fridge."

After double-checking the boat was well tied and concealed by thick underbrush, the two men hefted their gear and set off on foot.

The angle made hiking halfway down the city side of the levee's sloping surface difficult, but Abe wanted to avoid silhouetting themselves on the peak as well as escape the water at the bottom. The earth was soggy, both men adding a layer of boot-mud to their burden.

The pavement below gradually became drier, and after several blocks, they descended to the nearest sidewalk. Abe spotted high-water marks on several of the buildings they passed. A damp, moldy smell permeated the air, accented by the occasional whiff of raw sewage. The blackness of the night, absence of traffic, foul odor, and complete lack of human occupation provoked a sense of foreboding in both men. Their childhood neighborhood seemed dead and abandoned – a modern ghost town of immense proportions.

The men were less than four blocks away from their father's home when shots rang out. Sensing instantly that the gunfire was a considerable distance away, both men reached quickly for their pistols. When the wavering sounds of human screaming reached their ears, Abe uncased his rifle and began ramming shells into the magazine.

Finally, they stood in front of Mr. Edward Hendricks's humble abode. The two-story, quaint Victorian with a full-width front porch and white picket fence appeared undisturbed in the moonlight, the vision giving relief to both men.

"We'd better knock and yell," Charlie noted. "The old man's probably on edge and might take a shot at us."

"Be my guest," Abe smiled, motioning with a hand through the air.

Were it not for the nightmarish surroundings, Abe would have smirked at his brother's cautious approach. Stalking slowly up the front walk and gingerly mounting the stairs leading to the porch, Charlie positioned his body to the side of the door before knocking.

After banging three times on the frame, Charlie's voice rang out, "Dad? Dad? It's Abe and me. We've come to make sure you're okay."

In the quiet, seemingly unoccupied neighborhood, the sound of his brother's voice startled Abe. Compared to the noiseless background, the racket Charlie was making seemed like a riot. Abe began nervously scanning the area, checking to see if anyone had taken notice of their arrival.

In the otherwise still night, Charlie repeated his clamorous greeting, sending another jolt of hysteria through his brother.

Abe spied a sliver of a flashlight's beam pass by one of the curtains, soon followed by a challenge from behind the door. "The hell you say," bellowed the senior Hendricks's grouchy voice. "My boys are up north. Now who the hell are you?"

A few minutes later, the three men were clustered on the veranda, hugs and relief all around. With emotion in his eyes, Mr. Hendricks's only words were, "Am I glad to see both of you."

Zach's drive to New Orleans was a nerve racking, 16-hour adventure that exposed the Texan to the chilling cocktail of fear, paranoia, and near-anarchy that gripped Louisiana. He'd been forced to show his badge and credentials no less than six times.

On half of those occasions, the letter of introduction from the governor of Texas had been required for passage. At one roadblock, an officer had gone so far as to call Austin to authenticate his documentation.

But it was more than overly cautious law enforcement. Deep-seated fear was as thick as the late summer humidity. The people were burdened with confusion and frustration – emotions that were quickly morphing into anger and rebellion.

He saw it in the faces of a group of National Guard troopers mulling around a truck stop, waiting for someone to order them somewhere... anywhere.

The deputies manning the countless blockades went about their duties with curt voices and faces colored with apprehension. It was if the entire region was experiencing a collective bout of anxiety.

His truck stop meal was spent listening to a neighboring table of drivers; all of them furious over FEMA's lack of clarity regarding where they were supposed to deliver their cargos of water, blankets, and other emergency supplies. One man claimed to have been waiting for almost three days, another voicing his irritation over having been turned back from New Orleans twice.

As he drove, Zach thought back to Houston and his quip to Putnam. He *had* been recruited by the FBI. A Masters in Criminology, combined with an undergraduate degree in Forensic Chemistry, tended to open many doors. But what really set the young Texan apart, besides his GPA, was the fact that he'd financed part of his college education with a baseball scholarship. Brains and athletic talent were a winning combination for any wanna-be cop.

Despite the bureau's energetic recruitment, Zach yearned to be... had always longed to be a Texas Ranger. The solitude of the Louisiana highway brought back a rush of memories – engrained visions from long ago.

Zach had been just old enough to see over the dash. Riding with his father in the ancient Ford pickup, the two had been on a rare errand to the feed store in Fort Stockton.

It wasn't often the young Bass had the opportunity to visit the "big city," the event worthy of his wide-eyed, curious gaze taking in every detail of the journey. He could still remember the Country and Western song playing on the rambling old truck's AM radio. The cab smelled of hay and his father's Old Spice aftershave.

"Looks like the law is on the job today," his father had said, nodding toward the flashing lights of a police car ahead on the shoulder. The scene piqued Zach's inquisitive nature, his spine stiffening as he leaned forward to take it all in. The boy couldn't believe his luck, thrilled by the opportunity of watching a real Texas crime fighter in action.

Mr. Bass was more than aware of his son's fascination with cops and robbers. The lad was constantly behind on his chores, often immersed so deeply in the fantasy world of play that his assigned tasks were forgotten. Occasionally, a sharp word was required to bring the boy back to the reality of a working West Texas ranch.

But it was a small transgression. Mr. Bass was proud of his son, watching him grow straight and tall, enjoying his easy laugh, and reassured by the lad's honest conscience. Mrs. Bass had surely chosen well in naming their newborn son; he often observed.

She had taken one look at the infant's eyes and noted the resemblance to his great grandfather. Through the years, the namesake would demonstrate his predecessor's resolve as well.

The original Zachariah Bass had traveled west and settled in a harsh land. Despite the struggles of the drought, the Great Depression, and finally the Dust Bowl, the Bass homestead had survived.

Hoping to allow his son plenty of time to view the roadside police officer, the elder Bass had slowed the pickup considerably more than necessary. It had been a life-altering decision.

"Why is the policeman on the ground, daddy?" young Zach had asked. "It looks like he's shooting at somebody."

"Stay down!" the normally calm father had shouted, swerving the vehicle harshly to the side of the road.

Ignoring his dad's warning, young Zach couldn't help but peer over the cracked plastic of the dash. The officer was lying on his side, firing a pistol at some unseen antagonist. A pool of red grew under the downed lawman, puffs of dirt marking incoming bullets.

Zach's father reached across the bench seat and shoved his son to the floor. "Stay down!" he repeated.

In a flash, the old pump shotgun was out of the Ford's gun rack, the seasoned weapon occasionally employed in pursuit of hungry coyote or an errant prairie dog. Zach could remember the fear in his father's eyes, his shaking hands struggling to load shells into the scattergun's tube. And then he was gone, the pickup's open door bringing the sound of multiple gunshots roaring into the cab.

Zach couldn't stay on the floorboard. It was an impossible demand.

He watched his father rush to the policeman's side, quickly dragging the wounded officer to the rear of the police cruiser and out of the line of fire.

For some reason, Zach's naive mind assumed it was over… that the danger had ended. He could see his father was rendering aid to the cop, and the incoming shots had stopped. Zach wanted to help, too.

Reaching for the door handle, movement from ahead stopped him cold. Two men appeared, advancing toward his father with raised weapons. Zach knew they were bad guys in a glance. He bellowed a warning, "Dad! Look out!"

It all became a blur. Mr. Bass glanced up from the stricken man he was assisting, reaching for the nearby shotgun just as the first criminal fired his pistol. Zach remembered his father flinching, a slight hesitation in his reach, a pained expression in his eyes.

The 12-gauge sang its song, a cloud of white fire and smoke erupting from the muzzle. Zach had never seen his father work the pump so frantically.

And then it was over… the cloud of dust, cordite smoke, and confusion drifting away in the early morning breeze. Horror filled the young Bass's eyes – four men were lying on the ground.

He was out of the cab and sprinting to his father as fast as his legs would answer his panicked brain's instructions. Pale gray skin like he'd never seen on a person before, the color of his dad's countenance initially startled the boy. The raw flesh and pulsing crimson on his pop's shirt explained everything.

"Radio," came a croaking voice. "Call for help on the radio," the policeman said weakly, pulling Zach out of his trance.

The young Texan located the microphone, hooked to the dash above a cluster of lights and knobs. He'd seen enough television to know how it worked. "I need help!" he shouted after pressing the button. "My dad and the policeman have been shot. They need help."

"Who is this?" came a strong female voice. "This is a law enforcement frequency. You shouldn't be playing on here, son."

"My name is Zach Bass," he responded in a rush. "My dad and I were driving into town. The policeman told me to use his radio to call for help. There are men shot all over the road. Everybody's bleeding."

"What policeman?" the voice responded. "Where are you?"

Zach threw down the microphone and sped to the rear of the car. He looked at the officer's name tag, seeing the words, "Sgt. Hargrove," engraved in the shiny metal. But Zach couldn't read yet.

He rushed back to the mic and again pushed the button. "The policeman's name is S-G-T-H-A-R…" the young voice continued, spelling out the letters. "And we are going to Fort Stockton," he finally finished.

The dispatcher was still skeptical. "Where are your parents?"

"My mom died a long time ago, and my dad is bleeding behind the police car. He's dying! Please send help right now!"

"Okay… settle down. I need to know what road you're on. Do you see any signs along the pavement?"

Zach looked up, not being able to see anything. The windshield of the cruiser was a spider web of shot-up glass. Poking his head outside, he glanced up and down the flat road but couldn't see anything that would help.

"No," he broadcasted again. "I can't see any signs. I'm on the road that goes from our ranch into Fort Stockton…. That's all I know."

There was a long pause before the now-softer female voice came through the speaker. "Do you know your home address?"

Zach smiled. His father had made him memorize their address a long time ago. He blurted it out with pride.

After a few moments, the dispatcher responded. "Okay, I know you're on Highway 112. I'm sending help right now. How many men have been shot?"

"Four," Zach responded. "My dad used his shotgun on the two bad guys that had already shot the policeman. But pop got hit, too."

"Can you tell me where they are bleeding? Are they breathing? Talking? Moving?"

It occurred to Zach that all of the men around him might be dead. He might be alone, and that concept was more frightening than all of the blood and violence. After glancing around at the remote, desolate landscape, he started crying.

The young boy tried to answer the radio's question, but could only sob into the microphone.

"Stay with me, Zach. Hang in there," sounded the kind voice. "A lot of policemen and ambulances are on the way."

Zach dropped the microphone, hurrying back to his father. He noticed his dad's chest still heaving, but the pool of blood under his father's prone body was much larger.

"Dad? Dad, can you hear me?"

A wave of relief flushed over Zach when his father's eyes fluttered. It took several moments, but the elder Bass finally focused on his son's anxious face. The old rancher managed a slight smile. "Hi, Zach," he whispered.

"Dad, the lady on the radio said help is on the way. She's sending ambulances and more police."

"Good, son. You did good," came the whispered response.

Zach sat down on the pavement, not knowing what else to do. He lifted his father's wrist and squeezed tightly, wrapping both of his small hands around the older man's palm, waiting for help to arrive.

As time passed, he found himself watching his father's labored breathing, praying each exhalation wouldn't be the last. The entire world was defined by his dad's expanding and contracting ribcage.

One of the criminals lying in the road eventually moaned, the animal-like growl bringing the realization that the bad men weren't dead. Zach hefted his father's shotgun, changing his position so he could watch both his dad and the wounded villain. The lad was familiar with how to use the shotgun, having watched his father fire and clean the weapon.

The child had no idea how much time passed before he heard the first siren. Soon afterwards, the quiet, desert morning was completely inundated with the wailing of approaching responders.

The first to arrive was a deputy sheriff, the uniformed officer rushing forward with his gun drawn and sweeping the area. He spied Zach sitting with his legs crossed, the loaded 12-gauge resting in his lap while he held his father's hand.

"Drop that weapon!" the deputy commanded in a stern voice, pointing his pistol at Zach.

"Not until those crooks are dead or gone," Zach responded, never taking his eyes off the nearby shooters. "Those men shot my dad."

The deputy took a step backwards, his posture making it clear he was preparing to engage the boy. He inhaled deeply and screamed, "Drop that weapon now!"

"No," Zach calmly replied. "I have to protect my dad," he said bravely.

Another man appeared, moving to the deputy's side and placing a calming hand on the younger officer's shoulder. With a motion of his head, he made it clear that he didn't want a pistol pointed at the young boy – shotgun or no. The new arrival was wearing a white western hat, string-tie, and jacket. There was a silver star with five points prominently displayed on his belt.

"What's your name, son?" asked the hat's owner.

"Zach, sir."

"Zach, I'm a Texas Ranger. I need that weapon, son," the lawman said gently, approaching cautiously with his hand extended outward.

Again, Zach nodded toward the two criminals in the road. "Not while they can still hurt my dad," he replied with valiant resolve.

The ranger seemed to understand. Diverting to the prone bodies, he bent and checked each, kicking away their handguns. He then rose and then looked Zach in the eye. "I give you my word as a ranger, Zach, they aren't going to hurt your dad anymore. Now please hand me that shotgun."

Zach studied the approaching lawman. There was a projection of confidence, kindness, and earned authority in the man's demeanor. It made the boy feel safe. It was the first trust he'd felt since his father had been wounded.

Zach nodded, lifting the scattergun as if to hand it over. As soon as the ranger took possession of the firearm, he moved to the wounded police officer and then Mr. Bass, broadcasting a status on his radio the entire time.

Police, ambulances, and even a volunteer fire department's EMT unit began arriving. Vehicles, shouting voices, and running men were everywhere.

When the two EMTs tried to reach Mr. Bass, Zach wouldn't budge. Again, the ranger stepped in, pulling the worried son gently away while promising the ambulance crew would help his father.

Amidst the whirlwind of activity, lights, and rushing responders, the ranger managed to get Zach to take a seat in his truck. Slowly, with a kind tone and careful words, he pulled the story out of the frightened boy.

When he spotted his father being lifted onto the stretcher, Zach tried to exit the cab. "Don't worry; we'll follow the ambulance in my truck. I promise I won't let it out of my sight," reassured the lawman.

And he kept his word.

The senior Bass survived the encounter, as did the state trooper they had rescued. But Zach's father had taken a bullet to the spine and lost the use of his legs.

Being confined to a wheelchair was too much for the once able-bodied and powerful rancher. Over the next few years, Zach watched helplessly as his father's outlook deteriorated as much as his lower body. Bitterness, hard liquor, and remorse ruled the Bass household. Despite the awards and appreciation heaped upon the handicapped man, he couldn't deal with the stigma of being dependent. Mr. Bass's health dwindled away, declining until pneumonia finally took him to the grave just three years after the incident.

Zach's grandparents assumed the responsibility of raising the youth, the elderly couple moving back to the ranch from their retirement cottage in the Texas Hill Country. It was a struggle, but throughout it all, Zach knew he was loved. He also knew from that point forward that he wanted to be a Texas Ranger.

As the years passed, Zach replayed that fateful day a thousand times. The two men who had attacked the state trooper were escaped convicts from Oklahoma. With a stolen car and firearms, they were making a run for Mexico. Both had been lifelong criminals, neither surviving the encounter with Mr. Bass's 12-gauge.

Of all the memories and impressions, it was the ranger's presence that most impressed the young Bass. He began to read and study everything he could find about their organization. While other teenagers were interested in cars, the latest music group, or social media, Zach studied and read everything he could about the history and legend of the Texas Rangers.

Maturity led to understanding. Fate had been cruel that day, the odds of the encounter occurring in the remote lands of West Texas in front of father and son beyond calculation. It was a struggle for Zach to avoid the pitfalls of blaming God or feeling cursed for the misfortune.

A key weapon in his fight to remain optimistic was the memory of the ranger's actions that morning. Zach fully understood the difference between the deputy's pistol pointing, near-panic response, and the calm, in-control attitude of the senior lawman. It was a dichotomy that he often referenced when presented with challenges throughout his high school years. It was a model of exemplary, strong character - an example of ultimately good judgment.

Baseball was the other salvation in Zachariah's life. Tall and lanky, his frame wasn't suited for the more popular sport of football. But his whip-like arm could heave a rock or ball with dizzying velocity.

By his junior year in high school, Zach was drawing the attention of national scouts. As he began the 12th grade, the primary decision facing the young man was college or semi-pro. While the future was bright and clear, the decision troubled him. His grandparents pined for school; his pocket longed for the dream of money and the satisfaction of being paid to throw a baseball.

Toward the end of his senior season, Zach was putting the finishing touches on a three-hit clinic he was throwing against a rival team. The final out had gone down swinging, and after a brief celebration at the mound, the victorious pitcher headed for the dugout to pack his gear.

He was a few steps away when a tall, thin man appeared in his path. Zach recognized the gentleman immediately – a face forever engrained in his memory – the ranger from that day on the road.

"Hello, Zach. Nice game," greeted the lawman.

"Thank you, sir. Are you…" Zach questioned, the shock of the encounter making him doubt his own recollections.

The man nodded, smiling warmly. "Yes, I am. Do you have time to take a walk with me?"

"Yes, sir," the young man managed, a thousand questions tumbling through his mind.

"I've been keeping my eye on you, Zach. I travel out this way now and then, and I've tried to make a point of catching a few innings or driving by your family's place. I retired last month from the Texas Rangers, and in all those years, that day out on 112 sticks with me more than any other."

"That makes two of us, sir," Zach replied.

The older man snorted with a nod. "I suppose it does. But you've done well for yourself, young man. You're tall and strong, and from what I hear, a person of character."

The compliment, especially from a man Zach had considered a role model for so many years, made the young Bass flush. "Thank you," he muttered shyly.

"So what are you going to do, Zach? Rumor has it that you've been offered a solid scholarship at Texas Tech. I also understand the Houston Astros would like to have you in their farm system. These must be a heady times."

There it was again – that undefinable factor of trust. Zach had dozens of people spouting their opinions at him every day.

Everyone from his loving grandparents to his high school coach's secretary was giving advice on a regular basis. He couldn't walk into the diner without someone offering him a suggestion... couldn't read quietly in the library without a teacher or fellow student lecturing on a personal perspective of how the pitcher's opportunities should be played out. Why was he eager... no, anxious to hear the wisdom of a man he hadn't seen in almost 10 years? He didn't even know the ranger's name.

"It's a really important decision," Zach finally said. "I feel like I'm at a 'Y' in the road. If I choose the wrong path, I'll mess things up forever."

Again, the gentle chuckle. "That's understandable. I don't know if I'd use the word 'forever,' though. I'm sure it must seem like that... that it's critical you get it right."

"What would you do?"

The ranger strolled a few steps without responding. He finally stopped, looking Zach directly in the eye. "My daddy always said that an education is the only thing in life that can never be taken away. Money can be stolen or spent. Freedom can disappear. Friends come and go. Love can evaporate. But knowledge and learning are a man's possessions forever. I think that was pretty sage."

"So you would go to school?"

"Yes, I would. It may set you back a few years if professional baseball is in your future, but what are a few years? On the other hand, that sheepskin makes for a strong backup plan. You and I both know life can change at any moment. We both saw that out on the highway the day we met."

Zach absorbed the ranger's words, a nagging question rising to the surface. Without thinking, he blurted it out. "What was so special about that day on 112? You must have seen worse carnage... in the grand scale of an officer's career, that day couldn't have made the highlight reel. Why does it stick out in your mind?"

The ranger grunted, shaking his head with uncertainty. "I've asked myself that a hundred times, Zach. I don't have a very good answer for you. The image of a brave, 6-year old boy brandishing a shotgun and staring down a deputy might be part of it. Your loyalty to your father is no doubt worthy of note. But, I think what really etched that entire episode in my mind was the fact that you didn't crumble... didn't panic... didn't fold up the tent of your mind and disappear into a mental wilderness. In my line of work, mental toughness and loyalty are at the top of the requirement list, and you learn to respect those attributes above all else."

It was Zach's turn to grunt, his forehead wrinkling in thought. "Funny. From where I stand, I didn't do anything special or different. My dad needed help, and I went to his side."

"Did you know we found two bullet holes in your dad's truck?"

"No."

"You were taking fire, Zach, and you didn't even know it. Have you ever listened to the recordings of your exchange with the dispatcher?"

"No."

"Look me up after you have a child of your own, and I'll play that tape. You can decide then if you did anything special or not."

"I don't even know your name," Zach replied, still reeling from the encounter.

The ranger reached into his pocket, producing a business card. Before he handed it over, he placed a hand on Zach's shoulder. "My advice is to enroll. Let them fill your head with whatever keeps you awake in class. No one... not God, the devil, or the government can ever take it away from you."

The lawman presented his card and said, "Good luck, Zach." Pivoting, the retired ranger made for the parking lot, leaving a confused teenager in his wake.

Three months later, his chest-busting, proud grandfather had delivered Zach to the campus of Texas University.

In his junior year, a torn ligament announced the premature end to his baseball dreams, the extent of the injury beyond surgery's means to repair. It was another low in Zach's life.

Again, the words of the ranger drifted back into his head. "That sheepskin makes for a strong backup plan," he remembered. Again, the Texas lawman had been spot-on with his advice.

At graduation, the feds came calling. Zach had pushed aside the barriers of lower pay and lack of promotional opportunities, accepting the offer to join his home state's Department of Public Safety, the parent organization of the Texas Rangers.

It was the only choice that felt right.

After the academy, he'd begun his post-graduation law enforcement career driving a patrol car marked "State Trooper." During that first year, he began to realize that a career in law enforcement wasn't at all what he'd expected.

There had been a few occasions when Zach basked in a strong sense of job satisfaction. These rare episodes typically occurred when a case or incident involved protecting the least of the state's citizens from the worst. Serving the common, everyday folks, as they tried to better what was often a difficult life in West Texas was remarkably rewarding to Zachariah Bass.

But those instances were few and far between. He quickly found that a percentage of the population resented authority, while others couldn't seem to function without it. When he wore the uniform, people treated him differently, and it troubled Zach to no end.

Ranger Bass quickly found himself smack in the middle of what he eventually christened the "triangle of despair."

On one side of his imaginary, geometric figure stood his fellow cops. He had anticipated working with honest men who relentlessly upheld law and order, regardless of the sacrifice required. Instead, he found tainted individuals who often felt as persecuted as the criminals they pursued. So many of the elder, more-seasoned, officers were filled with a genuine disrespect for their fellow human beings. Having seen and experienced the worst mankind had to offer, they were beyond caring about justice, right, or wrong. Only survival and camaraderie of their fellow officers seemed to matter.

Zach thought back to his decision to fire Tusk's pistol – just to cover his tracks. Just to be safe. Technically, he hadn't done anything unjustified during the showdown with the gangbanger, but that fact might not matter if the wrong people started getting nosey. In that one fleeting moment, he'd actually committed a serious felony. And that single mistake ate at his personal fortitude. Was he as disenfranchised as the rest of his comrades after only a few years on the job?

The citizenry formed another side of the triangle. After first donning the uniform, it had taken Zach weeks to adjust to people's reactions. He recalled meandering into a restaurant and wondering why the ambient background noise of conversation suddenly decreased. Why did people stare at him when he stopped at the local grocer after his shift? What was the big deal about a guy in uniform pushing his cart up and down the aisles? Did they all feel guilty over something? Were the local cops so corrupt they were publically scorned? The isolation he began to experience led directly to withdrawal, a feeling of disembodiment from the population at large.

The final leg of the triangle consisted of the elected officials, more precisely the prosecutors. Zach had lost count of the number of times he'd witnessed overzealous district attorneys use the state's resources to hammer some poor guy into a plea. Guilt versus innocence had lost meaning at some point; only winning the contest seemed to matter.

The people's defenders liked their position of power and prestige. They wanted to be elected over and over again, and that meant being perceived as "tough on crime." That also resulted in a callous, uncaring attitude regarding justice and individual rights. A conviction rate was all that mattered come ballot time.

And, the law of the land made it easy for all three sides of the triangle to feed off each other.

Zach remembered one of his law professors lecturing on the subject, the bearded intellectual claiming that there were over 27,000 pages of federal laws, with that figure quite literally growing by the minute. A huge chunk of those laws referenced more than 100,000 federal regulations, and those often changed without a congressional vote.

"The average American commits three felonies per day," the professor had touted. "If that citizen drives an automobile, you can raise that number to six. The government can arrest any of us, at any time, and put us behind bars. We walk free only by the benevolence of men who are elected to fill the jails. Now I ask the class, is this a recipe for justice?"

More than once, the young ranger considered resigning. Late at night, when the day's adrenaline had finally burned off, he'd often pondered changing careers. But that train of thought always ended in the same place – fear.

Fear of being on the other side stopped him cold. The vulnerability of being outside the machine made him shiver. He knew what could happen to any citizen – had seen it with his own eyes. The American justice system had become an uncaring, unforgiving, out-of-control meat grinder, and her citizens seemed well equipped to provide an unending source of beef.

It was better to be a minor gear in an out-of-control machine, than a rusting piece of scrap. He'd stay in the machine. Perhaps one day the opportunity to make things better would present itself.

"Could the FBI would be a better choice for me?" he mumbled to the empty cab. "Maybe I'm not made of the right cloth to work the streets. Maybe I should consider an FBI lab instead of patrolling the desert."

He was right in the middle of an intense mind-movie, trying to visualize a life where his hat and boots were replaced with a white lab coat and rubber gloves, when the New Orleans skyline appeared on the horizon.

The sheer scale of the flooding amazed Zach. Despite the hurricane's making landfall more than a week before, the elevated interstate passed over block after block of standing, deep water. The destruction seemed to stretch for miles in all directions.

As his truck ventured deeper into the city proper, he could make out more details of the devastation. The glass was missing from practically every first-floor window. Household garage doors were buckled in half from the water's pressure. More than a few homes had been moved several feet off their foundations by the fast-moving currents.

Some streets were lined with the hulks of already-rusting cars; other avenues appeared to be entirely devoid of any sign of life. Light poles, street signs, and corner newspaper boxes had simply vanished.

The melancholy atmosphere was further darkened by the minimal traffic he spied on the roadway. Military vehicles, patrol cars, and government sedans dominated both lanes, the occasional 18-wheeler rolling one direction or the other. It quickly became apparent that every single semitrailer was being given a police escort in and out of the city. *Rule of law must be in jeopardy*, Zach realized. *They wouldn't be using valuable resources for convoy security if it weren't so.*

Numerous columns of smoke rose into the morning horizon, their ominous presence accented by the dozens and dozens of helicopters whirring over the stricken city's skyline. It looked like a war zone and smelled like one, too.

The stench of stagnating water, burning rubber, wood ash, and rotting garbage assaulted his nose. Some stretches of highway smelled like dirty athletic socks, others emitted the earthy odor of rotting flesh.

He'd been given detailed instructions at the last checkpoint, a handwritten, turn-by-turn handout someone had copied so it could be issued to rescue workers and the massive inbound federal response.

His orders were to locate the mayor, or if he was unavailable, the chief of police. Zach figured City Hall was the place to start.

For the most part, the government of New Orleans had been relocated to an upscale hotel just a block from the water-damaged municipal building. As Zach searched for a parking spot, he spotted a sprawling group of reporters, cameras, and bright lights assembled on the massive structure's front steps. "Now we're getting somewhere," he mumbled.

In a few minutes, he was eavesdropping at the edge of what was obviously a press conference. A large man in ornate uniform continued his address of the national media. "In this time of crisis, the safety of our citizens and first responders is our immediate priority. Therefore, no civilians in New Orleans will be allowed to carry pistols, shotguns or other firearms," declared the government official. "Only law enforcement is allowed to possess weapons. We believe this action will help keep our population safe."

A barrage of questions was shouted from the onlookers, but Zach didn't hear any of them. Exhausted from what had essentially been a three-day drive from Alpine, his weary brain was trying to wrap around such a violation of the Second Amendment. *They're confiscating private firearms?* he pondered. *How do you get a warrant to cover that? They'd never get away with that in Texas.*

Zach waited until the media event was over, trailing a small huddle of law enforcement officers inside the hotel's lobby. He caught the eye of one of the senior aides and flashed his badge. Extending his hand, Zach initiated introductions, "Howdy. I'm Ranger Zachariah Bass from Texas. I've been sent by the governor as a liaison for either the mayor or the chief of police."

"You don't say," the pessimistic voice responded. After grasping Zach's offered hand, the local continued, "I'm Captain Harold Baines, NOPD. You're in luck – the commissioner just concluded a press conference. I am sure he has nothing better to do than to entertain guests from neighboring states. Hold on though; maybe we can catch him."

Captain Baines didn't wait for Zach's response, instead pivoting quickly in an attempt to catch up with his boss. The visitor from Texas hustled to keep up.

The commissioner was surrounded by a whirling multitude of uniformed and civilian humanity, many of whom seemed to be vying for the head-cop's attention. For the most part, the city official ignored the shouted questions, camera flashes, and stacks of paper being shoved in his face as he slowly managed his way toward a bank of elevators.

Evidently, Baines was a trusted aide. After elbowing his way through the throng, he whispered a quick word into his boss's ear. Zach saw the commissioner glance in his direction and nod.

Finally reaching the refuge offered by the elevator, Zach attempted to push his way into the upward bound car, his exertions blocked by four huge NOPD cops who were obviously tasked with keeping out the riffraff. Baines again came to the rescue, his arm reaching out to pull the ranger inside just as the doors were moving to close.

"Texas, huh," the commissioner said, looking Zach up and down with a critical eye. "Ranger Bass, huh? Wasn't Samuel Bass a notorious outlaw and gunslinger over in your state?"

"Yes, sir, he was. No relation though."

With a dismissing wave of his hand, the top-cop continued, "No matter. So tell me, what the hell is a Texas Ranger doing in my city, taking up my valuable time?"

What city? Zach started to respond, but thought better of it. Instead, he unfolded the letter from his governor, handing the document over without a response.

A chime sounded, and the doors opened onto an upper floor, the procession shuffling into an oversized, plush hallway. Zach's boots sank into the carpet just as the head lawman finished reading the letter.

"Bullshit," he exploded, his intense gaze rising from the document and boring into Zach. "I don't know if our friends over in Texas have been keeping up on current events, but we've got a hell of a mess on our hands, young man. For the governor to insinuate that we're purposely dumping our prisoners in your lap is insulting... damned insulting."

"I'm not here for political reasons, sir," Zach responded. "I'm here to offer any assistance possible that will improve the processing of the evacuees. My company's major was very clear on that point."

"Process?" the man laughed, "What in the hell makes you think we have any sort of process? I've got hundreds of thousands of desperate people on my hands. Procedure drowned in the floodwaters. We're just trying to get as many to high ground and under a roof as possible."

"I understand, sir, but our jails are full, and my superiors don't want to turn your criminals loose on our innocent population."

Again, the commissioner cackled from his impressive belly. "At least you *have* jails, son. I would hope your superiors understand the hurricane that just kicked our ass could have easily ventured a couple of hundred miles west and slammed Houston. I hope my law enforcement comrades in the Lone Star State realize our roles could very easily have been reversed."

We wouldn't have fucked up so badly, Zach thought. *And I seriously doubt you would have offered any help.* But he didn't say it.

The commissioner interpreted the lack of response as the end of the conversation. Passing the letter back to Zach, he grunted with disdain and started to turn away.

"Sir," Zach stated with a firm tone that halted the retreat. Leaning in close to the man's ear, he whispered, "My major said he will set up a roadblock and turn away every pickup, van, bus, bicycle, and pedestrian trying to cross into Texas from Louisiana - if we don't determine a way to keep the criminals out. And I believe him, sir."

The commissioner's eyebrows rose, his brow wrinkling in anger. Zach's message, while obviously pissing him off, had struck a nerve. For a moment, the ranger thought the man might even order his arrest or deportation.

"I see," the commissioner finally whispered, much of his bluster fading. "And what would you suggest, young man?"

"Let me get the lay of the land, sir. For a few days, let me see what's happening in the streets and how the evacuation is being handled. I can voice any recommendations after I get a feel for what is going on."

The remaining anger dissipated from the head-policeman's face at that point. Turning to Baines, he ordered, "Assign our new friend to one of the confiscation patrols. Let him see that what we're facing up close and personal."

And then returning to Zach, he finished, "I'll look forward to your recommendations, Ranger Bass."

Once again, Zach was given directions and a handwritten note of introduction. He found the NOPD sub-station thirty minutes later. It looked more like an Army base than a police operation.

Camouflaged Humvees and patrol cars encircled what had been an elementary school before the storm. Zach didn't have to ask about the real station – he'd driven by enough flooded-out structures to guess.

Not only were military vehicles in abundance, so were soldiers. Clamping his badge in a clearly visible location on his belt, Zach exited the truck and began walking toward the main entrance.

The place was bustling with activity; National Guardsmen, police officers, and men whose jackets were embroidered with the initials of just about every federal agency he'd ever heard of rushed here and there. Almost everyone was heavily armed, plenty of M16s, shotguns and other tactical weapons on display.

He found the watch officer just inside the door. Ten minutes later, he was being introduced to a burly, barrel-chested NOPD sergeant named Roland "Butch" Ford. At well over 6 feet tall and sporting a closely cropped crew cut, the gent reminded Zach more of a Marine Corps drill instructor than a beat cop.

"We can use all the help we can get," the bleary-eyed, four-days-beyond-fatigued policeman commented. "We're understaffed, patrolling three precincts with less manpower than what we'd normally have for one. Most of my guys haven't slept for more than a couple of hours since the levees were breached."

"Looks like you've got a ton of guardsmen here. Are they taking any of the load?"

"Some," Ford replied, "but they're not experienced in the finer points of law enforcement. Those guys help some with the search and rescue, but handling any manner of criminal activity is still on us. The lieutenant has taken to pairing us up, which helps if a gunfight breaks out."

"Have you seen a lot of that?"

"Not in the last few days. At first, it was like living in a B-rated, Wild West movie, but currently we have the dry areas almost under control. And now with the mayor's new order for mandatory evacuation, I expect we'll see even less violence."

"How are you going to force them to leave?" Zach asked, trying to get a read on his new comrade's attitude.

"If we take their firearms, they'll leave. It's still not a very safe place to be around here at night, and everybody knows that. We'll push hard for an evacuation, and take their guns away at the same time. Hopefully, our fine citizens will get the hint."

"Doesn't confiscating guns bother you at all, Sergeant? I mean, I know things are dire here, but the Second Amendment? Warrants? Due process?"

Ford waved off the concern. "We're damned if we do, damned if we don't. We can't protect *them*... or their *property*, especially at night. The people screaming at us about looters during the day are out pilfering and shooting at shadows after dark. If one of them blows off his own foot, we'll be ridiculed for not being able to provide ambulance service. If they set their own homes on fire by shooting at a looter, we'll catch hell for not having a fire truck handy. Yet, when the fire department does respond to a blaze, some asshole snipes at the responders. If you throw in the burden of rescuing the thousands still trapped in attics and on rooftops, we're so shorthanded, it's ridiculous."

Zach could understand the attitude. He'd felt it a dozen times in his dealings with the public. The stress, extra hours, lack of sleep, and desolate surroundings were amplifying frustrations that practically every lawman experienced at one time or another.

Sergeant Ford informed Zach that a foot patrol would be forming up shortly and invited the ranger to join in. While the Texan's primary interest was what happened to potential evacuees after they were identified and marshaled, he didn't want to sit around the HQ and play with himself. "Sure, I'll tag along," he replied to the local lawman.

It was the wee hours of the morning before the Hendricks men had settled down. Each had a story to tell, adrenaline to burn off. At one point, after hearing his father's recounting of the looting he'd witnessed locally, Charlie determined it would be wise for Abe and him to retrieve their boat. "It might be our only way out of here," he commented.

Significant time and effort were required to carry the 18-footer to the backyard.

Sleep didn't come, even after the exhaustive physical outlay and the inevitable emotional valley that followed the reunion's high. Distant gunfire and the occasional drift of human shouting led to a nearly sleepless night.

Mr. Hendricks didn't want to leave his home, regardless of how passionately his sons argued their case. "I've watched gangs of young men break into every empty house on this block," he stated. "They only plunder the empty homes. If I leave, they'll ransack this place in a heartbeat."

"How long will it be before they start coming into occupied homes, Dad?" Abe asked.

"They'll find their ass full of buckshot," came the bravado response.

"You've got to sleep sometime. You'll be outnumbered… and probably outgunned. There's nothing here worth dying for," Charlie reasoned.

"That's easy for you to say, son. It's not your house and your memories. I'll be fine. You two head on back to your families."

And so it went. Both of the younger men knew their father well – it would take a little time to reason him out of his entrenched position, but eventually he would heed. Abe, after the ruckus of the previous night, prayed it wouldn't take too long.

The following morning passed without incident, Charlie mixing bottled water with instant coffee to greet the day. He made sure to point out the dwindling java supply. "We might need directions to that new Starbucks, Dad," Charlie needled, driving his point home. Abe reiterated their lack of rations, noting the few eggs left in the carton and the startling absence of pepper bacon. Mr. Hendricks pretended to ignore both of them.

Early in the afternoon, Charlie snapped to attention at the sound of a commotion coming from the neighbor's house. Broken glass, loud voices, and light banter drew the younger Hendricks to the front porch. The five young men who exited the unoccupied homestead collectively hefted four stuffed pillowcases, a gaming console, and laptop. At first, they didn't notice the two Hendricks brothers. The band of thugs hopped the picket fence and strolled across the yard.

It was Charlie's chambering a round in the 12-gauge that stopped them short. "What are you boys up to?" Abe questioned, standing next to his brother.

The young men didn't respond, instead choosing to back away several steps before turning calmly and sauntering down the street. Abe watched their retreat with a wary eye, their casual attitude as troubling as the occasional bout of laughter rising from the gang.

After that incident, all three of the Hendricks men decided that vigilance deserved a higher priority in their lives. The two sons took advantage of the escalation of security as well, making sure to point this out to their father at every opportunity. They even started a fake argument over who would lose sleep while keeping the late night watch.

"I'm really worried about dad," Charlie whispered when his father was out of earshot. "He is not taking the hint. We may have to hogtie and carry him out of here."

"I'm worried about all of us being carried out of here... in body bags," grunted Abe.

There were eight of them: three NOPD officers, three National Guardsmen, Sergeant Ford, and Zach. With the exception of the visitor from Texas, all the others were armed with long guns, body armor, and tactical vests.

They drove several blocks toward a neighborhood that, according to Ford, hadn't flooded. "Everyone knows this area is dry, so this is a prime target for looters."

On the way, their convoy of patrol cars and Humvees pulled into the parking lot of a national sporting goods chain store. Not wanting to be the aggravating new guy, Zach watched in silence as Ford approached the front door, pulled a key from his pocket, and unlocked a heavy chain. "I'm going to get you a shotgun," he turned and announced to the Texan. "The last thing I need is an ass-full of paperwork if you get shot. Pump or semi-auto?"

The ranger's foul expression was evident, clear enough for Ford to read. The local cop smiled and explained, "We have permission from the store's owner to take what we need. I'm not a looter, Mr. Texas Ranger; I'm keeping a record of everything the department takes. We'll reimburse them for every penny."

"Pump is fine with me," Zach responded, slightly embarrassed over his presumption.

Ford reappeared from the dark interior a few minutes later, a brand new 12-gauge pump and four boxes of shells in his hands. As he handed the weapon to Zach, one of the National Guardsmen asked, "Hey, what are those guys doing over there?"

All eyes traveled to a van idling a block away, the logo of a cable news network boldly painted on the side. Two men stood next to the vehicle, one of the onlookers hoisting an oversized camera on his shoulder.

"Hey!" shouted Ford, taking a step toward the camera crew and waving his arm. "You're not supposed to be down here!"

Realizing they'd been spotted, both of the newshounds rushed for their ride and jumped inside. The van barked rubber as it sped off.

Frustrated, Ford turned to Zach and bellowed, "Shit! I'm sure there'll be a video of the dirty New Orleans cops looting a sporting goods store. They'll splash it all over the 6 o'clock news. And of course, my captain's explanation of our agreement will be ignored. Some days, this job sucks."

"Just curious, why aren't they allowed in this area?" Zach asked.

"Because this region was a battlefield. One of the crews came under fire from a gang of looters, and we don't have the manpower to escort them everywhere they want to explore. There's supposed to be a procedure in place where they can get permission to tour the city, you know, so that local law enforcement is aware of their presence. But with all that is going on right now, I don't think it's a priority for the guys downtown."

Zach shook his head, "Damned if you do, damned if you don't."

The NOPD patrol was unlike anything Zach had ever experienced. With four men on each side of the street, they moved like a rifle company through the mostly unpopulated neighborhood.

Only occasionally did they spot anyone outside, and when they did, Sergeant Ford was aggressive, in-their-face pushy, leaving no room for doubt that the authorities wanted everyone to get out of New Orleans. Everyone.

Their first stop was to chat with an elderly couple fanning themselves on their front porch.

Zach was shocked when the members of his group pointed their weapons at the clearly harmless senior citizens. Ford was barking like a junkyard dog, growling orders like the residents didn't have any choice in the matter.

Still, despite the pressure, the old fella stood his ground. "We ain't leaving. We got no place to go."

Acting as if he was pissed, Ford then started grilling the couple about firearms. Both the woman and her husband denied having any weapons on the premises.

Again, Zach was stunned when Ford turned and ordered two of the guardsmen to search the house. No warrant, no probable cause, no hesitation. The troopers found nothing.

The sergeant was a perceptive individual, quickly noting Zach's discomfort. "A state of emergency has been declared," he reminded Zach. "The mayor has ordered all weapons be confiscated, and so has the chief. That's good enough for me."

"What about the Constitution?" Zach asked, unable to shake off the unsettling feeling in his core. "I don't think a declaration of emergency overrides any of the amendments."

Ford was clearly puzzled by Zach's reaction. "It's better for these people to get out of here," he reasoned. "They are risking their lives if they stay. Who the hell knows how long it will be before things get back to normal? I'm only trying to make sure they are fed and safe."

"It's your town, Sergeant. I'm only here to observe."

Soon, the entourage encountered a man sprinting down the street toward them. After finally getting the fellow to settle down enough to talk, he explained that the wall of an apartment building had collapsed just a few blocks away. The witness claimed he'd heard a voice yelling for help. He wasn't sure, but he thought he heard children crying, as well. He had run to find someone to help mount a rescue.

They joined the runner immediately, the man leading them through a neighborhood marked by deep but narrow, rectangular clapboard homes, modest in detail and a prevalent style of the area. Constructed early in the 20th century and seemingly of identical design, they lined both sides of the avenues in a very orderly fashion, only occasionally interrupted by commerce. Three blocks from their original position, the men reached a 1950ish, two-story apartment building, surrounded on two sides by the rising floodwaters. Sure enough, the ground had substantially eroded underneath part of the foundation. Ford motioned for everyone to be still.

A faint voice drifted from underneath the mound of concrete, wood framing and drywall. "Can anybody hear me? We need help! My children and I are trapped in here! Help, oh please God, someone help."

Zach couldn't pinpoint the exact source of the plea, the surrounding infrastructure and urban concrete making it almost impossible to judge the distance and direction of the sound. Sergeant Ford got on his radio, asking for backup and giving the street names of the nearest intersection.

"Let's see if we can get them out ourselves," he commanded. "Who knows how long it will be before someone responds?"

The entire team wasted no time digging in, pitching aside concrete blocks and large sections of plasterboard. Zach and one of the troopers put their backs into prying a support beam aside. Other men were using a long section of pipe to leverage debris on the opposite side of the mound.

One of the guardsmen pointed to the far side of the building, "Sergeant, I think we'd have a better angle if we went over there. That water doesn't look very deep."

Ford didn't want anyone wading out into the water, a warning of toxic pollution and unprocessed human waste being passed around to all rescuers just that morning. The team leader glanced at his own hands, already lined with small scratches and cuts from moving the hefty chunks of concrete, realizing the wastewater was a recipe for disaster. "I don't think risking the water would buy us much," the big cop said, wiping the sweat from his forehead. "I want everyone staying high and dry."

A process soon developed. The men would dig furiously for three or four minutes, and then Ford would whistle a halt. Everyone would remain absolutely still while the NOPD officer would exchange shouted words with the trapped victims.

"Oh, please, sir... save my children," the progressively weaker voice entreated. "They were already feverish when the building caved in."

"We're coming, lady; hang in there."

About then a large section of wall collapsed, several hundred pounds of brick and drywall just missing two of the men. Rather than retreat, Ford ordered several of his crew to brace the wobbly structure with whatever materials they could salvage from the rubble. Zach expected to be buried alive at any moment.

They put eyes on the woman ten minutes later. Her two preschool-aged children and she were pinned in what had been their kitchen, trapped in a small pocket between an overturned refrigerator and a stout breakfast table.

As they began to dig the mother out in earnest, the firemen arrived. Using crowbars, axes and other equipment, they took to the task while Ford's team stepped back. The crowd of responders breathed a collective sigh of relief when the first tot was passed up and out of the wreckage.

A Coast Guard helicopter appeared over the scene, circling once and then landing in a nearby parking lot. It wasn't long before the medics were evaluating all three victims. After a few minutes of frantic activity, Zach watched as the crews began loading the family onto the bird, preparing them for the flight out.

Word got around that one of the kids had some internal bleeding, and the mother suffered a compound fracture, but they all were expected to survive. Several of the firemen approached the law enforcement officers and praised Ford for his team's good work. Spirits were high all around. In the midst of chaos and mayhem, they had made a difference.

After the rescue crews had cleared, the sergeant's team mulled around, dusting themselves off, guzzling bottled water, and generally cooling down. Ford allowed his men a 15-minute break and then motioned for them to form up. It was time to get back to work.

Abe and Charlie were quietly huddling in the kitchen, plotting their next move to get their father to evacuate with them voluntarily. Dad was catching a nap on the couch.

The sudden banging on the front door spiked the brothers' adrenaline, the shocking racket so loud and unexpected it sounded like a bomb had exploded on the front porch.

Charlie reached for the nearby shotgun as Abe moved to see who would dare be so bold as to splinter the front door. As he passed into the living room, he was surprised to see his father reaching for the deadbolt.

"Who is it?" the elder Hendricks shouted, turning the knob just as Abe screamed for him to stop. It was too late, a large man in a blue uniform pushing his way inside.

"New Orleans Police Department!" the intruder shouted, repeatedly bumping the elderly homeowner backwards with his chest. Before Abe could do or say anything, a stream of uniformed bodies poured in behind the huge cop, the living room soon filled with armed men and rifle barrels sweeping in all directions.

Still in a state of disbelief, Abe could do nothing but hold up his hands in the classic, *"Don't shoot,"* position.

"You have to leave," the bull-cop began shouting. "The mayor has ordered all residents to evacuate. Now!"

"We're not going anywhere!" Mr. Hendricks responded, finally recovering. "Get out of my house."

Abe noticed the intruders spreading out, one man in an Army uniform slowly moving to get behind his father. Another cop who shouldered a shotgun was making for the staircase.

"Do you have a warrant?" Abe barked, not sure what else to say.

One of the two NOPD officers stepped closer to Abe, poking him in the stomach with the barrel of an AR15. "This is our warrant," smirked the cop.

"Are there any firearms in this house?" the lead man asked. "We've been ordered to confiscate all weapons."

"You can't do that," protested Abe, "That's illegal as hell. Get the fuck out of our house."

"Yeah... what the hell is wrong with you guys?" Mr. Hendricks demanded, regaining his composure and stepping toward the big policeman. "We've got rights here... you can't just barge in here and...."

A lightning storm charged with events erupted. Placing a hand on each of Mr. Hendricks's shoulders, the big cop yanked the old man savagely to the floor. Abe's natural reaction was to help his father, but he didn't manage a single step before the closest invader dove into his mid-section, slamming him brutally to the carpeting.

Someone was trying to pull Abe's arms behind his back as the room filled with the bedlam of shouted commands and confusing orders. Swirls of fast moving bodies, firearms, and his father's screams of protest made it impossible to discern what was happening.

"Where are the guns?" someone kept shouting. "Where are the guns?"

Two of the soldiers started for the kitchen. Abe's eyes followed their movement, despite being pinned on his stomach.

The kitchen door flew open in slow motion, the barrel of Charlie's shotgun rising frame, by agonizing frame. Abe wanted to shout a warning, tried to fill his throat with the words that would cause his brother to stop. But it was too late.

The 12-gauge exploded, pellets of buckshot driving into the nearest soldier's chest. Abe saw his brother's face wrinkle in pain and confusion as a series of bullets ripped through his torso. A cloud of red mist appeared behind the younger Hendricks as his body twisted and vibrated from the impacting lead.

Abe recognized his own voice screaming, "No!" while his little brother sank to the floor. As he went down, another jet of red fire sprayed from Charlie's shotgun. Someone howled in agony, the sickening wail overriding the earsplitting thunder of gunfire and the blaring shouts of men in combat.

And then Abe was free.

The man holding him to the floor rolled away, seeking cover when the firefight began. Still in shock over watching his brother cut to pieces, Abe rose to his knees, thinking only of gathering Charlie's limp body in his arms.

Movement drew Abe's eye, his father finding himself unburdened as well. Ed Hendricks was reaching for something, extending his arm in Charlie's direction. Too late, Abe again tried to mouth a warning for his dad to stop.

More thunder filled the Hendricks's living room, one of the cops believing Mr. Hendricks was reaching for Charlie's shotgun – or so they assumed. Abe watched in absolute horror as his father's head exploded in a geyser of tissue and bone.

"You sons-ah-bitches!" Abe screamed, finally managing his feet. "You murdering pieces of shit," he cried, staggering toward his father's body.

And then his way was blocked by the hulking shape of the bull policeman, the man raising a shotgun toward Abe's midsection. The remaining Hendricks knew he was about to die.

A flash appeared out of nowhere, the outline of a human arm entering Abe's narrowed view of the weapon that was going to claim his life. Striking the barrel just as a fountain of white fire erupted from the muzzle, the mysterious hand somehow managed to push the shot wide.

Blinking in surprise, both Abe and the big cop glanced up to see a man in a cowboy hat stepping between them. "Enough!" screamed the hat. "Stop this!"

Sergeant Ford blinked, looking into Zach's eyes as if he didn't know where he was. "Cease fire! Everybody! Secure your weapons – now!" screamed Zach. "Cease fire!"

Abe again tried to move to his fallen father's side. He managed a single step before a jolt of agony shot through his head, and then the world turned black.

The fog of shock and confusion in the Hendricks's living room was as thick as the cordite gun smoke. After a few moments, Zach's reeling brain registered the absolute blanket of silence that covered the area. It took him a few seconds more to realize the quiet was due to his ears being overwhelmed by the close-in gunfire.

The rest of Sergeant Ford's group appeared to be in some form of trance as well. One trooper stood and fidgeted with his M16, another man's eyes darting rapidly from body to body strewn about the floor. Ford was statue-still, his mouth moving, but no sound coming from his throat. One of the guardsmen rushed to the front porch to wretch.

"Are they all dead?" Zach finally managed to ask, his voice roaring inside of his skull as he tried to overcome the ringing in his ears.

The question seemed to break the spell, the men moving quickly to check pulses and listen for beating hearts. The news wasn't good.

Both of the civilians were dead. The guardsman hit by Charlie's initial shotgun blast had taken the blunt of the load in his body armor but was bleeding from several smaller wounds on his arms. The NOPD officer, caught by the scattergun's second shot, had a thigh full of buckshot and was hemorrhaging enough to turn his pants leg a glistening red.

The home's third resident, lying at the feet of Ford and Zach, was still alive, but bleeding from a nasty gash on his head – courtesy of a cop's rifle butt.

"What the hell happened here?" someone finally asked. "How the fuck did this spiral out of control so quickly?"

And then it seemed everyone wanted to talk at once.

Ford was the first to realize the ramifications. As the soldiers worked on the two wounded team members with their first aid kits, Zach could tell the sergeant was already formulating how he would frame the incident in his report.

Moving from team member to team member, the senior officer barked very pointed questions, such as, "What did you see?" and "Who fired first?"

When it was Zach's turn, the ranger answered in a neutral tone, "I didn't see shit. I was the last one in, so I have no idea what happened." It wasn't exactly the truth, but not entirely a lie. Besides, Ford's attitude was beginning to seriously concern the Texan.

Emotions continued to build throughout the group, an initial wave of anger quickly replaced by a current of remorse and chagrin. But then the tide started to turn.

"That guy from the kitchen fired first," someone protested, self-preservation finally taking hold of the herd's mentality.

Regret at the loss of human life was quickly cast aside. "What fucking choice did we have?" someone else chimed in.

With the exception of the Texan, it became evident that every man in the room was having negative thoughts about his career, reputation, freedom, and future. Each individual's emotions began feeding off the others, eventually building into a crescendo of convenient truth.

"We all acted legitimately," flowed the conversational logic. They were the law, and the dead occupants of the house had resisted and then attacked them. Right was right.

Abe's moaning from the floor again silenced the room, all of Ford's team nervously glancing at each other, questioning what to do with the one non-member witness. Zach didn't like the desperate expressions forming in their eyes.

"Since I didn't see shit, I'll take this man and go find him some medical care while you guys finish up here," Zach stated.

Before anyone could answer, he managed to lift Abe onto his shoulders in the classic fireman's carry, heading for the front door. No one stopped him.

Zach was three blocks away, straining under the weight of Abe's unresponsive body, when he spied a small convoy of Humvees rolling down a cross street. Setting the still-unconscious man on the sidewalk, the ranger waved down the military vehicles with his badge flashing in plain sight.

After turning over his wounded charge to the military patrol for transport to a nearby medical facility, Zach found himself walking toward the sub-station. He desperately wanted to get back to the truck and away from the team. For some reason, he glanced over his shoulder, back at the house where it all went down.

A thick column of smoke was rising into the air, Zach having little doubt that the scene of the incident was now completely engulfed in flames. Sighing, he decided the officers were overreacting. Or were they?

Inside the Texan, tumultuous divide grew incrementally as he navigated through the devastation that was once the crown jewel of the South. Ford and the others were all good men, asked to do an impossible job in unforgiving circumstances. Zach could relate; recollections of his own little "indiscretion" with Tusk resurfacing.

The men he'd been patrolling with had been pressed to the brink of human endurance, thrust into a desolate, seemingly hopeless situation. They weren't criminals by any measure, yet two people were dead. Two fathers, husbands... innocents who were only protecting their property and liberty.

But that's just your opinion, he thought. *The authorities here... the ones who serve this city think otherwise.*

Zach couldn't reach a conclusion, failed to span the chasm of his internal divide. He, too, was at the end of his rope, the travel, lack of sleep, and draconian surroundings taking their toll.

"I'll find a quiet place to hide the truck," he whispered. "I've got to get some sleep."

Abe never saw what happened to his father and brother's bodies – couldn't recall being driven to the airport. Flashing, brief images of a stretcher came to the surface, and then a howling wind and sense of weightlessness.

His first clear recollection was of a man in an Army uniform pressing a cold stethoscope against his chest.

"How are you feeling?" the doctor asked.

"Been better," Abe mumbled. "What happened? The police…. Where am I… my dad and brother?"

"You took a nasty blow to the head, sir," the doctor began. "I don't have any information about your family or what happened down in New Orleans. Right this moment, you're at an emergency triage center in Baton Rouge. They flew you in on a helicopter about 15 minutes ago."

The physician shined a bright light in Abe's eyes, shaking his head. Turning to some unseen assistant, he said, "We're looking at a pretty severe concussion here. I've got uneven dilation. Let's get some x-rays ordered."

The memories flooded Abe's mind, visions of his father lying in a pool of blood, his brother's chest being ripped wide open. He tried to rise from the cot, a strong pair of hands pushing him back down. His head was throbbing, lungs unable to pull in enough air.

"Murderers!" he screamed, trying again to move from the cot. "Those murdering sons of bitches!"

Through the trauma, Abe felt a sharp prick on his arm. He looked down to see someone poking him with a syringe of clear liquid. Almost instantly, a feeling of euphoria filled his previously troubled mind, and then the light began to fade.

After sleeping a few hours in the reclined driver's seat, Zach was stiff and sore. Needing to stretch, use the facilities, and hopefully locate a cup of coffee, he wandered into the substation.

The duty officer noted his arrival, waving the visiting ranger over. Handing Zach a slip of paper, the NOPD lieutenant announced, "This came in for you a couple hours ago."

Blinking the fog from his eyes, the Texan studied the cryptic message in a whisper. "Influx of refugees has halted. Number of potential refugees vastly overestimated. Report to Company E earliest. Current assignment canceled."

"I think your commanders thought we were going to be sending another 50 or 60,000 people to Texas," the duty officer observed. "We didn't have quite as big a problem as we thought, so the invasion from Louisiana has stopped. Good news for everybody."

Relieved, Zach decided that a steaming mug of java would taste even better now. He meandered through the maze of temporary desks and cubicles, following a cold trail of Styrofoam cups.

He discovered the pot, a two-inch thick black line of sludge in the bottom. Sniffing the brew, he tried to ascertain its age, and then settled on not caring. *Wine improves with age, maybe coffee does, too,* he conjectured.

He'd just finished pouring when he sensed someone standing close by. He peered up to see Sergeant Ford and one of the other NOPD officers. "Good morning, Ranger. Everything okay?"

"Is it morning?" Zach yawned, sipping the strong brew. "I had no idea."

"I heard through the grapevine that your assignment's been canceled. Heading back to Texas today?"

"Yup. Wish I could hang around to help you guys out a little…. You've got one hell of a job ahead of you, but my orders were explicit. You know how it is when they use the word, 'Earliest.'"

Ford chuckled, and then his face became serious. "I'm filling out my report, Ranger Bass. I wanted to double-check… make sure you hadn't recalled any additional details that I should note."

"No, officially I have nothing to add. As I stated previously, I was the last man in and didn't see much of anything."

Ford smiled and nodded. Extending his hand, he said, "Well, good luck then."

Zach accepted the offering but didn't let go of the man's hand. Instead, he pulled the NOPD officer close and whispered, "There was a crime committed at that house, Sergeant, and we both know it. The only reason I'm not sticking my foot in that sewer is because I don't think you or the other men are the guilty parties. From my perspective, the numbskull who ordered the confiscation of private firearms should be charged with murder. And if you ever meet him, you're welcome to let him know that I said so."

Releasing his grip, Zach swallowed another mouthful of coffee and smiled at the stunned sergeant. "Good luck, Ford," he said and headed for the truck.

Chapter 3 - Prosecution

Two years after Katrina...

The prosecutor shoved the pile of documents across the courthouse table, his expression one that failed to mask his disgust. "This sickens me, Mr. Hendricks," the state's attorney hissed. "You should be locked away in a federal penitentiary, not walking free."

"You call *this* justice?" Abe growled back. "Do you really believe *I'm* the criminal here? My father and brother were murdered, my family homestead burned to the ground to cover the acts of overzealous policemen and thugs. If you honestly believe *I* am the bad guy, then there is something horribly wrong with our system of justice."

The government lawyer bared his teeth, moving forward in his chair as if he were going to lunge over the mahogany conference table and assault Abe. But he didn't.

Taking a deep breath instead, he gathered himself and spoke calmly. "The Attorney General of Louisiana has agreed to drop all charges against you, Mr. Hendricks. In exchange, you will agree to dismiss your punitive actions against the city of New Orleans, Orleans Parish, and all involved in the alleged incident that occurred at your father's home. In addition, all records, proceedings, depositions, and other evidence collected by each party will be destroyed. All official court documents are to be sealed."

"And the gag order?" Abe's attorney questioned.

"A federal judge will issue a gag order, instructing that all parties are never to disclose any of these proceedings in public or private," the state attorney snapped, his voice seething with disdain. "Your record will be expunged, Mr. Hendricks."

Even though he had been warned of the parameters of the impending offer, the government lawyer's proposal spilled over Abe like a bucket of ice-cold water, awakening him to the stern reality of his situation. In that brief span of time, his last speck of hope was relinquished, the grim reality that he would never procure justice for his family settling like a rock on his chest. It was a head spinner, but on top of it all, Abe found himself being defamed, denigrated, disgraced. Now, the best that he could expect was to save himself. He couldn't believe it had all come down to this.

"My record..." Abe mumbled, shaking his head to clear the fog of incredulity that clouded his thoughts.

"I'd like a few moments with my client," Abe's lawyer said. "In private."

Without another word, the prosecutor rose and strode out of the room, leaving Abe, his counsel, and Kara staring at the pile of documents on the table. It was Abe who finally broke the silence.

"I can't believe this is happening," he whispered. "Not in the United States... not in America."

Kara reached across, gently squeezing her husband's hand in support.

The lawyer's tone was soft, "Abe, I know you don't like this. I fully understand why you feel that justice isn't being served, but this is the best possible outcome I can conceive. While it's true these guys have a burr up their collective ass, in reality it's much more than just our case. The city is in grave financial crisis, defending itself against an avalanche of lawsuits and legal actions. They'll come after you if you continue to raise a stink, and we both know it."

Abe nodded; he'd heard the argument before. It still wasn't right. "My father and brother were slaughtered," he protested. "They were shot down like a couple of dogs in the street. They died because the city issued an illegal order to confiscate weapons – an order that has since been ruled unconstitutional in federal court. And then... to make matters worse... the men who executed my family tried to cover up their heinous act by committing arson, intentionally setting a fire that burned my family homestead to the ground. Give me one good reason why I shouldn't feel like the scales of justice are tipped against me?"

But the odds *were* against him, a fact that everyone else seemed to grasp. Even the lawyer was melancholy, his eyes etched with a sadness deeper than the wrinkles that surrounded them. "I know, Abe. I understand your disappointment," he lamented. "I sympathize with your case more than any other in the 30 years I've been practicing law. But the other side tells a different story. Even you admit your brother fired the first shot, and that your father was resisting the officers. We cannot prove our case. We cannot win. Here, look at these files."

Abe watched as the counselor reached for a stack of folders residing on the table. He pulled the top one off and showed it to his client.

"Sergeant Roland 'Butch' Ford, New Orleans Police Department," he began reading, "seventeen years a cop, four promotions, five awards for distinguished service, married 22 years, three children. A deacon in his church and on the board of directors for a major local charity. This isn't the profile of a mass murderer, Abe."

When Abe didn't reply, the attorney pulled the second folder from the pile. "Master Sergeant Terrance P. Hull, Louisiana National Guard, U.S. Army Reserve. When he was with the regular Army, he served two tours in Iraq. Awarded the Bronze Star, Purple Heart, and three unit citations. Married, two children. A perfect service record and considered an upstanding citizen by everyone my investigators have interviewed. This man isn't a criminal either, Abe. I could go on. All of the files are there."

Kara leaned in close, kissing her husband on the cheek. "You can't bring them back, Abe. I'm so very, very sorry this happened, but the truth is that they're gone. And there's nothing you can do to change that. If you choose to fight this, and somehow prevail, will seeing the men in those folders go to prison fix anything? Will ruining their lives make our lives any better?"

Still, he wouldn't accept the cold, harsh reality of life. He scolded them, "I can't believe you two. I can't believe any of this is happening."

"I've known this prosecutor for years, Abe," the lawyer stated in a firm tone. "He believes you are the dangerous element here, honestly sees you as the ongoing threat to society. He will pursue the listed charges, and no one knows how a jury will find if the case goes to trial. It's not worth the risk. Take his deal and go on with your life. The only thing worse than the men who killed your family going unpunished would be you losing your freedom."

"What freedom?" Abe grunted.

The Orleans Parish, Office of the Prosecutor had charged Abe with numerous felonies and misdemeanors, including resisting arrest, conspiracy, assaulting a police officer, sedition, and accessory to attempted murder.

When Abe's allegations had first surfaced, the NOPD had claimed that no record, report, or other evidence existed. Later, the city prepared a virtual menu of excuses for the missing documentation; citing the state of emergency, flood-damaged police stations, lack of computer access, and general mayhem. But to Abe, the answer was much simpler; the authorities were trying to cover up the events after Katrina.

Abe kept digging, the effort rewarded as small details began to emerge. Sergeant Ford had indeed filed a full report, including the death of Charles and Edward Hendricks. The officer's account of the incident included statements by two other policemen and two members of the National Guard. Ford claimed that the resulting fire had been ignited during the gunfight.

Abe had pressed hard, poking copious holes in the handwritten report. The case seemed to finally gain momentum when his attorney was granted a subpoena to depose the witnesses. Abe was confident the felons' accounts would never match given the pressure of formal interviews and statements.

But then the prosecutor struck back, filing an exhaustive list of charges that resulted in Abe's arrest. The momentum of Abe's lawsuit never regained traction again. Instead, the legal contest raged for over six months like two men arm-wrestling to a draw.

And then there were the legal bills. The government lawyers had filed a cacophony of meaningless motions, maneuvers designed to bury Abe's legal team in a flood of paperwork deeper than

Katrina's storm surge had ever been. Whoever postulated that, "You can't fight city hall," must have realized that the government has much deeper pockets than its citizenry. Despite the insurance money from his father's policy, if the dispute went to trial, Abe and Kara would face bankruptcy.

Abe sighed, shaking his head in disgust while reaching for the papers. He peered at Kara, wanting one last confirmation that she supported his signing of the offer. She smiled and nodded, whispering, "I love you, Abe. Let's go back home and get on with our lives together."

Abe began signing the papers, the scratching of his pen the only sound in the room.

He was putting his signature on those documents for a variety of reasons. Kara and he needed a life without an extended legal battle. What kind of marriage could they have if she were lying awake every night, worrying about her husband becoming a convict? They had dreams of a home and family, not an empty bank account and looming jail time.

Abe continued in silence, signing page after legal-page of paperwork.

Old Tom Henry didn't believe in all-terrain vehicles, choosing instead to put his faith and trust in horseflesh, a well-worn saddle, and a bridle in his hand.

"Them gull-dern, gas-powered machines got no place on a proper ranch," he'd informed Zach at the corral. "I know every mother's son south of the panhandle uses those buggies to work their ranches, but I just can't see it. Their constant buzzing commotion disturbs the livestock, and fuel is more expensive than hay."

The old timer paused, moving to the other side of his mount to adjust the stirrup. "Two winters ago," he continued, "a diamondback snuck up and kissed me on my right leg." The ancient rancher then patted his mare gently on the neck, "Ole Daisy Mae here got me back to the house even though I was passed out in the saddle. Ain't no fancy contraption from Japan going to do that for a man."

It had been a while since Zach had ridden a horse, even longer since he'd steered one of the beasts over rough terrain. And rough it was.

The Lazy H ranch occupied some of the most cantankerous topography in Company E's region, the property occupying a space near both Big Bend National Park and the Black Gap Wildlife Management Area.

"How did you find the body?" Zach asked.

"I didn't," replied the weathered, old rancher. "I lease this section to hunters from back east now and then. You should've seen those two greenhorns, racing up to the farmhouse like they were being chased by the devil and a herd of demons, all pale and shaky after finding the deceased. They were like a couple of schoolgirls who'd never seen a dead body before."

Zach grunted, easily fashioning the image in his mind's eye.

"Then they had the gall to look down on me, like I was some coldhearted, senile fool because I didn't go rushing around like a freshly branded calf. I told 'em... we find corpses all the time around these parts. Ain't no big deal. Ya know, the coyotes cut and run if they see the border patrol closing in, and sometimes they can't round up all of their sheep again. We find them later… when the vultures are circling."

Zach wasn't surprised. Ranchers along the Rio Grande frequently happened across dead immigrants whose chosen path to freedom wound through some of the most desolate landscapes in North America. Most died from dehydration; some succumbed to violence.

The two men rode along silently, climbing ever higher into the craggy, steep cliffs. The trail was narrow, barely wide enough for a single mount to pass. Tom caught the ranger peering over the edge, a 70-foot sheer drop just inches away.

"Don't you worry none, Mr. Texas Ranger, sir," the rancher chuckled. "White Lightning is as sure-footed a steed as any. Ya know, I've seen lots of tenderfeet toss their cookies on a ride like this. Don't reckon many folks got the stomach for this kind of trail."

"Well, I have to say, it doesn't look like this path sees a lot of traffic," Zach responded, his back beginning to ache from bumping along at the steep angle of ascent, his mouth dry from inhaling trail dust.

"See what I mean? That's what is so odd about this corpse," Tom mused. "This trail dead ends up on Apache Ridge. There's no way anyone could have walked in from the south. This person had to come in from the north or west. Either that or this traveler was a mountain climber of some skill. Or maybe he was part goat."

Scanning the surrounding vista, Zach had to agree. Water wouldn't be the primary challenge here – the unwelcoming terrain would deter most interlopers, a high percentage of those who forged forward anyway being claimed by the desert. No question now why the county deputies had called in the Texas Rangers. Standard procedure would have been to simply let the county bury the dead and hope some next-of-kin eventually came looking for a lost loved one. But this... this was a puzzle.

The two riders continued their trek, passing through narrow canyons and traversing through fields of black, volcanic rock. Zach lost count of the switchbacks, at one point questioning if he could've found his way back to the ranch.

Eventually, they entered flatter ground, the plateau offering a splendid panoramic view including the distant Chisos Mountains. Emory Peak, the 7800-foot centerpiece of Big Bend Park, was clearly visible on the horizon.

Tom wasn't in the mood to sightsee, turning Daisy Mae and pointing toward a low formation of rocks, he announced, "It's over there."

A few minutes later, Zach dismounted, his eyes focused on the yellow bones and scraps of clothing still surrounding the body. The elements, birds, and insects had scoured every bit of flesh from the skeleton. The ranger knew that in this unforgiving environment, only a few weeks of exposure could have produced this result, but estimated these remains had been here for a much longer period of time. Windswept dust had partially covered some of the smaller bones, and the lightened hue indicated a year or more of bleaching by the sun.

He slowly circled the remains, not expecting any investigational epiphany, more so to get a feel for the position of the body and its surroundings. His methodology was to construct a story that explained the scene, but what lay before him contradicted the stereotypical demise of an undocumented alien. He noted the conspicuous absence of any satchel of clothing, empty water jugs, or food wrappers in the area – garbage that typically accompanied those trying to sneak across the border.

She had somehow hiked to the spot, an almost certain fact. Given the nearly flat surroundings, this outcropping would have been the only shady spot in the area. It was easy to imagine a thirsty, hurting woman struggling with each step. The sun, combined with her ever-thickening blood, would cause an extremely painful headache. To escape from the heat would have appealed to her.

She sat down to rest with her back to the rocks. Allowing for the position of the body and the respective angle of the sun, Zach estimated her arrival at late afternoon. She had never managed her feet again.

The lawman pulled his camera from the saddlebag, powering up the device and snapping a series of photographs from every vantage.

Moving in closer, his eyes scrutinized each small section of her skeleton, starting from the feet and moving up. The first thing he noticed was the absence of any shoes. Even the poorest, most desperate border crashers know not to attempt a desert crossing without protecting their feet.

Zach squatted down for a better view, clearly intrigued by the deepening mystery.
Maybe someone robbed her and took her shoes, the ranger reasoned.

She was young, he guessed, that determination gathered from a pelvis that displayed no telltale indicator of childbirth and the condition of her teeth. There was no way he could determine her actual age without lab results.

A faded swath of cloth caught the ranger's eye. Removing a pencil from his pocket, Zach gently brushed aside a thin layer of dust and sand, finally exposing a two-inch length of material. Holding the decomposing fabric in the light, he could identify a strip of elastic bordering a thin, almost sheer material. There was still enough dye left to detect a colorful pattern... a pattern with balloons.

I've seen this before, he suddenly realized. *The hooker... Tusk... the woman I accidently shot.*

Shaking his head, Zach dismissed the thought. Hundreds, if not thousands, of female panties may have been manufactured with that design. It was probably just a coincidence. *Still, she was probably about the right age...*

He continued examining the body, his next discovery even more troubling. She wore two rings on her right hand, one of them containing a sizeable amount of gold. *Well, whatever happened here, this definitely wasn't a robbery*, Zach pondered. *Thieves would have snatched that jewelry before her body was cold.*

The ranger finished his work, returning to the packhorse and retrieving a thick, plastic body bag and a shovel. They would haul her back down and send the remains to Austin for a complete autopsy.

With the body bag riding unceremoniously in the bed of the truck, Zach placed a call the minute he had cell service.

"Officer Hinton here, how may I help you," answered the polite voice.

"Hey copper, it's Zach Bass. How's tricks?"

"Well, my, my…. What a pleasant surprise, Ranger Bass. To what do I owe the pleasure?"

"Do you remember that woman I turned over to you in Alpine a few years back? At the hospital? The one I found with all that cash?"

There was a pause, the state trooper trying to recall. "Yeah! Sure do. You were off to solve the problems of the world, and I was supposed to clean up after your messy ass. Why?"

"Whatever became of her?"

"Your boss bailed you out, Bass. About 10 minutes after you left me carrying your bags, Major Alcorn showed up and took her off my hands. He said he was taking over the investigation, and I should resume my regular duties. That was the last I saw of her."

Zach was a little taken aback by Hinton's answer, his mind swirling as it assimilated the new information.

"Zach? You still there?"

"Yeah, sorry Hinton. I just wasn't expecting that answer. No biggie, though. Hey, thanks, man. Talk to you soon."

Zach continued driving into Alpine, wondering if his morbid cargo had made the same trip two years ago, chauffeured by the same ranger.

The riddle bothered him so much, that he decided to go out on a limb and dial Major Alcorn.

"What can I do for you, Ranger Bass?" came the gruff answer, the major no doubt having figured out how to use caller ID.

"Sir, sorry to bother you, but I am working a case and had a quick question. Do you recall the incident with that cartel goon named Tusk about two years ago?"

"Yes. Yes, I do."

"I just talked with Trooper Hinton, and he informed me that he turned the witness over to your custody that day. I was wondering if you could fill me in from there?"

Across the cell connection, it was difficult to be sure, but Zach sensed Alcorn was uncomfortable with the question. After clearing his throat, the ranger commander responded with a question of his own, "Where are you now, Zach?"

"I'm bringing a body into the morgue at Alpine. A rancher down by Black Gap found the deceased yesterday, and the circumstances were unusual enough that the deputies called me in."

"I'm in Fort Davis," announced Alcorn. "I can meet you there in about an hour. Is it the same girl?"

Zach actually pulled the phone away from his ear, staring at the device in shock. *How could you possibly know that?* Zach marveled.

"Ranger Bass, are you there?"

"Yes, sir. Sorry, I lost you there for a second. Cell signal out here is spotty," Zach lied, trying to buy time to think.

"Is the body you found the same girl?"

"There's no way to be sure, sir, but there is some evidence pointing me in that direction."

"I'll meet you at the diner in Alpine in an hour," the senior man stated and then disconnected the call.

"This day is going to be more interesting than I thought," Zach mused.

Major Alcorn strolled into the greasy spoon right on cue. Zach had dropped the female remains at the morgue, signed the paperwork, and was swallowing his second cup of coffee.

The two peace officers checked the menu, both ordering the lunch special of chicken fried steak, green beans, and mashed potatoes.

"On the day you left for New Orleans, I changed my mind about assigning the case to Trooper Hinton. He's a good man and a fine officer, but since there was a shooting involved, I thought it best if we handled the case inside our own department."

"Makes sense," Zach replied, trying to appear casual about the whole affair.

Alcorn continued, "I took the witness back to the scene. She walked me through what had happened so I could give the most accurate report possible."

Sipping his coffee, Zach met his boss's gaze over the rim of the cup. Alcorn seemed pissed.

"Why did you feel it necessary to taint the crime scene, Ranger Bass?"

Zach's heart stopped, a perceptible streak of icy cold surging through his core. "Sir?"

"Oh, come now, Ranger. Do you think I'm a fool? It was your bullet that hit that woman," the supervisor demanded, swallowing a bite and noisily flinging the fork on the ceramic plate. "And while that's not any big deal, your sloppy attempt to modify the evidence could have been. Thank gawd that cartel enforcer died; I can't imagine exposing your story to the scrutiny of a trial. You fucked up in so many ways, son. You should consider yourself lucky that I did the follow-up and not someone else." Alcorn paused his lecture, sipping from the mug before initiating somewhat intimidating eye contact with his charge.

Zach shifted his gaze to his lunch, choosing that moment to carve the rest of his meat, opting not to respond. He couldn't tell where his boss was going with all this, couldn't judge how much trouble he was in. Yet, the incident had been two years ago. Why hadn't Alcorn said something before now?

Realizing his subordinate wasn't going to comment, the major continued. "I corrected a few of your mistakes, Zach. It took a bit of work and time. When I left the trailer, the girl was gone... and so was the money."

Zach's pupils dilated as big as his coffee saucer, but he still kept his mouth shut.

Alcorn grunted at the younger man's reaction and then pushed some green beans around with his fork. "So I inherited quite a mess, Ranger Bass. I found myself with a rookie ranger who'd clearly screwed the pooch, but seemed to have done it with good intentions. My witness was missing, wandering the desert and probably making a run for the border. Given she had enough cash to retire to the Mexican Riviera, I wasn't overly worried about her safety. I was in possession of a dead cartel assassin, a fine gentleman who was carrying what appeared to be a down payment for causing my ultimate demise. You, sir, were in New Orleans and completely out of reach for consultation."

"So what did you do, sir?" Zach asked, unable to hold his tongue any longer.

"I filed a report on the incident, leaving no doubt it was a righteous shoot. Other than that, I didn't do a damned thing. There's no official mention of the witness, money, or anybody's attempt to tamper with evidence – yours *or* mine."

"Thank you, sir," Zach replied, his voice barely above a whisper.

"Look, I've kept my eye on you, Zach. Had to... given this little episode. I never noticed any other indiscretions," Alcorn announced, signaling the waitress for a refill on his coffee. "I know you are frustrated with this job. If you're like any other cop, you see and do some things that are... err... questionable at times. You've gotta make peace with that and draw your own line in the sand. Beyond that, young man – every law enforcement officer goes through those periods of doubt. That's why our community is so tightly knit. That's why we are held together with a unique bond. You should never forget that, Zach. Never."

"Yes, sir."

The two men parted company, Zach still deep in thought as he watched his boss drive away from the parking lot.

"Maybe I misnamed the triangle of despair," he reckoned. "Maybe I should call it the triangle of survival."

Chapter 4 – A Not So New Life

8 years after Katrina...

Abe steered through the neighborhood, a classic rock tune jamming through the speakers and a Cheshire cat grin painted on his face. The late afternoon sun blanketed the widely spaced homes, each centered on its own multi-acre lot, and separated by thick woods.

When Kara and he had decided to start anew and escape from the memories of Louisiana, the real estate agent had carefully considered their needs. His wife was a country girl, Abe a sportsman who had always taken every opportunity to get away from his father's suburban residence. The realtor had shown the couple a new development on the far north side of Houston, beyond the subdivisions comprised of tract homes and yet still within reach of the city.

"Houston's growing northward," the agent had informed the wide-eyed duo. "Grab this land now before urban creep makes lots this size unaffordable."

And so they had.

The couple had settled on a strategy of turning negatives into positives. The insurance money and modest estate Abe inherited provided the seed money for their little share of the American dream. Abe designed their home, his fledgling engineering start-up managing the project between paying customers.

He still experienced a flush of pride every time he pulled into the driveway.

With his briefcase in one hand and the long, narrow box of the new rifle in the other, he negotiated the sidewalk. After pausing to scan the backyard, his mood was elevated even more via the smooth carpet of lush green. The yard guys must have just made their weekly visit.

The back stoop was partially blocked by white trash bags, evidence of Kara's cleaning activities, and a strong hint for him to do his share. He was too excited by the afternoon's earlier events to tote the garbage out right now, making a mental note to perform the chore before another project commanded his attention.

"Darling, I'm home," he announced, stepping through the threshold.

"Hey," she replied, glancing up from a paperback and her steaming cup of tea. "How did it go today?"

Abe strolled to the couch where his soul mate had reclined, gently placing a hand on each cheek and kissing her forehead. "Oh, sweetheart! I had the greatest day, and I love you to pieces!"

Setting her book down, Kara returned the peck, a genuine smile illuminating her face. That reaction was quickly replaced with a frown when she noticed the rifle box. "Oh, Abe... not another one?"

It took him a moment to digest her remark, following her gaze to the cardboard package under his arm. "Oh, that. No, no, no, that's not why I had a great day," he said, waving off her concern. "This is just a deer rifle I ordered a month ago. I had a great day because we won the Morrison contract!"

The grin returned to Kara's face, "Oh, honey, I'm so happy for you! I know you've been working so hard on that bid."

"But that's not even the best news," he beamed. "We had 47 people show up at the 'Patriots Now' meeting this afternoon."

"Really? That's a new attendance record, isn't it?" she asked.

"Yeah. I think we're onto something here. People are so fed up with Washington... it seems like they really want to make a change. We registered five new voters today, and several people told me they were going to invite friends for next week's meeting. You should come."

Kara shook her head in disagreement, "Now why would this liberal girl want to go and mingle with all those conservative types? I'd be like a fish out of water."

"We're attracting more than just right-wingers. Two of the people who registered today were Democrats. And I'm trying hard to keep right and left out of the meetings – we're just people who want to see a change. You'd be fine; I promise."

Wrapping her arms around her husband's neck, Kara moved against him in a warm hug. "Abe, you don't know how pleased I am to see you so involved and happy in all this. After everything we went through in Louisiana, it's good to see you hit your stride. You've worked so hard – you deserve some success."

He returned the embrace, kissing the top of her head. "*We've* worked so hard, my wife. You've stuck with me through the lean and the mean, and I would never have made it through if you weren't right here beside me."

Kara kissed his cheek and then winked. "Perhaps a little wine is in order after dinner... then a celebration after that," she offered in her most sultry voice, seductively slipping her camisole strap over her shoulder.

Abe responded with an eyebrow waggle, "Now that would be the icing on the cake."

She moved to the kitchen counter, fiddling with her tea and the sugar and then giving the chili a quick stir. Nodding toward the rifle box, she announced, "I'll be an even happier girl when you stop bringing those home. With the company growing like a weed and your newfound political endeavors, when are you going to have the time to kill poor little Bambi?"

Abe shrugged, "It's just a hunting rifle, not a manifestation of paranoia." Sighing, his mood and demeanor changed immediately. "Are we going to have this discussion again? I like guns. I'm a man who works hard in an office all day, with my nose to the grindstone. Just daydreaming about spending time outdoors frees up my brain from the corporate games and bullshit. Besides that, you do not want me hiking in the wilderness unarmed where the feral hogs outnumber me a hundred to one. It's harmless, my love."

With a light chuckle, Kara turned and picked up a stack of envelopes. "Speaking of paranoia, there was a letter in today's mail from the IRS. It might be that certification you've been waiting on."

"This day keeps getting better and better," he said, reaching to accept the envelope. "If this is what I think it is," he continued, looking around for a letter opener, "I'm going to have even less time for hunting. 'Patriots Now' needs its non-profit status so we can actually start growing."

"I don't understand. It is going to be some sort of charity?"

Abe, finally locating the dull blade, looked up to answer his wife. "No, nothing like that. Being a non-profit allows us to reach out and involve more people. One of our members wants to rent busses and travel to assisted living facilities so the old folks can attend meetings and have a ride to vote. But we can't afford the insurance on the busses unless we're a non-profit."

Kara nodded her understanding, allowing Abe to return his attentions to the government correspondence. She watched as his face changed, a frown forming on his lips, quickly followed by a full-blown scowl as he continued to read the letter.

"Not good news I take it."

"This is bullshit!" he snapped, examining the paper with unbelieving eyes. "They can't do this!"

"What? What's wrong?"

"The IRS wants a list of all of our contributors, including their names, addresses, social media sites, and social security numbers. They want a signed affidavit from each member of our board of directors, testifying that Patriots Now isn't promoting a political agenda or participating in fundraising for the Republican Party. What crap! They can't do this."

Kara moved to her husband's side, scanning the document. "That does seem a bit harsh," she commented. "Maybe this is some new law or something."

Abe tossed the letter onto the counter. "I'm not going to let it ruin my day. I'll turn it over to George and let him look at it from an accountant's point of view. Maybe he knows something I don't."

He then moved with purpose to the rifle box, hefting the new weapon and turning to exit the kitchen. "I'm going to go put this in the gun room."

Kara watched her husband walk away, her attention then focusing on the government document. She couldn't avoid feeling troubled, almost as if the letter were a forecast of impending misfortune.

It had been a wonderful sight to see her husband turn his frustrations into something positive. After the incidents in New Orleans, she had watched him try several cures.

Initially, he'd rechanneled his anger and grief into the business, working incredible hours and enduring multiple sacrifices. While the new firm had succeeded, it still hadn't provided refuge from the demons that tormented her husband's soul.

Then he switched gears, attempting to exploit hunting, camping, and rock climbing as an outlet for his mental angst. She'd been worried, Abe seemingly discovering some resolution in firearms and shooting. Gently questioning his newfound love of destructive, killing machines, he'd waved off her concerns.

Over time, that fancy had faded as well, his gun cabinet and hiking boots covered in a fine layer of dust.

He did an excellent job of covering the fury that simmered inside. So skilled in fact, that Kara often wondered if time was actually healing her mate. But then something would shake his calm facade, some news story, Christmas card from an old friend, or television show. Abe would become sullen and moody, sometimes pacing around the house as if he were wrestling old demons and talking to the ghosts. She knew he was tortured at the worst of times, scarred at the best.

But then along came Patriots Now.

"The legal system failed me," Abe explained. "The justice system didn't work. I need to do something that gives me a respite from the sickening feeling that no meaning has come from my father and brother losing their lives. I have to find a way to turn bad into good, and I think the political route is the best option I've found."

And it seemed to be working. Kara had watched her husband throw his heart and soul into the organization – volunteering his time, purchasing equipment, supplies, and other necessities. Even the smallest milestones seemed to peg his gratification meter.

"I hope you're not a brewing storm," she scowled, peering at the letter. "I hope you're not another Katrina building strength out in the Gulf. My Abe has already suffered enough for any ten men... please leave him alone."

Given the late hour and remote location of their subdivision, the sound of the front doorbell brought both Kara and Abe to answer. Glancing through the peephole, Abe spotted two men with suits standing on his front porch.

Shrugging his shoulders in answer to Kara's inquisitive glance, Abe said, "Who is it?"

"Internal Revenue Service," came the response. "Agents Dunworthy and Hammond."

Abe flashed pale, the scene reminding him of New Orleans and the image his father must have seen before letting the policemen into his home.

"Are you okay?" Kara asked, not liking her husband's color.

"Yeah. Yeah, I'm fine."

Abe opened the door, making sure his posture let it be known that the two agents weren't welcome inside his home.

"Yes."

The man in front flashed his ID, including a badge. "Sir, we're here to speak with Mr. Abraham Hendricks. Is this the correct address?"

"Yes, I'm Abe Hendricks."

There was an uncomfortable pause, as if the agents expected to be asked inside. After it had become clear that Abe wasn't going to issue an invitation, the man asked, "May we come in?"

"No."

Abe's response drew a frown, the two men on the porch glancing at each other. "We won't take up much of your time, Mr. Hendricks. I think everyone would be more comfortable if we could sit and go through our questions."

"Gentlemen, I don't mean to be rude or uncooperative, but I learned a long time ago to exercise my right to remain silent. If you will hold on just a moment, I'll get my attorney's phone number and address. You're welcome to ask him any questions concerning my taxes."

The man in the back stepped forward, his voice projecting authority, "Why so uptight, Mr. Hendricks? You're acting like a man who has something to hide. You do realize that your actions will just make the service dig deeper?"

Abe bristled at the threat. "Are you saying that by exercising my constitutional right, I'm inviting my government to treat me differently than any other citizen?"

The man shook his head, "Describe it however you like, Mr. Hendricks. The fact remains that in the vast majority of cases, any taxpayer who lawyers up is hiding something… something significant. It is a statistical reality that our enforcement personnel can't ignore."

"I'm hiding nothing, sir. Now let me retrieve my lawyer's contact information."

Abe closed the door, turning to find a troubled look on his wife's face. "Are you sure we just shouldn't invite them in and see what they want to know?" she asked, her voice barely above a whisper.

"Yes, I'm sure," he responded, stalking off to retrieve a pencil and paper.

A minute later, Abe opened the front door, surprised to find only a single agent on his porch. A quick glance confirmed the nondescript government sedan sitting in the driveway was empty. "Where is your buddy?" Abe asked.

The agent didn't answer, but Kara did. "Abe, one of those men is in our backyard."

"Shit," he barked, pointing a finger at the remaining agent on his porch. "Get the fuck off of my property, right now, young man. Here is my attorney's name and number. Don't come back here without a warrant."

"Are you threatening a federal agent, sir?"

"I am warning a trespasser. I'm not going to ask nicely again."

"We'll be speaking very soon, Mr. Hendricks," the agent replied with a menacing tone.

Abe watched the two men leave, a very panicky Kara under his arm.

It took a few hours before the Hendricks settled down, Abe reassuring Kara that he'd done the right thing and that their financial records were in order. "I pay our taxes," he promised, "and I don't play games with any of the rules. It's just not worth losing any sleep over, especially for a guy who's seen how punitive our beloved government can be."

The entire incident was almost forgotten when Abe left for work the following morning, his 30-minute commute to his Woodlands office consisting mostly of a pleasant country drive.

Strolling through the mid-rise's lobby, Abe rode the elevator up to the third floor and entered Hendricks Engineering, Incorporated just like any ordinary morning. He stopped mid-stride, finding a rather large gentleman pointing a gun in his face.

"Who are you?" the big man growled.

"I'm the owner," Abe stuttered, finally noticing the embroidered initials "IRS" on the man's jacket. "What do you want?"

His question was ignored. Instead, the man lowered his weapon and demanded, "Do you have any cell phones or weapons on your person?"

"What are you doing here?" What's this all about?" Abe protested, his anger beginning to build.

"I asked you a fucking question!" the IRS man screamed at the top of his lungs, again raising his pistol.

"Yes, I have a cell phone. No, I don't have a weapon. Now, I want to see your warrant."

"Hand over your cell phone, sir, or I'll arrest you for failure to cooperate with a federal officer."

Abe shrugged, reaching into his pocket for the smartphone he carried there. Taking it from his hand, the IRS agent then motioned for Abe to follow.

He was led into the employee break room, finding all of his staff seated around the small tables stationed there. Everyone looked absolutely scared to death.

"I want to see the warrant," Abe demanded again. "You have no right to intrude on my…."

Agent Hammond appeared, unfolding a three-page document and shoving it in front of Abe's face. "Sit down and shut up, Mr. Hendricks. Here is our warrant. We are seizing all computer hardware, filing cabinets, and any records on the premises.

While we are boxing these items up, all of you must remain in this room. Your private cell phones will be returned to you when we have finished."

"I want to call my lawyer," Abe snapped. "This is outrageous."

"You are welcome to call your attorney as soon as we've finished gathering the evidence. That should only take a few more hours."

In reality, it was actually two hours and thirty minutes before the IRS agents finished their task. Abe watched in horror as every computer, copy machine, telephone, and file was boxed and carted off.

He counted at least fifteen agents roaming through his offices, three times the number of people employed by his tiny firm.

While they waited, the IRS men entered the break room twice, once to ask if the bookkeeper was present, the second time to announce that they were leaving. Tina, the receptionist, wasn't even allowed to go to the restroom during the entire ordeal.

And then they were gone, leaving behind a ransacked, hollow shell of what had been a bustling little enterprise.

Abe's first call was to his lawyer, his second to Kara. Neither answered.

His next priority was his employees. Most of them seemed to be in a daze, ambling around the office without purpose, staring at what had once been their livelihood. Abe didn't blame them.

"If I were in their shoes, my first priority would be worrying about my job," he whispered. "I need to reassure them and then give them something to occupy their minds."

After calling them all together, he pulled a company credit card from his wallet. "I want you all to hop in Tina's minivan and head over to the computer store. Everybody's wanted new laptops anyway, so we might as well seize this opportunity to upgrade. I'm going to call our telecom company and get a few phones over here right away. If we do this right, we'll only lose a day or two of downtime and may come out the other end even stronger."

His quick action seemed to dissipate some of the stress, the half-smiling employees dividing the assignments among themselves.

Abe, mind racing with thoughts of anger, revenge, and fear, half-heartedly went about tidying up the mess the government goons had made of his office. The ringtone of his cell phone brought more bad news. "The company credit card isn't being accepted," Tina informed him. "Do you think they've frozen all of the corporate bank accounts?"

"Damn, I never thought about that. Come on back over. I keep some cash at home, and we'll use that in the morning. Tell everyone they can have the day off with pay," he added before hanging up.

Now Abe was scared.

His attorney finally called back after Abe had driven halfway home. At least a dozen times the lawyer replied saying, "They did what?" and "They can't do that," while his client relayed the story of the IRS visit that morning.

"I'll get on this first thing in the morning," the lawyer promised.

"You'd better. I can't do business without phones, computers, or bank accounts."

"It's Patriots Now, Abe," the attorney replied. "I'm hearing all kinds of rumors about the feds getting nasty with Republican-leaning grassroots organizations. The IRS seems to be the enforcement agency of choice."

"They wouldn't do that," Abe replied. "Everybody would go nuts if the government started using the tax guys to leverage politics."

"The next election is going to be close, my friend. Politicians have done worse things to stay in power. Remember a guy named Nixon and Watergate?"

It took Abe's attorney six days to free up the company's bank accounts. Hendricks Engineering was forced to put up a $50,000 bond before the federal judge would release the company's funds.

"Mr. Hendricks is a flight risk," the IRS representative had told the judge. "It will take the service several weeks to examine all of the seized records. However, by documents submitted to the IRS under Mr. Hendricks's own signature, his firm has known business dealings with several international customers. We, therefore, request that he be considered a flight risk and ask that his passport be surrendered."

It was another five weeks before a rather harried man wearing the uniform of a delivery service entered the firm's reception area and announced that he had a truck full of boxes for delivery, courtesy of the Department of Treasury.

Abe's legal bill consumed practically the entire $50,000 bond. In addition, the IRS found $137 in questionable expenses, which with penalties and interest amounted to a new tax bill of just over $200 dollars.

No sooner than the last box was unpacked, Abe received a call from one of his most active supporters at Patriots Now. The man was being audited.

Within a week, three more of the founding members received visits from the IRS, all of them near panic after hearing Abe's story.

Patriots Now was disbanded 45 days before the November election, Abe convinced that his labors were all for naught.

Abe retreated into the dark recesses of depression. His business had been severely damaged, his bookkeeper recommending bankruptcy, or at least extreme measures of austerity. That meant letting employees go – people that had stuck with him during the lean times, folks whose entire families he knew by name, age and scout merit badge.

Kara tried her best, remaining upbeat and optimistic, pretending she didn't notice the depth of his funk.

He was parked on the couch one night, watching an old movie, unable to sleep. Nothing was on but a spy flick with a mediocre plot and B-grade acting.

The protagonist stumbled upon a government secret and couldn't resolve his conflict with the authorities. Instead, he spent the next hour and a half of the movie dodging hired assassins.

As a last, desperate resort to save his own neck, the hero turned over critical documents to the *New York Times*, hoping the exposure would keep the well-armed wolves at bay.

As the credits scrolled across the screen, Abe couldn't help but compare his life to the actor's role. He'd tried the legal system... and gotten screwed. He'd tried the justice system... and had almost gone to jail. His latest attempt, the political system, had almost resulted in the loss of his income.

But what about going to the press?

Like the guy in the movie, Abe knew what he considered a terrible secret. Yes, he'd signed a gag order, but so had the government... and they had surely violated it. Abe was convinced that his fledgling political organization of less than 50 members was no major threat to big government and could not command an audit by itself. It was extremely unlikely the IRS would have invaded his business without a more evocative catalyst - New Orleans. No doubt someone violated the federal order and bird-dogged those agents on Abe's company. The resulting audits were merely the method for delivering the governmental wrath.

"What's good for the goose is good for the gander," he whispered.

Sleep still wouldn't come, regardless of the hot cocoa and mind-numbing movie. Abe laid wide-awake, weighing his options.

He considered the risk he was taking, exposing the illegal duplicates of the documents he'd managed to sneak out of the New Orleans courthouse. All copies of those papers were supposed to remain sealed, never to see the light of day again.

Abe had watched the clerk wheel out the heavy cart housing several boxes of papers, all associated documents and records having been surrendered to the court as part of the binding agreement. The final signatures and instructions having just been completed, Abe felt a wave of nausea roll over him. Fearing he would lose his lunch then and there, he excused himself from the judge's chambers to splash some water on his face and collect himself. On his way to the facilities, he had passed by a small room, the clerk's cart resting unattended next to a massive shredding machine.

To this day, he couldn't explain why, couldn't justify the risk. Maybe it was the thought of losing the paper trail of his father and brother's demise. Perhaps, it was his way of retrieving the last evidence of his family honor. Maybe he was just a sore loser. For whatever the reason, those documents seemed like a magnet tugging at his very soul. With a racing heart, he'd reached inside, pulled the top two folders from the stack, and stuffed them in the small of his back under his jacket.

Shortly after moving to Texas, he had rented a bank lockbox, guilty of even more crimes in doing so. Using a copy of a driver's license provided by a job applicant, coupled with a fake address, he secured the box. He dropped in once a year, paying cash for the annual rent. There, he had stored the evidence of the injustice done to the Hendricks family.

So was it time to expand his life of crime? Was it time to throw a federal judge's orders out the door and contact the press with those documents?

Maybe he was being a little melodramatic? Maybe he could pass the documents along anonymously? Maybe he could be like Deep Throat from the Watergate era, and no one would guess his identity.

The fantasy pleased Abe, allowing him to drift off with happy thoughts of politicians scrambling to cover their asses, powerful, influential people quaking in their boots.

In his magnificent dream world, Abe gloated over the damage his information would inflict, visions of his favorite news programs carrying his release of documents as their lead story. He would have his day in court yet... in the court of public opinion.

Tomorrow, he would figure out how to contact a reporter and read about how to cover his tracks just in case it all didn't work out.

Over breakfast, Abe decided that purchasing a burner phone from a local box store was his best chance at remaining anonymous. A few quick internet searches armed him with enough knowledge to stop by a national chain on the drive into the office.

It took three phone calls to the Houston Post, the first two resulting in unfulfilled promises that someone would call him back.

Finally, after making an ass out of himself on the third try, Abe was passed on to a weasel-sounding kid working the city desk.

Despite having visions of some indifferent, pimply-faced journalism student, Abe relayed the highlights of his scoop. The response was less than enthusiastic.

"So let me get this straight," the reporter responded. "Your brother and father were killed by the New Orleans police right after Katrina. There was a shootout in your father's home. When you sued the parish, they had you arrested on what you believe are trumped-up charges. Do I have this so far?"

"Yes."

The reporter actually yawned before continuing. "In the end, the prosecutor decided to offer you a tit-for-tat deal - everything would be dropped by both parties, and everyone would live happily ever after. So far so good?"

"Yes," Abe replied, a sinking feeling beginning to fill his gut.

"And then, six years later, the IRS comes down on you like a ton of bricks. You believe it's because you were forming a voter registration political group and the agency had access to what are supposed to be sealed records."

"Yes, there's no other reason for them to have acted the way they did."

"Did they say that to you?" the kid asked.

"No, but…"

"So you don't know… you can't be 100% positive that's why they crashed your business – right?"

Abe was beginning to seriously regret making the call. "No, I have no proof of that connection."

"Sir, I don't mean to be rude, but it seems to me that you should be talking to an attorney, not the press. I don't think your account is something that would interest our readers. If you feel there's been a violation of your previous agreement, then a lawyer is who I'd be calling."

"But that's not really the point. They murdered my father and brother," Abe pleaded. "They killed two men in cold blood and then covered it up."

"But you signed an agreement with the court. You said yourself, at the beginning of this call, that you couldn't divulge your name because of a federal judge's gag order. So I do not see any cover-up or conspiracy. If a judge was involved, then it must have been an above-board deal. Thanks for calling."

And with that, the reporter hung up.

At first, Abe was embarrassed. Hearing that voice on the other end of the line retell his story, the entire affair didn't seem all that noteworthy. The fact that his business had practically been destroyed didn't mean anything. Many businessmen claimed the IRS was doing them wrong, yet when the truth was finally uncovered, some level of tax cheating was usually involved.

Abe looked around his office, deciding he'd be more comfortable licking his wounds at home. Maybe Kara and he could take a walk to clear his head.

After advising Tina he was out for the rest of the day, Abe began driving home. He'd managed less than 10 minutes on the road when a sign touting "Grand Opening – Guns and Ammo," caught his attention.

"Can't hurt to stop in," he thought, switching on the turn signal.

Abe entered the store, intent on browsing for a new shotgun. He'd seen a few articles about the latest recoil-absorbing designs and was considering a bird hunt later in the fall.

The young man behind the counter was friendly enough, letting Abe gaze at the long rows of rifles displayed on the wall. Like most gun stores in the area, this shop had a large section of tactical rifles and accessories.

Abe typically ignored such trinkets, unsure of any practical use, considering them mostly for show. "So what's the big deal with those battle rifles?" he asked the salesman in a somewhat surly tone. "What good are they anyway?"

Much to Abe's surprise, the young man's answer made absolute sense. "A lot of people buy them because they don't trust the government," came the response. "I'm not much of a conspiracy theory guy, but I have a few myself. For some reason, I feel more secure knowing they're in my safe at home."

Abe tilted his head, the guy's words resonating with his deflated mood. "Can I hold one?"

"Sure, let me show you our most popular model. This is an AR15, one of the most configurable rifles in the world. It is the civilian model of what our military uses in battle."

Abe hefted the piece, listening intently as the man behind the counter itemized the features and described the blaster's capabilities.

For some reason, Abe felt more secure holding the carbine. In the grand scheme of guns, including almost every other weapon warehoused in his safe, the AR15 wasn't very powerful. In fact, it was downright anemic compared to the majority of his hunting rifles.

Nor was the AR light, easy to handle, or as simple as most of his collection. Yet, there was something about the rifle that made him feel secure, empowered to protect himself against the worst the world could offer.

The array of available accessories and configurations was another surprise. "These grooves here, along the barrel, are called rails. One of the reasons why these guns are so popular is because you can mount all kinds of goodies there. Lasers, lights, optics, night vision, thermal imaging, slings... you name it. Each AR15 is configurable to what the owner needs, and it's a snap to change things up depending on those requirements."

Another customer appeared, a man about the same age as Abe. Flashing a familiar smile to the fellow behind the counter, the newcomer chimed in, "Government conspiracy theories aside," he began, obviously making fun of the salesman, "it's the flexibility of that rifle that I like. I can mount a flashlight for nighttime hog hunting and then turn around and attach a high-powered scope for deer season. Don't let all that military-looking apparatus fool you, that gun is one of the best small game rifles ever made, and probably the best home defense configuration in the world. I have a couple of them, and the rest of my collection gathers dust in the safe. It seems like I am always reaching for one of those 'evil black rifles,' first."

After being shown the necessary controls, Abe didn't want to hand the weapon back. Its weight and balance felt comfortable in his hands, the capabilities and ruggedness of the design obvious even to his uneducated touch. He was tempted to purchase the gun right there.

Finally passing it back, Abe motioned to the long rack of similar looking rifles. "Are all those the same as the one you showed me?"

"No, not really. There are multiple calibers, different barrels lengths, and features all around. There are a thousand different options."

"Let me do some research before I turn my credit card into a slag heap," Abe teased. "But I have to say, I'm impressed. Who knows, I might even become one of your best customers."

As he left the weapon emporium, Abe remembered seeing a variety of magazines at the local bookstore, entire shelves plastered with pictures of battle rifles and tactical gear. He would pick up some more information and educate himself on the AR.

"I haven't felt anything like that in my hands before," he whispered, pulling into the book peddler's lot. "It was so... so... so liberating."

His elation continued, even as he plodded along through afternoon gridlock. Gone was the belittling he'd received from the reporter, the frustration of his plight pushed back into the far recesses of his mind.

Pulling into the driveway, he made a decision. There was no way to explain this newfound sensation to his wife – no way she would understand. "I'll just keep this private," he convinced himself. "It's not like I'm having an affair."

Stuffing his stack of research material in his briefcase, he informed Kara that he had a ton of work-related analysis to finish. "Sorry, babe. I'm going to be stuck in my office slaving over this stuff for a while. Would you mind ordering a pizza tonight?"

Abe felt only a small pang of guilt over the deceit. Kara hated guns, and any interest in military grade weapons would only send her spiraling into an orbit of worry.

Chapter 5 - Awakening

Eleven Years After Katrina...

Zach inserted the key and entered his apartment. He could tell by the faint whiff of perfume that Cheyenne was already there.

Moving to the small breakfast bar, he sighed with relief as he unholstered his weapon and spare magazines, depositing the tools of his trade on the counter. The gentle rustle of footsteps announced her approach from behind. Wrapping her arms around his chest in a welcoming embrace, she balanced on her tiptoes and whispered in a sultry voice, "Welcome home, Ranger."

"How long have you been here?" he asked, pivoting to return the hug.

"I got off an hour early and decided to surprise you," she responded with a suggestive wink.

In a glance, Zach understood her meaning, the tall girl clad in nothing but one of his dress shirts. "I know that officers of the law don't like surprises, but I have a sneaky suspicion that today will be an exception," she flirted.

Zach needed no more prompting, pulling the girl tight against him, his passions escalating. Much to the ranger's surprise, Cheyenne gently pushed him away with both of her palms against his chest, saying, "Before you get your horse into a full gallop, cowboy, there is something I want to ask you about."

Puzzled, Zach tilted his head and asked, "What's up?" And then with a slight grin and an adjustment to the front of his jeans he added, "Besides the obvious, I mean."

Sliding her hands to his cheeks, she clasped his chin on either side, enabling her to peer directly into the lawman's eyes. "Zach, I am worried about you. When I borrowed this shirt from your drawer, an envelope fell to the floor, and I opened it. When did you plan to tell me that you intend to resign from your position?"

Anger flashed behind Zach's eyes, his posture stiffening as he pulled away from the girl. "Since when is it okay for you to open my private correspondence?"

Cheyenne, placing her hands on her hips, responded, "Zachariah Bass, I have been sharing your bed since Texas Tech, and your thoughts since we were kids. Any other red-blooded cowboy would have wanted me in his corral a long time ago. You can't blame a girl for seeking information where she can find it. Now 'fess up. Just what is going on with you?"

His explosive outburst was out of character. "Work is work," he snarled. "Play is play. You are not welcome to pry into my affairs."

At 6'4" and well over 220 pounds, most folks would withdraw from an angry Zachariah Bass... not so with Cheyenne. "You can snort like a mean, old bull all you want, Mr. Lawman, but I care about you, and you and I need to clear the air."

"You're damned right; we need to settle a few things," he snapped back. "A man needs a woman he can trust not to go nosing around in his work."

"Bullshit!" Cheyenne responded. "A hundred years ago, my granddaddy might have gotten away with talking to my grandmother using that caveman mentality, but that is not the way a modern relationship works."

Zach turned away, removing his jacket and tie without another word.

Cheyenne's tone softened, "Zach… seriously… you've wanted to be a ranger since you were a boy. I know it's not always been what you've expected, but no job is. I hate the thought of your throwing it all away."

He relaxed, staring into space for a moment before responding. "Do you remember when we were kids, and I used to make you play the damsel in distress so I could be the Texas Ranger coming to rescue you?"

Nodding, Cheyenne smiled. "Yes, I also remember when you tied me up and then couldn't get the ropes loose. I had a heck of a time explaining those wrist burns to my daddy."

Zach grunted, the episode making him smile. "You were so bony back then - all lanky elbows and knees. Every time I tried to tie you up, you would wiggle out of my knots. I was *bound* and determined to make you stay put."

Striking a model's pose, Cheyenne pulled the shirt tight across her significant breasts, the white cotton in contrast to her darkly tanned, slender legs. "We've both come a long way," she teased. "I remember when you were so skinny that you had to run around in the shower to get wet."

Zach had to agree, "Yes, we've both come a long way, but I'm not sure this path is the right one for me. My annual review is in a few weeks, and I typed up that letter because I think there's a chance the boss might ask for my resignation. I wanted to have it ready."

"What happened, Zach? You were so thrilled when you got your badge. You were strutting around like a cocky rooster with a bevy of hens. And then it seemed like everything changed... and now... now it's like you're just going through the motions."

"That's not fair," he started to protest. "You don't know what it's like. You shouldn't judge me without walking a mile in my shoes."

"It's not just your job. It's our relationship, too. Do you really want to know why I opened that envelope? I pried because I thought you might be trying to cull a different filly from the herd. The way you've been acting, I was worried there might be someone else."

"No, there's no one else."

Cheyenne's exasperation was evident, but she was undeterred. After waiting for the lawman to continue, she resolved to milk it out of him, bit by bit. "Why are you worried your boss is going to ask you to resign?"

That was a difficult question for the Texan, one he'd tried to answer himself for years. The words just wouldn't form sentences, his thoughts too scrambled to manufacture paragraphs of cohesive thought. He was sure Cheyenne just wouldn't understand.

Where had it all started going wrong? What was it that kept him from accepting promotions, from following up on opportunities that could lead to advancement? Cheyenne was right; he was only going through the motions - not a bad enough actor to get fired outright, just treading water and watching the time pass by.

How could he explain the episode with Tusk or the guilt he'd felt over the New Orleans incident? What words could he use to describe the dozen other small episodes that soured his soul? And perhaps more importantly, would such disclosures change the way his life-long love looked at him?

"Nothing went wrong," he finally answered. "I'm coming to the conclusion that I'm not cut out to be an authority figure. I've developed a strong cynicism toward my fellow man. Somewhere along the line, I've lost all respect for the legal system, and worst of all, I suffer bouts of incredible guilt over being a part of the whole damn mess. Now, are you happy? Satisfied with my confession?"

Shaking her head, Cheyenne responded, "I think I understand. I really am trying to. If it's that bad, why haven't you resigned already and moved onto something else?"

Because I'm scared, he wanted to shout. *Because of fear. Because I know what it's like being on the other side, and I'm frightened to exist in that place.* "Because the only thing I have going for me… the only thing that keeps my head from exploding… is the community of my fellow rangers. I'm now a member of a fellowship… a due paying affiliate of an exclusive club. If I resign, then I'm carrying around all of the garbage I've collected without any of that support. Living that way scares the hell out of me."

Again, Cheyenne's hands landed on her hips. "The *only* thing that keeps your head from exploding? What about *us*, Zach? What about our relationship? I'm feeling a little like chopped liver here. I've been putting up with a moody, sometimes sullen man for years, hoping and praying you'd come out of it. I've excused so much shit from you, telling myself that you needed me… that you wanted me… that if I played it the right way, you would open up, let me in, and I could help. Now I'm wondering if it all hasn't been a waste of time."

He didn't reply. She watched him saunter casually to the refrigerator and pull out a beer. He popped the top, meandered to the couch, flopped down, and fumbled for the television remote.

She waited, hoping for eye contact, a smile, wink… something. The only thing she sensed was a clear signal that the conversation was over.

Cheyenne disappeared into the bedroom, emerging a few minutes later fully dressed and carrying a small gym bag. "Zach, I'm leaving. I'm not getting any younger. I'm going to head back to San Marcos and visit my folks for a bit. Good luck."

He didn't react, his eyes remaining focused on the television as if he didn't hear her words.

She strolled over, bent at the waist, kissed his forehead, and then she was gone.

Abe resisted the urge to put a boot through the television. His hand, trembling with anger, managed to set the remote gently on the coffee table. It wouldn't do any good to damage the electronics – wouldn't change a thing.

Exhaling in a subconscious attempt to slow his racing heart, he sat quietly watching the now dark screen. Rage boiled to his core; frustration pounded in his head. It *was* going to happen – she *was* going to be elected the next president of the United States of America.

This evening's nationally televised debate had been the last hope. Glued to the boob tube for over three hours, he'd watched with more anticipation and angst than any Super Bowl in memory. But in the end, the underdog had fallen, and the analysts had been unanimous – she *was* going to win.

With a supreme effort, he suppressed the fury. It was time for clear thinking and cold analysis, not irrational, ire-inspired ramblings of emotional thought.

It was still a few weeks before the election, but there was little hope of either candidate changing the math. The computer models, polls, and state-by-state prediction of the Electoral College left little suspense regarding the ultimate outcome. *She* was going to be the Commander in Chief.

Abe held no personal grudge against Heidi Clifton. He'd never met the woman. Nor was it the Democratic Party that motivated his disdain. Conservatives and liberals had been duking it out for decades. At his age, he'd observed the ebb and flow of power in Washington change directions many times. But this was different. This election signaled a fundamental injustice, and it repulsed him.

No, he reiterated for the hundredth time; it wasn't just the Democrats, or their politics, or the left-leaning policies embraced by Mrs. Clifton that disturbed him. What was so troubling was his fellow countrymen's ignorance concerning the erosion of their liberties. To make matters worse, most of the talking heads on television believed that the Republicans would hold both the House and the Senate. They acted as if this should be some grand salvation for those on the right of the political spectrum. Abe knew it wasn't true – he had firsthand experience that both sides cared little for individual rights. If anything, the division of power meant more gridlock, bickering, division, and inaction.

It all served to feed the carved-out, hollow feeling in his soul.

But what really tore him apart was the injustice. Heidi Clifton's victory was a reward - a prize given to those who didn't deserve it.

Abe rose from the couch, ambling toward the study. Since Kara had left him six months ago, the house seemed more than just empty. Despite the same furniture adorning the rooms, the same pictures hanging from the walls, there was a difference. During the divorce, his wife of 13 years hadn't shown any interest in obtaining her share of their physical possessions. She hadn't wanted any of it. Nor had she tried to clean him out financially. Her attorney had offered a reasonable, fair settlement of their assets, and then she had simply disappeared from his life.
But in reality, she had taken so much from him. The place was now devoid of her sounds and smells, missing her spirit and ambiance. His heart was just as empty.

As he wandered down the hall, he stopped at the usual place. A montage of pictures greeted him, memories from happier times. There was Charlie, grinning with a huge catfish he'd pulled from the bayou. Right beside the image of his brother was his favorite photograph of his dad. Mr. Hendricks was dressed to the hilt, enjoying the festivities at his retirement party.

For the thousandth time since the incident after Katrina, guilt racked his being. Not only had he failed to prevent the deaths of his father and brother, but had eventually sold out, sacrificing their memory and the family's honor.

He abandoned the wall of memories, sauntering on to enter what had been his favorite room. The dark wood panels covering the walls advertised the space as a serious abode of male dominance – a place where business was conducted. The substantial, heavy desk accented the same theme. Bookshelves lined one wall, hundreds of bound volumes facing outward, signaling a belief that knowledge was a tool. A modern laptop rested nearby, the dark screen and keyboard seemingly unoffended by the more oft-used books.

This had been a retreat and preserve, an office, library, and his only personal space in their sizable dwelling. Kara had avoided the room, even the smallest hint of a woman's touch invoking a notice of trespass from her husband. "Hang what you will, wherever you want," he had informed with a smile. "The rest of the house is yours. You can color, paint, decorate and adorn anything and anywhere except for my study. I need a bastion of testosterone, a small cave of primitive, bad taste and dull hue."

Now the entire home was his, a somber overcast prevalent throughout. The study had been stripped of its unique personality. While Kara's love of colors and texture still lingered on the physical surfaces of his home, the décor was flat, singly dimensional, and lifeless without her.

The rifle was right where he'd left it, leaning against the wall in stoic solitude. He hefted the weighty piece, respecting what he considered a masterpiece of engineering, craftsmanship, and technology. His latest acquisition... it was called a Trackerpoint.

There were many more firearms in the nearby closet. Expensive weapons acquired over the years for whatever hobby or desire filled his fancy at the time. A catalog of calibers, styles, and capabilities resided in the specially constructed gunroom, a collection any respectable dealer would sincerely appreciate.

There had been periods when sport was at the forefront of his attentions. Mountain hunting, waterfowl, competitive skeet, and even a few trips to exotic lands had constituted recreation for the man seeking to experience joy again. Through his adventures, he amassed quite a collection of specialized weapons for all manner of hunting and shooting.

The rifle he held now was different from all the rest. It was extraordinary, and served only one purpose – the taking of life at extreme distances.

It was a new breed of firearm, a marriage of technology and ultra-precise machining made possible only by digital equipment. Rather than highly polished wood, a stock of black plastic extended from one end. Anodized aluminum and layers of ceramic coatings surrounded the inner workings. The traditional tube of a high-powered scope had been replaced with a boxy-looking apparatus, complete with buttons, wire-jacks, and a battery compartment.

Even the trigger had a different shape, feel, and most importantly - purpose. This weapon no longer directly engaged the firing pin, that task now controlled by one of the many computer chips built into the unit.

This gun was exceptional on so many different levels.

For over 400 years, a rifleman did his best to estimate how far his bullet was going to drop and spin. He would center on a point of aim and then pull the trigger. The better marksmen were capable of judging distance, wind, humidity and other factors that affected the bullet's ballistics. World-class shooters could hold the aim true until the lead had exited the muzzle.

Now, with the technology he held in his hand, none of that was necessary. Laser range finders, GPS sensors, target acquisition software, and computer chips executing several million instructions per second had all but eliminated the human from the loop. The trigger no longer engaged the firing pin because the digital system was better at the task. A man wasn't necessary to judge distance – the laser being far more accurate.

Abe grunted, thinking about the first time he'd taken the new rifle to a range. With even the finest of his hunting rifles, a shot at more than 600 meters was difficult. With the computer's help, that distance was now child's play. It had required driving to his cousin's farm to find a practice area with enough distance to push the limits of the new tool. Striking targets at over 1700 yards… a mile… 17 football fields… was now within his grasp.

Chambered in the .338 Laupa Magnum Modified, the weapon was capable of more than just long distance shots. It could deliver a mid-sized hunk of lead at high velocities, impacting the target with a significant level of kinetic force. Because of its considerable abilities, the military classified the .338 LMM as both anti-personnel and anti-material.

He returned the rifle to its resting place and then moved to the computer. A few keystrokes later, he began studying Mrs. Clifton's publically displayed campaign schedule. Nothing had changed since he'd last checked. She would be coming to his hometown four days before the election.

Sighing, Abe leaned back against the headrest, his eyes focusing on an empty point in space. For a moment, he questioned why he was even entertaining such heinous acts.

Since that day in New Orleans, the ghosts of Charlie and his father refused to rest, haunting him at every step. Their troubled souls pined for justice, their voices demanding some meaning come from their early deaths.

Was there any stone left unturned? What other recourse was left for him?

The answers to his questions came quickly, a harsh mental salvo firing painful realizations at his doubts. It was more than just the murders of his family members. He had tried the justice system, the legal system, politics, and the press. Each attempt had been met with inequity and malaise, sweeping him away to a place of irrelevance and misery. The system no longer functioned, and those who had broken it were about to receive a reward of nearly unlimited power.

"So you are what the end of the rope looks like," he said, addressing the nearby rifle. "This is what it feels like to have no other choice, to have exhausted all other sensible possibilities. I've done everything a reasonable man can, and every single time justice, morality, and liberty were denied."

"They, however, underestimated me," he declared with passion. "They expect me to fade away, to stumble into an abyss of numbness and despair. They anticipate my retreat. They assume that I'll hobble off, a beaten man limping away from the fight with his spirit broken and head hung low."

"Well, I have a surprise in store for them," he calmly told the weapon. "Maybe the very heart and soul of the United States has already perished, and if that is true, then I'm already as good as dead, too. So why go quietly? Why go down without a fight? Maybe... just maybe... I can spark a change. I've got a chance to open people's eyes and raise their awareness. I might still salvage a great destiny for America's citizens, recapture the unique and valuable essence of what was once the land of opportunity."

"You're up another point in the latest poll numbers," floated the aide's voice. "We're dumping a ten million dollar media buy into south Florida starting tomorrow, but there's no guarantee that will accelerate the trend."

Heidi rubbed her eyes, the motion confirming what everyone at the table already knew. She wasn't sleeping well, the endless campaigning, 16-hour non-stop days, and constant pressure taking a toll. One of the media experts quickly scribbled a note: *No close-up television appearances this evening.*

"Didn't we just do a big spend in Dade county a few days ago?" the candidate asked.

"Yes, ma'am. But our opponent scored well with senior voters during the last debate. We feel a strategic 30-second spot will clarify your position."

The gathering was interrupted by the low voice of the plane's captain sounding over the VIP terminal's intercom. "Ladies and gentlemen, we're going to have a slight delay before boarding. The Houston controller just informed me that the traffic pattern is full for the next several minutes. We should be able to let everyone board shortly. Thank you for your patience."

After a low grumbling over the delay, the crowd of staffers surrounding the candidate began to disperse.

Thank God, Heidi thought. *I can relax for a few moments.*

Closing her eyes, she attempted to clear her mind and prepare for the next speech in Dallas.

She felt a rustling in the next seat, the familiar scent of Polo aftershave infusing the surrounding air. *Aaron.*

She kept her eyes closed, hoping his seating selection was based on comfort, and not due to any pressing need or issue. Playing possum didn't work.

"I know you're not asleep, Heidi," he announced in a low voice. "I've watched you day and night for the last year, and you hold your lips differently when you're in dreamland. We need to talk."

Mrs. Clifton opened her eyes, not sure whether to laugh or scold her chief of staff. "What's so important that you won't let a girl catch a little down-time?"

"What's *wrong*, Heidi? You're going to be the first woman president of the United States of America. You've wanted it for so long, worked so hard, and now that we're just about across the finish line, it seems like you're having doubts."

"I'm fine, Aaron. Peachy keen. Now quit being an old worrywart, and let me rest my eyes."

"I don't believe you, ma'am. I can see it, and if it's that clear to me, then our staff, volunteers, and contributors can see it as well. I've already been asked by two members of the press if you're feeling under the weather. Another asked me if the hostile elements in the crowd today had shaken your resolve."

Heidi sighed, shaking her head before focusing her gaze on him. "Okay, you're right; I'm not on Happy Street, not even close. Our country is just so divided, Aaron. Half of the people look at me with hate and rage in their eyes. What's really bothering me is that I'm going to end up just like our current chief executive – paralyzed and hamstrung by a Republican House and Senate. I'm going to spend the next eight years accomplishing nothing. Look at how those people reacted to my words today. It was the first time I've been booed onstage since we started. You and I both know that I have little chance of making a difference."

"And this is news?" the political expert answered. "You can't tell me you're just now realizing this? As far as those couple of jerks today, it's Texas – what do you expect?"

Her expression changed, a veil of sadness dropping over her eyes. "A month ago, it still wasn't real. I kept waiting for something to happen... some other incident to derail the campaign and divert our attention. A short time ago, it finally dawned that the dream is going to come true – this really is going to happen. So then what? I want my campaign speeches to be more than just rhetoric. I want to help our people – lead our country... make a difference. But that's just not going to happen, and it's pulling me into a weird place mentally."

Aaron waved her off, dismissing the candidate's concerns with a chuckle. "You can reach out to the other side of the aisle. Your husband is still a powerful man in Washington, and he can help.

We can work hard to lure the moderate Republicans into a coalition. It can be done, ma'am."

It was Heidi's turn to laugh. "I know you're one of the most brilliant political minds on the planet, Aaron. I also am quite confident that a full pound of bullshit just flew out of your mouth. Coalition? That's ludicrous, and we both know it. They will have the Senate back after Election Day, and I'll be lucky to get new dogcatcher legislation through either chamber. It's a sad state of affairs for our citizens."

The campaign guru stared at the floor for a moment, remembering the reaction today to Heidi's speech... wondering how much her demeanor was influenced by the heckling Texans.

Aaron didn't hesitate, "Let's cross that bridge when we come to it. Job One is to get you into the White House. I've got a few ideas floating around in my head that might help with our nation's gridlock."

"Oh? And what might those be?"

Flashing a sly grin, he chuckled, "First of all, we can let Texas go... give them the option to secede. You know that a week from now they will be passing around that sour grapes petition again, just like the last time they lost the executive branch. Without Texas, the Republicans won't be so obstructive. Gonna be a pain in the ass reprinting all those maps of the USA, redesigning the flag.... Oh my gawd, we are going to have to revise all those IRS forms, too."

Heidi knew he was kidding, or at least hoped he was. Before she could reply, the captain's voice again sounded over the loudspeaker. "Ladies and gentlemen, it looks like the traffic pattern is clearing. Please proceed to board the aircraft."

Her campaign staff quickly hustled to form a cue, the boarding process for a chartered flight much less formal than any commercial offering. A few minutes later, the staff and press were marching across the tarmac and up the mobile staircase.

As was her tradition, Heidi lingered toward the back, always one of the last to board the aircraft to take full advantage of the sunshine and fresh air. Clearing his throat, Aaron announced, "I'm going to stay here in Houston and catch a later commercial flight. I've got some housekeeping to do with the local press. I'll meet you in Dallas tonight."

Heidi nodded, happy that her odds of catching a nap on the short flight had just improved.

Her chief of staff continued, "Good luck, and knock 'em dead."

Heidi maneuvered up the aisle through the shuffle of bodies, gradually making her way toward the front of the aircraft. She forced a fake smile as she passed through the small section reserved for the press corps, nodding at a few of the familiar faces.

Her first genuine relief of the day occurred when she passed through what had been the commercial airliner's first-class divider and entered the VIP cabin. Reserved for only the most senior campaign staff, here was a sanctuary. Here was peace and quiet.

Her seat was wide and soft; the comfortable, reclining unit installed specifically at her request. While serving as Secretary of State, she had flown hundreds of thousands of miles on various government aircraft and had grown to appreciate the expensive unit's features and design. There was a private washroom, complete with shower. A leather settee along one wall ran into an oversized wardrobe for her clothing. A large, state-of-the-art flat screen television and media center rounded out the refuge. Designed for international travel, the VIP cabin wasn't quite as luxurious as the accommodations on Air Force One, but it was far from roughing it.

Fastening her seatbelt, Heidi thought back to those days when her husband had been the president of the United States. She had learned to sleep while flying, one of the many acquired skills necessary to survive in the age of long-distance air travel. Little had she known how critically valuable that expertise would become in the future.

Her trip down memory lane was interrupted by the captain's voice, "Ladies and gentlemen, we've been cleared for takeoff. Please verify your seatbelts are secure."

The Secret Service detail assigned to campaigning candidates wasn't nearly as large or capable as the teams protecting the actual Commander in Chief. Abe knew this.

Even if Mrs. Clifton's plane had been the actual Air Force One, he still didn't believe the agents would extend their perimeter beyond a half mile... maybe three-quarters at best.

He was just inside a mile, exactly 1,690 yards from the end of the runway, according to the digital display in the rifle's optic. The wind was calm.

The original Linux software controlling the rifle's brain had an artificial limit programmed into its system, disabling the mechanism from calculating the lead for any object moving at over 10 mph.

It had been child's play to bypass the limitation.

He adjusted the bi-pod's position and then scanned the immediate area one last time, just to make sure he hadn't been spotted. There was no one around.

The new subdivision provided the perfect cover. Banging dump trucks, hammering, sawing, and nail guns were all an everyday occurrence, common until 5:00 PM. If anyone did hear his weapon's report, he hoped it would be ignored, written-off as over-time construction work. He'd arrived at 5:15, hidden his truck in a half-complete garage, and climbed to the second floor.

From there, pulling down the attic's access ladder had provided an even higher roost, a vent making the perfect hide. The elevation, combined with the flat landscape of north Houston, allowed him an unhindered field of fire toward Bush Intercontinental Airport.

For a moment, he experienced a wave of doubt. Even the planes looked like matchbox toys from this distance. Clifton's aircraft would be rolling at over 150 mph when he took the shot. The bullets seemed so tiny for such a far reach.

But he'd done it before. He'd practiced at much longer ranges than this, and a jet engine was a huge target.

His second bout of insecurity arose when the flight was delayed. According to her schedule, Heidi was to speak in Dallas in just over 90 minutes, yet the plane was clearly visible, sitting at the

VIP terminal with the bold logo, "Clifton Express," painted on the tail.

Fifteen minutes after Abe's math had calculated the scheduled departure, he exhaled in relief when the big aircraft started moving across the tarmac.

There was a line of planes waiting to take to the skies. He observed the chartered 757 inch forward, his heart rate increasing as the moment drew closer.

And then the aircraft taxied onto the runway and began creeping a little faster.

Abe put his cheek against the stock, exhaled, and closed his left eye. He centered the cross hairs on the fuselage first, the larger target easier to find. Moving the rifle to follow the plane's ever-increasing speed, he pressed the zoom button on the optical computer.

The image displayed in the view screen grew 35 times in just over two seconds, allowing a clear picture of the starboard engine. He aligned the registration mark on the leading edge of the turbofan and pressed the target selection button.

A green bracket flashed around the Pratt & Whitney engine, telling Abe that the optic's brain acknowledged his selection. He scrutinized the scope-computer's display as it calculated the target's speed, watching the red numbers increase as the pilots applied throttle.

The numbers continued to increase, 100... 110... 130... and then Abe squeezed the trigger, but, as expected, the weapon did not discharge.

A green arrow appeared, telling the shooter to raise his aim higher and to the right. It would take the 250-grain bullet almost three seconds to travel the distance to the target, and during that time, it would drop several hundred inches.

Abe did what the computer instructed him to do, moving the optic higher and in front of the speeding aircraft, his finger keeping the trigger taut.

Inside the electronic optic, several calculations were being processed at the speed of light. The target's distance, speed, and elevation were combined with the atmospheric conditions of wind, temperature, and humidity. Even the Coriolis Deflection, the rotation of the earth, was accounted for.

The weapon and optic worked together as a system, waiting for its human master to point the barrel at just the right time and place in space. When Abe finally aligned the muzzle where it was necessary, the rifle fired.

Like always, Abe jumped as the surprisingly loud report echoed over the empty subdivision. Despite having fired hundreds of practice rounds through his space-age blaster, he just couldn't get accustomed to the computer controlling the actual shot.

Wasting no time, he repeated the process as quickly as possible, managing a second shot before the first bullet impacted. He glanced at the target speed indicator just after the follow-up round exited the barrel, satisfied his timing was close enough.

Sighing, Abe hit the zoom button again, decreasing the magnification so he could witness the results of his work.

The first bullet struck harmlessly on the lower, rear edge of the turbofan's housing, poking a hole slightly larger than a third of an inch and causing minimal damage to the engine's critical function.

The second shot was devastating.

Striking with far more kinetic energy than any bird-strike, the 250-grain bullet sliced through the jet's aluminum skin and wreaked havoc on the hyper-rotating blades.

Shards of metal exploded outward, a cloud of shrapnel enveloping the inner workings of the engine and the control surfaces on the wing. A moment later, a secondary explosion ripped through the tortured machine, misting jet fuel providing the necessary pyro-inducement.

The cockpit instruments went insane.

The pilot's first inclination was a bird aircraft strike hazard (BASH). He was just lifting the front wheels off the ground when his aircraft shuddered violently and then pulled hard to starboard. Warning klaxons, blinking lights, and flashing displays immediately told him his aircraft was in trouble.

A 25-year Air Force veteran with multiple combat tours, the captain's reflexes were keen and proper. He didn't need to digest any computer displays or gauges to know his plane was no longer airworthy.

Lightning fast, his right hand yanked the throttles back at the same moment he applied the flaps and brakes. His eyes focused on the end of the runway and the rapidly approaching line of trees beyond.

"Mayday! Mayday! Mayday!" he anxiously broadcasted, just as the front wheels slammed back into the concrete runway. One of the dual front tires exploded on impact, the strut supporting the landing gear snapping in half a fraction of time later. Men no longer controlled the massive machine.

The 757 was nose down, scraping along the runway at over 160 miles per hour. She began to pull right, the forces of gravity and motion turning her into a giant, slow-spinning Frisbee. Her groundspeed was still in excess of 130 mph when her tortured belly vacated the concrete, now skidding across grass and weeds.

She was still doing over 80 when she slammed into the woods that surrounded the airport. The port wing snapped off, a fiery ball of red flame and black smoke exploding as the full tanks of fuel ignited.

Bleeding off velocity, the fuselage began climbing the trees, rather than crushing them, a growing pile of wood, plowed earth, and debris gathering under the body.

Finally, half tilted onto her starboard side, she came to rest.

Despite the spectacle lasting only a few seconds, Abe experienced one of the most intense emotional rollercoasters of his life.

He first flashed with anger, thinking he'd missed both shots. That feeling was quickly replaced with fury... the elevation and distance making it seem like the pilot was actually going to keep the aircraft under control. A microsecond later, when the flames appeared on the wing, he relaxed.

Bliss ruled his heart when the aircraft began spinning down the runway, clearly out of control. Apprehension replaced elation when the stricken plane left his line of sight, shortly thereafter replaced with satisfaction when the huge ball of black smoke and bright flash of an explosion appeared on the horizon.

After experiencing such a broad range of emotions in a matter of seconds, he became rather stoic, lying in his hide, and taking it all in. "I should feel some guilt," he whispered to the empty attic. "But I don't. What have I become?"

Realizing it wasn't the time for deep soul-searching, he began packing his equipment. He pocketed the two discharged shell casings, glanced around one last time to make sure he wasn't going to make it easy for the authorities, and then proceeded down the ladder.

As his truck calmly passed through the subdivision, he chanced one last glance toward the billowing column of dark ash on the horizon. A smirk crossed his face as he imagined the flames and utter chaos inside the plane.

He visualized piles of charred corpses, unable to resist comparing the scene to that of his father's house so many years ago. His family members had burned after being torn apart by violence. It only seemed fair, a gratifying eye for an eye.

Waves of pain crashed Heidi's consciousness like a mighty tempest pounding ashore. The agony surging through her body demanded she inhale, but each lung-full burned like an internal inferno. Opening her eyes commanded similar torture, the cabin's air thick with smoke.

I'm going to die, she somehow reasoned through the fog of physical torment.

And then someone was there. She was aware of the touch of human hands followed by a sense of weightlessness. Another throbbing shock rattled her brain when someone lifted her from the seat... and then was carrying her like a small child.

The Secret Service agent who found her was an ex-Division I linebacker, just a hair too slow to make the pros. Mrs. Clifton's weight was nothing to the stout man, his primary problem being the inundated cabin, boiling-thick with toxic fumes and unbreathable air.

It was a heroic effort, the lopsided passageway, unbolted seats and scattered bodies providing a horrific obstacle course. His muscles pumped with adrenaline-powered determination. The goal was the exit – he had to make it.

Finally, the red sign came into view, its appearance announcing nothing less than a new chance at life.

He set his protectorate down, leaning her body against a pile of crumpled seats. Flames licked at his suit, the jacket-wool on his back beginning to steam with the heat. It felt like someone was holding a blowtorch against his skull.

He identified the emergency handle and pressed it, but it didn't budge. He kicked with all of his weight, forcing the door to spring on its hinges. He heard, more than saw, the emergency shoot inflate.

Sunlight appeared through the portal, a wisp of fresh air providing relief to the agent's tortured lungs. He snatched up Heidi, turned to the yellow emergency slide, and jumped.

The steep angle and rapid descent left them in a tangled heap at the bottom. Ignoring the pain of his own injuries, the agent gathered himself and found his feet. He scooped Heidi into his arms, an overwhelming desire to gain distance from the fire driving his legs.

The escape was encumbered by snapped tree trunks, furrowed earth, and hunks of aircraft metal. He climbed, scampered, strained, and fought his way through, all the while carrying the nearly unresponsive woman in his arms.

His muscles finally gave out, the two survivors collapsing in a heap. After several deep inhalations, he looked down to see the candidate staring up with a smirk on her face. "Thank you," she croaked in a weak voice.

The news outlets got it wrong at first. The initial reports coming from local Houston stations were that a plane had merely skidded off the runway.

Within five minutes, it was being reported that the aircraft had burst into flames. Shortly thereafter, first responders began talking about casualties. That's when the national stations preempted their coverage.

A technician in a cable newsroom, monitoring the local feed, was the first to notice the charred emblem on the aircraft's tail. A quick call to his editor led to a hasty confirmation that the scorched plane was in fact Heidi Clifton's.

Like the firestorm consuming the interior of the plane, the story outside spread just as quickly. The entire nation seemed to pause mid-stride, suddenly glued to the nearest media outlet, waiting to hear the status of the woman who was most likely going to be the next president of the United States.

Confirmation of Mrs. Clifton's surviving the crash came from her campaign headquarters. The severity of her injuries was unknown.

Helicopters descended on the now-closed airport, every available airborne ambulance in the city dispatched to the scene. High magnification television cameras zoomed in on the massive streams of foam arching through the air to douse the flames. A sea of red emergency lights blanketed the area. Ambulance after ambulance was shown speeding from the crash site, all of them escorted by police cruisers.

And still America waited, suspended in a torrent of analysis, projections, experts, and file footage. How badly was Heidi injured? Would she be able to fulfill the role of Commander in Chief? What had caused the crash?

Military bases around the globe went on alert, fears of a terrorist attack reverberating through the Pentagon's commands. Federal and state government offices as well as local law enforcement intensified their diligence. Specifically, the agencies of the Department of Homeland Security went ballistic with activity.

Speculation exploded through the American media. Everything from sabotage to an assassination attempt was discussed, dissected, and dispensed. It was a broadcasting circus on a scale seldom witnessed before.

The first real information regarding Clifton's health was almost overlooked. A low-level hospital spokesperson released a statement via a medical service that Heidi Clifton had been admitted to the facility's emergency room an hour before. Apparently, she was undergoing a series of x-rays and other tests to determine the extent of her injuries. Her condition was listed as stable.

Until that point, the facility had been ignored, most of the newshounds favoring the larger medical centers where the majority of the wounded were said to have been transported. Once the communication had been processed, the media's rush to descend upon the remote hospital produced several fender-benders. Tow trucks from all over northwest Harris County rushed to remove the crumpled vehicles and establish order on the roadways.

Fortunately for the doctors and staff, the Secret Service had arrived first, a considerable security force in place before the invasion of the reporting hordes.

Once it was known that the candidate was alive and seemingly in no danger of losing her life, the media directed its attention to the cause of the crash. Ratings were at stake, billions of dollars of advertising revenue in play, and the conjecture ran unchecked.

Americans, glued to their television screens, were exposed to the full gauntlet. One cable news outlet went so far as to blame Texans for the incident, Heidi's recent debate victory and subsequent lead in the polls obviously rankling the Lone Star State to the point of retribution. Another commentator spewed pure speculation, telling her audience it was possible some right-wing mechanic sabotaged the plane... or perhaps some lunatic, radical-Republican air traffic controller had been the culprit.

This, of course, ginned up the leadership on the right. Salvo after salvo of accusation, innuendo, and political mud flew back and forth across the airwaves, deepening the chasm of an already divided American population.

It was early the next morning when an excited FAA inspector showed his supervisor the bullet hole he'd discovered in the plane's starboard engine. Within an hour, the world knew that someone had indeed tried to assassinate Heidi Clifton.

Not since the attacks of 9-11 had any event shaken America so deeply. Like watching a volcano spewing smoke and ash, the country stood back and held its breath, anticipating a dreadful eruption. They didn't have to wait long.

Abe carried his sandwich to the living room and switched on the television where he observed what could only be described as a political riot. He knew the authorities would be ringing his doorbell soon, his preparations completed long before he'd fired at the plane. There really wasn't much else for him to do but sit and witness the madness.

At first, he'd been a little disappointed when the news confirmed Heidi had survived the crash. While the outcome of his strike wasn't what he expected, he realized it really didn't matter all that much. The goal hadn't been to kill the woman. No, his objective was to draw attention, to make America stand up and take notice, to initiate change in a population content with an unhealthy status quo.

Once everyone realized that terrorism wasn't responsible, the pundits quickly turned their attentions to the distinct possibility of assassination. When the discovery of the bullet holes was finally made public, all hell broke loose.

Vicious, flagrant attacks flew left and right, the battleground of national media playing host to combatants. Warriors from both sides of the political spectrum wielded their weapons of choice. The Internet bloggers were the foot soldiers; talk radio and television hosts served as the officers, with the political parties filling the role of general staff.

Just as Abe had anticipated, the first shot of the war came from the advocates of stricter gun control. They fired the almost-predictable volley, using past mass-shootings, the nation's murder rate, and heavily skewed statistics as their ammunition. Within hours, battle rifles and handguns were flying off the shelves in record numbers as gun enthusiasts anticipated the backlash of a weapons confiscation.

The pro-gun lobby responded with an equally absurd barrage, claiming that the crazed acts of individuals were logical justification for arming every American.

The conflict quickly escalated, each side utilizing the attempted assignation as a platform to support not only its position on gun control, but also every other controversial issue plaguing the nation.

Abe sat in silence, disinterested in the theatrics, waiting for the true issue – government tyranny – to make the headlines.

At the Bethesda Naval Hospital, Heidi was watching the drama unfold from her hospital bed. After the local Houston doctors had pronounced her stable enough to be moved, the Secret Service had demanded she be transported to the DC area where they could provide the securest environment.

With the election now only three days away, Mrs. Clifton's staff had been eager for the move as well. The national press was concentrated in nearby Washington, a fact they felt might become critical should their candidate require extended medical care.

In fact, Heidi was relatively unharmed, at least physically. A few lacerations, a mild case of smoke inhalation, and a sprained shoulder were the worst of her injuries. She had even joked with some of her staff, "The things a woman has to do in order to get a little rest these days."

But those that knew her well sensed something more was wrong. Her attitude seemed reflective, her mood brooding. A few of the inner circle wrote it off to the aftereffects of a traumatic experience, others worried about the long-term impact.

When Aaron appeared at her bedside, it was if an enormous weight had been lifted from her shoulders. She had forgotten he had a last minute change in plans and thus was unharmed.

After visiting with his boss for over an hour, he finally determined it was time to deliver the bad news. "We lost several staffers," he announced, knowing she demanded the truth, positive or negative, delivered straight up.

"How many?" she asked.

"Twenty-four," he replied, "Another six are still in critical condition, but all of them are expected to survive."

The candidate looked away. While her face remained stoic, Heidi's eyes told a different story, a deep sadness consuming her normally temperate countenance.

For a moment, her reaction worried Aaron. The attempt on her life, combined with the shock of surviving a plane wreck, was enough to alter anyone's outlook. He examined her closely, praying the Heidi he knew and respected hadn't sequestered herself in some remote corner of her mind.

"And what about the election?" she quipped, her voice sounding as if she really didn't care about the answer.

Aaron steadied his tone, avoiding the attempt to escalate the conversation to a fruitless tiff. "I'm not sure. Nothing like this has ever happened before. I've got a call with the party leadership in two hours. I'm supposed to report on your condition, and more importantly, your mindset. I'm going to recommend they begin the process of rescheduling the election... moving the date out a few weeks."

"No," she responded immediately, a hint of the old fire in her voice. "I think that would be a mistake."

"I agree," sounded a new voice from the door.

Heidi and Aaron both glanced up to see Mr. Clifton standing in the threshold, a bouquet of flowers in the nook of his arm.

"I thought you were in Europe," Heidi stammered, truly surprised to see him.

"I was, but as soon as I heard the news, and the Secret Service cleared it, I headed back," the former president stated, strolling into the room. "How are you, Heidi?"

Aaron was confused by what followed. Despite spending practically every waking hour over the past year with Heidi, he still didn't understand the Clifton's relationship. There had been nationally reported acts of indiscretion on his part, less substantiated rumors circulated about her. Like all of the campaign staff, he had never seen anything but hard work and a dedication to politics from either of them.

Yet, there was something odd about the couple. They were separated for months at a time, each jet setting around the globe in the name of government service or personal advancement. She rarely spoke of him, either positive or negative, and never invoked his counsel on matters political or strategic. It would be easy to classify them as two people who had grown apart but never divorced, staying together for convenience, out of habit, and perhaps the occasional circumstance.

But there was a contradiction to that line of reasoning. Despite living two seemingly separate lives, neither would hesitate to drop everything and rush to the other's side in moments of crisis or need. It was just plain weird, but it seemed to work.

After the greetings and polite chitchat had been exhausted, Mr. Clifton got down to business. "Right now, you have the sympathy of the American people. There is an outpouring of concern. I want to tell you... make sure you understand... having their compassion doesn't mean you have their vote."

Heidi nodded, but Aaron didn't understand. "Sir, I've just checked the latest poll numbers, and Mrs. Clifton's popularity has surged three points since the incident. I don't quite follow what you're saying."

"Son," the former president began, his smile and slow drawl managing to keep the term on the politically correct edge of derogatory, "the average American feels sorry for Heidi – right now. The man in the street doesn't like anyone being shot at... or injured. Polls will indicate outrage over those who lost their lives. But that doesn't mean they'll vote with that emotion. A lot of people are going to wonder about Heidi's mental state, her capability to lead, and how she's going to handle the entire affair emotionally. Trust me here – this attempt on my wife's life will ultimately result in doubt, and that's not a positive thing so close to the election."

Aaron was taken aback by the words, Mr. Clifton's pronouncement going against what his heart alleged and the polls confirmed. On the other hand, Jefferson Clifton was regarded as one of the most astute political minds of the last century. His ability to perceive the electorate's mood was legendary, his skill at maneuvering through minefields almost mystical. Anyone on the national stage would be foolish to ignore the man's sage counsel.

"What would you recommend, Jeff?" Heidi asked from her bed.

"I would get up from that horizontal position and in front of the cameras as soon as I could walk. I would bring in the best makeup artist I could find and let them paint me up like an Indian brave going into battle. And here's what I would say..."

When he had finished, Aaron understood why Jeff Clifton was so highly regarded. His recommendation was straightforward, direct, and extremely poignant.

"Let me get some people working on this," the smiling campaign manager stated, pulling out his cell. "It's brilliant... absolutely brilliant."

The FBI, Secret Service, and FAA pulled out all the stops. Within hours, a lab technician was entering forensic data into a computer simulation, creating a 3-dimensional model of the attack on the chartered aircraft.

The plane's speed was known from the flight data recorders, as was the exact position on the runway. These parameters, combined with the entry angle of the first bullet, allowed the authorities to determine the shooter's vector to within a few points on the compass.

But there were still missing pieces to the puzzle.

"The digital model shows a downward trajectory of over 20 degrees," noted one of the FBI specialists. "Either our shooter was a couple of hundred feet in the air, or that bullet was dropping off a cliff."

"Maybe he was firing from an extreme distance," commented another analyst. "Any conventional bullet drops at a significant pace as the energy bleeds off."

"That is impossible. That aircraft was moving at over 160 mph and accelerating. There's not a sniper in the world that could hit a target moving that fast from long range."

One of the techs moved to a nearby computer and started pecking on the keyboard. A series of graphs and tables filled the screen. "I've accessed the ballistic performance database for all of the standard 30-caliber cartridges. Let's start running them against the model and see if we can find a match."

There were dozens of cartridges that fired a bullet .30 inches wide. Some were household names, such as the 30-06, while others were more exotic, such as the .300 Winchester Magnum.

One by one, the computer eliminated the options, some attribute of the round's performance making it unsuitable or extremely unlikely to have been used against the aircraft.

After an hour of number crunching, one potential match had been identified, but even that result was rejected by the FBI's experts.

"There's no way. None of this data makes any sense. It would take a radar guided, anti-aircraft gun to hit that plane from a mile away. We're barking up the wrong tree."

From the edge of the huddled onlookers, a new voice sounded. "I know a rifle that can make that shot. We've been evaluating a couple of them for our hostage rescue teams. It's called a Trackerpoint, and it's made by a company in Austin."

Again, fingers flew across the keyboard, the monitor quickly displaying an image of a computer-controlled, extreme-range rifle for the gathered techs. During the next 10 minutes, several sets of eager eyes studied the weapon's characteristics and performance.

Mumbling, "Holy shit," the lab's manager picked up a nearby phone.

"Get me Judge Mason, please. I need a search warrant."

The senior officer at the Austin office of the ATF didn't need to read the address of Trackerpoint's headquarters. He was well aware of the small company's developments, having watched their achievements with mixed emotions.

On one hand, from a "gun guy's" perspective, their technology was amazing. He could see incredible advantages for law enforcement and the military.

As a federal agent charged with enforcing the law of the land, the weapon's capabilities scared the hell out of him.

Now, given the headlines and the warrant he held in his hand, there was no doubt that his fears were justified.

The company's staff didn't want to hand over a list of its customers. Even when presented with a federal judge's signature, the CEO had pressed to call his corporate attorney before revealing a single name.

"We can do this two ways," responded the lead AFT agent. "I can walk out of here with every computer, hard drive, file drawer, and box... or... you can hand over that list, and I'll be on my way. Your call."

The thought of having his business ransacked, combined with the potential of a hostile relationship with the ATF, convinced the executive to hand over the customer list. There were 741 names on the printout, many of the disclosed buyers representing government and military agencies. Less than 400 individual civilians had coughed up the money for a rifle costing in excess of $20,000.

The list of potential assassins was further narrowed by the caliber of weapon purchased. Only four of the newer, modified .338 caliber had been ordered.

One customer was an 88-year-old millionaire and collecting enthusiast. Another was a civilian contractor charged with evaluating technology for the Special Forces at Fort Bragg. That left two likely candidates.

When the Houston area address of one Mr. Abraham Hendricks appeared on the computer monitor, all of the agents in the room knew they had their man, but proximity wasn't enough.

"I want a complete database search on this individual," ordered a supervisor.
The digital report began scrolling in 15 minutes, a multi-screen display profiling every aspect of Abe's life. When the gathered agents spied the results of the IRS tax audit, motive was established.

Everything from tax returns to cell phone activity appeared, including the make and model of the late year vehicles registered to the suspect.

Only five minutes passed before the FBI was on the phone with the company that provided the GPS-controlled, roadside assistance technology that came standard on every one of the automobile manufacturer's models. Practically all modern cars and trucks were equipped with these features.

It was a little known fact that these newer vehicles constantly broadcasted their locations, the data normally used to provide convenience services, such as navigation, collision detection, and anti-theft protection. Some units could even have their engines remotely disabled in the event the vehicle was stolen. Abe's truck was equipped with such technology.

A stream of data was soon being transmitted to the federal agency, a historical record of everywhere Abe had driven on the day Heidi's plane had been attacked. The destination and timing of his presence so close to the Houston airport was damning.

One last bit of information sealed Abe's fate. His smart phone also squawked its location on a regular basis. For this evidence, the FBI didn't have to contact the carrier or obtain a warrant - the NSA maintained a complete history.

A small army of agents was soon on the move, heading with a purpose toward a suburb in Northwest Houston.

The staff and administration at Bethesda were accustomed to the fact that their patients often required extreme security measures and large contingents of bodyguards. So common was the requirement, the hospital's heavily restricted VIP floor was equipped with special lounges set aside for non-medical personnel.

During Heidi's stay, Aaron soon discovered that the Secret Service had somehow managed access to a supply of the world-renowned White House coffee. A fresh pot was always on a burner right down the hall from his boss's room.

Ignoring the harsh looks expressing the agents' disdain for his intrusion into their semi-private domain, Mrs. Clifton's campaign manager had taken to filling his cup with the excellent brew. Aaron was putting the final touches on his third cup of the day when he noticed the open laptop sitting on a nearby table. A quick glance at the nearby restroom's closed door indicated the computer's owner had evidently abandoned the machine to answer nature's call.

Throwing the plastic stir-straw into the trash can, Aaron made to return to Heidi's side when the image on the laptop's screen made him freeze mid-stride. There was a picture of a man... a man he knew from long ago.

The Secret Service agent opened the door, drying his hands with a brown paper towel. He found Aaron fixated, gaping open-mouthed at his laptop.

"Sir, that's confidential information," the agent began to scold. "I would appreciate it if you would..."

"I think I know that man," Aaron whispered, ignoring the agent's protest.

"You do? How?"

Aaron recovered quickly, blinking away the shock. He turned to the agent and said, "You first. Why is the Secret Service interested in this person?"

"This just popped up not five minutes ago. The investigation team in Houston flashed this profile to see if our protection detail had any experience or knowledge of this individual. I believe he is a suspect in the attempt on Mrs. Clifton's life. If you know this guy... have any experience with him at all, I need to know about it. Right now."

Aaron knew damned well who Abe Hendricks was. In fact, he probably knew more than the FBI and the Secret Service combined. He also knew to keep his mouth shut.

"I can't be sure," he feigned, now hesitating. "Are there any more pictures?"

"No, at least not yet. Do you know him, sir?"

Aaron pretended to study the photograph, furrowed his brow as if trying to concentrate. "I just can't be positive. It seems like I've seen his face before."

"We should have additional information in short order. If this is the man who attacked the aircraft, he could've been stalking Mrs. Clifton for months. Perhaps you remember his face from a campaign event or fundraiser."

"Perhaps. Please keep me in the loop, and I'll do the same. Maybe it will come back to me," Aaron lied. "I would like nothing more than to see the man responsible for the deaths of my staff to face justice. That, and I'm sure we will all sleep a little better knowing an assassin isn't roaming around free." The agent nodded his agreement. Aaron pivoted and left the lounge, forcing himself to walk calmly back to Heidi's room.

Despite every fiber of his being screaming for him to rush from the medical complex in a panic, Aaron killed time. Heidi was off having some test performed, her unoccupied room providing a welcome sanctuary.

While he'd never considered the Secret Service personnel as intellectual giants, they weren't stupid either. A mad dash from the facility would be noticed, logged, and possibly analyzed at some future date. That was a series of events he simply couldn't afford. The smart move was to stay put and act like everything was normal.

Yet he had to do something.

He used the forced period of inactivity to think, constantly reassuring himself that his mental firepower would eventually provide a solution. Pretending to be consumed by a report retrieved from his briefcase, Aaron flipped the unread pages, all the while considering his options. After plotting every conceivable alternative, he finally concluded there was only one viable course of action. The answer made his stomach heave.

Finally, Heidi was wheeled back into her room. After being helped into her bed, she made eye contact with Aaron and immediately frowned.

"You look like shit," she announced.

"Just a little tired," he said, dismissing the observation. "You've got to admit, it's been a hectic couple of days."

Mrs. Clifton didn't buy it. "You look green around the gills, Aaron. Why don't you go get a few hours rest before the big event this evening." Aaron pretended to protest while secretly welcoming the opportunity to return to his apartment.

He dreaded making this call... didn't want the man who would answer to be involved in his life.

After the short cab ride, the familiar surroundings of his private abode helped build his confidence. He trudged to the bedroom, digging a no-contract, unregistered cell phone from his underwear drawer.

"Just when you thought you'd dodged a bullet," he whispered to the flat, "just when you thought you were free and clear, this bomb explodes."

He flipped open the cheap phone, punching the numbers from memory despite having never used them before.

Heidi Clifton's political wizard, one of the most powerful men in Washington, had trouble pushing the "send" button. His finger, shaking with rage and fear, finally managed to strike the right key.

"Yes," answered a mildly annoyed voice.

"It's me. I've got a problem, and I'm not sure who else to call."

There was a complete change of tone from the other end. "Tell me about it. You know I'm always here to help if I can."

"There is a paper trail that I suddenly wish didn't exist. I thought with your connections, it might disappear."

"Go on," came the reply.

Poot Terrebonne's index finger slowly traced the outline of her naked hip, his hungry eyes assessing every aspect of the curve and angle constructed by the underlying bone and muscle.

"Time's a wasting, Poot," she stated with an impatient voice. "I charge by the hour, ya know. Girl's got to make a living."

"Shut up," he snapped. "I'm flush with cash and intend to take my time. Been a while since I had a lanky one like you."

"How'd you fill your pockets so quick? I know you just got out of Huntsville last month. You got work already?"

"Ain't none of your business," he replied coldly. "I did a job over in Houston, so you'll get paid. Now just lay there and be pretty... and quiet. I hired you for those legs and what's between 'em – not engaging conversation."

Rolling her eyes, the hooker smirked, "No need to be short with me." She regretted the words immediately.

Poot inhaled sharply, slapping her face with a lightning-fast strike. "Bitch!" he hissed, eyes wide with rage.

Rubbing her stinging cheek, she instantly apologized. "I'm sorry, Poot. I didn't mean anything by it. It's just a saying."

Like so many vertically challenged men, Poot was well known for his uppity attitude and quick temper. The Cajun's appetite for tall women was legendary as well, more than a few of the escort services in New Orleans familiar with his tastes and desires.

Despite the arrogance and obvious compensation for his lack of stature, Poot had a fair reputation among New Orleans's working girls. He didn't get too rough, nothing too kinky, paid in cash, didn't last long, and preferred his female companions to be lean and leggy.

Her customer's frustration was further elevated when his cell phone sounded from the nightstand. Already thrown off his game plan, Poot reached for the annoying device as if he was going to fling it against the wall.

One glance at the caller ID changed his demeanor immediately.

Holding a "be quiet" finger to his lips while nodding at his companion, Poot answered with a congenial tone. "Yeah."

His eyes lost focus as he listened in silence. A minute later, he swung his legs over the edge of the bed, losing all interest in the woman beside him. "Yeah, I'm available," came his less than verbose reply.

"Baton Rouge?" the prostitute heard him say.

"Just the files? That's all they want?" he uttered a few moments later.

"I'll need the money up front to pry them loose," Poot continued. "Probably take five to ten large for a federal case. Meet me in the Quarter at the usual place... 20 minutes. I'll head up to Baton Rouge first thing."

Poot punched the "end" button, staring blankly at the phone as he gathered his thoughts. He then stood abruptly, reaching for his trousers.

He flipped three one-hundred dollar bills at the girl, growling, "Get dressed, and get out of here. Right now."

Smiling at the unearned bonus, she shrugged and began to comply. "Call me any time, Poot. You got my number."

A mob of reporters gathered in Bethesda's pressroom - standing room only. First up was the candidate's primary medical doctor, the distinguished gentleman providing a positive report on Heidi's physical condition.

The campaign then pulled a huge surprise on the media, parading out the always-popular President Clifton. With his customary smile and high-handed waves, he spoke to the throng as a relieved husband and caring family man.

Somehow, the ex-chief executive managed to pull off a conflicting message, convincing the onlookers that his wife was in excellent spirits, while at the same time expressing her remorse at the loss of life resulting from the incident. Walking the razor's edge as if it were a casual stroll in the park, he portrayed Heidi as strong, resilient, and ready to lead, yet deeply touched by the deaths of her co-workers.

Aaron was always amazed at Jeff Clifton's performances. The press seemed to suffer from amnesia regarding his indiscretions while serving in the Oval Office. One radio commentator had dubbed the former chief executive "the Teflon president," and the handle seemed to fit. Clifton's famous denial, "I never had sex with that woman," was now commonly used as a punchline, signaling a big lie that had resulted in practically no consequence. "I never inhaled," was another of the former president's oft-referenced jewels.

And then came the encore.

With perfect hair, flawless makeup and her typical conservative dress, Heidi authoritatively strolled out on the stage. There was one small bandage on her temple, her left arm in a sling.

The room went crazy, blinding camera flashes coupled with a hundred inquiries bellowed at once. She teased them, acting as if she had no intention of speaking or taking any questions. Jefferson Clifton moved to her side, taking a posture that appeared as if he were trying to protect his vulnerable spouse from the baying wolves of the press.

Grinning and nodding, she ignored the barrage of questions. It was a re-creation of Ronald Reagan stepping onto the balcony after the failed attempt on his life, waving and smiling to reassure the people.

Just when the reporters thought she was going to disappear from the stage, Heidi again shocked the crowd by stepping up to the microphone.

"If I am elected president of these United States," she began, "I will most likely have to endure even greater remorse than what I feel at the loss of my comrades in Houston. As Commander in Chief, I may be required to order our brave men and women into dangerous war zones where they risk the ultimate sacrifice. Some may not come home."

She paused to scan the room, her eyes focused and clear. A slight grimace had formed on her lips before she continued. "And yet, the president of our great nation must continue on. The chief executive is required to ignore personal grief and lead our people. Countless times throughout our history, our leaders have been forced to push aside individual remorse and wounded emotions in order to stay a steady hand at the helm. It's part of the job, part of our heritage, and why we live in the greatest nation on earth."

The fact that Heidi wasn't reading from any prepared remarks made her words appear even more sincere, projecting a confidence that resonated across the nation's television screens. No one had noticed her husband leaving a sheet of paper on the podium before he'd stepped away.

Mr. Clifton, standing in the shadows, swelled with pride. She had pulled it off perfectly. But then, rather than walk away, she remained at the microphone, her expression making clear she wasn't finished.

"I also want this episode in Houston to be a catalyst to reevaluate the Second Amendment of our Constitution. My fellow Americans, it is past the time to initiate this critical debate. We, as a nation, have witnessed the massacre of children at the hands of deranged individuals who can legally possess weapons of mass destruction. And we did nothing. We have watched our sons, daughters, family and friends cut to pieces because a few individuals are afraid of their government. They quote our founding fathers, spewing antiquated rhetoric from over 200 years ago that is not at all applicable to modern society."

She glared at the press corps, almost as if she were daring anyone to challenge her words. Her passion, anger, and determination were obvious in that moment – evident to the millions of Americans watching.

"Do we settle our political differences with rifles? What kind of society determines the winner of a disagreement via the bullet?

To the people who shout 'liberty,' and 'freedom,' I ask you – what kind of liberty do those 24 dead people on that airplane have now? What kind of freedom are their children, spouses, and parents enjoying? This has gotten ridiculous, and if I am elected your Commander in Chief, I will do something about it."

Heidi took a deep breath, pausing to grip both sides of the podium. "I have supported universal background checks since before the campaign began. I voted for every gun control measure that came across my desk as a U.S. senator. I ask my fellow Americans to reflect on our current situation as they watch the funerals of the fallen over the next few days. Please, help me add some small sense of meaning to their sacrifice... help me ensure a tragedy like this never happens again. Thank you."

The former president almost choked, stunned that his normally on-message wife had left the carefully planned parameters of the appearance. Despite the sick feeling building in his stomach, he smiled at Heidi as she left the stage, congratulating her on a job well done.

He glanced at Aaron, making eye contact as the entourage headed back toward her hospital room. The ex-president shook his head, a frown governing his expression. "She just fucked up," he mouthed.

Chapter 6 – The Siege

They had arrived.

The first hint was the repeated sound of a helicopter passing over the area. A single fly by wasn't anything unusual – such things occasionally happened. On the second pass, Abe's senses snapped to full alert. The third pass was confirmation. He was sure his property was being scanned with a variety of airborne instruments.

Next, he spied Mrs. Fuller peeking through her drapes, the nosy woman's attention focused on the end of the street, well out of his range of vision. *That's where the initial patrol cars will be gathering, blocking traffic and mustering their forces,* he conjectured.

His lack of fear was a bit of a surprise. Despite the realization that dozens of law enforcement officers were preparing to storm his residence, he felt little emotion. Neither anger nor foreboding dominated his mood. It was the first calm he'd felt in years... since New Orleans.

He knew they would attack the front and back simultaneously. It was only common sense. What he wasn't sure about was which end of the house would receive the most attention.

"It doesn't matter," he proclaimed to the empty home. "I've got a whole series of surprises for them."

He tried to visualize what they were doing. "Probably scouting the lay of the land," he decided. "No doubt putting some long range shooters on the water tower, maybe commandeering Mrs. Fuller's spare bedroom up on the second floor as they evacuate the neighborhood."

He pressed the remote to turn on the television, switching to the channel that displayed his security cameras. A few days before, he'd discretely altered their direction, pointing them outward so he could enjoy the show. He didn't have to wait long for the opening act.

The first to enter his field of view were mere uniformed patrol officers. There were six in all, sidearms drawn and taking up positions along his back fence. After a few minutes, it was obvious their job was to block any escape route.

"You guys are wasting your time," he whispered to the television. "I'm not planning on going anywhere."

Movement drew his eye, the camera on the front porch detecting human shapes pressing toward the house, working along the edge of the street. "Ahhh. Now we're getting serious," he observed.

The advancing group contained five officers, all wearing body armor, tactical vests, and Kevlar helmets. All of them carried long guns, the familiar outline of at least three M4 rifles discernable on the grainy image. The bright, yellow letters "FBI" were stenciled across their chests.

Those first five, probably one of the FBI's Hostage Rescue Teams, paused by the low wall bordering his front yard. They were soon joined by three additional officers, two of them carrying shields, the third hefting what appeared to be a heavy battering ram.

In a flash, they were through the front gate, quickly approaching up the sidewalk and then spreading out on the front porch. Despite observing their progress, the loud banging on the door startled Abe. The sound instantly diverted his mind's eye to the memory of being in his father's home – 11 years ago.

"FBI! We have a warrant! Open this door! Police!" screamed the voice.

Before Abe, or any other reasonable person, could have answered or opened up, an even louder crash sounded as the battering ram slammed against the reinforced threshold.

At least you have a warrant this time, Abe thought, as he casually reached for the extension cord at his feet. Without hesitating, he plugged the red wire into the socket just as the ram impacted again, shaking the wall so violently one of Kara's favorite photographs fell to the floor.

The whine of a small pump drifted in from the garage, a slight odor of gasoline accompanying the noise. Abe smirked as his hand reached for the switch that controlled the front porch light.

Only two days before, he'd replaced the factory-delivered bulb with a modified version – screwing in a unit with exposed wires that would generate a shower of sparks. The ram struck the doorframe again.

The pump was connected to what had been Abe's mister. Used to spray a refreshing fine cloud of cold water during those intolerable summer months, he had installed the system a few years ago so Kara could enjoy the porch swing, even during the sweltering Houston evenings.

Instead of water, the pump now drew from a 5-gallon can of gasoline he'd kept in the garage. A mist of explosive vapors soon began falling around the agents trying to breach his home.

Evidently, they realized something was wrong. He could hear excited voices on the other side of the wall, the assault against his door now halted. Shifting to watch through a tiny slit in the shutters, he flicked the switch.

A ball of flame engulfed the verandah, its red and yellow center expanding in a brilliant flash. Like the whoosh of an over-fueled BBQ grill being ignited with a match, the roar of the flames was quickly overridden by cries of shrieking, horrified men.

Abe watched as they scrambled from his porch, two of the policemen partially engulfed in flames, a third stumbling badly as if he were blind. Other officers rushed to help their injured comrades while still more policemen pointed their weapons to cover their retreat.

Abe flipped the second wall switch.

It took a few seconds for the scavenged heating elements to ignite the smokeless powder packed into the three canister bombs. He'd purchased two 8-pound containers of the propellant at the local gun store a few weeks ago, joking with the clerk about how reloading his own ammunition was the only way he could afford to target practice.

The heating elements were scavenged from inexpensive coffeemakers, inserted directly into the gunpowder. The local home improvement store had provided the pipe, electrical wire, and nails.

Each of the foot-long, steel tubes contained almost two pounds of explosive, another two pounds of nails wrapped around each. Given the dense landscaping at the front of his home, it hadn't been difficult to reroute the electricity and disguise the devices.

Despite the amount of powder, Abe was disappointed in the size of the blast. Still, the air was filled with a hailstorm of shrapnel, four of the policemen in his yard going down, at least three staggering backwards.

Clouds of smoke and dirt rose into the air as the rumble of the explosion rolled down his usually quiet, suburban street. The echo hadn't yet faded before he was throwing open the storm shutters.

The AR15 was equipped with an infrared optic and holographic sight. Abe shouldered the weapon and began scanning through the thermal imager. His vision was filled with an odd combination of amber, crimson, and ash. The outlines of several human shapes were clearly visible, despite the thick fog of smoke and debris still fouling the air.

He spotted a handful of wounded men on his lawn, some lying prone, others trying to crawl away from the carnage. Abe wasn't worried about the officers on his property. They most likely weren't going anywhere.

He moved his aim toward the end of the street where several responders were scampering toward their downed comrades. He began firing.

At first, they didn't seem to understand that they were the targets, many of the agents continuing to charge directly into his line of fire. That situation quickly changed when men began to drop from his rapidly barking weapon.

He switched positions, redirecting his aim to the opposite end of the street. Here there were fewer targets, but still enough to warrant the remaining 15 rounds in his magazine.

Abe pulled back, speedily slamming the heavy shutters into their locked positions. It had only taken a few seconds to fire the 30 rounds, but the smoke was beginning to clear, and he didn't want to tempt the snipers who were no doubt covering his home. He was reasonably confident they had thermal technology as well, but had gambled they wouldn't typically use the devices in broad daylight.

He slammed a fresh magazine into the AR, returning his gaze to the security cameras and the backyard. A smile crossed his face – the back of his home was void of any intruders. The cops had either learned their lesson or detected the explosive devices covering that side of the house. Abe wondered if they had the technology to spot the laser trip-wires.

For a brief moment, he thought about engaging the wounded men still on his property, but dismissed the urge. Dealing with their downed comrades would take resources. Plus, the remaining cops wouldn't be so brash after seeing their mauled co-workers carried past. It was a small mercy – one the New Orleans police hadn't shown his brother or father.

After another quick scan of the security cameras, he decided a cold drink was in order. Besides, they would be cutting off the electricity any minute, and he would need to preserve the generator's gasoline supply. He knew that the refrigerator would soon be a luxury.

After opening a bottle of frosty water, Abe grabbed his pack and prepared to head upstairs. The armored vehicle would be next, and he could best deal with it from an elevated position.

Before he reached the bottom step, the power blinked once, twice, and then the room became dark. The police had cut the electricity. He had little doubt his cable TV, water, and natural gas would soon follow. The phone was questionable.

A grin crossed his face when the electrical switchgear in the garage did its job, the slight whine of his generator engaging just before the lights came back on. He wouldn't even have to reset the clocks.

As if on cue, he heard the downstairs phone ring. It was either a solicitor or a police negotiator. Neither was welcome.

Sighing at the distraction, he decided to get it over with and answer the call.

"Hendricks residence," he answered with a polite voice.

"Mr. Hendricks, my name is Sal Perkins… Special Agent Sal Perkins of the Houston FBI office."

"Hello, Agent Sal Perkins," Abe responded with a pleasant tone. "I'm glad you called. There have been several men trying to break into my house, and I believe they should be arrested."

"Those are federal law enforcement officers, sir, and you know that. I'm calling to ask you to surrender peacefully. Unless you do, this can only end one way."

Abe chuckled, the response genuine. "The last time I had a bunch of cops at the door, it didn't work out so well. I'm not going to make that mistake again."

"There's no need for you to die, Mr. Hendricks. No reason for more loss of life. I'll personally guarantee your safety if you surrender peacefully. I can be there to meet you. You have my word that none of my men will shoot."

Abe was already tired of the conversation and saw no reason to be polite to the cop on the other end of the line. Pulling the phone from his ear, he bent slightly to return the headset to its base. The wall beside him exploded in a shower of plaster.

A string of bullets ripped through the air, a steady cadence of high-velocity lead slapping, banging, and popping into the living room.

Confusion reigned in Abe's mind for a microsecond, his body instinctively ducking the growing cloud of grit and debris flying from the wall. Awareness came to him in slow motion, his senses so acute that he could actually hear the bullets punching through the shutters before they slammed into the walls and furniture surrounding him.

Not realizing he was still gripping the handset, Abe scrambled across the floor on his hands and knees, desperately trying to escape the wave of destruction tearing into his home. Vases exploded, picture frames shattered, and wooden chairs vibrated with the impact. The air quickly grew thick with a fog of dust, drywall, and furniture stuffing.

They're using the phone to track my position somehow, he realized. *Amazing.*

And then the barrage stopped.

"You've just made a big mistake, Agent Perkins," he said breathlessly into the phone, his body hiding under the coffee table. "There are some very good reasons for me to sacrifice my life. You're going to have to come in and get me, and I'll give you fair warning – it's not going to be Mardi Gras."

Abe yanked the phone's cord from the wall and rolled away – unsure exactly what technology allowed them to locate him so precisely, but not wanting to take any chances. It took him a bit to gather himself, rising cautiously and ready to dive for cover just in case the cops still had a bead on him somehow.

But nothing happened.

Replaying the incident, he grew angry. He concluded that the conversation with Agent Perkins was yet another example of over-zealous, totalitarian response. Then again, what else should he expect?

"I'm going to make them experience helplessness," he whispered. "I need to make them understand what it feels like to see people you care about die right before your eyes – and there's not a damn thing you can do about it."

Returning to Heidi's hospital room, Jefferson Clifton wanted desperately to kick his wife's ass, but it didn't happen. First came the personal physician's insistence on checking Heidi's status. It had taken stern words and outright bullying before the medical staff had given its *Good Housekeeping* seal of approval to walk the short distance to the pressroom. Now, the doctor wanted to make sure she hadn't suffered from the effort.

President Clifton's patience was stretched even thinner by Aaron's continued presence. His wife's chief of staff seemed determined to hang around, making things worse by reinforcing Heidi's performance with a fountain of glowing, supportive praise.

I need to be calm, Mr. Clifton thought. *I can't scold Heidi in front of her people. I'll just loiter and play the role of supportive husband until that young staffer moves along.*

When a very bossy nurse appeared, demanding everyone vacate the room and give Mrs. Clifton an opportunity to rest, his head nearly exploded. He was already livid with Heidi, incensed by her seemingly careless act. He believed her unwillingness to ignore her impulsive nature was her primary weakness as a politician.

Eight years ago, it had been her passions that had propelled her to the lead of the Democratic-pack. That same enthusiasm had been at the center of her downfall as well. And yet, incidents like today pointed to the conclusion that she hadn't learned her lesson.

Rash stunts like today's trumpeted remarks on gun control could lead the party's powerbrokers to withdraw their critical support. Her occasional outbursts of off-message ranting would surely put him in an early grave.

Time after time, he'd tried to coach her through it, but it just didn't seem to be doing any good.

This time, he was going to shove the message down her throat. He even considered turning on the television in her room, so she could watch the results of her own foolishness.

It had been decided over two years ago that gun control was not going to be a part of the 2016 campaign. Sage political minds had run the numbers, processed the polls, and gauged the pundits. Their recommendations had been unanimous - leave gun control out of this election if the Democrats wanted to hold onto the White House.

And Heidi had agreed, reassuring the influential individuals guiding their party of her resolve to remain on message.

Now, three days before the election, she'd gone flying around the pressroom on her broomstick, the wicked witch of stupidity. He was going to let her know, in no uncertain terms, how ignorant her decision was.

But he needed to do that in private. Despite his anger over her blunder, the event didn't warrant a public dressing-down. *Scolding her in front of her subordinates would only create more issues in the long run*, he plotted.

Disgusted, he'd eventually left the room, heading to a nearby lounge area where he knew there was a television.

The first image he spotted was an aerial view of some house. He could see tons of police cars lining the road beyond the roof in the center of the picture. The announcer was reporting about a standoff.

He quickly flipped channels, anticipating a replay of his wife's remarks while some network political analyst tore Heidi to shreds. Again, he discovered another video of dozens of cops rushing around with their guns drawn, expressions rife with urgency all around.

A hasty survey of the cable networks confirmed that they were all broadcasting similar footage.

"What the hell," Jefferson mumbled, not seeing what he'd expected. He adjusted the volume to better hear the journalist.

"All that we know at this point is that there have been over a dozen law enforcement casualties in this generally quiet neighborhood. I spoke with one of the local residents, and here's what she had to say."

The image zoomed in on an elderly woman, the name Carol Fullerton flashing across the bottom of the screen. "The police swarmed my house and told me I had to leave my home immediately. They rushed me out the back door so fast, I didn't even pick up my purse. About a half an hour ago, all heck broke loose over there. I heard hundreds of gunshots and explosions that lasted for some time. I can't imagine what kind of building could remain standing after such abuse. Everything I own is in that house. I just hope I have a home to go back to."

The network then switched back to the aerial view, a fuzzy, long distance shot of what appeared to be the roof, yard, and surrounding woods of a typical upscale home. The on-the-scene reporter's voice returned, "According to some off-the-record sources, the FBI approached this residence because the owner was a person of interest in the recent assassination attempt on presidential candidate Heidi Clifton. As of this moment, I've been unable to obtain official confirmation of that information."

The former president rubbed his chin, relieved that for once, the campaign had caught a break. Heidi's misstep at the press conference would be overshadowed by the events unfolding in Houston. If the gunman held out for a while longer, her words might be completely overlooked.

The upstairs bedroom was equipped with a security monitor as well. It had been a wise precaution, the central television downstairs now riddled with police bullet holes.

Four cardboard boxes, each filled with golf balls and lined against the wall, provided a bulletproof barrier.

Checking the placement of his makeshift shield, Abe couldn't help but smile at the memory.

His cousin had actually discovered the small miracle. Always a boisterous fellow, the mouthy-relative had issued a challenge of marksmanship – shooting golf balls. Several of the small targets had been strategically placed, and the contest begun.

After dozens of shots, the competitors eventually sauntered over to examine their accuracy. As they first approached, Abe was troubled by what appeared to be untouched targets. There was no way he could have missed every shot. Upon closer examination, they found that each ball had indeed been struck numerous times, yet each had maintained its integrity.

What was even more astounding was the fact that most of the bullets had created entry holes, but hadn't penetrated through the other side. That observation was confirmed after he sawed a few of the balls in half and found bullets lodged inside.

"We've discovered a new type of reactive armor," he'd announced to his cousin. "The military will be happy to know they don't need all of that expensive, heavy steel plating. They can just cover their tanks in golf balls and call it a day."

"And," replied his grinning relative, "If the battle lulls, the troops can always work on their slice. A multi-purpose piece of gear!"

Little had Abe known how important the role that small piece of ballistics-trivia would play.

The local driving range sold bags of "experienced" golf balls for a few dollars. A business down the street rented moving vans and sold boxes. Abe selected the tall, thin wardrobe packers so that they provided enough girth for the balls to rest three-deep. That was plenty of ballistic protection for what he needed.

The storm shutters had been installed years ago, designed to withstand the occasional hurricane that visited Texas every few years. In anticipation of this day, he'd modified a select few of the thick barriers, cutting a small rectangle into the wood at the very bottom of the window cover.

An inch wide and just over three inches high, it was the perfect shape, allowing his rifle barrel a clear field of fire while at the same time providing enough clearance for an unhindered view by the weapon's optic.

Abe thoroughly understood the wooden shutters wouldn't stop an incoming round from a high-powered sniper rifle. That fact had just been violently reiterated downstairs. That's what the golf balls were for.

He also understood the gamble involved in exposing himself, even though the opening was tiny. It was a calculated risk. It was well known that military and law enforcement shooters possessed extraordinary skills with their weapons. But hitting a 1-inch wide opening while under duress was unlikely, and he planned to put the men who opposed him under significant stress.

After verifying the lights were out, he pulled down the small cut of wood, making sure not to show any movement or color behind the opening. After a quick adjustment of the golf ball barriers, he unfolded the shooting sticks and set the Trackerpoint rifle into the stabilized platform. He was extra careful to keep the muzzle well back of the opening.

He began scanning his surroundings, paying specific attention to the areas where he'd hide if he were a long-range shooter. There really weren't that many options.

His neighborhood consisted of upscale residences, most sitting on lots consisting of 4 to 10 acres of land. Thick woods surrounded the well-manicured lawns, only Mrs. Fullerton's hacienda visible from his homestead. That's where he spotted the first FBI shooter.

Zeroing in with his computer-controlled optic, Abe had to hand it to the guy – he was extremely well hidden.

There were several vents on the Fullerton roof, spinning aluminum units commonly called "whirlybirds." One of the neighbor's wasn't turning, despite the heat of the day.

Abe would have passed right over the sniper, but the lack of movement seemed odd, drawing additional scrutiny. Upon further inspection, he noticed the proximity of the beach-ball sized vent to the stone chimney extending upward through the shingles. It just looked out of place, and that caused him to focus on the oddity.

The sniper had removed the whirlybird's upper section, resting it next to the chimney to provide excellent concealment. But it wasn't enough.

Abe pushed the target acquisition button, the green brackets flashing on the small gap between the metal vent and stone façade. He felt no guilt, having little doubt that the man on Mrs. Fullerton's roof would kill him without hesitation.

The laser registered the distance to the target at just over 300 meters, a leisurely shot for the fancy rifle.

For a moment, he considered scanning for additional shooters, but decided the delay was unnecessary. Once he fired on the closest man, the others would give themselves away as they returned fire. He prayed the police snipers would be unable to zero-in on the tiny slot carved in his shutter.

Abe pulled the trigger, the green guidance arrows instructing him to adjust his aim a few inches to the right, less than a foot higher. The electronic crosshairs were actually centered on the chimney when the powerful weapon roared.

Unlike the aircraft, the effect of this shot was nearly instantaneous. Abe saw the concealed government shooter jerk, and then his weapon clambered down the shingled roof. He immediately zoomed the optic out for a wider field of view and began scanning for anyone daring enough to return fire.

Like the shooter on Mrs. Fullerton's roof, the sniper on the water tower was also well concealed. Somehow, the man had managed to procure an off-white bed sheet that closely matched the paint on the steel tank. Only the appearance of a black rifle barrel gave him away, a mistake that would cost him dearly.

The range finder signaled 820 meters just as the first incoming bullet struck the shutter with a resounding "thwack." Abe ignored the broken glass and splinters, trusting in his bullet stop to keep him alive. Still, his fingers moved with nervous haste as he repeated the aiming process. Another round plowed into the golf balls at the same moment his .338 reported its deadly discharge.

A spectacular plunge confirmed he'd struck the target, the sniper's dark image rising briefly to its feet, and then plummeting over 60 feet to the ground. Before the already-dead man slammed into the earth, Abe was scanning for more work.

Standard law enforcement procedures stipulated a secure perimeter of 300-500 meters around any active shooter. The exact distance established for any operation was up to the local commander's discretion – terrain, population, and urban density all factors that were to be taken into account.

With Abe's counterattack on the FBI's over-watch personnel, he assumed they would rethink how close their assets were positioned. He was right.

From his elevated perch, he could examine movement several hundred yards down the thoroughfare in front of his house. Uniformed police officers were casually stepping to their cars, obviously heeding an order to pull back.

The feds were running this show. They had set up a blocking position along his street, more to keep innocent passersby safe than to confine the distant suspect. Perimeter duty was a boring, mundane assignment – rarely involving direct engagement with a suspect. Given the nonchalant manner of the officers' movement, they evidently felt secure, removed from the dangerous man who lived so far away.

Abe and the Trackerpoint turned their casual egress into a nightmare.

The fugitive began firing round after round into the helpless police cruisers, each of the 250-grain bullets delivering over 1,000 pounds per square inch of force. Automotive sheet metal was sliced like carbon paper, engine blocks providing only slightly more resistance to the living hell of Abe's incoming fire. Fuel tanks were punctured like water balloons, the volatile liquid dripping on the ground, elevating the danger even more.

Recovering from their initial surprise, many of the policemen sought cover by going prone or diving for the shallow ditch that bordered the road. It didn't do them any good.

So accurate was Abe's weapon, even the slightest exposure meant death. After several men were picked off, some of the survivors scampered from their hides to evade the rifleman's fury, hoping movement and distance would save their lives. Their escape plans failed.

Others made for the trees after seeing man after man fall to the unbelievably accurate fire being sent their way. The soft pines provided concealment, but little cover. Abe could spot their anxious, frightened, faces peeking from behind the evergreens. It reminded him of Charlie's expression as the bullets tore into his chest. He would deliver a similar experience to these brothers of the badge.

Even at 500 meters or more, the .338 could blow through a tree trunk and still maintain enough energy to penetrate a cop's body armor. Two more officers dropped before the others realized they might as well be hiding behind toothpicks.

Only the density of the forest allowed any survivors.

Chapter 7 — Hello, Sam

Zach watched her stroll across the hotel's lobby, resisting the urge to let loose with a proper West Texas wolf whistle.

The Texan wasn't sure of her genetic composition, had no idea what ancestry had produced Detective Samantha Temple's legs, but he knew he wanted to visit that country before he died. Hopefully, that wouldn't be today.

"I'd never guess you were a cop," the ranger said, a forced professionalism returning to his manner.

They moved to a secluded corner, well away from the constant traffic of guests, porters, and staff.

Moving one leg slightly forward, she lifted the short black skirt high enough to reveal a petite revolver holstered just above the top of her hose. Zach tried to look away, but she caught his glance. "Don't get any ideas, Mr. Texas Ranger."

"Yeah? Well, don't flatter yourself, Sam. I was just checking to make sure your equipment was proper," he replied, shaking his head.

Snorting, she looked away with rolling eyes, "I've never had any complaints about my equipment, Ranger. Don't concern yourself."

Zach believed her.

He'd met this example of Houston's finest just the previous day. He was trailing a suspected con artist, a rather crafty fellow whose most recent sin was an attempt to bribe a government official in Louisiana. When his offer of significant monetary exchange had been rejected, gunplay erupted, and the perpetrator allegedly bolted for the Lone Star State. Major Alcorn had assigned Zach to hunt the criminal down.

The trail had led Zach to a dead body and one very tall homicide detective. Sam's investigation of the murder made a temporary partnership unavoidable.

Zach's first impression of Detective Temple hadn't been a positive one. While the homicide gumshoe was clearly an intelligent, experienced investigator, she came across as big-city sophisticated - and more than a little snooty.

Nearly six-feet in height, she was definitely a tall drink of water, but from Zach's perspective, she used that stature to look down her nose at the planet's lesser creatures.

That first day, he'd watched her scold two uniformed officers at the crime scene, barking a harsh reprimand over a minor misstep with an evidence envelope. A few moments after she'd finished belittling the patrolmen, he overheard a lab technician receive a professional ass chewing via Sam's cell phone.

The local cops dubbed her the "Amazon Queen," a fitting handle if the ranger had ever heard one.

She was, as Zach would soon discover, the ultimate professional. Highly intelligent, detail oriented, and exuding boundless energy, Detective Temple had been issued a golden shield in record time. Her interpersonal skills, however, sucked.

Until this moment in the hotel hallway, he'd never considered her female attributes. On an average day, she dressed like a librarian, her casual work attire accented by hair pulled back into a neat bun and thick rim glasses. To complete her work uniform, she typically donned the kind of low-slung flats purchased more for orthopedic comfort than a heel's ability to glorify the line of a girl's leg. Now, going undercover as a call girl, he was beginning to wonder what else he'd overlooked concerning this complex woman.

Their suspect, as it turned out, had an appetite for high-end escorts. The boys over at vice knew the man by name and reputation – he favored tall, lithe-limbed beauties who weren't afraid to show a little thigh. The ranger had to agree with the gent's preferences – he had demonstrated a weakness for the same body type, as well.

The lounge at the Metro Hotel was well known as a welcoming location for professional women to advertise their wares. It had been Samantha's idea to go "under cover." Zach suppressed the nearly infinite string of one-liners forming in his throat. His partner had a temper, and she carried a gun.

Zach had staked out the hotel's lobby while Sam rushed home to change. She strolled into the lobby half an hour later, gussied up and sporting leg. A lot of leg.

Wearing 4-inch heels and dark, thigh-high stockings, Detective Temple did indeed command the room like an Amazon queen. She sashayed into the bar, selecting a stool like it was an old friend. The male population held its collective breath, spellbound as she ordered a white wine and crossed those seemingly endless limbs.

Zach had to admit he'd never seen God issue such a long shin to any human being. The distance between her kneecap and ankle was mesmerizing, the flesh of her calf seductively proportional.

Shaking his head in an effort to get back to business, the ranger continued scanning the lobby, waiting for the suspect to make a shopping trip to the bar.

While they waited, Sam found herself being approached by practically every cowboy in that watering hole. Zach watched from his distant perch, amazed at how deftly she dismissed each suitor with a smile and minimal conversation.

And then the man they lay in wait for appeared, stepping off the elevator dressed to the nines, and looking like he was ready to party.

Poot Terrebonne's stride indicated he was a man who was clearly pleased with himself. As the suspect strolled through the lobby, Zach had to wonder how the recently released convict could afford such fine duds, let alone a room at the Metro. This definitely wasn't a low rent, no-tell motel. And from what Zach could ascertain, the felon had been living pretty high on the hog in the French Quarter too... that is, of course, after he vacated the Lone Star State's hospitality suite at the Huntsville correctional facility.

It didn't take long for the flesh-hound to zero in on Sam. When she stood, leaning to reach for a bar napkin, Zach thought the fellow's head was going to explode. He was seated next to the detective in seconds, buying Sam a drink in record time.

Fifteen minutes passed before he rose, heading back to the elevator with a confident gait. Zach didn't understand, but didn't want to approach and blow their cover either.

Moments later, Sam sauntered to the lawman's perch as if she were reviewing one of the fancy canvases that adorned the lobby. "Follow me to the ladies' room," she whispered.

And so he did.

"It's all set," she reported, examining her appearance in the oversized mirror. "I told him I had to use the facilities and would meet him in his room in a few minutes. He's supposed to be freshening up and ordering champagne," she announced, reapplying a layer of pale pink lipstick and arranging her exotic tresses before making a slight adjustment to her stockings. Finally satisfied with her presence, she puckered her lips and blew him a kiss. "Ready, cowboy?"

"How much?" Zach asked, unable to stop himself.

"How much for what?" she smiled coquettishly.

"Your services."

Grunting, she batted her eyelashes and responded, "$2,000 for two hours. Nothing rough."

"Damn," Zach replied as they strolled toward the elevators. "This guy must have more money than sense."

"Fuck you," she whispered as they entered the car. "I let him talk me down from my normal rate of $1500 an hour."

Again, remembering the pistol strapped to her thigh, Zach decided silence was the better part of valor... and his health.

They exited into a plush hall, thick carpeting and tasteful art adorning the passage. "I'll wait out here with my ear against the door. As soon as you see that the money's inside, yell. If he gets the drop on you, yell. If anything goes wrong...."

"Yell," she finished for him. Then with a sly smile, her accent became laced with southern charm, her tone that of a helpless belle, "I think it's sweet that you're so worried about little ole' me. How nice it is to have a big, strong, Texas Ranger to protect me."

Without another word, she glided toward the crook's room, an exaggerated swagger in her hips. Zach ducked behind the ice machine.

Her knock was answered immediately. Light spilled out into the hall as she was invited inside. Zach waited a few moments after the lock had clicked and then stalked to the threshold to eavesdrop. He'd acquired a universal keycard from the front desk while Sam had been changing. He withdrew the plastic from his pocket … just in case.

"Show me the money," Sam urged, getting right down to business.

Poot glanced up from his champagne pouring and smiled at the crass demand. "Show me your tits first. I don't like fake ones."

"You don't see anything until I see the money," Sam countered.

Handing her a glass of bubbly liquid, his eyes lustily swept up and down her frame as he began to circle her like a ravenous lion preparing to pounce on an antelope.

Towering over the shorter man, Sam did her best to imitate how a real escort would react. "Okay, I'll flash the glands, but that's it. No more freebies."

"Deal," he responded, moving to the edge of the bed and taking a seat for a better view.

Sam unbuttoned her blouse, exposing her bra. Without unsnapping the undergarment, she pulled it up to expose her breasts. "Satisfied?"

Poot reached to examine a sample, but she backed away, covering the merchandise as she withdrew. "I thought we had a deal," she protested. "Show me the cash, or I'm out of here."

But he kept on coming, a greedy gleam in his eye. It was a mistake.

As he extended both arms to grab the detective, Sam ignored his left hand, focusing all of her attention on his right. Before Poot could react, she had a grip on his wrist and thumb, bending the digit back as she twisted the joint.

The Cajun conman howled in pain, Sam's downward pressure forcing him to his knees. She was just twisting his arm behind his back when Zach burst into the room, pistol drawn, barrel sweeping right and left.

"It's okay," she snapped. "I've got it under control."

"Where's the money?" he asked, ignoring the menu of smart-ass remarks that filled his throat at the sight of her unbuttoned blouse.

"I don't know. Mr. Horny here decided to get frisky before I saw the cash."

"Shit," Zach spit, glancing around the room for any sign of the evidence they so desperately needed. He finally spied a briefcase in the corner.

As he stepped to retrieve the leather attaché, Sam's prisoner surged with an angry roar, "Noooo!"

His elbow slammed into Sam's knee, causing the high heel-clad detective to lose her balance. Zach spotted the man reaching for the small of his back and realized his partner hadn't had a chance yet to search her captive. *This is going to get ugly*, the Texan recognized instantly.

As the suspect brought his weapon to bear, Zach's fist slammed into the guy's nose. In rapid succession, two more powerful jabs from the ranger ended all resistance, the stunned crook slumping to the floor as blood poured from his mouth and flattened snout.

"Well, that was a pleasant surprise," Sam remarked, rubbing her sore leg.

"What?"

"I thought all you West Texas cowboys shot first and asked questions later," came the detective's response.

"Nope," Zach answered with a grin. "We save our ammo for the interrogation. The state's on a tight budget, and bullets are expensive."

Sam grunted, staring down at the unconscious Mr. Terrebonne. "You may need those bullets to get this guy to talk. Looks like you broke his jaw."

"We've got wounded men lying all over the place up there," one of the officers shouted, his face flush with fear and anxiety. "We've got to get them out!"

Special Agent Perkins peered at his watch and shook his head, "We will have to wait. The Harris County armored vehicle won't be here for another 25 minutes. I can't order more men into the kill zone."

Another cop stepped forward, his expression and tone divulging the tortured nature of his soul. "Those guys will bleed out in 25 minutes. Even if they aren't hurt that bad, that fucker might decide to start taking out the wounded. We've got to get our people out of there."

Perkins was just as disgusted as anyone. "I know; I know. I've got people up there too. Anybody got any ideas?"

"We could form a wall with the shields," somebody suggested. "Put up a barrier while we carry the wounded out of his range."

"His *range*?" a deputy snorted, "That son of a bitch nailed my commander at 800 yards. I saw another constable fall beyond that, and he was at a dead run. How in the hell are we supposed to carry our guys that far? He's good enough to pick us off if there's even the smallest opening. I think it's suicide to go in there without armor."

Perkins had to agree, but was out of ideas. He continued to scan the anxious faces, hoping the law enforcement brain trust would generate a solution from its collective experience. It was then that he noticed the line of traffic that had formed, waiting to enter the now closed neighborhood. An oversized vehicle in the gridlock caught his eye.

Pointing, the FBI agent suggested, "What about the garbage truck? Can we use that as cover to go in and get our people out?"

Several heads turned to inspect what sparked Perkins' suggestion. "That might work," came a voice from the throng. "Let's see if we can get two or three of them. Give the EMTs some room to work on our guys," suggested someone else.

"Let's hurry," Perkins added, "They are going to need some modifications for this scheme to succeed. It's going to be night soon. I don't want our folks walking around with flashlights."

Ten minutes later, Abe recognized the sound of a large diesel motor in the distance. He'd moved to one of the other upstairs bedrooms, thinking any remaining snipers would have zeroed in on his previous shooting position.

"Finally," he proclaimed to the empty house, "Took them long enough to get some armor up here."

Again moving to a shooting slit, he scanned the street, expecting to see one of the county's armored cars. A questioning frown formed on his face when instead of a heavily plated battlewagon, he spied a short parade of trash trucks rolling slowly up the road. There were lines of policemen walking behind them.

"I've got to hand it to you, Agent Perkins," Abe observed. "That was clever... very creative."

Raising the Trackerpoint, he zoomed in on the lead truck, thoughts of plinking the driver circulating through his mind. He had to study the oncoming convoy before he realized the cops had up-armored the garbage haulers. He could see police shields tied to the windshields and grills, a sage tactic to protect the engines and drivers.

Mrs. Fullerton's residence was also active. Switching his angle, Abe observed three officers appear from the rear of his neighbor's home, each man brandishing a riot shield, together forming a wall of protection. Two additional officers crouched behind the barrier. Like crabs crossing beach sand, the little huddle moved forward as one, eventually reaching the downed sniper. Abe saw them quickly snatch up their comrade and then scuttle back to the safety of the backyard.

"The brotherhood of blue," Abe nodded. "I wonder if they would have done the same for my father and brother?" he whispered. "I bet they wouldn't be so brave if there had been just regular old Americans bleeding on the grass."

Zach sat on the hotel bed, absentmindedly listening as the Houston cops went about processing the scene.

He was profoundly perplexed.

They had discovered the money, part of the stash in the briefcase, a bit more buried in the closet. The manager, pissed that one of his better rooms would require new carpet, had discovered the rest of the bribe-loot in the hotel's safe.

But it was the bankroll's container that rattled the Texan's cool. The manager produced an old gym bag, faded from wear and age, sporting the emblem of the NY Jets. The Texas Ranger was sure it was identical to the satchel Tusk had been carrying ... the same bag Major Alcorn claimed vanished with the only witness.

The bad guy's gun appeared to be the perfect match for Sam's open homicide, the ballistics test likely to confirm the weapon had been involved in at least one murder.

While Sam's case was surely wrapped up tight and adorned with a pretty, pink bow, Zach's life had just gotten entirely more complex.

How in hell had that gym bag gotten back into circulation? What possible connection did a dead Latino girl and long-expired cartel henchman have with an H-Town conman? None of it made sense.

The crook had been watching television when the smoking hot detective entered his room, the muted set streaming a breaking news update during the entire forensic process. Zach's eye was suddenly drawn to the screen, the news station displaying a picture of a guy that seemed familiar. The name under the grainy photo read, "Abraham Hendricks."

"What the hell," the ranger mumbled, upturning couch cushions in his scramble for the remote.

One of Sam's coworkers was standing close by, Zach's flurry of activity diverting his attention from the laptop in his hands. "You haven't heard what's going on up north of the city? There's a standoff involving an active shooter happening right now. I heard over the radio that they've got a least 16 officers down. The nut job that tried to kill Clifton is holed-up and has the entire place booby-trapped."

"I know that guy from somewhere. Who is he?" Zach replied.

The officer started tapping on his keyboard, spinning the machine around to show Zach the screen.

"Says here he was born in Louisiana, moved to Texas a little over 10 years ago. No warrants, no arrests. Probably one of the Katrina transplants."

That was it! It all came flooding back to Zach. That was the bloody man he'd carried out of the house in New Orleans.

Turning to Sam, he pointed toward the television and asserted, "Hey, you are not going to believe this, but I know that guy... the holdout. Do you have any contacts working that scene right now?"

Turning to the television, Sam watched the broadcast for a few moments without comment. Finally staring down at the floor, she said, "Yes, as a matter of fact I do. Sal, the head FBI agent, and I have been dating on and off for a while."

Zach shook his head and thought, *I knew I should have gone with the FBI. They get all the perks.*

Memories of New Orleans circulated through Zach's head as Sam and he drove north toward the standoff. While the episode in Louisiana entered his mind now and then, he'd never taken the time to follow-up. The backlog of cases in the overworked El Paso office simply hadn't allowed it.

As the HPD teams finished up at the hotel, he made a call to his headquarters, requesting all available information be forwarded to his smart phone. There hadn't been much.

Sergeant Ford, the only name he could recall from that day, was still with the New Orleans PD, now a captain in their Rapid Response Unit – a kind of politically correct name for what was essentially a SWAT team.

Until the newscast, he hadn't even known the name Abe Hendricks.

When the emails from HQ began filling his inbox, Zach slowly filled in the gaps, creating a mental picture of the chain of events. Mr. Hendricks had survived his head injuries, but with some difficulty. He'd been hospitalized for over two months. Evidently, he'd hired an attorney because there was a sealed record of a lawsuit. Things got a little sketchy after that. There was another sealed arrest record for Abe, but no trial docket or list of charges. The lawsuit had been dismissed the same day as the charges had been dropped.

Since that time, the ranger knew that Abe had relocated to Texas, procured a driver's license, paid his property taxes, and kept his nose clean. Other than a divorce some months ago, there wasn't any other record of the man on any law enforcement databases.

"So fill me in, Ranger Bass," Sam began, "How do you know this man whose desire it is to make the Guinness Book for killing more cops than Al Capone?"

Zach told his temporary partner the story, filling in as many details as he could recall.

"I remember reading about that gun grab," Temple responded. "I was in college when that all went down, and one of my professors was going ape shit crazy over the whole thing."

"Yeah, I remember it not sitting right with me either, but if you had seen New Orleans after the storm... I'm not saying it was justified, but those cops down there were facing something no one had ever seen before. In some small way, I don't blame the mayor, or chief, or whoever came up with that plan. Their intentions were good, but short-sighted."

Sam seemed to be rolling his response around in her brain for a bit, staring out the passenger window as the city passed by. Finally, "Didn't they pass a new law a few years after that all went down? Seems like I remember reading about it."

"Yes, they did. There was an enormous legal debate over what powers government held when a state of emergency was declared. I guess no one had ever defined the rules as far as private firearms were concerned."

"The founding fathers didn't do such a good job of that either," Sam noted. "Just a few words here or there could have made the Second Amendment crystal clear and avoided a lot of disagreement."

Zach glanced over at his passenger and grunted. "Seems clear enough to me. The people have the right to bear arms. What more do you need?"

Sam sighed, giving the ranger one of her you-know-better-than-that looks. "I should have expected that attitude from you, Ranger Bass," she chuckled. "A hardline conservative, through and through. But your position oversimplifies the issue. The framers saw fit to insert the term, 'well-trained militia,' and that has opened the door to decades of debate."

"Not according to Alexander Hamilton," Zach fired back. "He said the government's army can never be formidable to the liberties of the people while there is a large body of citizens. Sure sounds like Alex intended for the people to be able to hold their own against either the feds or the states."

Detective Temple was impressed. "Why Zachariah Bass, I had no idea you were a constitutional expert. I could, however, counter that with a dozen other quotes that opposed Mr. Hamilton's point of view."

Zach shook his head, unappreciative of her challenging retort. "They all understood the need to walk that fine line between mob rule and tyranny. A military take-over was a real threat in their world. The only way to stop that was with a well-armed citizenry."

"Look, I'm as ardent a supporter of the Second as anyone else," Sam replied. "But I also know that we have to have limits. Weapons technology has advanced well beyond anything the founding fathers ever considered. We can't have unrestricted firepower in the hands of every citizen. The mess we're heading into is a prime example of that. The weapon this guy is wielding has already killed many good men. What if people could own battle tanks and fighter jets? There have to be some controls... some regulations, or we'll cascade into anarchy."

"I've got a funny feeling this entire mess leads back to some asshole's decision to confiscate arms in New Orleans. I can't put myself in Abraham Hendricks's head, but I bet I'm not far off base with that theory. When it comes to freedom and guns, I guess Patrick Henry summed it up best."

Sam interrupted, rolling her eyes. "Seriously? Are you some self-proclaimed expert on the Second Amendment? Why do I feel another verbose quote on the way?"

Zach laughed, but then his tone became serious, "Guard with jealous attention the public liberty. Suspect everyone who approaches that jewel. Unfortunately, nothing will preserve it but downright force. Whenever you give up that force, you are inevitably ruined."

Half-teasing, Samantha looked at Zach and said, "So you do think every citizen should be able to own a tank?"

"No," Zach replied. "But regulating everyone to a bolt-action, small caliber weapon isn't what the framers had in mind either. When tyranny arms itself with an M16, it's tough to resist with a hunting rifle."

"I'll tell you one thing, if I know Agent Perkins, the guy holding up in that house is going to wish he had a tank... maybe two."

The Harris County Sheriff's Department had long before enrolled in a federal program that provided surplus military equipment to local law enforcement agencies – free of charge.

The program, commonly referred to as 1033, had provided the local law enforcement agency with over $4 million dollars in weapons, body armor, trucks and other surplus military equipment.

The most expensive items were two "mine resistant ambush protected" armored vehicles (MRAPs). After insurgents in Iraq had taken to repurposing explosives into improvised explosive devices (IEDs), the Pentagon had rushed the development of a new class of military transport that could withstand these types of attacks. Several different versions of MRAPs had been purchased and deployed in the conflict.

Eventually, the Iraq war ended, and the military found themselves with an excess of the colossal machines. Rather than scrap the expensive behemoths, someone in Congress decided to offer them to police departments. The cops thought that was a good idea, too, given the steadily increasing firepower they faced on the streets.

The particular model in use by the local SWAT team was called a Caiman. With a 6-wheel drive, thick plating, and powerful diesel engine, the machine was built to withstand mines and ambushes conducted with military-grade firepower.

Abe heard the Caiman's rumble when it was still a half-mile away. From his second-story perch, he spotted it a short time later. It was an impressive machine.

He sat and watched its approach, marveling at the Machiavellian image – an armored machine of war traveling down a quiet neighborhood street. "I bet they wish they had those in New Orleans," he whispered. "They could have really gathered up some guns with a couple of those."

The Caiman slowed as it approached his driveway, almost as if it were a delivery truck checking house numbers. Abe was well aware of what it intended to deliver – a 10-member SWAT team concealed inside of its crew compartment.

For a moment, it looked as if the driver was going to spare the stacked stone wall that surrounded Abe's yard, but that assumption proved to be false. Gunning the engine, the 6-wheeled mammoth charged right through, the landscaping barrier providing no more resistance than a parking lot speed bump.

Abe reached for a nearby bag, his hand reappearing with a hockey-puck shaped disk. Repeating the process multiple times, he soon had nine of the small units spread on the windowsill by the time the Caiman was halfway to his front porch.

Originally, the small disks had been magnetic lights. He'd first purchased one of the handy little units to illuminate the bed of his pickup. Battery powered with an intense attraction to metal surfaces, they were designed to stick practically anywhere.

Now, the units in front of Abe no longer contained light bulbs, batteries, or switches. Most of their vacant, internal spaces had been packed with a homemade explosive, knowledge gained by Internet browsing. The medium velocity propellant was carefully inserted behind a concave-shaped disk of bronze.

It had taken some experimenting, but he'd found a solution in the plumbing section of the local home improvement store. The cup of bronze pipe elbows, after substantial trimming from his garage band saw, proved to provide the perfect dimensions for what was known in military circles as a "shaped charge."

A visit to a local hobby shop had provided the detonator – a model rocket kit containing not only the wireless control, but a second benefit as well. The rocket fuel could be purposed as an excellent igniter for his cookie-sheet explosives.

When Abe had first learned of his county's possession of the heavy military vehicle, it had put a serious damper on his plans. He'd been watching the nightly news report on a hostage standoff with an active shooter when the video zoomed in on the super-sized armored car rolling onto the scene.

It didn't take long to ascertain the make and model, nor did it require much research to determine the Caiman's weakness.

The V-shaped bottom was nearly impervious to mines… capable of dealing with explosions far more powerful than anything Abe could produce. The vehicle's sides were also designed to withstand more punishment that he could throw at it with small arms.

But the top, like most armored vehicles, was thin and vulnerable.

The sheriff's MRAP charged his porch, the leading wheels slowed by the three steps rising to his threshold.

Abe threw open the shutters, each hand wielding a magnetic "bomb-lette." With his arms a blur, he began tossing them like Frisbees, another and then another dropping from the window directly above the advancing armored car.

Some of the units bounced harmlessly to the ground, others stuck to the roof of thin steel plate. Reaching quickly for the hobby-store remote at his feet, Abe hit the switch just as several sniper bullets slammed into his golf-barrier.

The actual explosions weren't overly impressive, making far less noise than typical holiday fireworks. But the results were devastating.

Shortly before World War II, military ordnance experts had discovered that any explosive becomes far more effective against armor if it is "shaped" like a cone or possesses concave geometry. Abe had simply adapted designs that had been around for almost 100 years.

The bronze pipe melted as the explosive expanded, the kinetic energy forcing a jet of the liquid metal through the Caiman's skin at several thousand feet per second.

The driver, engine, fuel tank and several members of the SWAT team were taken out immediately. Ammunition and diesel fuel began to burn… the survivors in the back hitting the door release as black smoke began to fill their compartment.

They began pouring out of the back, more motivated to escape their burning transport than to assault the target. Flames were now licking at the insides of the critically wounded beast, a boiling dark fog rolling into the atmosphere.

Moving so as not to use the same window twice, Abe rushed downstairs, prepared to activate his mister or fire his AR15.

Neither was necessary.

Leapfrogging back toward the road, Abe spied the survivors of his attack retreating, two of their wounded being carried toward the rear of Mrs. Fullerton's home. He decided to let them go without harassment, now worried that the burning hulk resting right next to his porch was going to set his personal citadel on fire.

He had a thought, unsure if the police had managed to turn off the 200-foot deep well that provided water to his property. After checking the front and back yards for a secondary assault and spotting no activity, he scurried for the attached garage and switched on his sprinkler system.

Rushing back to the living room, he was relieved to see the pulsing jets of water arching in their pre-programmed circles. He hoped it would be enough to extinguish the flames.

Chapter 8 — New News

Given the political landscape and right-of-center mindset of most Texans, it was no surprise to spot a group of protesters milling about, facing a line of police officers who didn't seem amused.

Maneuvering the pickup through the gathering throng, Zach spied several handmade signs held in the air. "No Waco HERE!" read one of the larger examples. Another asked the reader to "Remember Ruby Ridge."

The ranger's favorite message read: "Feds: Take your heavy hand and go home!"

There were already two food trucks parked along the road, short lines of hungry protesters cued to purchase burgers and tacos. The congestion was further enhanced by a substantial number of television cameras, carefully positioned to capture the best angle should a confrontation break out.

It was a snarled circus of sound, color, and motion.

"Don't mess with Texas," he heard Temple mumble.

Zach and Sam approached just as Agent Perkins was pressing his earpiece in tight. "He did what?" the FBI man was saying, his voice clearly shocked at what he heard across the radio.

"Son of a bitch," Perkins continued, "This is worse than a Rambo movie. Who the fuck is this guy?"

His expression softened when he turned and identified Detective Temple, a slight smile flashing across his lips. "What are you doing here, Sam?" he asked, clearly under extreme stress.

"Hi, Sal. I want to introduce you to Ranger Zach Bass. I think he might be able to help you."

The frustration showed on the federal agent's face, his eyes boring into Zach as his mouth was forming a rejection. "We're getting our asses kicked right now, Sam. I don't mean to be rude, but I don't have time to…"

Zach stepped forward, inserting himself between Sam and the FBI agent. "I know the man inside of that house, Agent Perkins. I saved his life once. He might talk to me."

Perkins blinked, his gray matter taking a moment to assimilate Zach's words. "You what?"

"I saved his life once… a long time ago. In addition to that little tidbit, I can tell you why this guy has decided to tear law enforcement a new one."

"Okay… explain it to me."

And Zach did, relating the story of Abe Hendricks and post-Katrina New Orleans.

"Holy Shit," Perkins replied when the ranger had finished. "That does explain a lot. This guy's been stewing on this for 11 years. No wonder he's been one step ahead of us all the way."

"I can't tell you what pushed him over the edge," Zach continued. "Maybe it was the election… maybe his divorce… maybe a cop looked at him funny last week. But I saved his bacon in New Orleans, and he might remember me. He might talk to me."

Perkins looked around noting the fading light. "It's getting too dark to try anything now. Let's give Mr. Hendricks the night to wonder what we plan next. In the meantime, let's see if we can work out how to get your face in front of him without it being blown off. Otherwise, I'm going to have to call Washington and ask for military assistance. I can't risk any more men."

No sooner than Perkins had made his decision, than a voice sounded in his earpiece. "Sir, we are picking up electronic signatures inside the suspect's home. They correspond to a cell phone being used."

"A cell phone? You mean he's calling somebody? I thought we had his number rerouted through the Stingray?" Perkins asked, referring to the bureau's portable cell phone tower that could intercept any mobile phone.

"We do, sir. This phone must not be in his name or registered to the address. We'll have the number in less than a minute and cut it off."

"Don't," Zach said, stepping close to Perkins. "Let's see who he's calling. What can it hurt?"

Perkins didn't like the idea, standard procedure calling for any barricaded suspect to have all outside communications denied. But then again, nothing in the manual had worked so far. Speaking into the microphone, he said, "Don't cut off that number just yet. Can you tell me who he's talking to?"

"Yes, sir. He was connected with a local news station – Channel 3 to be exact. But the call has already ended."

It took Perkins all of five minutes to locate the Channel 3 van, sitting in a virtual parking lot of reporters from every local and national media outlet. Several heads turned in surprise when Perkins strode into their camp, the expression on the FBI agent's face making it clear his visit wasn't a social call.

After flashing his badge to a guy who looked to be in charge, the federal agent stated, "I understand your station just received a call from our suspect. I need to know what's going on... what he said."

"Really?" replied the surprised producer. "I thought that was a prank call. That was really him?"

"Yes, it was. What did he want?"

"He said he wanted Ross to come to his home and talk to him. He said he had documentation that would explain and justify why he was doing all this. We hung up on him... we thought it was a prank."

"Who's Ross?" Zach asked.

"Ross Garcia, our senior field reporter. Don't you watch the news, friend? Ross is probably one of the most recognizable faces in Houston."

Zach turned to Perkins and chimed in, "That explains it. He wants a face he knows... someone he's sure isn't an undercover cop."

Perkins began pacing, not sure how to handle this new event. Again, it was against procedure to allow any civilian to endanger himself. On the other hand, the reporter might be able to provide them with valuable information about the inside of the suspect's home.

"If I okay Ross talking to the suspect, would he be willing to do it?"

"I sure would," answered the new voice, a young man with perfect hair and bright, white teeth stepping around the van.

"You do realize this guy has killed over a dozen police officers so far? He's booby-trapped his home, yard and who knows what else. We're not talking about a stable individual here."

"I was embedded with the Airborne in the Iraq war. I reported from Afghanistan for 18 months. I know what the dangers are."

"Call him back," Perkins decided. "If your man is willing, I'll let him pass through. I want one thing though. I want him wearing a camera and a microphone."

"I don't think that will be a problem," the reporter answered. "I'll tell him I have to film the meeting for the station. He might not let me video everything, but who knows until we try."

"I get the tape," Perkins continued. "You have my word I'll return it as soon as the legal eagles allow it. You'll have an exclusive."

This time the producer spoke up, "No deal. You can have a copy, but we get to go with whatever our man brings out."

Perkins rubbed his chin, knowing it was a marginal call. In his years with the agency, he'd seen examples of press interaction that had ended up both positive and negative. Criminals would often confess to a reporter, but they also could muddy the waters. There was also the chance that this could morph into a hostage situation, and that would make things even more complicated. But it couldn't get much worse.

"Deal," the FBI man finally decided.

The producer dialed the station, a quick set of instructions resulting in the primary listed number returning Abe Hendricks's call. When he answered, the receptionist patched Ross in.

"This is Ross Garcia, sir. I'm sorry we got disconnected earlier. How can I help you?"

Despite only speaking to the suspect for a short time, Perkins recognized the voice on the other end.

"My name is Abe," stated the voice. "I have information that I want to be made public. I'm sure your station will find it interesting, to say the least. You have my word that if you come alone and don't try anything stupid, you won't be harmed."

"Okay, Abe," the reporter replied smoothly. "How should I approach your home?"

There was a slight chuckle on the other end. "Just walk up to the front door, son. You'll have to maneuver around this junk heap the cops just left sitting here, but there's nothing I can do about the mess right now."

"I'm going to bring a camera with me. I need to document our discussion for my producer."

There was a pause at the other end of the line, and for a moment, those gathered thought Ross had gone too far.

"I suppose that's okay," replied Abe. "But you can only film where I say. I know the cops are going to be studying that video, and you can't blame me for not wanting to help them end my life."

"When can I come over?"

"Right now is fine," the voice responded. "How soon can you be here?"

Zach stepped forward, whispering something in the reporter's ear. After a quick nod, Ross responded. "Abe, before we discuss that, there's someone here who claims to know you. He says he was in your father's home the day everything went wrong. He says he saved your life. He wants to speak to you."

This time there was a long pause, Perkins beginning to get angry over the interloper's unexpected and unplanned move.

"What's his name?" Abe asked, his voice hesitant and suspicious.

Ross held the cell phone out for Zach to respond. "Mr. Hendricks, I was the man in the western hat who pushed the shotgun aside. I know you may not remember, but I also carried you out of the house and found medical care."

Abe's response sounded shaky. "Yes, I remember. You were there... you were a witness to the whole thing. Who are you?"

"I am a Texas Ranger, Mr. Hendricks. My name is Zachariah Bass. I'm sorry I never followed up on your injuries or what happened that day in New Orleans. I was sent back to Texas the next morning, and quite frankly, I left it up to the local authorities to sort everything out."

"Tell you what, Mr. Texas Ranger, I'm actually glad you're here. You see, what I'm about to tell that reporter is going to be pretty shocking, and having a reputable eyewitness to back up my story can't do any harm."

"So how do you want this to play out, Mr. Hendricks? You have to know the FBI is going to get rough. You've already hurt them badly. How do we end this?"

"Send in the reporter... alone. I'll let you all decide how this is going to end after everyone has had a chance to hear my story."

Aaron was experiencing one of those rare moments where self-preservation was overriding the needs of his candidate. His reputation in political circles was that of a man who put "the job" ahead of any personal needs.

But not this evening.

Camped in front of the TV, intently watching the siege in Texas, he had played a nonstop game of political chess since learning the identity of the man in Houston. Moving the strategic pieces around the board of public opinion, he'd tried to anticipate every feint and counter.

The pro-gun lobby was zealous, powerful, and well-funded. Early on, Heidi's campaign had adopted a strategy to circumvent, avoid, and dance around the issue. Most of her inner-circle was composed of resolute believers in universal background checks, restricting military grade weapons, and limiting access to certain types of ammunition. However, the calculus-based marketing models had demonstrated that publicizing such a position would erode the delicate coalition of voters in her corner.

The issue was just another example of how fickle the American public had become. By a huge margin, most people supported some measure of extended background checks. By the same margin, Americans supported the interpretation of the Second Amendment that protected individual rights to gun ownership. For a politician, it was a maddening dichotomy.

Were it not for the standoff in Houston commanding the nation's attention, he'd be in full damage control mode right now. Heidi's words at the press conference had taken her out of the neutral zone, and already their opponent's camp was leveraging the opportunity.

Salvation, via spin, deflection, and a tug at the public's sympathy, was doable. He could easily explain her remarks away, the reaction of a distraught individual who had just suffered an attempt on her life *and* a plane crash. Who wouldn't be a little tainted? It was understandable and forgivable. They could release some vaguely worded outline of Heidi's position on gun control, and it would all fade quickly.

The potential exposure of Aaron's own involvement with the New Orleans gun grab skewed everything. While it hadn't received any media coverage just yet, the reverberations of that disclosure would be swift and harsh.

Aaron's mind conjured up images of his face plastered all over the media. "Meet the man behind the atrocities that occurred in New Orleans!" they would broadcast. "Here is the evil maniac who is responsible for Abraham Hendricks' killing dozens of people. And this demon is about to become the president's chief of staff and most trusted adviser! Off with Heidi Clifton's head! Hang 'em high!"

Am I overacting? he wondered. *Probably not.*

In the months that followed the New Orleans confiscations, any debate regarding guns in Washington had been fundamentally skewed. What had once been an unfounded fear of government tyranny now had a poster child, a factual, inarguable example. The great gun grab was thrown in the face of every legislator who even hinted at restricting Americans' right to firearms.

The Assault Weapons Ban had expired just before Katrina ravaged the Gulf Coast, the law's sunset clause making practically every type of semi-automatic weapon available to the public. Numerous attempts were made to reinstate the ban, but all failed. In every case, the New Orleans confiscation was used as a hammer to pound the reenactment of the law into dismal defeat.

If that wasn't bad enough, there were 22 state laws passed in the wake of what the pro-gun lobby had taken to calling, the "Katrina tyranny." In 2006, under extreme pressure, President Bush signed the Disaster Recovery Personal Protection Act, a new federal law that many in the gun control camp believed was a significant step backwards for their cause because it reinforced the most conservative interpretation of the Second Amendment.

By some people's perspectives, the local government's action post-Katrina was the single biggest setback for the gun-control cause in the history of the United States. Even the tragic, mass-killings that occurred at schools and theaters couldn't return the genie to the lamp.

"Insanity is repeating the same mistakes over and over again while expecting different results," he'd told Heidi early on in the campaign. "We have to remove gun control from our dialog. The party wants it that way. I want it that way, and the people obviously lean that way."

And it had worked – until now.

Watching the events unfold in Houston, Aaron felt the stirrings of anger begin to build. The networks were showing stretcher after stretcher being loaded into ambulances. The death toll was mounting; the dedicated men and women of law enforcement were being slaughtered in record numbers because a clearly deranged man had unfettered access to nearly limitless firepower.

"The NRA should be embarrassed," he whispered to the television. "The Senators and members of Congress that fought gun control should hang their heads in shame."

But it wouldn't play. Americans would be outraged for a few weeks, shedding tears as procession after procession of flag-draped coffins paraded across their television screens. Eulogies and funerals would tug at the hearts of millions, but it wouldn't be enough. After all, it wasn't the guns that killed those brave men and women; it was the lunatic who pulled the trigger. While emotions ran high today, that right-sided logic reasoning was sure to follow in its aftermath.

It was then that an odd thought occurred to Aaron. He found himself hoping the standoff in Houston would last, at least past Election Day. He felt a twinge of guilt over the realization that the carnage occurring in Texas would actually serve to help Heidi's cause while at the same time providing justification of his involvement in New Orleans.

The ringing of his cell phone pulled him away from his line of thinking. "Hey, Aaron," the voice of the campaign's lead pollster sounded. "I just got in a batch of new numbers. Heidi is up another point at the national level. Great news, huh?"

"Sure is. Let's just hope it stays that way."

"Neilsen and USA Today both have her holding at 53 to 47. Still inside the margin of error," continued the excited voice. "I don't think she hurt herself all that badly at the press conference."

Aaron managed a smile, not wanting to put a damper on the excited man's work. "I'll let Heidi know," he replied. "I'm sure the news will make her feel better."

He experienced a sense of relief after disconnecting the call, chiding himself over being paranoid and making a big mental ado for no good reason.

"Sometimes," he whispered to the television, "the smart move is to do nothing, but that's not a chance I can take...."

Ross drove his own personal car past the police barricade. One of the cameramen had provided him with a handheld digital camera, complete with microphone and light. Switching on the diminutive device, he positioned it on the dash, allowing the best vantage for recording the trip. It would make excellent background video.

His palms were wet on the steering wheel, a fact that didn't faze the experienced newsman one single bit. The source of his stress wasn't due to encountering the man who would surely go down as one of the most violent killers in American history. No, Ross was nervous because this was his chance at the big time... a doorway to New York and the national stage. He just couldn't fuck it up.

After passing through the perimeter of cops, it was just over a mile trek to the Hendricks residence. Driving through the upscale neighborhood of tree-lined streets and well-manicured yards, Ross worked hard to squelch his anxiety. He kept trying to occupy his mind with the rewards that would come his way if this interview went smoothly – kept telling himself that he'd been in worse places, taken bigger risks. When the address of the barricaded home appeared through the windshield, all attempts to control his fear quickly evaporated.

He couldn't help but draw the parallel to Iraq. There was a burned-out armored vehicle, black streaks of charred grass, and rubble from the crushed wall. He could clearly recognize the broken glass and splintered wood that dominated the front of the home. Trenches of disturbed earth offered evidence of explosions. It was a battlefield, no different from those that dominated the world's hot spots – right here in his hometown.

Parking on the street, he wiped his sweaty hands and exited the car. He had managed three steps before he realized he'd forgotten his camera. "Come on, you dumbshit... get your act together," he mumbled while retrieving the critical piece of gear.

His legs were weak and wobbly as he approached the porch. The smell of burnt rubber and thick cordite wasn't helping at all. Ten steps away from the stoop, he yelled at the house, "Mr. Hendricks? Mr. Hendricks? Ross Garcia here."

"I see you, Mr. Garcia," acknowledged the same voice he'd heard over the phone. "I've been watching you all along. Come on up to the porch and chill out – I'm not going to hurt you."

Ross did as he was told, stepping around the lifeless Caiman and continuing his hike up the steps. Once on the veranda, he noticed what sounded like a series of deadbolt locks disengaging, auditory evidence of a front door obviously secured to withstand a serious assault. He glanced down to spot the blinking light on the camera, evidence that it was already recording his journey.

The door swung open, the shadowy outline of a man at the edge of the threshold. "Step over here where I can see you, please."

The reporter watched as Abe lifted some device to his eye and scanned him up and down. After a few seconds, a bright light blinded the newshound, again the beam moving up and down his person.

"Please turn off your camera, Mr. Garcia. I'll let you turn it back on in a few minutes."

Ross did as instructed.

"Come on in," Abe motioned, never showing himself. "I apologize about the mess, but you know those police snipers... they're a messy bunch."

Ross stepped through the threshold, the destruction apparent even in the darkened interior of the home. "Follow me, please," directed the voice from the shadow.

Abe led the reporter through the shattered living room and into the well-appointed office. A computer screen's blue glow yielded the only light in the study. The host motioned for the journalist to take a seat, and then paced around the desk and perched in his ergonomically designed chair. The eerie light of the monitor provided Ross his first glimpse of the man who held center stage of news broadcasts from Maine to California.

Abe pointed at the laptop and apologized, "I hope you'll understand if I can't give you my undivided attention, sir. I'm monitoring a network of cameras and sensors – just in case my FBI friends down the street figure now is a good time to mount another attempt on my home. No offense, but I wouldn't put it past them to decide I was distracted by your visit."

Not knowing what to say, Ross merely nodded, waiting for his host to launch into what he anticipated would be some sort of political diatribe or paranoid manifesto.

"You can turn on your camera now, son. Let's get this over with," directed the calm voice from across the mahogany desk.

For the next half an hour, Ross listened to Abe's story. From the determination of two brothers to rescue their father through the killing of the two men, the digital camera recorded every sordid detail.

Abe was an excellent narrator, almost as if he'd practiced the telling for years. He never expressed opinion or made any political commentary – relating just the facts and raw emotion of a man who'd witnessed his family's demise.

And then the account and its tone changed. Anger began to creep into Abe's voice as he relayed the experience of being arrested in retaliation for his pursuit of justice. Tears formed in his eyes as he detailed the injustice, cover-up, and totalitarian actions by the government machine he was fighting.

Mr. Hendricks had trouble making it through the IRS's raid on his business without choking up.

With his experienced reporter's ear, Ross knew he was listening to solid gold. His primary audience was conservative and untrusting of big government. They would eat Abe's story like candy.

Abe editorialized toward the end, describing the ongoing guilt he'd felt over never clearing the Hendricks name... never restoring the honor of his family.

"My wife of 13 years left me six months ago," Abe admitted. "As she packed her things, she told me I had never been the same man after Katrina, and now that I think about it, she was a saint for having done her best to heal me for 11 years."

"So why now, Abe? Why did you try to assassinate Heidi Clifton after all these years?"

There wasn't an immediate answer, Mr. Hendricks seeming in deep thought. Finally, "I'm going to hold onto that little secret for a while, sir. It's my ace in the hole."

Ross started to ask more questions, but the storyteller stood, signaling the interview was over. Extending his hand, Abe closed, "Please keep in mind that from my perspective, I'm a revolutionary. This," he reiterated, spreading his hands to indicate the surrounding home, "is my Alamo... a modern day Concord or Lexington. Our government has slowly morphed into a tyrannical beast, in some regards more intrusive than the British Empire was at the beginning of our Revolutionary War. I am not some deranged individual who chose these extreme measures without reason or cause. I only expect that you will be fair in your reporting of this event. It was a pleasure meeting you. I doubt our paths will cross again."

The newsman understood the implication. "It doesn't have to end that way, sir. With this information and your testimony, a jury might have mercy. You'll go to prison for sure, but you still might be paroled in time to enjoy your later years."

Abe snorted, "No need for all that drama, young man. You see, quite honestly, our government has robbed me of every reason I had to live anyway. That is why I have chosen this path. And now, in bringing this totalitarianism to light, I've been responsible for the deaths of a lot of cops. I know what that means; and no, thank you. I'm sure the government boys will win, but I'm not going to make it easy for them. Now you'd better get going."

Zach was on the fringe of the gathering inside the Channel 3 van, the cramped space stuffed with federal officers and the station's staff. They were all huddled around a series of monitors, scrutinizing Ross Garcia's interview with the man who currently captivated the world's attention.

After the video finished, the reporter was hustled off to the mobile command center where the feds maintained a large camper-like trailer. Zach had toured a similar unit some time back, amazed at the technology they commanded at their disposal. Given the extended perimeter Mr. Hendricks's accuracy had necessitated, the ring of officers surrounding the area encompassed roughly 400 men and women, and that number was probably growing. Managing such a massive force required state-of-the-art communications, command, and control.

Zach and Sam lingered in the background, letting the feds do their thing. The Texas Ranger was sure the reporter was about to receive the grilling of his life, a thousand questions about every little facet of his adventure. Perkins would be looking for a weakness, any advantage he could exploit to end the standoff.

There was a deeper, more personal reason why the ranger withdrew. Waves of guilt rolled over the Texan, an undeniable crush of remorse. Zach felt a responsibility for all that had happened.

Why hadn't he followed up? Would it have taken more than a few minutes and a computer to investigate how the final chapter of the New Orleans episode had resolved?

Yes, he'd been busy. Yes, the entire incident had been out of his jurisdiction... far away from the demands of law enforcement in West Texas. But why hadn't he followed up?

Strolling around the law enforcement camp, the ranger's head remained in a daze for several minutes. Anger began to replace his remorse. The entire affair was a textbook example of the triangle of despair, and the ramifications were going to affect hundreds of innocent lives. He had to do something to break the cycle.

Flashing his ID, Zach approached the producer. "Could you give me Mr. Hendricks's cell phone number, please?"

After hesitating for a moment, the senior newsman shrugged and read the number off his phone.

"What did you do that for?" Sam asked, hurrying to catch up with him. "I've got a bad feeling you're up to something, and I'm pretty sure I don't like it."

Zach nodded but wouldn't confess. "I've got an idea rolling around in my head, but it's not ready for public discourse."

"I can tell you're accustomed to working on your own, Ranger," Sam teased. "I think it would be wise for you to trust my judgment on such complicated matters. That's what partners are for."

Yawning, Zach smiled back at her. "I need to catch some sleep. I'm guessing between all these cops and journalists, every hotel within a hundred miles is booked. Unless you're going to invite me over to your place to catch some shuteye, I'm going to have to sleep in my truck."

"No chance I'm inviting you to my place, Mr. Zachariah Bass. Forget about it."

"You should learn to trust my judgment on such complex matters," Zach replied with a grin. "After all, we're partners, ya know."

Chapter 9 – Damned Texans

Aaron awoke to the persistent buzzing of his cell phone. Finally shaking off the cobwebs of sleep, he managed to smash the correct button and growl a nasty, "Yes?" into the device.

"You better turn on the news, buddy," one of his campaign assistants said. "All hell has broken loose in Houston."

"What time is it?"

"It's 11 PM here. Were you asleep?"

Aaron replied with a curt, "Yes, I was," and disconnected the call. The television in his bedroom was displaying a cable news station a few moments later.

"Ross Garcia, a local reporter for the Channel 3 Action Team News in Houston, was allowed entry into Abraham Hendricks's fortified home this evening. He has filed this report," stated the excited anchor.

Aaron immediately recognized Mr. Hendricks's face, despite not having laid eyes on the man for almost 10 years. Sitting upright in his bed, he watched the 12-minute segment without comment or expression. When the local reporter had finished, the network cut back to the New York desk.

"We've invited a panel of political experts into the studio, despite the late hour," the anchor announced. "Let's start with how this is going to impact the Clifton campaign only two days before the election."

The station's self-appointed experts weren't far off; Aaron hated to admit. "Mrs. Clifton made her position on gun control entirely clear on television just last night. Let's face it; she seemed to mock those people who purchase firearms to protect themselves from government tyranny. Now, with the revelations rising out of Houston, we have an example of a citizen who suffered what can only be described as tyrannical treatment. I know this is going to sound sick, but put yourself in Mr. Hendricks's shoes. What other recourse did he have?"

"He should have used the courts!" shouted another panel member.

"He did," came the reply, "and was arrested on trumped up charges for the attempt."

"Then he should have fought those charges and used the system. Taking a gun and issuing violence is never the answer."

"Fighting city hall takes never-ending financial resources. I would imagine Mr. Hendricks was already broke, under arrest, and facing a very powerful, vindictive government machine. I ask again, what choice did he have?"

"He should have appealed the decision."

"No, he was under a court-ordered gag and would have been arrested for contempt if he had pursued it further. I hate to keep repeating this same thing, over and over again, but the question still stands; 'What choice did he have?'"

"He tried to go the way of democracy and work with the voting public, too. He received nothing but the heavy boot of government on his throat. Now, today, everyone knows that the IRS was being wielded as a political weapon. But when Mr. Hendricks was trying to get the press to champion his cause, such accusations were unheard of. No one believed him."

The show's host stopped the shouting match, introducing a spokesman for the NRA. "Oh... my... gosh," Aaron whispered. "Now we get to see some true craziness."

But the guy wasn't as over-the-top as Aaron had predicted.

"The National Rifle Association was involved in no less than five legal proceedings regarding the New Orleans confiscations. Less than two weeks after the police activities were brought to our attention, we filed a motion in federal court to block this illegal seizure of private property. We were granted that motion."

Reviewing his notes, the host prompted, "But that wasn't the end of it. Was it, sir?"

"No. We sued and won, but the city of New Orleans wouldn't return the confiscated weapons. We had to file another motion, this time receiving a court order. Again, the city still wouldn't return its citizens' property. A federal judge stepped in, issuing another court order, and still today, 11 years later, there are over 1,000 guns that have not been returned to the rightful owners."

"So you don't find Mr. Hendricks's story at all hard to believe?"

"No, not at all. There have been numerous cases involving law enforcement officers during that tragic period. Just last year, an officer was finally sentenced for having burned a car containing the body of a murdered citizen. To this day, that murder goes unsolved and unpunished. But the courts have sentenced a former police officer for torching the body. It seems igniting evidence was a common disposal method at that time."

It was over an hour later when Aaron finally switched off the TV. Padding barefoot to the kitchen of his Chevy Chase condo, he poured himself a glass of water.

After quenching his thirst, he set the glass down and peered at his watch. "The game will get serious tomorrow. I'd better get some sleep."

Aaron's head had just returned to the pillow when his cell began its merciless buzzing. "What the hell?" he grunted, reaching for the annoying device.

"Her numbers are dropping like a rock," sounded a worried voice through the tiny speaker. "I've never seen a reversal like this."

Aaron listened as his polling expert described the phenomena. "Heidi is big government, less state control, and anti-gun. That guy down in Houston just rammed a major wrench into her gears. This is bad timing, sir. Really bad."

After ending the call, Aaron paced the apartment. "Gawd, how I hate Texas," he spat. "Everything about that fucking state seems to want to screw me. Heidi's plane, this asshole gun-nut from my past, the media... and..." he didn't want to go there. Couldn't force his mind to list what he hated most about the Lone Star state – wouldn't say it aloud, despite being alone.

But he had to address it. There was no choice but to push aside his prejudices and control the anger.

Digging in a drawer, he again pulled out the no-contract cell phone and stared blankly at the device.

"This is twice in one week," he mumbled, feeling like the world was closing in all around him.

He didn't need to dial the number, the phone's memory containing the digits from the previous call. He pushed the send button, wincing when the same gruff voice answered.

"I thought you might be calling again," came the response. "It seems this man is the gift that just keeps on giving."

"I am running out of options on this end," Aaron said calmly. "You know I wouldn't ask if so much wasn't riding on..."

"Don't trouble yourself," came the gentle interruption. "I'm already on it. I'll take care of it once and for all."

Arriving at the Clifton campaign headquarters the following morning, Aaron wasn't surprised by the throng of reporters awaiting his arrival. A hundred voices erupted with questions as he made for the front door, all of the journalists seeking his attention at the same time.

Aaron ignored their desperate shouts and pleas until he was about to enter the office. Pivoting abruptly, he raised both of his arms to quiet the gathering. "I will take a few questions now. Please be polite."

Pointing to a nearby woman who he knew worked for a network friendly to his campaign, Aaron smiled and said, "Go ahead, please."

"Do Mr. Hendricks's revelations change your candidate's position on gun control?"

"No. Mrs. Clifton has been clear on her position since she was in the Senate. The fact that one individual has wrought all of this pain and suffering does nothing but reinforce her beliefs... and those of the majority of Americans."

Another reporter jumped in, firing off his own inquiry, "Early polling indicates a growing sympathy for Hendricks. Does the campaign have any comment on that?"

Aaron nodded, "We hope that Mr. Hendricks will surrender peacefully, without additional bloodshed. He has the right to face a jury of his peers. If his story is true, it is only human nature to feel remorse at his losses, but two wrongs don't make a right. The death of my coworkers, as well as the demise of all of those law enforcement officers in Houston, can't justify more killing and mayhem. Our society doesn't practice the Old Testament's 'an eye for an eye,' any longer."

"You worked in the Louisiana State Attorney's office post-Katrina, Aaron," yelled another man from the back of the crowd, "were you involved in Mr. Hendricks's case in any way?"

There it was. The question Aaron had been dreading – his worst fears come to realization. With every ounce of control he could muster, Aaron fought to keep his face neutral. It all was riding on his verbal response, as well as how well the press could read his body language. "I don't recall being involved in Mr. Hendricks's issue. What I do remember is the absolute bedlam we were all suffering at the time. Computer systems were down, communications practically non-existent. Mr. Hendricks may think there was some huge conspiracy... some authoritarian cover-up, but I doubt it. Most likely he misinterpreted an overwhelmed, local government that had been reduced to paper files, handwritten correspondence, and from a productivity perspective, had been transported back in time 100 years."

"Has the FBI contacted you or the campaign about the incident?"

"No."

He pointed to another reporter, shouting "Last question," above the din.

"Does Mrs. Clifton really want to modify the Second Amendment?"

Inside, Aaron smiled at the opening created by that last question. "I wouldn't use the word 'modify.' She feels it needs to be clarified. Despite what our opponents might say, she is a human being after all, and she is a product of her experiences. Mrs. Clifton is like most other Americans, wondering when the slaughter is going to end. When are we going to come to our senses? When will an unfounded fear of tyranny stop overriding the safety of our sons and daughters? Mr. Hendricks is a prime example of the downward spiral driven by the current interpretation of this amendment. His brother, by his own accord a conservative individual, apparently challenged police officers who were executing a lawful order. Based on some unfounded fear that they were trying to violate his liberty, he attempted to end their lives rather than conform. That horribly warped logic has now led to additional loss of life in Houston. Mr. Hendricks has admitted that the death of his family members has motivated him to kill over a dozen men – public servants whose only crime was to serve and protect other Americans. We must end this useless cycle of violence, and a vote for Heidi Clifton is a step toward that goal."

Aaron pivoted, entering the sanctuary of the office building without another word.

Sleep, as he had anticipated, never came. What he'd completely underestimated was the impact a lack of shuteye would have on his mind and body.

Abe rubbed his eyes, the burning sensation worsening by the minute. Glancing down at his favorite coffee cup, he made for the kitchen, throwing one last glance at the security camera monitor. They would be coming again, any time now.

But he'd been saying that all night.

The hotplate caused the generator to change its tune, the engine's baritone hum indicative of the burden the additional voltage required to heat the water. For the first time in Abe's adult life, he wasn't looking forward to the taste of coffee. How many cups had he consumed since this whole ordeal had started? Ten? Twelve?

A noise sounded outside, causing him to raise the ever-heavier AR15 and rush to the nearest monitor. *Nothing. Could have been a bird or a squirrel*, he realized, treading back to the coffee water.

It had been that way all night. Despite all of the automation, technology, and planning, his paranoia wouldn't allow him to trust his preparations. Even an hour's rest would make a difference, but every time he started to close his eyes, visions of federal officers pouring into his home denied the much-needed shuteye.

Death was no longer a concern; it really never had been. It was being taken alive that worried Abe the most.

"Are you sure?" he asked the coffee cup. "Are you still prepared to die?"

He carried the steaming mug to the front of the house, peeking through a narrow slot in the storm shutters. The Caiman was still halfway up his front steps, its partially scorched shell looming above all other features of what had been a beautiful front yard.

Kara's beloved flower gardens were a mess, courtesy of his homemade IEDs. The paint on the front porch's pillars had bubbled from the heat of his gas mister.

But what actually drew Abe's eye were the dark spots of crimson stains on his lawn. Blood, human blood – from men he never met and probably would have liked, if not befriended.

An uncontrollable bout of yawning interrupted his thoughts, quickly followed by itching, irritated eyes. "I wonder how much longer I can last," he whispered to the empty, bullet-riddled room.

The thought of suicide entered his mind again. He'd never understood why so many barricade situations were concluded by the holdout ending his own life. Studying everything from the authorities' response to the mindset of the siege, Abe had asked himself numerous times why those inside so often elected to end their lives. It was a human riddle that he'd never resolved.

Now he knew, understood fully, why so many had chosen that way out. It was a downward spiral of fear, depression, remorse, and worst of all – exhaustion. Lack of sleep tended to amplify emotions, and when those emotions were being driven by hundreds of armed men intent on killing you, the outcome was inevitable.

But he wasn't there yet. He was driven by a cause, better prepared and wiser than so many who had challenged their government's authority. *Not yet*, he resolved.

He moved back upstairs, the view of his lawn depressing in so many ways. After a quick scan of the upstairs monitor, he then made another tour, checking each window for some undetected approach. *They'll be coming soon*, he knew. *I wish they'd just finish this. I hope the pain is tolerable, and I go quickly.*

Fresh from a night's rest, shower, shave, and change of clothes, Zach was at the FBI's command trailer just as the sun broke in the east. The place was buzzing with activity, despite the early hour.

Toting a fresh cup of coffee and accompanied by Detective Temple, he waited patiently for Agent Perkins, listening as a large gathering of men were being briefed on the bureau's latest plan to dislodge one Mr. Abe Hendricks.

"Two Blackhawk helicopters are being flown in this morning, each equipped with FBI Hostage Rescue Teams. These birds will hover over the suspect's home while the teams insert via fast-roping onto the roof.

Perkins then pointed to a diagram of the Hendricks home, complete with detailed outlines of the doors and windows.

"After orienting post-insertion, the teams will assault three sides of the structure simultaneously. We believe Mr. Hendricks is capable of defending only one side of his property at any given time. Once inside the home, he will be quickly overwhelmed, and this episode will end. Any questions?"

Zach had a dozen questions, but it wasn't his place. Technically, he had no business even being in the area, let alone participating in a federal operation.

The meeting adjourned a short time later, providing Zach the opportunity to speak with Agent Perkins. "What time are the choppers supposed to arrive?" the ranger inquired.

"Two hours, give or take," Perkins replied. "This nightmare can't end soon enough."

"Until then, would you have any problem with my trying to talk Mr. Hendricks out?"

"Hell, yes, I have a problem with that. All I need right now is to end up with a hostage, or another dead body. Besides, what makes you think he'll listen to you?"

Zach rubbed his chin and then responded, "Because I saved his life. I think I could win his trust, and like you said, another dead body isn't going to do anyone any good."

Perkins clearly didn't like it, but something in Zach's manner led him to reconsider. "I suppose it would quiet down a few of the conspiracy nuts if we took him alive. Sure, Ranger Bass – be my guest."

Zach dialed Abe's cell phone, surprised when the holdout answered. "Who's this?"

"This is Ranger Bass," Zach replied. "The guy who saved your bacon in New Orleans. I want history to repeat... I want to save your ass again, Abe."

A deep chuckle sounded over the phone's tiny speaker, the belly-deep laughing followed by silence. "It's a little too late for that, isn't it? I don't think you can salvage my life now, Ranger. Things are a little different this time."

Sighing, Zach shook his head. "Let's be honest. Becoming a martyr this morning will not further your cause. I'm not going to lie to you – you're going to spend the rest of your life in a cell. But aren't you at all curious to see if your sacrifice makes a difference? They have televisions and newspapers in prison, Mr. Hendricks."

"I'll concede that point to you, sir. It would be interesting to see how this all plays out, but I would prefer to be dead than lose my freedom."

It was Zach's turn to laugh, "That sounds noble and brave, but from my way of thinking, it's a cop out. If you really believe in this movement... a cause you've deemed worthy of human life... then you should want to stick around and help it along. After all, you don't want your sacrifice just to be a flash in the pan, do you? You can write letters in jail, author books, and conduct interviews. If your objective is to initiate government change, then why not stay alive and keep up the fight?"

Zach knew his reasoning was working from the extended gap of silence that followed. The ranger's face broke out in a smile when Abe finally came back and asked, "And would you guarantee I would make it to jail, Ranger? I've hurt a lot of those lawmen... made them look bad. I'm pretty sure most of them would prefer to shoot me on sight."

Looking at a surprised Agent Perkins, Zach responded, "I'll come in by myself and bring you out, Abe. I'll be right there beside you the entire time. I don't know if you remember or not, but I'm a big son of a bitch and mean as hell. I don't think any of these federal boys will pick a fight with me."

There was laughter from the other end, quickly followed by the biggest surprise of Agent Perkins' extensive career. "Okay, Ranger Bass. Come on in and get me. I'll surrender to you... and you alone."

"See you in a few minutes, Abe."

Temple and Perkins were speechless, neither of them ready to believe it had been that easy. Sam finally spoke first, "Are you sure it's not a setup?"

"Could be," replied Zach. "But isn't it worth a try? How many more brave men might die in that airborne assault? For sure, Mr. Hendricks would perish, but I doubt your teams will get inside unharmed. I think we have to try reasoning with him."

A short time later, Zach was driving through the police barricade and on the road to Abe's stronghold.

Stopping in the street, the ranger left his truck running and preceded to stroll across the yard toward the house. He was almost to the porch when the front door opened, a tired, bleary-eyed Hendricks stepping outside. Zach couldn't see a weapon.

"You're making the right decision," Zach reassured the clearly nervous man.

"I suppose you're going to search me and then handcuff my hands behind my back."

Zach shook his head, "I need to see if you're hiding a weapon, but no, I didn't even bring any cuffs with me. Now once I turn you over to the feds, they will definitely want you restrained. I'll make sure they're professional about it."

"Thanks for that," Abe replied. "It will be nice to leave the old neighborhood for the last time with a little dignity."

Zach approached Mr. Hendricks and quickly patted him down. "Ready?" the ranger asked as soon as he was certain the man was unarmed.

"Now is as good a time as any," Abe responded and began strolling toward the idling pickup, Zach walking alongside.

A hissing noise split the early morning air, followed instantly by a loud thump. Abe's body jerked from the impact of a sniper's bullet, a small red circle in the center of his chest. Mr. Hendricks was dead before he hit the ground.

A swarming convoy of lights rushed towards Abe's house, law enforcement vehicles of every make, model, and description racing to the scene.

Agent Perkins was first, opening the passenger door of his government sedan before the driver had come to a complete stop.

The special agent, hustling toward Zach, found the ranger on one knee staring down at Abe's body lying in the grass. Hell's fury filled the Texan's eyes as he peered up at the approaching federal officer.

"What the hell happened here?" Perkins inquired. Before he could finish his interrogation, Zach's tall frame uncoiled, a snake-strike fist slamming into the FBI man's face.

"You lying son of a bitch!" Zach screamed, raining blow after blow onto the hapless agent's head. "I gave my word - you fucking piece of shit!"

It took three burly officers to pull the ranger off, the outcome of that encounter in question for a few moments. Zach's rage flourished, his desire to pummel Perkins so intense that the men pinning his arms were straining to maintain control. It was Sam who finally managed to settle the Texan down, stepping between the men and screaming, "Enough, or I'll shoot both of your stupid asses!"

Throwing off his own restrainers, a bleeding, bruised Perkins pointed a finger at Zach. "What the fuck is your problem, Ranger?" he yelled.

Again, the Texan tried to shake off the men restraining him, his face flush with the heat of anger and exertion, veins protruding on his temples and forehead. "You had that man killed, you piece of shit! I gave my word... the word of a Texas peace officer... and you murdered him while he was in my custody!"

"Bullshit!" Perkins screamed back, his own rage overcoming the shock. "Arrest that man for assaulting a federal officer!" he ordered, looking around at the rapidly growing throng of law enforcement personnel gathering on the front yard.

Two FBI agents moved toward Zach, one of them producing a pair of handcuffs. They were a few steps away when another voice sounded out, "Belay that order! You have no authority to arrest a Texas Ranger."

All heads turned to see Major Alcorn walking onto the grass, five large men in western hats, all carrying M4 rifles, accompanying the new arrival.

"Bullshit!" repeated Perkins, obviously losing control of his temper. "I'm a federal officer, and I have plenty of authority. Arrest these men as well," he shouted, pointing at the group of rangers.

"I wouldn't try that, son," Alcorn responded softly, his eyes boring into Perkins with an icy stare.

Sensing a confrontation, the surrounding group of cops, deputies, ATF, FBI, and visiting lawmen began to separate, some moving to stand with Perkins, others siding with Alcorn. A cloud of tension filled the air.

"Stop this!" Sam's voice cut through the air. "Have you all gone insane?"

Perkins blinked. Shaking his head in disgust, he looked over the crowd and said, "Forget about our hotheaded ranger, we've got a crime scene to process. I want the bomb squad to clear that residence, the forensic teams to cover every inch of this property after they're done."

Everyone exhaled, relieved that the unprecedented standoff hadn't escalated. Perkins, throwing one last harsh look in Zach's direction, pivoted and stormed off, a red handkerchief mopping the blood from his nose and lip.

No one noticed Ross Garcia, or his tiny digital camera. No one paid any attention as the sly reporter pocketed his recording device and slinked off, whispering about having hit the lottery two days in a row.

By Aaron's way of thinking, news of Abe Hendricks's death meant little as far as the campaign was concerned. He was wrong.

The public's reaction surprised Heidi's chief of staff, as well as practically everyone else on the national stage. Cries of conspiracy rang through the air, quickly followed by accusations of "Big government! Loss of Liberty!" and even a few radical elements claiming, "Abe Hendricks was justified!"

Those on the left rallied to the Clifton campaign's cause, shouting, "We need tighter gun control! Stop the killing! When is enough... enough?"

What shocked Aaron the most was the middle. The independent voters' reaction wasn't aligning with his candidate's position. The airwaves were packed with video of the confrontation over the dead man's body, courtesy of Ross Garcia. Bloggers lit up the information superhighway with boldly worded pieces, while several newspapers ran special additions.

The tide of public opinion begun to turn, quickly snowballing against Heidi Clifton.

The Clifton for President campaign possessed an unprecedented sophistication with regard to processing poll numbers and the public's overall mindset. Thousands of volunteers, researchers, contracted think tanks, and political experts monitored events in real time, utilizing state-of-the-art computer systems and heuristic software.

As the sun moved east to west across the land, Aaron sat and watched Heidi lose ground as more and more Americans became aware of the morning's events in Houston.

In the campaign's headquarters, the staff could see the transition as well, faces that had been sure of victory just a few hours ago, now beginning to wrinkle with worry.

But Aaron seemed to be taking it all in stride. Some of his direct reports wrote it off to his positive management style; others thought their boss was sticking his head in the sand, ignoring the tsunami that was preparing to hit their beloved Heidi.

By lunch on the east coast, Florida was in danger of turning into a red state. By early afternoon, two more battleground states were in the Republican column.

Right-wing talk radio hosts, Fox News, and conservative bloggers were having a field day at the political left's expense. "Wake up, America! Abe Hendricks was justified!" they shouted to anyone who would listen. "It was Heidi Clifton and her gang of liberal, gun-grabbing, constitution-busting, ideologues that caused the entire mess. What true patriot would have acted differently?"

Even the dead law enforcement officers in Houston became pawns in the political mudslinging dominating the electorate's attention. Both sides blamed the other for the carnage and loss of life, the two parties producing talking points to support their cause.

By mid-afternoon, several other "victims" of the New Orleans gun grab were coming forward, spouting their exaggerated tales of "government thugs," using excess force while confiscating their firearms... at least that's how it appeared to the folks on the left.

The eastern corridor between Washington and Boston rallied to the federal cause, the vast majority of the public calling for the Lone Star State to disband its "uppity" Texas Rangers.

There was an outcry from the geographical center of the country as well, many politically weighty voices calling for the rangers to be rewarded for their actions. California, four hours behind in the news cycle, sided with the opposite coast.

So passionate was the public's reaction, small skirmishes between the two opposing sides began to occur. A pro-gun rally in Kansas City turned into a riot when the attendees were confronted by marchers demanding universal background checks.

More and more reports flooded newsrooms across the country, Americans turning on each other over the issue, sometimes violently.

Senators and congressmen from both sides joined the fray, many issuing a thinly veiled lambasting of the opposition while pretending to plead for calm.

Atlanta experienced extreme violence, as did Austin, Texas - massive demonstrations turning into full-blown anarchy, complete with looting, burning and pillaging.

Aaron's cell phone rang, a quick glance indicating that Heidi had placed the call. Wondering what had taken her so long, he listened to her concerned voice. "You better get over here... right away," she said. "My husband is about to have a coronary, and I think we need to have a quick skull session."

With a smug grin, Aaron informed his assistant that he was heading to the hospital. "I may be there a while," he informed. "Don't let the senior staffers go home. I've got a feeling we're going to have a very, very busy night."

Heidi was in Aaron's face immediately, barking a harsh, "What the hell has happened to the American people?" before the new arrival could even say hello.

Ignoring the remark, Aaron stepped to Heidi's bedside and said, "How are you feeling?"

"She's feeling like shit," Mr. Clifton responded before his wife could form any words. "She always feels like shit when her ass is getting kicked all over the media, and the election is slipping away."

Pivoting with vigor, there was fire in Heidi's gaze as she glared into Aaron's eyes. "I can't believe people are reacting this way. How can anyone be a leader of this country when it is full of idiots? I knew this election was going to be rough, but the shit that is being spewed over this whole gun control thing is out of control."

"Whoa... hold on," Aaron said, holding up his hands to slow down the irate woman. "The election isn't over yet. You know how quickly these things can change."

His statement didn't seem to resonate with the former Commander in Chief. Grunting, Mr. Clifton shot back, "What election? There's not going to be any election tomorrow, son. There's going to be a landslide, with my wife's ass getting kicked, and the country subjected to another eight years of Republican rule. You both had better be finding a way to reverse this fiasco, and you better be doing it quick. Maybe you should consider resigning, Aaron."

Aaron's voice was calm in reply. "I serve at the pleasure of Mrs. Clifton," he maintained, shaking his head to emphasize his message. "If you want my resignation, I'll tender it immediately. But let's be clear about one thing, we can't sell our ideology out in the false pretense of compromise. I can't work for anyone who crumbles every time the Republican Party farts."

Heidi had heard enough. "Jeff, stop it! Aaron's right, the last thing any of us needs right now is a family quarrel. Are we so shallow that we are going to turn on each other when the road gets a little bumpy? We need to fix this, and fix it right now."

Her husband waved his hand through the air, a gesture clearly indicating it was a hopeless cause. "Save your breath, Heidi. This thing has snowballed out of control, and there's no way to turn it around in one day. Yet again, you've somehow managed to give away the Oval Office."

She glared at him from her elevated bed, the anger about to boil over. Aaron stopped the oncoming tirade with five little words. "I can fix this. It's easy."

Both Heidi and her husband blinked at the words, the skeptical expression on both of their faces making it clear they didn't believe him.

Reaching into his briefcase, Aaron pulled out a thin stack of papers, handing a few sheets to both Heidi and her husband. "This is what we're going to do," he announced with a voice exuding confidence.

Heidi skimmed the documents first, her eyes wide with surprise. She didn't say anything, looking up and watching her husband mouth the words as he read.

When the ex-president had finished, his face displayed a neutral, blank look. "I've got to hand it to you, Aaron. It's different... it's bold."

But Mrs. Clifton still wasn't convinced, her frown a prophecy of the words that followed. "You want me to announce my support for the secession of Texas? You want me to break our union? Are you insane?"

Aaron nodded, "Before you call for the straight jacket, just hear me out. We already know that the petitions have already started circulating, just in case you win – just a bunch of sore losers calling for Texas to secede. The exact same thing happened after the last presidential election." The campaign manager was grandstanding, yet timed his presentation well enough to resonate with the duo of political heavyweights. "You know what I am talking about. Eight years ago, it went so far that the governor publically announced that he would support such an initiative."

He paused after every statement, watching his audience carefully to ensure they were still with him before revealing the nuances of his idea. "Now, I'm not saying we should actually grant Texas its independence; I doubt very seriously that it would ever come to that. But if you declare your willingness to consider the idea, and communicate such a concept in the right way, you'll pull in a considerable number of votes from the center."

When Heidi shifted her weight, Aaron realized that she had reached a saturation point of discomfort with his plan. The savvy staffer anticipated her upcoming objection and answered it in advance.

"Stay with me here; I know this idea is a little radical. But historically this is a low risk plan; these things never pan out in favor of secession. Remember what happened when Britain gave support for Scotland to explore the idea of establishing it's sovereignty? The Scots ran the numbers, looked at all the impediments to independence, huffed and puffed and threatened to pull away from Britain, and in the end voted against secession. I believe this announcement would win the election in the short run and put this Texas independence idea to bed once and for all."

"And how would I go about flirting with the break-up of the United States of America?"

Aaron produced another report, the multi-page document containing an analysis of dozens of polls, surveys, voter responses. Pausing his sales pitch for a moment, Aaron gave the Cliftons time to scan a few pages. When he began again, his voice was almost a whisper. "The word 'United' in our country's official name has been a misnomer for over two decades. Our federal government has been ineffective for even longer. Our system is broken. In my opinion, as well as the scholars who compiled that report, our country requires drastic measures in order to correct our course. Yet, no one seriously believes we can pull it off in the current political environment. There has to be a bridge between the right and left.... We have to stop fighting each other. I believe the strategy I've outlined could be the catalyst to make that happen."

Heidi had to admit, the report Aaron had provided was shocking. Looking down at a page, she read, "Over 56% of liberal voters believe conservatives are more dangerous to our country than international terrorist organizations. Wow."

"So let's turn the tables. This time we scare them," Aaron continued. "We let this idea of secession run its course. In the meantime, you look like a hero, a president who is willing to work with the right. You're progressive, open to new ideas, serving in the best interest of all the people, not just the folks who voted for you. My hope is that the threat of splitting our country will draw the extreme elements in both parties a little close to the center.

Mr. Clifton looked up from his reading and said, "Okay, say Heidi goes along with this – what is the end game?"

"If she wins the election, we can pursue her promise until both sides realize how unrealistic the concept would be to implement. The extreme factions on the left, those who say, 'Let Texas go and good riddance,' will see the light – the whole is greater than the sum of the parts. On the other hand, those calling for an independent, conservative paradise will grow to understand they can't survive as a separate republic. With any luck, both sides will come to the conclusion that working together is by far the better resolution."

"And if they don't?" Heidi asked.

"Look at what happened in Canada back in 1995 when Quebec wanted to split off," Aaron continued. "And of course, Scotland went through the same exercise just a few years ago. In both of those cases, going to the brink resulted in concessions from both sides. There's no way Texas would ultimately vote to secede."

"But," responded Heidi, "central Europe did split into several smaller countries. Slovakia from Czechoslovakia, for example, occurred while I was at the Department of State. It can happen."

"In the unlikely event that happens, then let Texas go. Without Texas, the Democrats will enjoy control of both the House and Senate. You can pursue your agenda and help our nation thrive while our new neighbor to the south struggles. If they secede, I predict that by the beginning of your second term they'll want to rejoin the union with a mouth full of humble pie. Hopefully, everyone will have learned a valuable lesson, and we can close the divide that separates our people."

"It will never get to that point," the former president stated. "The right will take the argument to the edge... they may even stare into that abyss... but it will never happen."

Heidi looked at her husband, "So you're in agreement with this move? You think I should go on national television and state my support for this insane idea?"

Mr. Clifton nodded, a sly smile on his lips. "What do we have to lose? No offense, my dear, but you're too old to run again in four years. Admit it – this campaign has damned near killed you. Besides, as it stands right now, you are *not* going to win. I think it's radical, in-your-face politics, and maybe that's just what the country needs right now. I've not heard any better ideas."

Heidi evaluated her husband's words, saddened by the realization that as things stood, all of the money, effort, time, and energy she'd invested was about to be for naught. Her mind flashed images of the volunteers, those idealistic, young faces who had pledged their hearts and souls to see her in the Oval Office.

But what bothered her the most was the frightening image of a Republican president who controlled the House and Senate. She believed the people would suffer terribly under such rule, and that troubled her greatly.

"Let's do it," she calmly announced. "Somebody write me a speech."

Aaron reached inside his briefcase, producing a laptop. "I took the liberty of creating a draft, ma'am. It's on this machine. I'll be happy to work with you on any changes you see fit."

It had been easy to draw the national media. With the virtual feast of fast-moving news events of the last few days, the insatiable appetite of the 24x7-news cycle was still ready, willing, and able to gorge even further.

When Aaron had used the phrase, "The most important event in American history since Roosevelt's request for a declaration of war against the Japanese after Pearl Harbor," many in the press had rolled their eyes. Heidi Clifton wouldn't be the first campaigner to oversell an announcement, especially given that her lead had evaporated in less than 48 hours.

The soiree was scheduled at the National Press Club, programmed for prime time television and the source of continuous speculation and rumor.

The fact that Heidi was holding such an event on the eve of a national presidential election sparked even more intrigue. Normally, presidential candidates spent the last few days visiting contested hotspots and trying to woo those last few undecided voters.

With a rousing introduction by the chairperson of the Democratic Party, Heidi took the stage in a conservative blue pantsuit, white silk blouse and the all-important American flag pinned to her lapel. Her arm-sling was adorned with numerous small elephants, a detail that sparked laughter from the applauding crowd as she waved and smiled.

Ascending to the podium, her demeanor could only be described as optimistic, her eyes genuine.

"My fellow Americans," she began, "Over the last few days, we have seen an unprecedented series of events unfold. I, like many of you, have cried, prayed, cursed, and pondered the seemingly endless stream of headlines that has subjugated our lives as of late."

Making sure she stared directly into the cameras, Heidi continued. "But most of all, my mind has been focused on the reasons why these events have occurred. I've spent many hours talking to experts, interacting with the people, and most importantly, searching my soul for the root source of these troubles."

"But the 'why' isn't enough anymore. I've been seeking a solution... a fix... a course to steer our great nation on a path of justice, prosperity, and liberty for all."

Heidi took a deep breath, a pause to emphasize the importance of her next sentence. "And I'm pleased to announce to the nation tonight, that my staff and I have crafted what we believe is a revolutionary track that will resolve our political gridlock. I stand before you this evening, full of resolve and confidence, to communicate that I believe the crippling political divisions hamstringing your elected officials can be bridged."

Scanning the audience, Heidi noted a mixture of boredom and frustration through the ranks of the press corps. *I'll fix that*, she thought.

"I don't hate conservatives," she began. "I don't despise, belittle, or ignore their point of view. They are as important to America and any political persuasion or philosophy. And yet, our people have become so divided, so encamped in silos of heartfelt beliefs that our government no longer functions."

A lackluster round of applause rose from the crowd, Heidi deftly waiting for the support to fade.

"Each side of the aisle has become expert at sabotaging the other. Our two-party system has become a two-*warring*-party system."

Again, a bit more enthusiastic response arose from the hundreds of seated attendees.

"I have a message for the progressive citizens listening tonight – your conservative friends and neighbors aren't going to go away. You're not going to change their minds. Those of us on the left have long pushed for tolerance, an understanding that not everyone looks like we do, speaks the same dialect, or worships the same God. Yet, for all of our humanity, we will bare our teeth and attack the right without mercy – just because they think differently than we do. This, my fellow progressives, is hypercritical and destructive.

"And I have the same message for those who think more conservatively. Liberals aren't going away either. We have our beliefs and ideals. You aren't going to beat us down or convince us by argument or debate. We don't need your salvation."

A chorus of clapping filled the hall, a few members of the press beginning to show more interest.

"So how do we fix this?" Heidi asked the audience. "How do we address the social divide that grips our country, a chasm so deep and wide that it renders our great democracy ineffective?"

Pausing as if she expected an answer, Mrs. Clifton scanned the room with a twinkle in her eye. "My proposal is simple, historically successful, and should satisfy the most ardent on both sides of the political spectrum."

"Throughout the development of mankind, when there was a political, religious or ethnic division of the population, the people separated, the predominant groupings establishing their own homeland, kingdom, or country. Even the United Nations, as late as 1948, saw fit to establish a sanctuary for those of the Jewish faith – Israel."

Now she had them, several of the reporters perking with attention, a sea of pens scribbling notes.

"I have come to the conclusion that we, the United States of America, need to consider a similar solution. If I am elected president tomorrow, I pledge to all Americans that I will initiate an effort to grant the great state of Texas its independence as a sovereign nation."

Gasps, murmurs, and a few outright exclamations of surprise swept the room. Heidi didn't give the disturbance any chance at gaining momentum, increasing the beat of her speech and raising her voice to make sure she held the floor.

"I envision this new nation as a friend and ally. I see the rebirth of the Republic of Texas as a sanctuary for those who wish to be governed by like-minded individuals. I am convinced that the concept is worthy of analysis, the potential deserving of serious consideration."

Then, the one rough spot of the entire presentation occurred. Heidi paused as if she anticipated applause, but none came. It was a brief, but noticeable moment.

"Many historians have concluded that one of the primary contributors to the fall of the Roman Empire was the sheer size of her economic and geographical mass. I submit to my fellow citizens that we, as a people, are experiencing the same symptoms. It is a fair observation that the federal government has grown too large. It isn't unreasonable to question so much power being concentrated in Washington, DC. Our founding fathers debated this very subject for years, one of the most hotly contested issues being how much governmental control resided at the federal level versus each individual state. Our population, geographic territory, world influence, and economic engine are scales of magnitude greater than in those times. Have we become too large, too diverse, too secular to be governed successively by a single system? I feel this is an appropriate question for our elected officials to explore."

She then smiled broadly at the cameras, a slight grin turning at the corners of her lips. "Some pundits will say I'm crazy for going before the nation and floating such a radical concept. They'll claim I bumped my head in the plane crash and spread rumors questioning my sanity. But out-of-the-box thinking is what is going to save our great nation. New, revolutionary ideas are what helped us achieve a pinnacle, and I believe that same type of clean-slate creativity will be required to keep us there. If I am elected to the Oval Office, I won't be afraid to entertain any reasonable idea, regardless of its source or the ideology of the creator, and the American people can count on that."

Mrs. Clifton tidied up her papers, a sign she was about to conclude her astounding presentation. "My fellow Americans, I want to make a commitment, right here and now on this national stage. If I am fortunate enough to be elected your Commander in Chief, I will bring together the best minds available to study this option. I do this because I love my country and countrymen. I make this pledge to reassure all Americans that I want to fix our problems and improve your lives. Genuinely, from my heart, I want to see all of the people have the opportunity to pursue liberty and happiness. May God bless America."

The crowd erupted in applause, many standing to show their appreciation and respect. Heidi waved and smiled, walking from one side of the stage to the other, mouthing the words, "Thank you," over and over again.

Just when it appeared she was about to exit, another bolt of excitement shot through the throng as her husband appeared from behind the curtain, apparently anxious to congratulate his wife with a hug.

Just over 24 hours later, CNN was the first to call Heidi Clifton's victory, the other networks quick to follow. For the first time in recorded history, a woman was now the most powerful person on earth.

Chapter 10 – Madam President

President Clifton wasted no time.

Within a week of her swearing-in ceremony, she began avalanching Congress with a series of initiatives, bills, and budgets. Less than 30 days passed before she had signed her 10th executive order.

One Republican senator called the White House's barrage a "Salvo of Liberalism," and he was one of the more polite politicians on the hill.

All the while trumpeting a theme that touted, "Get something done for America," Heidi's staff opened with an appetizer of raising the minimum wage. The second course was immigration reform, quickly followed with an entree of reenacting the Assault Weapons Ban, complete with sides of universal background checks and limits to magazine capacities.

For dessert, she offered up a revamping of the Affordable Care Act, teasing those on the right with offers of accepting compromise and including Republican ideas into the revision. The White House tried to make political hay, claiming they were reaching out to the other side of the aisle and trying to avoid the inaction of the previous administration.

The effort, for the most part, was ignored.

With a Republican-controlled Senate, not a single one of her introductions reached the floor. The world's most exclusive club instead concentrated on a rash of hearings surrounding Abe Hendricks's death and the activities of the IRS. While it was all for show, the nearly continuous clamor did manage to keep the issue of big government in the forefront.

The media took great pleasure in the gridlock, the airwaves and print brim-full of mudslinging, finger pointing, and name-calling.

While the rest of America seemed to lose interest, it was the Texas representatives in the House that began to pressure President Clifton, using every opportunity to remind the chief executive of her campaign promise regarding the secession of the Lone Star State.

The NRA, fearing the Clifton anti-gun legislation, joined a small but growing chorus, applying its significant influence to remind Heidi of her commitment.

Several grassroots organizations in Texas, bolstered by Heidi's pre-election speech, were being taken more seriously. After all, if the president of the United States had entertained the possibility of an independent Texas, why shouldn't the residents do the same?

"This Texas thing isn't dying down, Aaron. I want your input on how to handle my scheduled call with Governor Simmons this morning," the president began, spreading a napkin across her lap and eyeing breakfast. "I was hoping our initiatives would capture the headlines, but they're not. I don't feel like we can procrastinate any further."

Aaron finished buttering his muffin before answering. "It's not a concern, ma'am. The latest poll numbers show that only 34% of registered Texas voters would support such a move. Let them schedule a referendum and get it over with."

"And if the polls are wrong? What happens then?"

Flashing a foxlike smirk, the White House chief of staff responded, "Remember Scotland's recent vote back in 2014? London got a little smug on that one… almost let it get away… but it didn't happen. We can do the exact same thing their senior officials did… scare the hell out of everyone, and then offer a few worthless concessions. We'll have a few of your supportive bank presidents drop predictions of runaway inflation, massive unemployment, and hyperinflation. They'll whisper gloom and doom into the *Wall Street Journal's* ears so it won't look like it's coming from us."

"And?"

"Then you swoop in, telling Texans that you don't want them to go. You flash patriotic, pleading that the country is better off staying together. We'll write up some stump speeches where you recognize the great contributions that state has made to the union. Then, you can promise them some high-sounding changes the federal government will implement so they can decide against the secession and still save face. Once the issue is shot down with a vote, hopefully, we can get a few concessions from the right and move on with our agenda."

Heidi nodded, consuming the remainder of her meal in silence.

After they had finished, Heidi pushed a button on her telephone and was answered immediately. "Yes, Madam President?"

"Get me the governor of Texas, please."

"Yes, ma'am."

Aaron couldn't help but feel a bit coy, eager to watch Heidi manipulate the hard-right buffoon over the phone. He didn't know Simmons personally but had watched highlights of the man's campaign. Setting aside the stark differences in political philosophy, he could tell that the governor just wasn't in the president's league, not that many were.

"Good morning, Madam President," greeted a southern drawl over the speaker.

"Good morning, Governor. I appreciate the opportunity to speak with you concerning the potential secession of your state from the union. I feel like the time has come to dig deep and explore this option."

"I agree, ma'am. What do you have in mind?"

Heidi shook her head, wondering how the man had been elected to such a vast and powerful state. "I'm willing to support a binding referendum, open to all eligible voters in your state. I think the sooner we schedule this event, the better."

There was zero hesitation in Simmons's reply. "Madam President, I'm afraid I can't support that plan. We're not going to make the same mistakes as Scotland and Quebec. If I may, I would like to offer an alternative suggestion."

For the first time that morning, Aaron grew concerned. Rising quickly from a nearby couch, he moved closer to the phone and his boss. A puzzled Heidi responded, "Go ahead, Governor; I'm open to ideas."

"We would suggest a special commission to study the issue. They would be charged with forming an outline of the process, including specifics on currency, taxes, banking, and commerce.

We agree on the state-wide referendum, but firmly believe our citizens should understand exactly what they're voting for."

"I'm not sure I agree with your reasoning, Governor," Heidi replied. "I ran on a platform of efficient government, and it sounds like your proposal would be not only wasteful, but a distraction from the more important issues facing both of us."

A grunted laugh came through the speakerphone, not enough of an outburst to be offensive, but still potent enough to send a message. The governor wasn't buying Heidi's argument.

"President Clifton, let's be blunt with each other. Before the election, you knew this initiative didn't have a snowball's chance in hell of succeeding. It was a brilliant move; I'll give you that, but there was… and is… a minuscule risk that the union will divide. My party is still stinging from being outmaneuvered, and the last thing I'm going to agree to is a less than honest effort. Yes, you'll have to work a little harder… pay a higher price to shoot the thing down. But you will still accomplish the same result and won't have our side of the aisle screaming to high heaven that we were screwed over in the process."

Heidi smiled, the governor's little sermon reminding her of southern politics at its finest – something she'd watched her own husband refine over the years. "Okay, Governor, let's say I agree to your plan. Who is on this Blue Ribbon panel? How do we select the members, and what is the composition?"

Aaron was close to being physically ill. He, more than anyone in the world, wanted the entire "Texas thing" to go away.

As Heidi and the governor hacked out the details, the chief of staff had to return to the couch and take a seat, fearing the excellent breakfast was about to come back up.

"Aaron? Aaron, are you okay? Your face is pale," Heidi gently checked.

"Something at breakfast didn't agree with me, ma'am. I apologize."

"No problem," the Commander in Chief responded, concern for her friend and subordinate sounding in her voice. "Why don't you go rest for a bit? I'll have the recording of my call transcribed, and we can review it later."

Too embarrassed to let his boss know he hadn't been intently listening to the entire conversation, Aaron nodded his agreement. "I'm sure I'll be fine soon, ma'am."

"Ranger Bass, I'm assigning you to the governor's security detail. You are to report to the Austin office first thing in the morning."

"But, sir, I..."

Major Alcorn didn't let the protest leave Zach's throat. "Son, your actions in Houston have caused a shit-avalanche of Texas-sized proportions. I've had everyone from the DOJ to the FBI's Washington office calling for your head. This all may boil down to our governor pulling strings, or perhaps even making it known he'll pardon you if it comes to that. Go guard the man, and make damned sure you befriend him. You may need it."

"Yes, sir."

"We'll bring you back here when this all blows over. Make sure it does."

"Yes, sir."

Stunned, Zach ambled out of his boss's office, thinking seriously about resigning. The FBI was crooked. The DOJ was worse. A man who surrendered to Zach personally was dead, and there was little hope of the killer facing justice.

While Perkins denied any knowledge of who the shooter had been, Zach didn't think the feds had put forth an honest effort to find the killer.

According to the official reports, several officers manning the perimeter had heard the shot but hadn't paid much attention. There had been a lot of gunfire around the Hendricks neighborhood, so one more shot from a noise-canceled weapon wasn't anything new.

The so-called investigation had been complicated further by the number of out-of-town policemen. It was simple math. The larger a perimeter's circumference, the more manpower that is required to keep the inquisitive public out and the criminals in. The city of Houston and its surrounding counties had contributed dozens of officers, but it still wasn't enough. Zach had heard reports of cops being sent in from as far away as Arkansas, but somehow the official logs and records of visiting officers had been erased. *Imagine that*, Zach mused. *How convenient.*

After throwing a few clothes in a bag, Zach filled up the truck and headed east. *Austin would be okay*, he figured. The food was excellent, the music great, and the people interesting. Besides, this assignment would be like a mini-vacation. After all, how hard could it be to guard one man?

"Why Texas?" the senator from Georgia asked President Clifton.

"Because geographically, it makes sense. Also, its history, culture, and size make it a viable option," Heidi responded.

Sipping his cup of exceptional White House coffee, the gray-haired gentleman peered over the rim of his cup at the newly sworn-in chief executive. "I have to hand it to you, Madam President; that was one crafty political play. Risky, but obviously worthwhile."

"It wasn't as political as you might think, Senator. I intend to keep my campaign promise and see this through. That's why I've asked you here for breakfast, to gauge your interest in joining our Blue Ribbon Commission and explore the concept."

Arranging his cup and saucer on the coffee table, the Senate Majority Leader sighed. "I have to tell you, ma'am; I've got a lot of extremely envious constituents. I've heard from thousands of voters who are asking 'Why not Georgia?' along with Texas. There have been many voices calling for the Old South to rise again. You've opened a huge can of separatist worms."

Heidi was smooth, "So I've heard. We anticipated such reactions and sentiment, but believe this will be limited in scope. One method to make sure we don't split the nation in half is to state clearly that there will be open borders between the two countries if there is secession. At any time the people on the right want to relocate, they'll be free to do so. Same goes for those on the left living in Texas. Remember, Senator, they have Democrats and liberals down there - millions and millions of citizens with progressive leanings reside in the Lone Star State."

"You sound like you really want this to happen. I'm surprised," responded the life-long Republican. "You know some in the press have started calling you the 'Anti-Lincoln.'"

Heidi laughed, "I've been called far, far worse. However, that just reaffirms the point. If you stand back and look at our system, the interaction of the parties, and the polarization of our citizens, there is logic to this madness. But even beyond that, I made a promise to the American people, and I'm going to keep it."

"I've got to admit, after the initial shock of your announcement, I found myself tempted to relocate. I probably wouldn't, being a Georgia boy through and through, but there is an appeal to living in a place inhabited by like-minded people."

Nodding her understanding, Mrs. Clifton continued, "We envision a relationship much like the European Union. Open borders, free trade, mutual defense packs... that sort of arrangement."

The senator extended his hand, "I'll agree to be a member of your Blue Ribbon panel. I'll enjoy the ringside seat for *this* show."

"Thank you," Heidi responded, accepting his handshake.

Aaron stood in the Oval Office, facing his Commander in Chief while he waited for her to complete a phone call.

"I've got to hand it to Governor Simmons, he sure is taking this game seriously," she said after disconnecting. "That was the Israeli Ambassador, requesting my personal approval for him to visit Austin. It seems the people of the Lone Star State are seeking Israeli expertise in establishing a new country."

"Makes sense," Aaron replied, shrugging his shoulders. "Other than the Soviet Bloc states that broke free, Israel is the last major country created out of thin air. If anyone knows how to do such a thing, it will be them."

Heidi stood, stepping from behind the desk. She settled at the window, crossing her arms and staring outside. "I thought this would be over by now. I thought common sense would prevail, and everyone would agree that this is a stupid and unnecessary exercise."

"It's only been a few months since your inauguration, ma'am. Give it time to fade away."

Heidi turned, her pivot just a little too fast, her body language a smidge too tight. Aaron knew instantly she was stressed over the subject. "I'm not going to go down in history as the president who destroyed the union. That's not going to happen," she declared.

Aaron held his ground, "Madam President, I just don't see it occurring... it's just not feasible. Please keep in mind why we announced this in the first place – it was to pull in undecided voters from the middle, and perhaps a few on the far right as well. It worked. All we're seeing right now is a bunch of blowhards trying to make political hay. Even that is fading. The amount of stumping on the subject, in Congress, is in decline."

The president shook her head, "I went along with this because I thought it would bring the two sides together. I had expectations that the right and left would see how ridiculous their partisan positions were and meet in the middle. But that's not happening. If anything, it has divided the country further – made the chasm deeper."

"You remember the budget stalemate from just a few years ago? How both sides took the government shutdown to the brink of disaster? Washington has seen this sort of gamesmanship for 200 years. Texas seceding from the union is no different, ma'am. Sabers will rattle until the last possible moment, and then the matter will die quickly."

"And in the meantime," Heidi responded with frustration, "Nothing is getting done. We've not even managed to push one single piece of legislation through committee, let alone signed into law."

"With all due respect, ma'am, nothing was getting done before you came into this office. If you recall, on the campaign this was one of your primary concerns. The gridlock we see today isn't any worse than your predecessor suffered for years."

Nodding her head, President Clifton acknowledged Aaron's point. "What do the latest poll numbers indicate from Texas?"

"Only 36% of registered voters are in favor of secession. Like I keep saying, it's not going to happen."

The small icon on Zach's cell phone signaled a new voicemail now resided in his inbox. Since there weren't any missed calls on his mobile, it had to be someone trying to reach him via the Austin office.

He dialed the sequence of numbers required to access the seldom-used feature, a computerized voice announcing that he had one new message.

An unfamiliar female voice came across the line. "My name is Kara Hendricks… well it used to be Hendricks…. Anyway, I found a letter today from my late husband, Abe. I think you were with him at the time of his death. I remember watching you fighting with that other cop on the day he was killed, and somehow I got the impression that you cared. I think this note might be significant. Please call me."

Zach wrote down the number, his mind racing with the woman's words. She answered his return call on the second ring.

"Ma'am, this is Ranger Zachariah Bass. I received your message."

"Thank you for returning my call, Mr. Bass. Are you the same ranger I saw on television when my ex-husband was killed?"

"I am, ma'am. To this day, we've not found his killer, but the case has never gone cold – at least not by my way of thinking. Could you tell me about this letter?"

"Abe and I had a beach home down at Gulf Shores, Alabama. After our divorce and then his death, I just didn't have the heart to visit the place. I rented it out over the summer and finally worked up the nerve to come down here for a few days. Evidently, one of our renters checked the mail and retrieved an envelope addressed to me from Abe. She must have forgotten to tell me about it, because I just found it on the counter in a stack of junk mail."

"And what does the letter say?"

"Well, that's just it. There is no letter, just a key and a sticky note. It's in Abe's handwriting, and it says, 'Kara – this is important.'"

Zach rubbed his chin, trying to figure out the next step. "Is there any sort of name or number on the key?"

"Yes, it has the word, 'Prime,' as well as a number, 00617134."

"And you have no idea what this key might be for?" the lawman queried.

"No. Since our divorce, I had only spoken to Abe once. He called me a few days before he shot at that plane and told me he was sorry for everything."

"Did he own any other properties? A lockbox? A storage bin?"

"Not that I know of. Our house in Houston was spacious, and Abe definitely wasn't a hoarder. About the only thing my husband held onto over the years was bad memories."

"Ma'am, I'm going to see if there's any reference or record for that key. It also might help if you could send it to me. I'd be happy to give you a FedEx account number and my address."

Kara agreed, jotting down the information and promising to send Zach the package next-day delivery.

After disconnecting the call, Zach dialed one of the lab technicians associated with the Department of Public Safety. "Can you do a database search on a particular key for me?"

The answer came less than an hour later. Abe Hendricks evidently had access to a bank lockbox in Houston – a lockbox that the FBI hadn't been able to find.

"Yet another wonderful gift you have delivered, Ranger Bass. And it's not even my birthday yet," Major Alcorn stated, sarcasm thick in his tone. "Technically, we should hand this information over to the feds and be done with it. However, for some reason, our colleagues in Washington have a hard-on for one of my rangers. I suppose it might have something to do with a public, full-frontal assault that ended up on national television, but I can't be sure about that."

Zach nodded, fully understanding his boss's frustration. He had apologized, more than once, and that was all he would offer.

"I could request the case files from Washington, but I'm sure that would garner unwanted attention as well. Those fellas don't seem to be a forgiving bunch. Regardless, without that supporting information, I don't see any judge authorizing a search warrant."

"Maybe the bank will let me look inside without a warrant," Zach offered.

"Unlikely," replied the major. "If it were some bumpkin-based operation out in the middle of nowhere, then perhaps. But this bank is in suburban Houston, and I doubt they'll be anxious to let you nose around. I think you're wasting your time."

Zach pondered his boss's recommendation but couldn't let it go. "I feel a sense of responsibility, sir. My path crossed with Abraham Hendricks twice. It's almost like a destiny or something."

Alcorn sighed, his frustration evident. "You have some vacation days coming, Ranger Bass. What you do on your own time is none of my affair. But be warned – don't get stupid. There's already enough tarnish on your badge. I won't tolerate any more."

Alcorn flipped Zach the key, "Report back here tomorrow, Ranger. I'll dock you one vacation day, and consider this entire matter as personal business. While I'm sympathetic to the frustration you've felt over Mr. Hendricks's death, we've got a governor to protect."

The drive from Austin to Houston was only a few hours, especially when the driver wasn't worried about the speed limits. On the journey across central Texas, an idea occurred to the Ranger, a thought that might salvage what was sure to be a wild goose chase.

"Detective Temple," Sam answered, picking up her cell phone on the first ring.

"Hello, Detective. This is Ranger Bass. How are things in the murder capital of Texas?"

"People are just dying to get my attention, Ranger Bass. What can I do for *you*?"

"I'm on my way to Houston, working on a case that might interest you. How's your schedule look this afternoon?"

Sam, as usual, was suspicious. "What case would that be?"

"I don't want to talk about it on the phone, Detective," Zach responded, knowing she would have trouble letting any mystery go unsolved.

"Okay. I'll bite. Where do you want to meet?"

Grinning, Zach looked at his watch. "I'll pick you up at the precinct in an hour."

With the Bayou City's traffic, it was closer to 90 minutes before Sam climbed into Zach's pickup. "How do you people handle this gridlock?" Zach complained. "It's no wonder there's so much crime in the inner cities. The bad guys know the cops will be stuck in traffic for two hours before responding."

"Nice to see you too, Ranger."

"Sorry," Zach smiled. "I'm just not used to it; I guess. Austin is bad, but I don't have to go downtown much. Anyway, I am well, Detective Temple. How might you be?"

"Same old grind, Zach," she smiled. "So what brings you to my lovely part of God's country?"

"Abraham Hendricks," Zach replied, and then proceeded to relay the details of his conversation with Kara Hendricks.

"And why, if I might ask, do the Texas Rangers give a rat's ass about that case?"

Zach frowned, taking a moment while he chose his words. "The rangers don't, but I do. That whole morning just eats at me, Sam. I've not been able to let it go. A man, innocent until proven guilty, surrendered to me. He was killed before facing a jury of his peers. That's not what I'm about... it's not what we're about."

Temple didn't comment at first, her analytical brain sorting through it all. Finally, she flashed Zach an odd expression and said, "You know, after the Hendricks incident, Sal just wasn't the same. He dove into the investigation, intent on finding whoever shot Mr. Hendricks. Despite you two having a schoolyard brawl, I think he felt the same way. I got the impression he was getting close, but then all of a sudden, he was promoted and moved back to Washington. Poof! Just like that."

"I take it things didn't end well between you two?"

"You could say that," she replied, a hint of frost in her tone. "The bank is over there... you'd better get in the other lane."

After parking, Zach pulled his jacket from the backseat and straightened his tie in the mirror. Detective Temple caught on immediately. "You don't have a warrant, do you?"

"Nope. This one is going to be via pure charm and charisma."

"We're fucked," Sam sighed, and then crossed her arms and feigned anger. "And I should be mad as hell at you for wasting my time on this ill-advised adventure. I thought you ranger-types were pros."

"Watch and learn, young detective," Zach grinned, pulling a briefcase from the back seat and opening the door.

They entered the bank, Zach flashing his badge and asking to see the manager. Immediately.

A middle-aged man appeared, introducing himself. Zach couldn't help but notice the fidgety fingers and sweaty palms as he shook the man's hand. "I'm with the Texas Banking Commission out of Austin, sir," Zach began. "It has come to our attention that your operation here hasn't been adhering to the regulations regarding the verification of customer identification."

"I don't understand, Mr. Bass," the now-perspiring banker responded as he hustled the visitors back to his office. "I assure you that we strictly follow the FDIC and federal banking laws to the letter."

Zach shook his head, pretending disappointment. "I have evidence to the contrary, sir, and depending on your cooperation today, we may or may not have to bring in the federal authorities."

Nervousness was replaced by outright fear on the manager's face. Spreading his hands in helplessness, he pleaded, "Please, Mr. Bass, the past few years have all been so confusing. No one has been in contact with my bank regarding any issues or irregularities. The laws keep changing, and it's nearly impossible to keep up. Just today, my regional manager described the current regulatory environment as 'pure chaos.'"

Zach switched gears, shifting from Mr. Hyde to Dr. Jekyll. "I understand. I certainly do. We're all a little frustrated by the volume of the updates as well. But still, just like you, I have a job to do."

The manager relaxed a bit, "I want to assure you, Mr. Bass, we want to remain in good standing with both state and federal regulators. What exactly are we suspected of doing incorrectly?"

Zach set his briefcase on his lap. After flipping the two locks, he produced a picture of Mr. Abraham Hendricks, as well as the lockbox key. "Do you know this man?"

The manager studied the photograph for a moment and then nodded. "Yes... he isn't one of our regular customers, but I do recall his face."

"And does this look familiar?" Zach asked, holding up the key.

"Yes... yes, it does. That's one of our lockbox keys."

"According to our information, you rented this man a lockbox without verification of his identification. His real name is Abraham Hendricks, but I'm quite sure you have no such person on file as having done business with your facility."

The fear was back in the manager's eyes as he turned to the computer residing on his desk. With a sad, almost desperate look, he answered a few moments later. "You're correct, Mr. Bass. We have no Abraham Hendricks on file. I'm not quite sure how this has happened, but I assure you we..."

Zach's tone growled low and mean as he interrupted the stammering banker, "This is a serious offense, sir. I think it's about time I introduced Detective Samantha Temple, Houston Police Department, *Homicide*."

Sam flashed her badge, her stoic, expressionless face signaling she meant business.

Zach, worried the bank manager was going to have a heart attack right then and there, continued. "What name did Mr. Hendricks use to rent this lockbox?"

The manager's hands were shaking so badly he had to make three attempts to enter the key's number into his computer. "Mr. Eugene Smith," he finally sputtered.

A barking laugh came from Zach's throat, the outburst causing the sweating manager to jump. "Mr. Smith? Really? Your staff fell for that one?"

"I'm sure our personnel followed all of the appropriate procedures, Mr. Bass. We can't be held responsible if someone has a fake...."

It was Sam's turn to jump in, her cold tone stopping the manager mid-sentence. "Google the name Abraham Hendricks, sir. You'll find about six million results. Compare the man in Mr. Bass's picture to the images you see online."

Without hesitating, the banker turned back to his computer. A few keystrokes later, he inhaled sharply. "Oh my God," the shocked man whispered. "That's the same man who tried to assassinate...."

"We need to see inside that box, sir. Right this minute. Because of your bank's sloppy procedures and failure to follow regulations, vital evidence may be have been withheld in this investigation."

The manager's face grew pale, his head nodding agreement. "Of course... of course, we want to cooperate fully with the authorities. I'll have our assistant manager bring you the box immediately."

Ten minutes later, Zach and Sam sat alone in the manager's office, peering inside the metal container at a single manila envelope. "Here goes," Zach said, reaching for the evidence. "I hope Mr. Hendricks wasn't into ricin or other poisons."

Sam chuckled, "I'd check it for trip wires... we know he was into those."

Releasing the tie-string, Zach reached inside and extracted a thick set of documents. A few moments later, the ranger sighed, shaking his head. "These are copies of Mr. Hendricks's sealed court papers. I don't understand. Why would he have sent his ex-wife the key and the note? Why go to all the trouble and risk of using a fake ID and renting this box, all just for these?"

"Didn't you say the note told his wife these were important?"

"Yeah," Zach replied, apparently puzzled.

"Then there must be something hidden in these documents. Something Mr. Hendricks felt was worth the trouble to hide."

"Great," Zach replied. "I was counting on taking you out to dinner for helping me. Now I guess I'll be reading court papers all night."

"And what makes you think I would've accepted your invitation to dinner, Zachariah Bass?"

"I thought all you big-city girls liked thespians. I figured after my little acting job today, you wouldn't be able to say no."

Sam laughed, pointing to the stack of papers. "How about Chinese take-out and the coffee table at my apartment? I am a sucker for a good mystery, so I'll help you look for the needle in this haystack."

The two law dogs managed to make a mess of Sam's usually tidy apartment. Thanks to the cardboard food containers, coffee cups, and stacks of papers, the upscale loft soon looked more like a college dorm room than the dwelling of a professional woman.

The evening's festivities had begun with reading. Sam, producing legal tablets, pencils, and her laptop, started by organizing her share of Mr. Hendricks's documents in neat stacks of priority.

Zach, on the other hand, sat with an open beer, quickly making a mess of his portion, randomly searching for something that caught his eye.

Breaking only to consume so-so noodles and insult the other's fortune cookie message, the duo continued to dig through a monotonous pile of requests, motions, statements, and depositions.

Zach leaned back, rubbing his eyes and moaning. "This shit might have been important to Mr. Hendricks, but for the life of me, I can't see why. Nor can I understand why the court sealed these files. The police report covering the incident at the house in New Orleans takes a few liberties, but I've seen worse. What are we missing here?"

"For once, I agree," Sam replied, stretching her arms high in the air. "It all looks routine to me. No smoking guns… no skeletons rattling in any closets."

Clearly frustrated, Zach said, "So where do we go from here?"

Reaching for her computer, Sam set the device on her lap and then passed Zach her share of the papers. "Let's take every name contained in those documents and do a search. A few years back, I solved a case by doing this. It might help."

Scratching his chin, Zach agreed, "Sounds interesting. Where did you learn this technique?"

"Watching cop shows on TV. They always cross-reference a database of names," she teased.

Shaking his head in disbelief, Zach decided it couldn't hurt. He began reading every name he could find on each page. Sam made a list, scribbling on a legal pad, occasionally asking for clarification of a spelling.

The next step involved the pair entering each name and searching both the worldwide web and a law enforcement database used by the Houston cops.

Some common names returned thousands of results. Roland Ford, a.k.a. the burly NOPD sergeant, filled Sam's laptop with pages of links and references. The clerk on record as having filed the case was even worse, given her name appeared on practically every court document filed over a period of 12 years.

They were on the edge of calling it a night when Sam entered the name, A.P. Miller into the search engine. Zach was already standing, pulling on his jacket before heading to the door.

"Hold on a second... this is interesting," she said. "Have you ever heard of A.P. Miller before?"

"No," Zach considered, trying to place the name.

"How about Aaron Miller?"

After a moment, the ranger's answer was the same. "Nope."

Sam turned her laptop around so he could see a picture on the screen. Zach recognized President Clifton immediately, but the man beside her didn't ring a bell.

"So?" he asked, still having no clue.

"I can't be sure it's the same man, but the White House chief of staff is Aaron Miller. The lawyer from the Louisiana Attorney General's office who filed the motion for all of Mr. Hendricks's files to be sealed was A.P. Miller."

Something in Sam's explanation registered with Zach. "Hold on a minute... I saw that name on one of these other papers."

It took the ranger another 15 minutes of searching before he found what he was looking for. "This is a deposition Mr. Hendricks's attorney conducted with Sergeant Ford. Look here, where he asked Ford if the NOPD had requested any legal opinion on the order to confiscate private weapons."

After taking the paper from Zach, Samantha began reading the record aloud:

"Sergeant Ford, did you or your superiors request any clarification when you received the orders to confiscate private weapons?"

Ford: "No, sir, we did not. The man who briefed us on the new directive was from the state's Office of the Attorney General, and he seemed to know what he was doing. He visited our temporary station and outlined our responsibilities."

Plaintiff Rep: "During this briefing, no one asked any questions?"

Ford: "No, sir, this attorney was passionate and thoroughly convinced that NOPD had the right to execute the confiscation. As a matter of fact, I recall this lawyer saying he had prepared the legal justification for the mayor and police commissioner. None of us gumshoes were going to question that."

Plaintiff Rep: "And who was this attorney from Baton Rouge?"

Ford: "I don't recall exactly. I think his name was Miller... something like that."

Plaintiff Rep: "Are there any other details of that meeting you can remember, Sergeant?"

Ford: "When the meeting was breaking up, I remember walking out behind this guy. He was talking to another officer. I heard him say, 'Anybody with a gun in New Orleans falls into the same category as a looter – lethal force is justified.'"

Sam looked up, shaking her head in disbelief. "If it is the same guy, we now know what pushed Mr. Hendricks over the edge."

Zach nodded, "We also have a pretty good idea why this was all sealed and hushed. The second most powerful person in the world... the guy whispering in the president's ear not only made a horrible call on the Second Amendment, but was overheard instructing a police officer to kill offenders. Wow!"

"That's not the worst of it," Sam noted. "The cover-up is more politically damaging. If this had been made public before the vote, it might have had a significant impact on the election. I think the trail of who shot Mr. Hendricks might have just gotten hot again."

"But the election is over," Zach replied.

"Not the referendum on the secession," Sam reminded the ranger. "This could still blow up in their faces."

Zach hadn't thought of that, his mind charging forward with the ramifications of their discovery. "So what do we do with this little nugget of truth?"

"Honesty is always the best policy," came the instant response.

"Bullshit," Zach countered. "Seriously, do we keep this under our hats? Report it to our superiors? What?"

Sam rubbed her temples, the potential reverberations causing her head to hurt. After a few moments, she stopped and shrugged. "Do you want Texas to secede or not? I'm just the good-looking sidekick in this adventure... the eye candy of our crime-fighting duo. You're the brains, Zachariah Bass – do you want to live in a state, or a republic?"

Zach pretended to be hurt by the analogy. "I thought I was the sex appeal of this outfit."

His response was a well-thrown couch cushion. "Get out of my apartment," she hissed, barely managing to keep a straight face. "Unlike some people, I've got to hit the office early. Now get!"

Zach stopped at three convenience stores before he found one with a copy machine. After acquiring a roll of quarters, he began the process of duplicating the pertinent pages from the lockbox.

Retiring to the truck, he then highlighted A.P. Miller's name on the copied documents, scrawling "White House COS," in block text along the margin.

After placing the copies in an envelope, he returned both sets to his briefcase and headed for home.

All the way back to Austin, the ranger mulled over the situation. The time passed quickly, the abrupt appearance of his driveway illuminated in the headlights' beam a small surprise.

"I think Sam asked the right question," he said to no one. "Do I want Texas to secede or not? This information is a game changer, and I can't take it lightly."

He exited the truck, taking in the small, rented home in the moonlight. The yard needed a good trim, and there were weeds growing up through the gravel in the drive. "How did I get myself into this shit?" he whispered.

Chapter 11 – Reaction

The special commission began its work, the final goal being to negotiate what became known as the Treaty of Secession, or TOS. Those disillusioned with the process began referring to the acronym as the "Ton of Shit."

There were 28 members, half of them Democrats, half Republicans. It was agreed that the White House would nominate 50% of the members, the State of Texas an equal number. A process identical to voir dire, the most common jury selection technique, was implemented.

Once formed, the new organization elected its own hierarchy.

In the end, the make-up of the commission was quite impressive. Comprised of economists, politicians, business leaders, two university presidents, and a former Supreme Court justice, it was difficult for either side to find fault with the members' credentials. One newspaper went so far as to call the membership "the greatest collection of intellectual firepower convened since the Constitutional Convention."

The secession movement attracted strange bedfellows, the camps for and against not at all what folks expected. The strongest supporters were on the liberal side of the aisle, the most vocal opponents on the right. The non-Texas Republicans possessed a strong, well-founded fear that Heidi Clifton would roll over the entire country with left-leaning legislation if Texas separated. Much to the offense and surprise of their brethren in the Lone Star State, the conservative right denounced the entire concept.

States like Wyoming, Tennessee, and Utah were the most vocal about "maintaining balance," and "stronger together."

Proponents argued that "the balance" had meant gridlock and inaction, and that "together," meant knife fighting in a phone booth.

Like almost every other major issue facing the United States in the last 12 years, gridlock ensued. The days passed, each bringing a new argument, point-of-view, or angle to the debate. The commission continued to move forward, however, working out of the limelight, negotiating the details, timelines, rules, and policies of the treaty.

It was a monumental undertaking, requiring enormous resources and expertise. The White House fought many battles, fending off repeated calls from Congress to stop the madness and quit wasting valuable resources. President Clifton would respond to her critics by requesting a status updating her proposed legislation, which of course, had gone nowhere.

"It seems Congress has nothing better to do," she said during one Sunday morning interview. "They aren't passing any legislation, not solving any of the nation's real issues, so why not dedicate resources to determine if the United States and Texas would both be better served by separating?"

Zach blinked hard, in an effort to clear the fog from his eyes. His head was pounding, the dial on his watch refusing to come clean and show him the time.

Finally, the numbers appeared.

"Shit!" he snapped, throwing back the covers and rolling his feet over the edge of the bed.

He was still trying to button his shirt ten minutes later, rushing out the door... the task made more complicated by the two hangover-reduction aspirins he clutched in one hand.

Throwing the truck in reverse, he almost didn't see Mr. Porter walking his dog in the pre-dawn coolness. It seemed like it took an eternity for the elderly neighbor to pass by.

Zach's head felt like it was being split with an axe, his eyes unable to blink away the alcoholic haze, the lights on the dash still not entirely clear. He searched around the cab, looking for his reliable stash of bottled water, but there wasn't any. With a scowl of resignation, he tossed the two tablets into his mouth and began chewing the bitter pills.

The fowl taste of rancorous, after-beer slime, combined with the chalk-like cure, made the Texan's stomach heave. He managed the side of the road, thankful for the early hour and the few passing drivers who witnessed his convulsions. The worst part was seeing the bits of aspirin floating in the sea of bile and realizing his headache would continue to rage unabated.

It was 30 minutes to the agreed upon rendezvous, Zach using the drive time to pine for something, anything, to rinse his mouth of the rotten taste. Looking in the mirror, he caught a glimpse of his own face, the image prompting another cramping pain in his gut.

Sleep deprived, bloodshot eyes peered back in the reflection, each orb surrounded by dark circles of too much beer and not enough shuteye. The worst was the second-day stubble on his face, a clear indication of a man who did not have his act together.

"That's not the image of a professional officer of the law," Zach mumbled, doing his best imitation of Major Alcorn and anticipating what would surely be his speech. "That's not how a Texas Ranger reports for duty."

"Fuck you, Major Tight-ass… *and* the Texas Rangers," he hissed.

Zach tried to make up time, using the lack of traffic and a break-neck pace to eat away the miles. Despite the effort, it was clear he wasn't going to make it.

"I need to call those deputies and tell them I'm running late," he mumbled, feeling his pockets for his cell. "Knowing those two gung-ho dicks, they'll get all puffy-chested and try to go in there without me."

Patting down his vacant pockets, Zach's hangover headache inevitably worsened. He didn't have his cell phone, the forgotten device probably resting comfortably on his kitchen counter. "Fuck!" he yelled at the empty cab, the outburst serving only to enhance his throbbing skull. "Did you forget your gun and badge, too?"

Zach reached his belt and double-checked that his pistol was indeed in its holster. The checkered grip of the .45 did little to reassure him. "What a sorry ass excuse you are for a lawman," he mumbled.

He'd been drinking way, way, too much since the discovery in Abe Hendricks's lockbox. The stakes were extremely high, the pressure of his knowledge nearly unbearable. Why didn't he listen to Alcorn in the first place? Why had he stuck his nose in where it didn't belong?

The ongoing national headlines regarding the secession didn't make things any easier. Any fool could see the country was a tinderbox, ready to erupt in an inferno. "And here I am, a drunken idiot, holding the match."

Lawmen were trained, steered, managed, and forced to keep secrets. Confidentiality was a trademark of the profession. Yet Zach struggled with the knowledge he possessed.

Yesterday, he'd made up his mind to tell the world. He had the package all ready for delivery, had a plan all worked out. He would disguise his face, approach the Houston television station in the wee hours, and drop off the envelope addressed to Ross Garcia. Zach had witnessed the man's star on the rise and figured he had the balls and wherewithal to make national noise.

His fortitude, however, had begun to waiver, his bravery leaking away. What if releasing the information locked away in his gun safe caused unrest or violence? What if his disclosure resulted in riots with people being killed or harmed? How many lives was this single Texas Ranger willing to impact? How much history did he intend to write?

The only thing that seemed to manage the weight on the Texan's shoulders was booze… a lot of painkilling alcohol.

Finally, the sign announcing the Rodriguez Garage and Body Shop came into view, the rusted blue metal advertisement hanging lopsided from an ancient, roadside post. Zach could see the county patrol cars parked underneath.

They had a warrant for one Robert William Carter, a.k.a. Buffalo. Mr. Carter was the new president of the Comanchero motorcycle club, a B-grade biker outfit, historically more of a nuisance than a serious threat. With a string of petty thefts, numerous disturbances, and the occasional assault attributed to the gang, law enforcement had always watched closely but didn't prosecute to the extreme.

Buffalo's appearance had changed the profile. Reportedly a recent immigrant from the Hell's Angels core management in Los Angeles, Mr. Carter was rumored to have been transferred with orders to shape up the lightweight, underperforming affiliate.

Zach visualized the suspect's file, the few photographs available making it clear how the man had earned his nickname. At 6'5", well over 300 pounds, and sporting a wild mop of tightly curled hair, Buffalo truly looked like... well... a buffalo.

Always understaffed and underfunded, the rural sheriff's department was ill equipped to penetrate the organization, nor could it deploy any of the sophisticated surveillance techniques available to larger law enforcement departments.

It was Zach who managed to dig up some dirt on Buffalo, finding a failure to appear warrant issued some years before in San Diego, California. The ranger had used the minor offense to convince a county judge to issue an arrest warrant.

Alcorn had insisted on Zach being there when the warrant was served. "We think old Buff is establishing relations with the cartel boys," the boss had stated. "I want a ranger's eyes looking around inside that biker's nest. Make sure those fine, young deputies don't miss anything."

Coming to a jerking halt behind the rear patrol car, Zach's temper flared when he saw both deputies had already entered what was essentially a compound – part junkyard, part garage, and supposedly the flop for the suspect.

The freshly cut, dangling chain at the now-open front gate confirmed the two eager-beaver officers had already forced their way into the premises. Zach drew his pistol, just sliding through the narrow opening when he heard a loud banging sound.

"Police! We have a warrant!" a voice shouted. "Pol…"

The second announcement was interrupted by a loud blast, Zach's pickled brain somehow identifying the report of a shotgun.

Adrenaline kicked in, the ranger's fog clearing instantly. He had managed three running steps before the second shot rang out, quickly followed by two smaller popping noises that were most likely from a pistol.

Zach rounded a small row of sheds and an old wrecker, his legs pumping at full speed. The two deputies came into view, one sprawled on the ground, writhing in agony, the other bent over his comrade, attempting to render aid.

The uninjured lawman, startled by Zach's approaching footfalls, almost shot the ranger. Obviously near panic, the deputy lowered his pistol and returned to assisting the downed man.

"How bad is he?" Zach barked, taking a knee, his pistol sweeping the doors and windows of the nearby building.

"He took a 12-gauge blast to the chest," came the frightened, stuttering voice. "He's bleeding."

Zach scanned again for the shooter before glancing down to assess the injured lawman. With immediate relief, he realized the majority of the buckshot had struck the local deputy in his Kevlar vest. A few pellets had hit an unprotected shoulder, a couple more striking his face.

"He took the blunt of it in his armor," Zach announced. "He's going to be sore as hell, but I think he'll be okay."

"It hurts to breathe," groaned the downed man. "Hurts like hell."

"Drag him out of here," Zach ordered. "Go back to your car and call for an ambulance. Where's the suspect?"

"He gave us both barrels and then scrambled around the building," came the rushed response. "I think he was making for the junkyard out back."

"Get him out of here," Zach demanded. "Call for help. I'll go take care of Mr. Buffalo."

After verifying the uninjured deputy was capable of dragging his comrade to safety, Zach scanned the area again and moved out, heading for the spot indicated.

With weapon high and ready, Zach found himself trekking through caverns of stacked, junked cars. Access paths had been left between the rows of scrap metal, the resulting maze providing a thousand places to hide.

Staying close to one wall of the rusting steel hulks, Zach progressed slowly, trying to keep his footfalls silent. *It could take a dozen men all day to find that asshole in here*, Zach thought. *He could be anywhere.*

The ranger proceeded cautiously, not really expecting to locate the suspect, hoping Buffalo was as stupid as most criminals and would make a mistake.

After stalking the first row and finding nothing, Zach's patience was wearing thin. More than anything, the lawman was mad at himself for being late. His lack of professionalism had damn near cost that young deputy his life.

He was mid-way through the second aisle when the scraping of a footstep sounded across the yard.

"Carter! This is Zachariah Bass, Texas Ranger. We've got a battalion of lawmen on the way here. Come on out, and it will go easier. Make us come in and get you, and an accident might happen."

The lack of a response didn't surprise Zach. He rounded a corner, wishing his tortured brain could come up with some clever logic to talk the thug into surrendering and save everybody a lot of time.

A shadow of movement caught Zach's eye, just a hint of discoloration at the peripheral of his vision. The ranger dove for the ground as a spread of buckshot ripped through the air, tearing into the sheet metal door of an old pickup.

He landed badly, his right wrist going numb, his .45 clanging into a nearby pile of rims, fenders, and engine parts.

Zach rolled hard, eyes scanning for any nook that might offer cover. Small geysers of dirt erupted where the ranger had been just a split-second before, the thunder of the second blast echoing through the canyons of discarded steel.

Buffalo, seeing his opponent was unarmed, held his ground. The huge biker flashed an evil grin as he broke the old double barrel in half, the two spent casings arching through the air. Zach saw the man's hand disappear into his pocket, digging out the bright, red plastic of two more shells.

The ranger charged, roaring a battle cry at the top of his lungs.

The gang leader was startled by the move, fumbling for a moment as he shoved the reloads into the breech. Zach was six steps away when the massive man's hands snapped the weapon's fore end back to ready.

Four strides separated the two when the barrel started to rise. As if in slow motion, the ranger's brain processed every minute detail of the attacker's movement, very much like the televised replay of a critical sports moment.

The hairy knuckle of a forefinger was moving for the trigger at two steps. Zach dove, his knees and calves protesting at the strain of launching his body with every ounce of energy he could muster.

The ranger's hand was almost there, his extended arm reaching for the barrel, mere inches away. He wasn't going to make it, time slowing enough to eye that finger pulling back on the trigger.

Zach felt the barrel's impact on his outstretched hand at the same moment the skin on his face burned with the heat and light of the discharge. And then his shoulder was slamming into the biker's chest, either the collision or buckshot originating intense waves of pain through the lawman's frame.

A blur of clenched hands and punting legs consumed Zach's field of vision as the two men tumbled across the ground. He thought he heard Buffalo grunt, but the sound could have come from his own throat.

The ranger's next image was of a sizeable fist flying toward his face. Only an instinctive reflex allowed his jaw to avoid punishment, the blow landing on Zach's shoulder instead. It was a small salvation, streaks of pain shooting through Zach's ribs, his lungs struggling to draw air.

A tattooed arm was driving an elbow at the lawman's nose, the massive, bony appendage moving at incredible speed. The Texan took the majority of the strike on his forearm, the deflection no doubt saving some teeth, but still initiating reverberations of agony through his frame.

Finally, the lawman saw his chance. The biker was off balance, overextended. Zach's boot landed a savage downward kick on the side of Buffalo's knee, the popping of tendons accompanied by a deep-throated howl of pain.

The ranger threw his hand at the big man's throat, the web between his thumb and finger landing solidly against the behemoth's Adam's apple with a sickening crunch.

Buffalo went down, collapsing in a heap of panting, wheezing misery.

Sirens sounded in the distance, ambulances and lawmen rushing to answer the call for reinforcements. Zach loomed above the biker, hands on his knees and breathing hard to catch up.

The lawman managed his handcuffs despite the numbness still governing his right arm and hand. A few moments later, Mr. Carter was secured on his stomach, still trying to suck oxygen into his massive girth, the effort hindered by a larynx that was most likely going to require surgery. Zach didn't give a shit if the son-of-a-bitch died right there in the dirt.

He stumbled off, aiming to retrieve his weapon and at least part of his dignity. He'd just returned the .45 to his belt when a half dozen officers rushed on the scene, weapons drawn.

"He's going to need an EMT," Zach announced, his voice raspy and low. "And I need a fucking cup of coffee."

Pivoting to return to his truck, Zach ran headlong into Major Alcorn, the presence of his commander shocking.

"What the hell happened here, Ranger?" Alcorn snorted.

Zach didn't respond at first, still getting over the surprise of seeing his boss in the field, 50 miles from where he was supposed to be... and at just after sunrise.

"Do you require medical attention, Ranger Bass?" Alcorn asked.

"No, sir. I require coffee."

Zach half-staggered back to his truck, every muscle in his body protesting the stroll. The sight of the EMTs working on the wounded deputy prompted him to detour for a prognosis. Feeling more than a little guilt over his tardiness, the ranger was glad to see the man clear-eyed and responding to the medical technicians.

"Did you get that fucker?" the cop asked when he saw Zach approaching.

"Yes, he's in custody... probably on his way to the ER any minute now," the ranger responded.

"Good... I hope you kicked his ass good and proper," the injured man croaked.

Zach patted the man on his unharmed shoulder and started to turn away when the deputy called out. "Ranger," he said, trying to rise up from the stretcher. "I don't think you understand. He knew we were coming."

"Huh?"

"Buffalo knew we were coming. He was waiting on us.... I heard a cell phone ringing as we approached the door. A guy like that sleeps in.... His business doesn't actually encourage his being a morning person."

Zach nodded, "I'll make a note of that, deputy. You work on healing."

The ranger watched the EMTs shove the stretcher into the rear of the ambulance, one of the medics crawling in to ride with the patient while the other rushed to the front to drive.

Zach turned, continuing back to his pickup, stopping only to borrow a bottle of water from another officer. The ranger drank the refreshing liquid quickly, sitting in his truck and trying to regroup. He kept replaying the wounded man's words over in his head.

At first, Zach concluded that the guy was just trying to justify a sloppy approach. The ranger had seen many people attempt to explain away bad luck, stupidity, or improper techniques with theories of conspiracy or skullduggery.

But the deputy did have a fair point – the entire reason why warrants were exercised at the break of day was to catch suspects unaware. Most people weren't at the height of alertness at such an early hour – an advantage for the lawmen.

Now curious and recovering, Zach made for where he'd left Buffalo. He wanted to see if the man had a cell phone hidden somewhere on that massive body.

The ranger was halfway to the spot where he'd left his captive when he spotted the EMTs struggling to push a heavily burdened stretcher across the dirt surface. There was a sheet completely covering their cargo. Buffalo was dead.

"What the fuck happened?" Zach snapped, stepping in front of the medics.

"He was dead when we got there," one of them answered. "Looks like he suffocated by the color of his face."

Stunned, Zach stepped out of the way and let them pass. Major Alcorn and the other officers followed, the senior ranger making a beeline for Zach. "Was that man breathing when you cuffed him?"

"Yes, sir. I didn't hit him hard enough to close his throat… at least it didn't feel like that. He was wheezing, but still breathing."

Alcorn looked Zach up and down, the ranger's dirty, torn clothing a visible indication there had been a serious scuffle. "Make sure you get pictures of any wounds, bruising, or other signs that he resisted," the major ordered.

"Yes, sir, will do. Did the suspect have a cell phone on his person, sir?"

Alcorn tilted his head, "No. I'm sure he didn't. After I found him unresponsive, I patted him down personally."

Another deputy approached the two rangers, a twinkle of excitement in the man's eyes as he pointed toward the clipboard in his hand. "We found a bunch of stolen merchandise inside," he proclaimed. "There's even a truckload of flat screens from that warehouse robbery over in Midland. Another of the trailers is stuffed to the gills with electronics that appear to have been destined for New Mexico. Looks like these guys were regional players."

"Did you find the suspect's cell phone?" Zach asked, his reaction bursting the officer's excited balloon.

Looking down at his papers, the deputy responded, "No… no cell phone listed here. We're still going through the storage rooms though. It might be back there."

"Thanks," Zach replied, wondering if the wounded cop had actually heard a phone at all.

"You better get to the ER," Alcorn stated. "I want pictures and a doctor's report detailing your injuries. Since our friends were doing business across state lines, the feds might be joining our little party. I want everything dotted and crossed."

Zach nodded, pivoting to return to his truck. The major's voice stopped him mid-stride. "Ranger Bass," came the stern voice. "From now on, I'd appreciate a clean, shaven face and ironed clothing. Carry on."

Zach did as he was ordered, driving off in a huff. As he motored toward the ER, he contemplated the source of his ire. It wasn't the scolding by his boss, nor was the violence at the junkyard to blame. It was a nagging, little voice in the back of his head telling him that something just didn't quite make sense.

The deputy's remark about the warning call was troubling. Suspects generally fled when they got warnings; they didn't stay to shoot it out with law enforcement. So why didn't Buffalo run? He had time, given that the deputies waited a few minutes before entering, waiting for Zach. And if the ranger had not been tardy, he would have been the man in front. It was always that way, the senior man taking the lead, especially if he was a Texas Ranger. If someone had made a warning call, he might have been the intended target.

It was all too much. Considering the hangover, sleeping through his alarm, forgetting his lifeline-cell, and the enormous pressure of the Hendricks documents, Zach's reasoning arrived at the worst-case conclusion. "Somebody is trying to kill me," he hissed, an internal rage growing by the second. "I don't know who, or why, but they better eat a big breakfast before coming after me. I'll be watching now... I'll be ready."

Governor Simmons followed the state-provided sedan as it entered the half-circular drive, eventually passing the uniformed Department of Public Safety officer stationed at the gate. A few years ago, while the governor's mansion was under renovation, some asshole had tossed a Molotov cocktail and damn near burned the place to the ground. Ever since, the people had been burdened with the cost of protecting the national historic site.

It wasn't long before the visitor was mounting the front steps. Simmons, stepping from between the Greek Revival columns, extended his hand.

"Thank you for coming so late, Doris. This exhausted public servant surely does appreciate it."

"No problem, Governor. My staff has finished the evaluation of the state's global corporations, and I knew you wanted this report as soon as possible."

They entered the foyer, grand marble, historical artworks, and an assortment of antiques from the proud past aesthetically displayed. Neither party paid much attention, the governor passing through almost every day, the state's comptroller nearly as often.

They stepped down the hall, eventually arriving at the mansion's library, both taking familiar seats. Digging through her attaché case, the state's financial wizard dug out two copies of a report.

A smug smile formed on the governor's lips. "I bet all of our corporate friends are as giddy as we are about the possible reemergence of the Republic."

Frowning, Doris shook her head, "Surprisingly enough, sir, that's not the case. I had my people double-check the results, and quite frankly, the numbers are all a little troubling."

"Troubling?" grimaced Simmons, "What do you mean? I figured all those big business honchos would be chomping at the bit, waiting for our independence day. What's got their saddle blanket in a wad?"

"It seems the majority of the CEOs interviewed were very concerned about infrastructure and bureaucracy. They mentioned tax law, collection, and processing. Others wondered about Food and Drug regulation and enforcement. All of the federal agencies, administrations, and bureaus that are part of their everyday business processes have no Texas equivalent. That means they would face an unknown, and nothing worries executives more than uncertainty."

The governor rubbed his chin, clearly puzzled. "I hadn't thought about it that way. Face-to-face, they all buck and moan about the mammoth federal bureaucracy in Washington, how it eats profits and gives nothing but headaches in return."

"Yes," replied the comptroller, "That's true. But they *know* Washington. They know the game. If Texas becomes an independent nation, the dust won't settle for quite a long time, and they are well aware of that fact. Their operating environment would become an unknown."

Nodding his understanding, Simmons seemed disappointed, "We've been working with the assumption that all the major corporations in America would be stampeding our borders, anxious to get the heel of Washington's boot off their throats. From what you're saying, our friends in the business world are going to hang back for a bit and see how we set things up."

"It's more than just the bureaucracies, sir," she added, flipping through the report. "Several mentioned the court systems. They seem concerned that the existing state infrastructure isn't prepared to take on the federal workload. But... the single largest concern in their minds was currency and banking. Practically every interviewee asked if Texas would print its own money or if there would be a system like the Euro. Will we have a central bank, insurance like the FDIC, and a stock market? How long will all of that take to establish? What happens in the meantime?"

"Those are reasonable apprehensions on their part, no doubt about it," the governor agreed. "I wonder if all those people who went around demanding Texas pull out of the union had any clue how complex all this was going to be. Here they were, signing petitions and writing Internet blogs like this was as easy as baking a batch of cookies."

"It is an enormous undertaking, Governor, no doubt about it. And if we simply duplicate what Washington has created over the years, aren't we going to end up in the exact same place? Out of control debt, overregulation, and an infrastructure that is self-destructing?"

Simmons nodded, "I understand. What would be the point if we simply mimicked Washington? They might as well stay put if there's no advantage in pulling up stakes and moving south."

"Whatever the experts decide, sir, it has to be new and improved. But aren't we all hoping for that very thing?"

Red watched the gas pump's numbers roll, a little worried that he might overdraw his checking account with the fill-up. Mary needed diapers and some hotdog buns for the cookout at her mom's this afternoon, but he had a twenty to take care of his wife's shopping list.

The sound of crunching gravel caused him to look up, an old Chevy pickup rolling to the island on the opposite side of his Dodge. Nodding at the driver, he wondered if Steve knew one of his running lights had burned out.

"Morning, Red," greeted the new arrival, swiping his card and then pulling the hose from the pump.

"Morning, Steve," came the reply. "How's that GM product treating you these days?"

"I've got over 97,000 on her the last I looked, and other than being a hungry beast, she's still running strong."

The two men filled their tanks, small talk of family, fishing, and the big sale advertised at the Martin's Tractor Supply permeating the Hancock, Mississippi air.

Red, having a head start, heard his pump snap off first. After returning the hose, he pulled a pen and piece of scrap paper from his pocket and wrote down the total. The receipt printer hadn't worked in two years.

"Hey, Red," Steve called, peeking around the pump, looking for the windshield squidgy. "What do you think about this whole Texas thing?"

Hooking his thumbs in his pockets, Red spat and then answered, "I don't like it much. But truth be told, I've not considered it a whole lot. I've got a bearing going out on the Deere, and the small silo's blower motor is on its last leg. Thinking about those Texans bailing out on us hasn't been high on my list as of late."

"Claire and I were talking about it this morning. She wants to put our place up for sale and move to the Lone Star State if it happens."

The statement surprised Red. "Really? Things that bad, Steve?"

"No, no worse than normal. I'm just sick of busting my ass on that patch of dirt I call a farm, and never seeming to get anywhere. I'm not getting any younger, and Claire is convinced Texas is going to be a boomtown if this deal goes down."

"But your family has lived here for what… four generations? We've all seen some tough times. I have to say I'm kind of shocked to hear you speak those words."

Steve's pump picked that moment to finish its work, the conversation put on hold while he returned the hose to the cradle. Rather than let the discussion end, he moved to the back of the truck and leaned against the fender, a sure sign he was serious about the subject. "What worries me the most is how this country will fare after Texas pulls out. The House will turn back over to the libs… probably the Senate, too. Claire is worried the whole damn place will become some sort of socialist mecca."

Red looked down, scuffing his boots in the dust for a moment before responding. "I know this sounds bad, but two years ago... during the worst of the drought, Mary and I had to take assistance from the county. The harvest wouldn't pay the mortgage *and* put meat on the table. If it weren't for the food stamps, I would've lost my place to the bank. When I think about this supposed conservative paradise called the new Republic of Texas, I wonder if such a thing as food stamps will exist there. I worry about what would happen to folks in my situation... people who hit hard times and need a hand."

Steve seemed a little surprised by Red's story, "I had no idea. I knew things were tight for you guys, but didn't think it had gotten so bad."

"We only needed a little help for about three months, but with a new baby on the way and no rain, we were thankful. That episode changed my outlook on things. The Republicans can stammer and wail at the heavens about welfare fraud, cycles of dependency, and sucking from the government's tit all they want. I used to agree with them wholeheartedly. But then when it hits you... when it's your family that's hungry... well, a man's perspective can change."

Steve waved off his friend's concerns, "There's a difference and a big one. You've always been a hardworking man, paying his own way. I don't know of a single conservative that would have denied you that help. It's the people who game the system that raise their dander."

Nodding, Red took a step toward the combination convenience store and post office, his friend moving to follow. "I don't have any answers. I'm just a dirt farmer trying to get by. But I'll tell you this, if I had a vote, I'd cast my ballot against it. The U.S.A. has accomplished more than any other country on earth, and we did it standing together. I don't see any good reason to have a divorce now."

"I guess we'll just have to wait and see," Steve replied, his mind moving on.

On the way out, Red held a small stack of mail in his hand. "Hey, Steve," he called to his friend, holding up the envelopes. "Do you think they'll have mail in Texas?"

"Probably," came the frowning response.

"Dang... without the mail, there wouldn't be any bills. Now that might convince me to pack up and move."

"Mexico will kick their asses within three months," spouted the state congressman from Delaware. "They'll be back, begging to rejoin the union as soon as the first Mexican division crosses the Rio Grande, and as far as I'm concerned, we should tell them to go pound sand in their asses."

One of the representative's aides cleared his throat, "Actually, sir, according to this fact sheet, if Texas were an independent nation, it would have the 13th largest economy in the world - ahead of Spain and South Korea, and much larger than Mexico."

Waving off the statement, the congressman retorted, "All the more reason for Mexico to try and retake what they consider to be their territory anyway. A sizeable economy doesn't equate to an equally large military."

"I don't know. From what I see here," replied the aide, pointing to the latest documents from the president's commission, "Texas would actually have a significant military presence, roughly equivalent to Great Britain. Not a pushover by any sense."

"How? When we pull the U.S. men and equipment out of there, how are they going to build up a military force so quickly?"

"That's my point, sir," replied the nervous assistant. "This report indicates that Texas would retain 9% of the current U.S. military hardware. That includes planes, ships, armor, personnel... even nuclear weapons."

"What? That's preposterous! The American taxpayer footed the bill for all of that, and now the president is going to give away part of our arsenal?"

"They've paid for it too, sir. According to these numbers, Texas contributes 9% of the U.S. population and funds 9.2% of the tax revenue. I think the president is only considering what would be their fair share."

Snorting, the congressman countered, "Then give them 9% of the federal debt, too. Fine with me."

"You know, this is really interesting. I'm reading here that the Pentagon is seriously concerned about the secession. It seems that while Texas is only 9% of the population, they make up almost 13% of the military personnel. The Joint Chiefs are predicting manpower shortages for at least six years."

The first tee at Almaden Country Club was more than just a launching point for an exclusive round of golf. Its proximity to the oversized putting green allowed casual connections between members, often leading to informal gatherings while the next foursome waited its turn to ply the links.

The long, narrow tee-box was located just off the primary cart path; a busy thoroughfare used to access the driving range, snack bar, and nearby locker room.

Well-dressed members, brandishing the absolute latest in golfing style and technology, often huddled at the #1 tee. It was a social hub, a place where old friends exchanged casual waves, warm smiles, and lighthearted harassment so common amongst competitive men.

Nestled between San Jose, California and the foothills of the Santa Cruz mountains, Almaden wasn't the most exclusive club in the area. That title was reserved for the invitation-only echelons of the super-wealthy, such as the San Francisco Golf Club or Cypress Point on the Monterey peninsula.

No, the club was a haven for northern California's working millionaires, men who had started businesses and made them grow with sweat equity, hard work, clear thinking, and being just a little faster than the opposition.

Entrepreneurs felt a natural kinship at the facility, regardless of their trade or specialty. The CPA, who 30 years ago branched out and started his own firm, was right at home playing alongside the owner of a distribution company. How you made money wasn't important here. Success was the social equalizer, good taste and professional behavior more important than one's alma mater or political affiliation. Many of the rank and file were street fighters, elite warriors and survivors of the ultimate conflict – business. They were welcome.

On an ordinary Friday afternoon, the primary topic of discussion would have involved handicaps, hefty wagers, and strokes given or received. On occasion, the subject might be the markets, the club's latest board meeting, or an investment opportunity being considered or proposed. Rarely were partisan issues topics of conversation here, seldom were international events dissected.

The proposed independence of Texas had changed all that. Not for the political ramifications, nor for the social implications. The buzz was, as usual, about what it all might mean for commerce, trade, and the bottom line of the members' broad range of businesses.

Andy stood on the back of the tee-box, absentmindedly swinging his driver through the air as he waited, watching the group ahead search for a lost ball.

"Hey Paulie," he said, turning to address a member of his own foursome, "Am I going to have to file an international tax return if this Texas thing goes through?"

"Probably," came the CPA's grinning response. "I'm already talking to my people about doubling our fees. I'm projecting this secession-thing will be like rocket fuel to our bottom line."

"Double?" chimed in David. "Hell, Paul, I'd get him for at least triple. International tax is a complex animal, isn't it?"

"Don't give him any ideas, David," Andy replied. "And besides, don't you have an office down in Dallas... another in Houston?"

"Sure do, but I'm going to move my primary residence down there so I can lower my tax bill all around. How do you think I'd look playing golf in a cowboy hat?"

"Do you think it will help your hook?" came Jimmy's voice, pulling his own driver from a bag riding on the back of a cart.

"Nothing will help that hook," added Andy. "But seriously, has anybody heard how they plan to regulate cross-border commerce? Some of my biggest customers are in Texas."

All eyes turned back to the group's expert on things financial and accounting. Paulie shrugged, "If it's like Mexico, it won't be a big deal. If it's like Canada, it will suck. That's not counting the whole NAFTA mess. If Congress opens that beauty up, all bets are off. But it's not happened yet, so I wouldn't worry about it."

The group in front of them had finally moved on, allowing Jimmy to tee up his ball. After a few warm-up strokes, he settled in, launching the drive a little left, flirting with the lake that adorned that side of the hole.

David was next, pegging his Titleist and setting up to draw the shot. The metallic ping of solid contact sounded, the ball's initial trajectory looking sweet. Mid-flight, it took a hard left turn, diving for the ground as if it were a falcon swooping in on a field mouse. "Damn it!" he growled. "Maybe I *should* try that cowboy hat."

Paulie was next, eyeing David's short drive with a sly grin. "If you do move to Texas, my golf earnings are definitely going down the tube. You better fix that hook, or I'll be filing bankruptcy papers on your behalf. You'll qualify for Chapter 18."

"Chapter 18? What's that?" David responded, still glaring at his misbehaving ball.

"Default by golf debt. Wagers lost over 18 holes," came the chuckled reply.

"Seriously, Paul, you don't think they'll secede?" Jimmy asked.

The answer didn't come immediately, Paul's drive splitting the fairway. "Short, but in the middle," he mumbled. "The story of my golf game... and sex life."

After returning his club, Paul watched his partner hit a solid shot, then cringe as the ball drifted right, rolling toward a fairway bunker that seemed to possess an almost magnetic attraction to the sliced ball.

Paul spoke up, "You just answered your own question, Jimmy. I think the country is like that tee shot you just hit. It tends to drift to the right, and often ends up in a bunker. Maybe letting Texas go is the bunker this time... maybe not. I'm not going to worry about it until I see papers being signed."

And so it went, the electric whine of cart motors intermingled with curses, boisterous laughter, and the occasional celebration as the group toured the course.

It was traditional for the men to gather in the club's bar after their round. There were bets to be paid, drinks to be bought, stories to be told.

"David, you're not really thinking of moving to Texas?" Jimmy asked.

"No, I couldn't handle the weather there. San Jose has spoiled me. But it is tempting. One of my sons lives down there, and he doesn't pay state income tax. The same house that costs $4 million here, you can buy down there for $500,000 dollars. The difference in the cost of living alone is astounding."

Several heads nodded around the table, signaling their agreement. Andy spoke up, "David doesn't need the money," he noted, "but a lot of people do. My biggest concern over this entire Texas thing is that droves of people start moving there, either sick of liberal thinking or wanting the economic advantages. I heard one news commentator claim that every millionaire in the country would move to Texas; every person on welfare would move out. If that happens, the rest of the country is in big trouble."

Jimmy dismissed his friend's concern with a wave, "Never happen. Look around us. The girl who brought us these drinks isn't well off. The grounds crew mowing the putting green this morning isn't wealthy. You have to have a mixture, or it doesn't work. Even the most exclusive, expensive locales have all different levels of income. No reason why Texas wouldn't be the same way."

David nodded, "I'm with Jimmy on this one. How many times have we all sat around bitching about an increase in California's tax... or fees... or whatever pocket-robbing scheme those assholes in Sacramento were dumping on our heads? All of us could have afforded to move anytime we wanted. I could have pulled my company out of here and into Nevada in a heartbeat, and it would have saved me plenty. But we didn't. None of us did, and I bet most people will decide against pulling up stakes and heading to Texas."

"I get so tired of the liberals that run this state," Paul confessed, looking around to see who might be in earshot. "If it's not some harebrained environmental program, it's social engineering, or gun control, or some damn regulation that takes money out of my pocket. I'm sick of living in a place that's always on the brink of financial ruin, yet won't control its own spending. If the State of California were one of my companies, I'd have fired the manager or sold it off years ago. But David's right. I won't move either. At least not until the lack of water forces us all out."

Andy sighed, "I'd go," he announced to the surprise of his friends. "I feel like a man without a country. I'm white, middle-class, male, Christian, and over 40 years old. I no longer feel like I belong... like I'm no longer in line with the mainstream values of this nation. Everywhere I turn, the country's problems are being attributed to my race, gender, and religion."

Paul nodded, "Well of course you're to blame. Don't you watch the evening news? You earn too much, don't pay enough in taxes, worship the wrong God, and are generally to blame for every historical wrong over the last 1,000 years. Slavery was your fault. Poverty and discrimination were your gifts to the world. Social inequalities, injustice, and unrest were all the result of your actions. Because of your race and success, you automatically hate women, minorities, immigrants, and anyone else who doesn't look like you."

While Paul's monologue generated a few chuckles, every man at the table could relate to his words. They had all felt the same way at one point in time or another.

"I do get a little tired of being labeled evil, hurtful, and destructive," David continued. "I'm a little fed up with everyone thinking it's wrong to base wages on skills or expect people to pull their own weight. Is it intolerant to demand rule of law? Is it really greedy to amass wealth?"

Paul shook his head, "Texas leaving the union won't fix a thing. They may not have the same problems, but they'll have their share. Just because you draw a line on some map and put a different bunch of crooks in charge won't change a damn thing. I can see no reason to jump from our liberal frying pan into their conservative fire."

After three months, the TOS commission released the final results of the negotiations.

President Clifton and Governor Simmons, in a joint press conference, announced the date of the election for all of the residents of Texas to determine if they wanted to secede. The people would be given 30 days to study the treaty before the vote.

A few astute politicians and commentators began to notice what they termed, "Treaty fatigue." The American public had grown tired of the constant bickering, had lost interest in the back and forth repartee.

That night, a poll found that only 41% of Americans knew that Texas would decide on her own whether or not to leave the union.

Chapter 12 – The Issue

It was a rare occasion, Zach unlocking his front door at a reasonable hour. It wasn't an accident or random occurrence.

His day had been consumed by appearing as a witness in a trial… the constant breaks, objections, and meetings at the bench dragging the entire affair out. By the time he was dismissed from the stand, there wasn't much time left to do anything in the field.

"You're shitting yourself," he informed the empty home. "You're having trouble handling the load those documents are putting on your back."

And it was a tremendous weight.

The entire courthouse had been abuzz over the Presidential Commission's report. Like most Texans, Zach had been following the entire story day-by-day, gradually accepting that his home state might actually become a country.

Unlike the people around him, Zach knew he could drastically influence the outcome.

Despite maintaining an outward appearance of supporting whatever the people democratically resolved, he was still unsure of how to handle the secret locked inside his gun safe. When someone mentioned the nationally televised debate scheduled for that evening, he'd decided a little TV time might help him make up his mind.

"You're bullshitting yourself again," he cursed. "You're hoping one side will kick the other's ass tonight and let you off the hook."

Unscrewing the cap from a cold beer, he reached for the remote just in time.

"Tonight, we are bringing you a special edition of the *World News Today* program. This extended broadcast will focus exclusively on the proposed secession of Texas and more specifically on the recently released results of the President's Blue Ribbon panel. The debate between Governor Simmons of Texas and Senator McMillian of Illinois will follow."

With flawless hair, conservative blue suit, and nationally recognized smile, the anchor appeared at his usual desk, a graphic in the background depicting the United States being split in half.

"We begin our broadcast tonight with a look at the future of our nation if Texas were to secede. Our first report has been filed by our Washington bureau chief and deals with how the political landscape would be altered by the event."

"Good evening. As of today, there are 36 members of the House of Representatives from Texas, with only seven of those being Democrats. Potentially, the greatest short-term impact for the U.S. would be the Democratic Party taking back control of the House. Currently, Republicans enjoy a 28-seat majority, but with 29 of their rank no longer serving, Nancy Pelosi would once again be primed to become the Speaker of the House."

The image then shifted to the Senate, a set of numerical columns overlaying the chambers of the higher house. "The same result would occur in the Senate," the announcer continued. "After the last election, the Republicans managed to pull off a single seat majority, 50 to the Democrat's 49, with one independent serving the esteemed body. If Texas leaves the union, along with both of her current Republican senators, the GOP would again find itself in a minority position."

A video clip of President Clifton began to roll, the chief executive smiling and waving to an adoring crowd. "This bears well for the president," the voiceover continued, "as most political experts believe she has little to no chance of achieving any significant legislative accomplishments with the current division of power in Washington."

Zach watched the broadcast with a keen eye, trying to gauge where the whole thing was going to fall, and more importantly, trying to figure out how he really felt. The issue was obviously complex, nowhere near black and white. *Wasn't that the way with everything these days?*

The ranger continued to absorb the broadcast, surprised at some of the predictions the commission had committed to paper. Other tidbits of information were just common sense.

He yawned his way through the segment concerning the Supreme Court justices, and how a U.S. government dominated by the left would appoint like-minded judges. *Duh.*

Despite being a native, a few of the facts revealed in the report were a surprise to the Texan.

"Texas is the third largest producer of electronic components of all the states," said one industry analyst. "It is by far the largest exporter of such products."

"Texas will be one of the largest export economies in the world," announced the reporter. "With excess cattle, oil, and agricultural produce, the new republic would export more goods than California and New York combined."

Zach continued watching, several of the statistics making him proud to be a resident of the Lone Star State.

"Texas has the 3rd largest reserves of uranium in North America," said one of the experts. "In addition, the state ranks 5th in coal reserves, and has significant reserves of other critical metals."

The network special then turned to the more difficult questions, a reporter grilling Governor Simmons with a rapid-fire barrage of questions for over ten minutes.

"What about the people receiving Social Security?" poked the newsman.

"Social Security pays regular benefits to Americans living outside the United States today. Why would Texas be any different? The same can be said of retired military and government workers. They can live in any country and still receive their benefits."

"How would Texas pay for its share of the federal debt?"

"We would be happy to make payments on our portion of the debt. The commission agreed that Texas is 9% of the population, so we will have to inherit 1.15 trillion, or the same percentage of the debt. But, we will also receive that same percentage of gold reserves, military hardware, and federal assets. It must be a fair exchange, as the people of Texas have paid for roughly 9% of the federal apparatus with their income taxes over the last 100 years."

The reporter didn't like that answer, the scowl on his face making that clear. "And a constitution?"

"We will immediately adopt the U.S. Constitution, with only minor changes. The Second Amendment, as an example, will be clarified. All changes will be approved by a state-wide referendum within 12 months of independence."

Zach was bored with it all. He was reaching to turn it off, when he heard the word taxes, closely followed by the reporter's eyebrows shooting skyward.

"We will have no income taxes," Governor Simmons announced proudly. "My staff submitted a plan that will provide more than enough revenue without corporate or individual incomes being garnished. Our new system will also provide a solution for one of our nation's largest issues – immigration."

Shaking his head, the reporter couldn't make the connection. "I'm not sure how taxes and immigration affect each other, Governor."

"Like Canada, Germany, and many other countries around the world, we are going to sell citizenship. Any non-criminal, from any nation, will be welcome in Texas. For the undocumented workers already in the state, we have a solution... a simple, easy path to becoming a citizen."

"Go on, sir. You have me intrigued."

"We will establish a quick, 3-day documentation process, not unlike the current day green card. The immigrant will pay income taxes for a period of years, at a rate similar to what the U.S. taxpayers are burdened with today. After seven years, the green card holders will become citizens. This way, the state receives income, and we don't have people risking their lives to sneak across the Rio Grande."

"And so you plan to tax these poor people enough to pay for a new national government?"

Simmons growing frustration with the man's biased attitude was clear, but he kept his temper in check reasonably well. "Of course not," he said, dismissing the reporter's spin with a wave. "We will fund our nation's federal needs via currency control and the existing income from tariffs that will come to Austin rather than Washington."

"So you're just going to print money? Won't that lead to inflation and devaluation of Texas's currency?"

"No, that's not our plan. Any government that has controlled its own currency in the past has failed miserably. We're not that stupid. Our plan eliminates the role of controlling the money supply, as it is currently fulfilled by the Federal Reserve Bank. We will utilize an independent central bank with elected officials. Rather than give an expanding currency supply to private banks, like the U.S. does today, the government will inject that new money into the economy to pay its obligations."

"I don't understand – you'll still be printing money to pay the government's debts, won't you?"

Simmons shook his head, "No. The number of notes being printed will be legally limited to the growth in the economy. If Texas grows at 3%, then the government will receive that same 3% to spend. If we only grow at 2%, then our budgets will be limited to that amount. There will never be any out-of-control inflation. We're not going to make the same mistakes that have plagued Washington."

Zach was impressed. A country without any income taxes? He made a note to check his paystub and compute the increase in his monthly take-home.

He also liked the governor's idea of fixing the immigration problem. So much of his work in law enforcement was due to illegal activity by folks trying to cross from Mexico. On the other hand, the Latino influence on much of Texas was clearly a positive. Maybe the Lone Star flag would fly over the new melting pot of the West?

Zach had made up his mind before the debate began, that portion of the broadcast merely confirming his decision. Switching off the television, he opened the safe and withdrew the envelope containing the copies of the Hendricks documents.

He'd make an unscheduled trip to Houston in the morning, the address of Channel 3 News already embedded in his memory.

For a moment, he considered calling Sam. The thought of meeting her for lunch made him smile, but then he changed his mind. He was treading on dangerous ground, convinced the records had something to do with the incident involving Buffalo. There was no need to drag Detective Temple into the deep water with him.

"Sorry, Sam. You're just going to have to go a few more days without seeing my pretty face," he whispered.

Chapter 13 – Trail of Tears

Samantha Temple studied the body, or what was left of it, with a keen eye. Even for the experienced, homicide detective, the scene was shocking.

"I found the arms!" shouted a patrolman, some 30 meters away.

The area was on the edge of Harris County, thick with underbrush and scrub trees. A citizen hunting his lost dog had found the pooch – and the body.

Thankful she opted against high heels today, Sam trekked down a seldom-used lane, the thigh-high weeds only slightly lower along the two parallel paths where a car's tires would pass.

She found the officer standing with his back to the grisly discovery, the youngish man with a green face merely pointing to the remains.

Sam could understand why. The two arms, separated at the shoulders, were lying about six feet apart. Ropes were still attached to the wrists, the lanyards no doubt hastily cut away from the vehicle that had been used to pull the victim apart.

"Not a good way to die," Sam commented to the pale officer. Bending closer to examine one of the limbs, she continued, "From the looks of his wrists, they were torturing him... pulling him apart slowly."

Her comment tipped the scales between full on nausea and his current hue, the young HPD officer rushing away, coughing and gagging on his own vomit.

Sam ignored the upheaval, moving to examine what was once a left arm. "Nice watch," she noted, using her pencil to brush away a small clump of grass. "You weren't some homeless guy... or a doper who owed money to some vicious loan shark."

The crime scene investigation unit arrived a moment later, high-end digital cameras snapping photographs of every possible piece of evidence. Sam noted her footfalls on a diagram and then instructed one of the technicians to do the same for the still-puking officer.

"This happened less than 48 hours ago," announced another agent. "From the rope burns on the hands and wrists, I'd say the victim died slowly. He was being tortured... maybe interrogated."

"I bet he talked," Sam observed. "I bet he told them anything they wanted to know."

"He lived for about 1 minute after his arms were dismembered," noted the medical expert. "Actual cause of death most likely due to hemorrhaging. He was brutally beaten as well, the disfigurement of his face and skull the result of a blunt instrument... maybe a blackjack."

Satisfied that the surface area and near-proximity to the body had been detailed, the CSI officer gave Sam the okay to search the body.

"Who *are* you?" she wondered, taking a knee and patting down the corpse's pockets. The first thing she found was a press identification card. Wiping the blood from the plastic encased ID, Sam inhaled sharply when she read the name. "Ross Garcia," she said aloud. "Now who did you go and piss off?"

Fifteen minutes later, Sam was on the road, driving to the victim's home address. On the way, she couldn't dismiss the commonality of Abe Hendricks, Ranger Bass, Sal Perkins, and the now-deceased Ross Garcia. She reached for her phone.

"Hello, Detective Temple," Zach answered in a cheery voice. "What can this Texas Ranger do for you?"

"I just finished working a crime scene, and I ran into an old friend of yours," she answered. "I'm sure you remember Ross Garcia, the man who became famous for interviewing Abe Hendricks and flashing your fistfight all over the national media."

"Yes," Zach replied, his tone cautious. "And what did Mr. Garcia have to say?"

Sam ignored the question. "And when was the last time you encountered Mr. Garcia, Zach?"

"I've not laid eyes on the man since that morning in Mr. Hendricks's yard. What's going on, Sam?"

"Someone tied ropes around Mr. Garcia's ankles and wrists, and then proceeded to pull him apart. My guess is they used a pickup truck, and the culprits most definitely did it nice and slow."

"When?"

"The medical examiner thinks it was less than 48 hours ago. Anything I should know, Ranger Bass?"

The gap of silence on the other end told the detective that Zach was choosing his next words carefully.

"As I'm sure your brilliant mind had already deduced, I sent Mr. Garcia an anonymous copy of Abe's papers. Other than that, I've not had any contact with him since that morning when your ex-boyfriend and I had our minor altercation."

"No contact?"

"No, none. And if I were you, I wouldn't rush to the conclusion his death is related to those documents. There's no way anyone could know he had them. I just dropped them off yesterday morning at the station."

"And you didn't tell anyone what you were doing?"

"No. I started to call you, but decided against it. I didn't want to involve you in something that might be over-the-top dangerous. I'm pretty sure somebody's been trying to take me out."

"Now that's stunning news – someone wants to kill Ranger Bass. I'm utterly shocked. Why would anyone want to end the life of such a nice, polite, low-key guy like you?"

"I know," Zach teased back. "I guess they heard that the good die young."

"And you were going to fill me in on this little tidbit at what point in time? Or had your brilliant deductive skills already eliminated the possibility that someone might associate me with you, and thus concluded I was not in danger?"

"I think you're jumping to conclusions," Zach replied. "It's entirely plausible that Mr. Garcia's murder was due to a completely unrelated story he was covering. He was, after all, an investigative reporter. This might have been purely a coincidence. Where are you now?"

"I'm heading over to Mr. Garcia's home. He resided on the west side… out in Katy. Are you in Houston?"

"Not yet. I'm still about an hour outside of town. The governor is going to be visiting your lovely city in the next few days, and I've been assigned to do a little pre-arrival screening. Why don't you give me the address, and I'll meet you there. It's on the way, after all."

"Suit yourself," she replied. "I suppose you might get lucky and notice something I've missed."

An hour later, Zach's pickup rolled up next to Sam's city-issued car. "Was Mr. Garcia single?" the ranger asked.

"Divorced," Sam replied, eyeing what should be an empty home.

They discovered the front door locked, two days' worth of mail still crammed in the box. Working their way around the exterior of the upscale homestead, Sam was a little surprised when Zach drew his weapon. "What?" she mouthed, reaching for her own pistol.

Nodding toward the back door, Zach whispered, "The glass is broken out… right above the lock."

"I need to get Katy PD out here," the detective nodded, raising her cell phone.

After Sam had called for backup, the duo decided to go ahead and enter the Garcia residence.

From the moment Zach set foot in the rear entryway, it was obvious the place had been tossed. Papers, dishes, pans and the contents of each drawer and shelf were scattered on the floor. Every container of food in the refrigerator had been searched and discarded, the stench of spoiled groceries mixing with a stream of soured milk running across the floor.

The couch and chair cushions had been dissected, every picture on every wall pitched into the middle of the floor.

"Somebody was definitely looking for something. I wonder if this was before or after he was murdered."

"The forensics team should be able to tell from the spoiled food," Sam replied.

They entered what had been Ross's home office, the paneled walls and built-in shelves lined with books accenting the massive desk, printer, and filing cabinets. Zach peered inside an open closet door and then shook his head. "This happened after he was murdered. The safe is open, and it wasn't cracked. Whoever was torturing the man managed to get the combination."

Sam was at his side a moment later, her eyes scanning the safe and the litter of papers scattered around the opening and floor. "Do you see the copy of the documents you sent him?" she asked.

Zach glanced around, finally shaking his head. "Nope. Don't see them. But we have no way of knowing they were ever here."

Throwing the ranger a dirty look, Sam bent, her hand seeking a thin coating of white dust she spied on the baseboard. After rubbing a finger through the substance, she took a sniff and frowned deeply.

"What?" Zach asked, now clearly intrigued.

"It's fingerprint powder," she announced. "We use aerosols nowadays, but I'm sure that's what this is. Someone with access to a fingerprint database surely can procure aerosols. That's just weird."

"There's another use," Zach sighed, rubbing his chin in thought. "You can tell how recent a copy was made if you mix the right chemicals together."

"Shit. You're right. How did you send Garcia those documents?"

"I delivered them to the Channel 3 offices, slid the envelope through the mail slot."

Sam shook her head, deep worry evident in her eyes. "Well, whoever pulled Mr. Garcia apart at the seams now knows those were recent copies. They also know someone has the originals. I'd be watching my back, Ranger."

"I have been, Detective. Believe me, I have been."

"What are you going to do?"

Zach rubbed his chin, trying to think it all through. "Right now, nothing. The governor is coming to Houston, and from there we're flying to Washington. At least the trip will give me some time to come up with a plan."

"I will keep working this end, but I don't expect to find much. Whoever did this was a pro. I'll let you know first thing if I get lucky."

Zach removed his jacket, draping it over the hotel chair without ceremony, not giving a shit about potential wrinkles. Next came his boots, shoulder holster, tie, shirt, and finally the soft-sided body armor that was now like a second skin.

He was in the shower moments later, hot water pounding against his exhausted shoulders and tense neck. The last two days had been a non-stop whirlwind of stress, and Governor Simmons's itinerary wasn't even one-quarter of the way complete.

"At least the Secret Service guys are pros," he muttered through the warm spray.

Taking off from Houston had been bad enough, every security man in the world developing a sudden aversion to flying since the incident with Abe's rifle and President Clifton's plane. Landing in DC hadn't been a bucket of beer.

Then came a seemingly endless agenda of dinners, meetings, diplomatic functions and other activities associated with a man who had recently exploded onto the national stage. The fact that Simmons could soon be a head of state made all the pomp and circumstance even more intense.

Tomorrow morning, Simmons's entourage was heading to New York and the United Nations.

Not only were Zach's duties mind numbing, his responsibilities allowed for zero personal downtime. The motorcades had driven by some of the Washington landmarks he'd read about since he was a kid, but there wasn't a spare second to even look, let alone sightsee.

His boss had visited the White House and Capitol Hill, had been granted access to the innermost sanctuaries of power - places Zach had never imagined he'd see. Now, lathering the day's toil from his body, he couldn't remember a single detail of the West Wing. His mental bitch-session continued, the negative thoughts much deeper than a lack of time to snap tourist-type photographs.

"This is just like becoming a cop," he mused, rinsing the fancy smelling shampoo from his hair. "It's not what it seems from the outside at all. No glory. No glitz. No appreciation. Just sore feet, a tired back, and one tiny-ass paycheck."

A trip to the hotel lobby seemed in order. He was off duty for a whole 10 hours, a cold beer and a proper dinner sounded like culinary therapy for what ailed him. He'd eaten his last several meals on the go, the short breaks allowing only cold sandwiches and lukewarm coffee.

He stepped off the elevator, taking a moment to orient himself in the expansive lobby. There were three restaurants and four saloons within the hotel, according to a passing bellman. "These boys in Washington have their priorities straight," the ranger mused, heading toward the recommended watering hole.

More than a few eyes redirected Zach's way as he entered the establishment. His tall frame, western garb, and well-worn boots were out of sync with the $3,000 dollar suits and Rolex watches adorning the locals. But he didn't care.

He decided on a seat at the bar rather than occupying one of the many tables, an isolated stool far more inviting than sitting alone at a booth. Besides, there was a baseball game on television above the colorful rows of liquor bottles. He couldn't remember the last time he'd watched America's pastime. *I wonder what Texas's pastime will be?*

The 20-something girl behind the counter was pretty. Damn pretty, with straight teeth, clean skin, and shiny hair. She handed him a menu, enough of her scent drifting past the Texan to cause his mind to wander for a moment. Her genuine smile didn't help his focus.

"Are you with that group from Texas?" she asked, clearly plugged into the hotel's gossip loop.

"Yes, ma'am, I am," Zach replied, desperately straining to keep his eyes above her high-riding breasts.

"I've never been to Texas," she grinned. "Is everything really bigger *down there?*"

Damn, Zach thought, her words catching him off-guard. *Either this gal is an expert in the flirt-for-tips trade or she has some weird cowboy fantasy.*

Deciding laid-back and humble was the safest plan of action, Zach smiled and replied, "Texas is just a place, ma'am. Nothing more, nothing less than most states."

The bartender seemed momentarily disappointed by the answer. She quickly moved on to explain the dinner special, which was some fancy pasta dish Zach had never heard of and couldn't spell. The prices printed on the menu were shameful, some of the listed wines more than a week of his pay. Zach nearly panicked before recalling that the state treasury was picking up the tab – as long as it was "reasonable."

"I'd like to start off with a cold draft," the Texan announced. "And your best steak, medium pink, and throw a reasonable pile of veggies on the side."

With beer in hand, Zach watched the baseball game, waiting patiently for his plate.

"My, my... would you look over here," a voice sounded over the ranger's shoulder. "This place has surely gone to hell in a hand basket. They even let criminals sit at the bar."

Turning, Zach found himself staring at Special Agent Perkins and two other probable FBI types. "How's the nose?" Zach responded smugly.

He hadn't seen Perkins since their encounter in Abe Hendricks's front yard. There had been threats of prosecution, nasty letters to Zach's commander, and even a couple of phone calls from a federal prosecutor. But the incident had never been pursued further.

Abe Hendricks's killer had never been found, one of numerous sore spots that festered inside Zach's head. Like so many things in the ranger's life, it was still an open chapter – closure unlikely and frustration accumulating over time.

Any assault on a federal officer was a serious offense, but the lines of authority were blurred between the Texas Rangers and the FBI. Zach had moved on, assuming either his superiors were running interference or the FBI wanted to let the media circus die down given they never identified the shooter.

Most guys would have walked away, content with the sharp exchange. But Perkins wasn't that type of fellow. "I'm just standing here thinking I should have you arrested, shackled in irons, and dragged down to the bureau's headquarters for an intense interrogation session. I still have some questions for you, cowboy," the clearly agitated man stated.

"Your dick isn't big enough, Agent Perkins," Zach responded, calmly sipping his beer. "Now if you'd like to lay our badges on this bar and go outside for a moment, I'm game. But you don't have enough political ass to arrest me, and we both know it."

"Bullshit," the FBI man hissed, taking a step forward. "You're in my territory now, asshole, and I have just the perfect lockup in mind. We apprehended a rather large gentleman just this morning, and I'm sure he would enjoy your company as his bunkmate."

Nodding their agreement, the two men bookending Perkins seemed to find the vision amusing.

Zach stood, uncoiling his frame from the stool and coming nose-to-nose with the FBI man. "Go ahead, numb nuts... whatever sends a tingle through your stones. Cause an incident if you want. It's your ass."

Perkins blinked, not sure what his next move should be. Zach's imposing posture and sneering expression baiting the fed to make a move.

Somehow, Perkins managed to move his nose closer to Zach's, barely any air between the two as it was. Both men continued to stare, hatred filling the narrow gap between their eyes.

It was one of the FBI men accompanying Perkins who broke the spell, hooking arms with Perkins and pulling him away. "Our table's ready," the man stated calmly. "I'm hungry, and this isn't the place for a showdown."

The bartender picked that moment to deliver Zach's plate, her cheerful voice giving the Texan an excuse to break contact with the slowly retreating agents.

"Do you know that guy?" the barkeep asked.

"Yeah... we go back a long way."

"If he's bothering you, I can call hotel security."

Zach grunted, wondering exactly how Agent Perkins would handle such an interruption of his meal. "No," the ranger finally replied, "that won't be necessary."

As he sat and enjoyed what was a medium quality, vastly overpriced steak, Zach replayed the confrontation in his head. He didn't blame Perkins for being upset – being bushwhacked in front of your subordinates tends to do that to the alpha-types in law enforcement. But there was more to it than just ego.

The federal guys had always considered themselves a notch above any state employed comrade, regardless of skills, position, or performance. And it wasn't just the FBI.

Zach had seen ATF, the IRS, NSA, BOLM, and other alphabet soup agencies conduct themselves as if they were not only the ultimate legal authority, but also the moral sovereigns of the species. Nowhere was that attitude more evident than with Department of Justice prosecutors.

Forking a mouthful of stir-fried vegetables into his pie hole, Zach chewed slowly, wondering if he needed to be concerned about

Perkins causing more trouble during the Texas delegation's visit.

He'd noted much of the nation's capital seemed to have its nose out of joint, especially when it came to Texas. The reactions he'd witnessed ranged from a thin veneer of dislike to outright hostile glaring. Even the staff at the White House had seemed unwelcoming.

Twice, Zach had found himself in the same room with Aaron Miller. After the first encounter, Zach's untrusting mind was convinced that the president's right-hand man knew the ranger possessed Abe's documents.

Don't be silly, he'd finally convinced himself. *There's no way that guy knows what you're holding.*

The second brush with Miller had left the ranger more at ease. Major Alcorn seemed to hit it off with the powerful politician, Zach having observed the two men laughing privately in a back hallway.

The humor between Alcorn and Miller had seemed genuine, dispelling Zach's suspicions of the chief of staff. *If he were really onto me*, Zach thought, *he would try to discredit me with my boss instead of swapping jokes with him. Someone else must want my head on a silver platter.*

The plush mattress and white noise of the hotel's air conditioning allowed a fitful night's rest, and Zach awoke before dawn.

By sunrise, he'd had downed the hotel's continental breakfast of fruit and coffee. There were still two hours before he was scheduled to report to Alcorn.

He pondered a trip to the facility's gym, but decided a run through the streets of Washington would be the better option. A little sightseeing along the route would satisfy the tourist in him.

It was still reasonably cool when he exited the front doors in sweat pants and sneakers. After a series of stretches, he began a slow jog toward the National Mall.

Traffic was already heavy, despite the wee hour. Zach had been in town long enough to know absolute gridlock was only an hour away.

He picked up the pace after four blocks, working at what he estimated was a six-minute mile. It felt good to use his muscles, the circulation and deep breathing like a drug to the Texan. He actually smiled when the first drop of perspiration ran down his forehead.

Just then, a DC cabbie with a bad case of road rage angrily honked his horn while slamming on his brakes hard enough squeal the tires... all the while screaming profanities at a black SUV. Turning and running backwards so he could see what sounded like an accident, Zach watched as the driver of the massive vehicle continued through the red light, ignoring the oncoming traffic that clearly had the right-of-way. One offended commuter was shaking a fist out his window, smoke still curling off the guy's tires.

The SUV's behavior drew the Texan's eye. Using the reflection provided by the glass storefronts, Zach watched as the suspicious vehicle seemed to be tailing him. *Perkins*, he thought, *that man just can't leave well enough alone.*

It was another block before Zach spotted the opportunity to test his theory of surreptitious surveillance. He was approaching a small park, an area with enough foliage around its perimeter to block the view from the street.

Zach cut off the sidewalk, increasing his speed as he sprinted through the well-manicured grounds.

Chancing a casual glance, Zach relaxed a bit as the SUV passed on by. *Paranoia will destroy ya*, the ranger mused, slowing his pace again.

He continued his trek out of the park, still on edge, but enjoying a good laugh at his own expense. Six blocks later, the hairs on the back of his neck began to stand on end, his sixth sense fully engaged. The black SUV was back, trailing behind him.

Somehow, he'd missed the other car. It was an old surveillance trick, employing more than one vehicle, each taking turns in close proximity to the suspect. He should have been more careful – if the tail were Perkin's Feds, they would be pros.

Zach dropped out of his running stride, thinking he should conserve energy and take a little time to think. He wasn't doing anything illegal, and while he'd been bluffing in the hotel's bar, any headline involving the delegation from Texas was bound to stir a reaction neither side wanted. Still, it bothered the Texan that someone would put a team on him.

The more he walked, the greater the resentment grew. Perkins was an ass, no doubt about it. Guys like that gave law enforcement a bad name. Zach decided to have a little fun.

The first step was to identify the second vehicle. There might be three, but that was unlikely given how fast the SUV had returned to the close-in position.

Zach decided to make his followers nervous. Stopping mid-stride, he spun quickly and stared hard at the SUV. Again, the vehicle passed him by, the windows too dark to see who or how many were inside.

He started walking again, paying particular attention to the cars behind him. At the next intersection, he took a quick right, moving quickly down a quiet side street and then ducking into the doorway of a closed shop.

A dark green sedan passed, followed by a red sports car and finally a smaller SUV. Zach pivoted, intent on reversing course and continuing toward the Mall.

The brick next to the Texan's head exploded with the impact of a bullet, shards of mortar and stone stinging Zach's face as he ducked away.

He heard two more bullets crack through the air as he scrambled for the corner, barely catching a glimpse of the green sedan racing in his direction. The window was down, a hand holding a noise-canceled pistol protruding from the opening.

Zach sprinted like the wind, praying the busier street and presence of so many pedestrians would keep the shooter from sending more lead his way.

He dashed at full speed, trying to look more like a serious runner than a guy fleeing for his life. Another turn and he was on the Mall, the area inaccessible by automobiles.

The Washington landmark was already busy with pedestrian traffic, hundreds of people hustling here and there, most probably on their way to government offices. Zach spotted an old oak and put his back against it, casually scanning while he pretended to adjust his shoe. Bending low, ready to either go prone or flee, the hammerless Smith and Wesson revolver felt reassuring in the ranger's hand. He stayed right there, waiting for his new friends to show themselves.

They didn't.

Time to draw them out, he thought, again performing a very public stretching routine like he was going to start running again. It worked.

He saw two men glance in his direction, then turn away quickly, making for a nearby parking lot. Zach could see the black SUV occupying a handicap spot.

The ranger charged directly at the two fellows, racing as fast as his legs would pump. He was twenty feet away, and they still had their backs to him, stepping briskly toward their ride. *Most suspects wanted to get away from shooters – not attack them,* Zach mused. *Makes me think I should have stayed at the hotel for the continental breakfast.*

Ten feet and one of them began to turn, probably alerted by Zach's pounding sneakers.

Five feet and the Texan was flying through the air, nearly horizontal when his shoulder slammed into the closest man, driving his victim into his own partner. It was a spine-crushing tackle that would have made any NFL safety proud.

Surprise was always the worst enemy, and Zach leveraged his advantage. In less than a second, three powerful jabs jolted his adversary's face, each impact rocking the man's head backwards. A shower of blood was spewing from his crushed nose, his eyes closed before his head bounced off the sidewalk.

Before the second tail could make his feet, the ranger was on him, raining blows and kicks. The brawl was over quickly.

Well, this doesn't happen every day. What is my next best move? Zach thought, weighing his options. He scanned the area, noting several people with frightened looks raising their cell phones to their ears. Now was not the time for an arrest or even an extended visit with the Capital Police. Any delay would cause Alcorn's already short-handed security detail to work additional shifts and overtime hours. Plus, he had gotten what he wanted – to get a look at the men who had been shadowing him. After all, it wasn't like he could really file charges against them for spying on his marathon training. The man with the pistol had been in the sedan, not the SUV, and the ranger had no evidence tying the two together.

Headlines were another good reason to avoid the local authorities. The country was on edge, tempers near the surface. No, it wasn't a good time to hang around and explain it all.

He patted down the man at his feet quickly, fully expecting to find an FBI service weapon and ID. He found nothing.

Glancing back over his shoulder, he could see cops running his way, still a football field's distance from the scene of the crime. Giving the antagonist one last kick to the ribs, Zach trotted off, throwing his sweat jacket into a trash barrel to confuse any witness's description. He chose a zigzagging route back to the hotel to avoid being linked to the brawl.

Fifteen minutes later, he passed through the lobby, opening his room with the magnetic card. Before jumping into the shower, Zach paused, his mind racing with possibilities.

A million questions surfaced in Zach's brain, demanding to be processed and assimilated, but all of them began with the sure knowledge that someone was plotting his demise.

Was Aaron Miller behind all this? The man was certainly powerful enough to control local muscle. But a public hit on a visiting dignitary's security detail was risky, and Zach believed most politicians to be risk-adverse individuals. No way would the man in the White House open himself up for the exposure if things went wrong.

Agent Perkins is no fan of mine either, the Texas Ranger considered. Again, the FBI agent had a lot of influence locally. If there had been a single shooter, that scenario might have been more believable. But, like Aaron Miller, it didn't make sense. One rogue agent or thug that owed Perkins a favor might be trustworthy enough to pull off a public killing – but not three. Three men constituted a conspiracy. Three men were a cell. Three men tripled the odds that someone would talk, get drunk and brag, or come back later and ask uncomfortable favors in exchange for silence.

Before he knew it, there wasn't any more time to ponder the episode. Simmons's flight was scheduled to leave in 45 minutes, and he needed to be in the parking garage and ready to go. He would file a report with Alcorn as soon as the plane was in the air. Other than that, any additional crime solving would have to wait.

Zach found his boss at the rear of the aircraft, checking a laptop computer in the small cubbyhole that served as Alcorn's office. "Sir, there was an incident in DC that I need to report," the ranger began.

The major didn't even bother to look up from his spreadsheet, no doubt absorbed in the security arrangements for the next leg of Simmons's trip – the Big Apple. "Go ahead, Ranger Bass," Alcorn mumbled, clearly in a tense mood.

"Perhaps later would be a better time," Zach offered, not entirely pleased his boss wasn't giving his full attention.

Alcorn seemed to sense Zach's frustration, finally looking his subordinate in the eye. "Now is as good a time as any; go ahead."

Zach made his report, providing the major with all of the critical details regarding the incident in the nation's capital, careful not to disclose any possible connection to Abe Hendricks. Alcorn, for his part, sat calmly and listened without comment.

When Zach had finished, the major shook his head. "Interesting. We had no threat analysis from the Secret Service for the governor, nor did they indicate there was any issue with the security detail. Are you positive this wasn't just a random robbery attempt?"

"They seemed reasonably skilled in surveillance, sir. They also used a noise-canceled weapon and knew the area quite well.

Until they started shooting, I thought it was Agent Perkins just trying to harass me for old time's sake."

Alcorn grunted, "No matter where you go, Ranger Bass, you seem to drum up trouble. Have you been sampling any married women since we've been in Washington?"

Laughing, Zach replied sarcastically, "Sure. Dozens of them, Major. What else would I be doing with all of the free time your scheduling has blessed us with?"

"Well, somebody sure-as-shit doesn't like you," came Alcorn's reply. "I don't know what we can do about it right at this moment. Give me a full, written report, and I'll send it to the Secret Service and FBI as soon as we land in New York."

"Yes, sir."

Chapter 14 – The Third Storm

Zach was happy to see Texas again, his first trip to New York and Washington lacking both in entertainment value and rest.

After sleeping 20 hours and consuming an entire pot of coffee, he felt enough relief from the jet lag to get back at it. His first stop was the Texas Ranger's Austin headquarters.

While the computer had never been one of the lawman's primary crime fighting tools, Zach fully understood the capabilities of the digital world.

It didn't take long to find out who was the top dog, hotshot reporter in Dallas. Zach had decided on a change of venue for disclosing the Hendricks documents, his reasoning based on an in-depth understanding of the human animal. He surmised that the newshounds in Houston might not be enthusiastic when it came to undertaking a secret, high-level investigation of federal officials, especially after one of their own had recently been drawn and quartered with an F150.

A note from Major Alcorn reminded the ranger that he hadn't completed his annual firearms qualification. A crack shot, he supposed turning lead and paper into fire and smoke would improve his mood. After a quick trip to the range, he'd make up some excuse to head for Dallas. Once there, he would drop the bomb.

His drive to the qualification range was interrupted by a call. Zach hadn't seen Cheyenne's number appear on his phone in weeks. For a moment, he considered letting it roll to voicemail, but then changed his mind. It never hurt to mend fences with a pretty gal.

"Hey there, stranger, not heard from you for a while. How are you?"

Every muscle in the Texan's frame tensed when a mechanical-sounding voice responded. "We have the girl. We want those papers. Listen closely if you ever want to see her again."

"Come alone. We're not stupid, and we have ears everywhere your voice can be heard. By yourself, bring the papers, and we'll let the girl go."

Zach couldn't help himself, "You are stupid. First of all, the girl means nothing to me. She left me weeks ago. Secondly, what if I've made copies of the papers? You're not exactly impressing me with your well-conceived plan. Let her go now, and maybe I won't bother to hunt you down and kick your ass."

The clearly altered voice smirked. "No one said we weren't going to kill you, Ranger. Time to make a trade - you and the papers for the girl. We'll take our chances on any copies."

"Where?" Zach asked.

"Here are the coordinates," and then the voice read off a series of numbers, the cross hairs of longitude and latitude. "When you arrive at that point, we'll provide additional instructions. Be there by midnight, or we will kill the girl and start working on your family." And then the call ended.

Zach entered the coordinates in his GPS, not surprised to see a remote location display on the map. It was across the border in Louisiana, smack dab in the middle of swamp country.

"Should have figured," he mumbled, "easiest place there is to get rid of a body or two."

Midnight. That was 11 hours from now… with a nine-hour drive. Not good.

His first call was to Major Alcorn. "Sir, I'm going to call it quits early today. I think the blue-plate special down at Carlos's Diner didn't agree with me," he informed the major's voice mail.

He was dialing Detective Temple's cell phone while entering the combination to his gun safe's lock, stuffing Abe Hendricks's papers into his briefcase.

"Why did I answer this call?" her voice sounded. "I should know better."

"I have a lead in the Ross Garcia case," he said. "I thought you might want to be involved in the take-down."

"Really." It wasn't a question.

"Really. Do you want to help or not?"

"The last time I helped you, Ranger Bass, I arrived late to work the next morning, was left with a huge-ass mess in my apartment, and worried for a week that my career would be over if that bank manager ever mentioned my badge number. That's not even taking into consideration having a role in splitting apart the good, ol' U.S. of A., or a man being drawn and quartered. You can surely understand my hesitation to partake in your little adventures."

"But the Chinese food was tasty, and we both expanded our investigational skill sets. Besides, I really need your help."

Something in Zach's voice told Sam that there was more to the story. "Okay, what's wrong, Zach?"

Driving east at a breakneck speed, he told Detective Temple about the phone call, including a short back-story on Cheyenne.

"So let me get this straight. You want me to be involved in what could be a violent incident outside my jurisdiction, illegally crossing the state line while acting as a law enforcement officer. I would be risking my own hide – all to save your ex-squeeze? Tell me, what is wrong with that logic?"

"Oh, come on," he chided. "It'll be fun. Where's your sense of adventure?"

There was a long pause on the other end, Zach not sure if the detective was going to make up some excuse, or just straight up tell him to go to hell.

"Okay," she finally answered. "I'm in. But you owe me a better dinner than take-out Chinese, Ranger. Go ahead and tell me this harebrained scheme of yours right now. That way, I'll have time to fill in all the gaps and miscalculations - and maybe save all three of our lives."

Zach's 4x4 was caked in muck, the results of having to cross into Louisiana using a logging road that was more liquid dirt than anything else. They had decided to sneak into Cajun country and avoid the main thoroughfares – Zach still concerned about a possible association with the NOPD or other local law enforcement.

It was an hour after dark when they finally managed to negotiate the great Piney Woods, emerging on a two-lane Louisiana state highway, both officers now officially out of their jurisdictions - nothing more than tourists.

Upon crossing the state line, Sam insisted they both wrap their cell phones in tin foil. After a few rounds of relentless teasing, the ranger finally conceded it was a good idea. Many models had non-removable batteries, and both had witnessed the FBI inexplicably acquire some amazing evidence on past cases.

"You think this is all Perkins's doing; don't you Zach?"

"Yes, he's the only person I know that has access, means, and motive."

"What motive?"

"He has got to somehow be connected to Aaron Miller. He was involved in Abe Hendricks's assassination. You said yourself that afterwards, he got a promotion, and poof, he was gone."

Sam grunted, "That's not motive; that's pure speculation. Besides, I knew Sal pretty well, and he always seemed like a straight shooter - probably too much so for his own good. My money is on the NOPD guys that were involved in the Hendricks incident. They're still trying to cover their asses."

The Texan shook his head, "I was headed that way, but that scenario doesn't logic check. How would they have known I was going to be in Washington? It's Perkins, has to be. He's the only guy with enough resources to assign that much manpower, and he would be able to process fingerprints."

They continued driving toward the coordinates displayed on the pickup's GPS system, Sam cross-referencing satellite maps printed from the Internet. "From what I can tell, the first stop is a roadside picnic area, just on the edge of the bayou. We can count on them having eyes on that area, just to make sure you come alone."

"I'll stop about 10 miles away... that should be far enough. You can hop in the back and hide until we know what the next play is. I hope you're not claustrophobic."

The detective half turned, glancing out the back window of the truck. A hard top, lifted via hydraulic struts, enclosed the pickup's bed. "It's called a Tonneau cover," he'd informed her earlier.

"As long as it's not airtight back there, I'll be fine."

The rest of the drive passed in silence, each law officer using the time to prepare mentally. Zach, as promised, pulled to the side of the road 10 miles away from the picnic area. "You don't have any cameras in the bed do you?" Sam asked, gathering her things to transfer to the back.

Zach laughed, "No. Why?"

"Because I'm going to change while I'm back there, and I don't want any video showing up on the Internet. I'm just not that type of girl," she teased.

It was a well-timed joke, serving to break some of the stress that was already building.

"If such a video were ever to come into my possession, you have my word as a Texas Ranger that I wouldn't post it on the Internet," he grinned.

"You pervert," she chuckled. "You'd keep it for yourself!"

And with that, she was out of the truck, lifting the cover and disappearing into the bed.

Zach approached the roadside picnic area slowly, letting his headlights do their work. The crawling speed also allowed him to scan the surrounding countryside with his night vision, but he could detect nothing.

The headlights illuminated the shiny frame of a cell phone, the unit left resting on top of one of the picnic tables. It was ringing before he exited the cab.

"Yeah," Zach answered.

"Open up all four doors on your truck and move away," came a robotic sounding voice.

Zach did as instructed, unable to resist scanning the area for the spotter as he moved to the back of the truck, sure Sam would be able to hear his voice. While he couldn't see anyone, it wasn't hard to imagine someone with a powerful pair of binoculars checking to make sure he hadn't stuffed a SWAT team in his backseat.

"You're a smart man," sounded the voice, obviously pleased to see the truck was empty. "Get back in and drive two more miles east. You'll spot a farm lane on the right. Turn in. We'll let the girl drive your truck out after we have you and the documents."

"Okay, a farm lane two miles to the east. I pull in, and you'll release the girl." Zach repeated for Sam's sake. The call was terminated.

Climbing in behind the wheel, Zach waited until he was back on the main road and then yelled to the back. "Ready?"

"Ready," the voice behind him responded.

Zach found the lane, cautiously turning in. He saw the reflection of several vehicles parked 50 yards away, two men with rifles standing on each side of a tall woman. The prisoner was Cheyenne.

He stopped the truck and dowsed the lights. Reaching for the folder of papers next to him on the console, he opened the door and stepped out into the humid Louisiana night.

He sauntered thirty feet toward the gathered kidnappers and stopped, holding up a folder in the bright moonlight. "What now?"

"Bring it over here," commanded a distant voice.

"Let the girl go. I'll meet her in the middle. I need to make sure it's her," the Texan answered.

Two of the vehicles facing the ranger turned on their headlights, the sudden glare temporarily blinding Zach. Squinting and partially turning away, he could identify movement ahead of the bright beams – the motion of someone walking toward him.

"Zach?" shrieked Cheyenne's voice. "Zach, is that you?"

"Yes. Keep on walking and get ready to drive the truck."

Her eyes were wide with fear as she drew closer, flashing an expression of relief and puzzlement as she passed.

Zach continued his steady march toward the kidnappers, holding the folder of documents. He managed another dozen steps when a shout issued another command. "That's far enough, Ranger," boomed a somewhat familiar voice. "Take off your jacket and show us you're not armed."

"Major?" Zach questioned, halting in the middle of the lane. "Major Alcorn? What the fuck are you doing out here, sir?"

The low chuckle that followed sent chills up Zach's spine. "Oh come on, Zach. I thought you would have put the pieces together by now. Who do you think killed Abe Hendricks? Think about when I walked up on you and that FBI puke having a free for all. You never even noticed the rifle I was holding, did you?"

Zach had relived that moment a hundred times. He searched his memory, trying to retrieve the image, but couldn't. "No, sir, I didn't. But I still don't understand..."

"You're about the luckiest son of a bitch I've ever seen, Bass. After you avoided Buffalo at the junkyard and my friends in Washington, I had to up my game. Those documents are never going to see the light of day. I just can't have that."

"I still don't get it, Major."

Again, a low, evil sneer echoed through the lane. "Zachariah Bass, you know you never spent much time at the head of the class. No matter – I'm done talking."

Zach heard the sound of a shotgun's pump chambering a round.

"Run, Zach!" screamed Sam's voice from the woods, followed instantly by the sound of a heavy object hitting the ground and rolling across the gravel.

Zach spun away, shielding his eyes as the flash-bang grenade exploded.

Despite his standing more than 20 yards from the detonation, the ranger was briefly stunned by the blast. Six million candelas of white light combined with 180 decibels of thunder split the air, enough released energy to temporarily scramble the brain of anyone nearby.

Zach was darting for the truck as best he could, his gait wobbly and unsure due to the jumbled fluid between his ears. The Texas Ranger sensed, more than saw Sam scurrying slightly ahead of him in the same direction after tossing the device.

"Go! Go! Go!" the two officers screamed at a still-bewildered Cheyenne. Sam reached the truck just then, hopping into the passenger side, front seat, slamming the door behind her. The movement of the truck provided just the catalyst the traumatized Cheyenne needed to snap her out of her daze. She jerked the truck into drive, the pickup's back wheels beginning to throw dirt just as Zach dove over the tailgate and through the narrow opening into the bed.

The ranger was tossed from side to side as Cheyenne fishtailed back onto the blacktop road, the sound of the squealing rubber and a racing engine making it clear that a high-speed getaway was in progress.

Jolted by the less-than cushy ride over the rear suspension, Zach managed to right himself and regroup, wondering how long it would be before Sam instructed his ex-girlfriend to stop and let him out of the back.

After a few minutes of obviously traveling at extremely high speeds, Zach began to worry. *Why weren't they stopping?* A distant popping noise, followed by the loud thwack of a bullet hitting the tailgate solved the mystery. Someone was shooting at them.

Zach pushed up the bed's cover with his head, the sound of rushing wind filling the confined space. Peering through the narrow opening, he immediately understood why Cheyenne hadn't let off the gas. There was a car just a short distance behind them, at least one more beyond that.

Two more bullets tore into the bed of the truck just as Zach spied the muzzle flashes and outline of a man firing from the pursuing car's passenger window.

Ducking back down, he reached for his .45, but then realized he'd left it in the cab. A few seconds later, his hand brushed against the rifle case.

Zach smiled, unzipping the AR15. With the kidnapper's urgent demand, there hadn't been time to return the carbine to his safe. For once, the combination of a hectic schedule, the firearm's qualification requirement, and his absentmindedness had paid off.

There were several full magazines in the case's side compartment. Slamming one into the rifle, he released the bolt and turned on the holographic sight. "I've got a very unpleasant surprise for you, traitor," he hissed.

Using his head to lift the cover just enough for the rifle's barrel to clear, Zach tried to center the red dot on the windshield of the pursuing sedan. The moving truck and bumpy road made holding his aim impossible, but the lawman didn't think pinpoint accuracy would be a critical consideration.

Flicking off the safety, he began squeezing the trigger.

Zach jumped at the report of his first shot, the confined space and metal walls of the pickup's bed amplifying the small carbine sound like a howitzer. He recovered quickly, the realization that being deaf and alive was better than the alternative.

He began firing again, unsure where his shots were impacting, but pouring round after round into the space between the chase car's headlights.

The driver's first reaction was to brake, but it didn't do him any good. Zach held his fire when the car swerved left, and then hard right into a field bordering the road. The change in direction was too fast, the momentum too great for the pursuer. The ranger smiled when he saw the vehicle's lights begin somersaulting across the crops.

Evidently, the driver of the second car didn't understand what had just happened to his mate. Now finding himself directly behind the prey, he accelerated to move up and continue the fight.

Zach's rifle began spitting high-velocity lead into the newcomer, just as Cheyenne drove over an extremely rough stretch of road. Cursing the Louisiana highway department for the lack of maintenance, the Texan tried his best to hit the pursuer, but doubted he'd done much damage.

The rough road and missed shots evidently prompted the chase car to realize what had happened to its friend. Zach was disappointed when his target slowed considerably, drifting back to a safer distance.

Deciding he was wasting ammo, Zach stopped firing, watching the headlights and contemplating what Major Alcorn would try next.

As they sped along with the pursuing car keeping its distance, Zach had the time to evaluate the situation tactically. He knew the trio had a couple of distinct things working in its favor. The first was his truck's size, its clearance, horsepower, and 4-wheel drive giving them an advantage off-road.

The second was that Sam's presence had surprised the kidnappers. The adductors had to be asking themselves where the detective had come from, and how many more helpers Zach had waiting in the shadows. A small thing, but helpful nonetheless.

His thought process was interrupted by the slowing of the truck. Zach's heart raced for a moment, thinking a stray bullet had damaged the engine or hit a tire. He readied to start blasting away at the distant headlights, but then felt the pickup sway as Cheyenne negotiated a curve.

He watched the lights following them blink and flutter, evidence of trees and other undergrowth hindering his line of sight now that the road wasn't perfectly straight. At one point, they completely disappeared for a few seconds.

Zach also noted there were still two cars in pursuit.

Sam's voice sounded over the wind, "You okay back there, Ranger?"

"Yeah, I'm fine. What's the plan?" Zach shouted back.

"We were hoping you had one," the detective responded.

"Keep heading toward Texas," he replied. "We need to take them off-road. We'll have the advantage then."

"Gotcha."

A few moments later, the truck slowed even further. "There's a little town up here," Sam yelled back.

Zach wanted Cheyenne out of danger. The girl was an innocent, and the chances of a stray bullet or a collision were increasing with every passing mile. An idea popped into his head.

"Let me out," he called, stuffing his pockets with spare magazines and a bottle of water. "You guys bust it for the border, and I'll hold them off. I'll make my way home somehow."

"Bullshit!" Sam yelled back. "I'm staying with you."

"No, you have to get Cheyenne back on our home turf. Once you're in Texas, you can protect her and send reinforcements if needed. Now stop this damn truck, and let me out."

For a moment, Zach didn't think the two women in the cab were going to do as he wished. He could see a scattering of houses, a church, and other signs of civilization passing by. Just as he was preparing to launch into an angry tirade, he felt the truck braking hard.

The ranger was hopping out of the back before the pickup reached a complete stop. He hit the pavement and instantly made a run for what appeared to be a closed gas station. At the early hour, no one had been privy to his exit.

Alcorn's posse wasn't that far behind, entering the town just as his pickup barked the tires, accelerating away in a blue cloud of burning rubber and dust.

Zach centered the rifle's red dot on the approaching car and then adjusted the shot according to his estimate for a reasonable lead. He started squeezing the trigger.

Nothing happened for the first few shots. Just when he thought his bullets had completely missed the racing car, the vehicle swerved sharply, scraping one of the town's utility poles along the passenger side. Zach rapid fired at that first car, his barrel tracing as the vehicle drew abreast and following with shot after shot as it zoomed by.

The second pursuer stopped well short of Zach's position, distant dome lights announcing that at least one person was exiting the vehicle.

Now with foes at two angles off his position, Zach decided to buy the girls some time, fading back into the shadows and sneaking into the town. With any luck, the gunfire would motivate the local residents to call the Louisiana authorities. He was pretty sure Alcorn and his henchmen wouldn't want to deal with the cops.

Zach moved down what could only be described as a typical, small town residential street, keeping away from the pools of illumination generated by the corner streetlights.

Dogs were barking all over town, a few windows glowing bright as the sleepy citizens tried to figure out what was going on.

The ranger kept moving, knowing time was on his side. A little less than 10 minutes passed before he heard the first siren, wailing its announcement in the distance. It soon had company.

"Heh, heh. That would be the calvary. Alcorn and his fellow criminals will bug out now," the Texan whispered to himself. "They won't want to explain what's going on to the locals."

He identified a good hiding spot, a small, dark grassy gap between two garages. *The perfect vantage, but thank gawd I won't have to be here long,* he mused. Putrid-smelling trashcans lined one exterior wall, offering excellent cover, and there didn't appear to be canines living on this block. One of the two houses attached to the garage hide was for sale and seemed to be vacant.

Ducking down behind the cans, Zach waited, heeding the symphony of sirens streaming his way. "I'd give anything to see Alcorn's face," he whispered.

The first patrol car rolled slowly down the street a few minutes later, its blue lights flashing, the driver-controlled spotlight searching yards and alleys. Zach considered surrendering, but decided to wait it out a little longer before making a move. Alcorn was one of the smartest men he'd worked with, and there was no telling what that crafty son-of-a-bitch would come up with.

Zach stayed put, seeing no reason to expose himself via any sort of movement. He had an excellent tactical position, good egress, and was within 100 yards of deep woods should he be discovered. He knew that most criminals gave themselves away by moving. He'd seen it a dozen times, the mere passing of a police car flushing out a fugitive like a bird dog scattering quail on the prairie. It didn't matter if it were a city street or the West Texas desert, criminals evidently became nervous, scared, or impatient and would flee a perfectly good hiding spot. He wasn't going to be so stupid.

One of the orbiting squad cars stopped directly in front of the Texan's refuge, the deputy inside patrolling with his windows down. Zach could hear the car's radio blaring through the opening.

The cruiser's headlight illuminated the base of a massive oak ahead, the driver mesmerized by the movement of what appeared to be an errant armadillo. Zach's jaw dropped when he recognized Major Alcorn's voice boom over the car's radio, "The suspect is wearing blue jeans, a white dress shirt and possibly a western hat and boots. He is well over six feet in height with a muscular build and closely cropped hair. He is armed with a shoulder-fired weapon and handgun. He may attempt to identify himself as a law enforcement officer. We have reports that he has even flashed a counterfeit badge. He is extremely dangerous."

Shit! Zach thought. *Alcorn's got the locals bamboozled.*

The ranger's frustration escalated quickly... and not only regarding his current situation. If Alcorn had alerted the entire state of Louisiana to his false report, Sam and Cheyenne's chances of getting home had just plummeted as well.

The deputy continued rolling through the subdivision, evidently satisfied that the local wildlife that had drawn his attention wasn't his fugitive.

A few minutes later, Zach's situation degraded even further. One block from his position, he watched another cruiser pass under the streetlight, the words, "K-9 UNIT" boldly stenciled on the side of the passing vehicle. "Not good," the Texan whispered, realizing the town wasn't big enough to hide him from dogs, at least not for long.

For a bit, he considered retreating into the nearby woods, but that plan couldn't stand up to the ranger's scrutiny. He had no idea how deep, wide, or long the patch of foliage grew. For all he knew, there could be a bayou or state police post just on the other side of the tree line.

After verifying there weren't any cops nearby, Zach slipped to the rear of the closest garage, staying low between the buildings. He almost tripped over the old push mower, the abandoned unit completely hidden by the darkness and knee-high weeds. He knew he needed transportation to stay ahead of the authorities. Carjacking sounded like his best option.

After momentarily cursing the old relic under his breath, an idea popped into his head. Slinging his carbine, Zach felt around for the tool's handle, soon verifying that all four wheels were still intact. The simple machine moved easily.

He reached into the trashcan, pulling out a white bag of garbage. The refuse rested securely on top of the antiquated mower's engine. Zach secured the handle upright using the trash bag's ties.

Next was the tricky part. With his new yard tool in tow, Zach returned to his vantage point, trying to decipher the grid being used by the patrolling cops. He was halfway up a small hill, the slope steep enough for the mower to roll a considerable distance unencumbered.

When the road cleared of traffic, Zach crept to the middle of the street, pulling his makeshift diversion along behind him. Again, the area in front of his trashcan outpost brightened, the headlights of an approaching police car divulging its position. Zach estimated there were at least six units patrolling the small community, probably more on the way. He waited until the cruiser was just in the right location, aligned the mower as best he could, and gave it a good shove.

The machine hadn't moved ten feet before Zach was diving back into his hiding spot.

He watched the little contraption rumble down the street, the white bag giving it a ghost-like appearance as it passed through the shadow of the streetlights. The cop saw it, too.

The deputy raced forward half a block and then stopped his car, exiting at the same time as drawing his weapon. The lawnmower had disappeared into a dark, shady yard, ramming into a thick line of landscaping bushes and vanishing from the lawman's sight. Approaching with his gun drawn at the same time as radioing for backup, the deputy never saw Zach sneaking up behind him.

For just a microsecond, the ranger deliberated the value of introducing the lawman's head to the butt of his rifle, but that course was dangerous. The local cop had no idea he was working for the wrong side, and it was extremely difficult to knock a man cold without causing long-lasting damage.

Zach chose a slightly different route, pressing the cold, steel barrel of his rifle against the deputy's ear.

Normal human reaction was to the turn. Zach was ready, poking the lawman forward and off balance. "Don't," Zach hissed. "Drop the sidearm."

The cop hesitated, at which point Zach's boot struck out, impacting his captive in the back of the knee. The joint buckled, and the man went down with a groan. A half-second later, the ranger wrestled the pistol from the grip of the aching cop.

Next, Zach pulled the mobile radio's plug from the battery pack on the officer's belt, yanking the microphone from his shirt and pocketing the critical electronics. The patrolman's Taser was next, Zach promptly pointing the disabling device at his captive's leg and engaging the trigger.

Before the unfortunate deputy had even stopped vibrating from the current, Zach was sprinting back to the idling squad car. The ranger was behind the wheel and rolling away a moment later.

Zach estimated he only had a few minutes before the deputy recovered. Maybe a couple more before the officer flagged down one of his comrades. "Give me four minutes," he whispered. "That's a four-mile head start. That's all I need."

Zach's instincts screamed for him to floor the cruiser and escape, but instead he advanced slowly toward the center of town, acting as if he were just another officer joining the hunt for the bad guy.

Two minutes had passed before he was on the edge of civilization, his boot pushing the gas pedal to the floor. Zach turned off the strobe lights, sure that any other responding units would wonder why his car was traveling away from the scene.

He was going over 100 mph at the four-minute mark, listening intently to the police radio for the announcement of his hijacking.

It was actually seven minutes before the near-panicked voice blared over the frequency, informing all responding lawmen that car number 115-8 now contained the fugitive. By then, Zach was looking for a side road that headed west and back to Texas.

The ranger knew all modern police cruisers were equipped with GPS tracking devices. It would take only few minutes more before the right people, with the correct passwords, could assemble at a computer console and begin vectoring the pursuit onto his stolen unit.

He spotted a country road heading in a westerly direction. Riddled with potholes, it was barely wide enough to accommodate the car, small limbs and weeds grabbing at the vehicle's exterior as it raced by. About three years past the point where the gravel should have been topped off, a fine cloud of sediment chased him as he bounced along, but it was the best option available. "I'll give it five minutes," he speculated to the empty cruiser. "After that, I'm on foot and praying Texas isn't too far away."

He couldn't speed as fast on this surface as the blacktop, the washboards and sparse stone layer limiting his pace. At four minutes, he spied a farmhouse and considered stealing another ride. He passed on by instead.

At five minutes, he slammed on the brakes, sliding to a halt alongside what appeared to be a thick wood. Zach popped the hood and trunk, quickly disconnecting the cables from both the primary and backup batteries. He wasn't for sure if that would kill the GPS or not.

The pine forest he entered was difficult walking, every low-hanging branch and vine slapping his face or tangling his feet. He kept pushing, knowing distance was his opportunity for salvation.

He encountered the game trail less than 400 yards into the undergrowth, the general westerly direction servicing his needs. Initiating a slow jog, the ranger metered his stride, conserving his energy. He estimated it was just over 10 miles to the Texas border.

Relief recharged Zach's spirit when he spied the power lines. The utility company had cut a swath through the underbrush and trees, the high-tension towers most likely heading to Beaumont, perhaps Houston. Zach increased his step, scanning his surroundings constantly, hustling for five minutes, hiking for five while he scoured for pursuit.

He happened upon the roadway, not sure if he had crossed the border or not. His feet were aching, legs tired, and throat dry. He decided to risk using the pavement, the early hour unlikely to produce any traffic.

The deputy was sitting just over a short rise, his car idling at an intersection as if he lay in wait of the inevitable speeder to blast past his position. Zach ventured close enough to identify the emblem on the side of the cruiser, recognizing the name of the county as belonging to the Lone Star State. "Home, sweet home," he whispered.

Zach observed the unmoving patrol car for several minutes, finally determining the deputy inside was taking a nap. *Slow night*, Zach mused. *I'll fix that.*

Reaching in his pocket, Zach pulled out his cell phone and unwrapped the tin foil. Despite his exhaustion, he had to smile at Detective Temple's antics. He found the number in his contacts, noting the 4 AM time and shaking his head at the need to make the call. He'd never dialed this number before.

The phone rang four times before the voicemail kicked in. Displeased, but not discouraged, Zach didn't leave a message, but disconnected and then immediately redialed. A drowsy, male voice answered the second attempt. "This is Colonel Bowmark."

"Colonel, this is Ranger Zachariah Bass, Company E. I have an emergency, sir, a situation that requires your personal attention."

"Why are you calling me instead of your commanding major, Ranger?" growled the man who controlled the oldest state law enforcement body in the United States.

"Sir, my major *is* the emergency. The man has turned, sir. Gone rogue, and I can prove it."

Zach's accusation was unheard of in ranger tradition and lore. Not since the 1800's had one of their own gone off the reservation.

"Son, you better have your shit in one single, neatly-packed bag before making that allegation. Do I make myself clear?"

"Sir, I have multiple, direct witnesses that will testify Major Alcorn has been involved in extortion and kidnapping. Furthermore, he is the prime suspect in at least one murder."

"And why are *you* making this *my* business at 4 AM, Ranger?"

"Because Major Alcorn is trying to kill me, sir. I need help getting in and didn't know who else to call."

"Where are you?" the colonel asked.

Zach watched the nearby deputy flash his headlights once, then a second time. Returning the cell phone to his ear, Zach said, "Thanks, Sheriff. Please make sure your man knows I'm walking in from the east."

Despite the colonel's attentions, it had taken almost an hour to roust the local sheriff, another 15 minutes before a radio dispatcher contacted the deputy Zach had been watching.

Strolling up to the patrol car, Zach nodded to the young officer behind the wheel and flashed his badge. *Sorry to interrupt your nap, buddy*, Zach mused.

"Have you heard anything about HPD Detective Temple?" Zach asked as he opened the passenger door, the dome light illuminating the cruiser's interior. The ranger couldn't help but notice the fellow sitting behind the wheel seemed barely old enough to shave.

"Yes, sir. She is at the sheriff's department in Orange, Texas. I've been instructed to take you there," replied the nervous rookie. It felt good to sit down, Zach taking the opportunity to lean back and close his eyes for a moment.

No sooner had he gotten comfortable than his cell phone sounded an annoying tone. The caller ID informed him it was Detective Temple.

"Glad you made it," he answered.

"Same back at ya, Ranger. We are safe and sound here, surrounded by adoring men in uniform who seem to be concerned over our every need."

Zach grunted, picturing Samantha Temple and Cheyenne descending upon the remote department in the wee hours. He was sure the few male personnel working the graveyard shift were convinced they'd died and gone to heaven.

Before he could think of a clever retort, Sam continued. "Any word about Alcorn?"

Zach sat upright, the mention of his rogue boss killing any comedic creativity. "No."

"The Louisiana State Police are looking for him. So is half of Texas. The last anyone laid eyes on him was over 20 minutes ago. Better watch your back."

After digesting the news for a bit, Zach nodded his head as if Sam could see his nonverbal response. The adrenaline rush was wearing off, his mind finally processing the irrational data it absorbed in the last few hours. The man he had reported to for years was as dirty as they come. Finally, he responded, "Yeah. Okay, I'll see you in a few minutes."

"You got any idea what you are going to do with those documents?" Sam asked.

"Right now, I need to sleep for about two days. I'll figure it all out after that."

The car slowed for an intersection, the deputy glancing both ways for oncoming traffic. Zach was stuffing his cell phone back in a pocket. The car started to roll.

It seemed like only a fraction of a second before Zach heard the driver's surprised voice, "What the hell...." And then the world exploded.

Zach's entire frame was slammed against the seatbelt, the nylon material cutting into his flesh like a dozen sharp blades. Before his body could react, the ranger's skull smashed into the window, white lines of agony pulsating through his jarred brain.

His vision returned a few moments later, the interior of the police car bathed with brilliant white light. Dazed and disoriented, Zach's head throbbed with even more vigor as he attempted to get a look at what had just happened.

For a moment, the ranger thought he was awaiting admittance at the pearly gates. Fluffy shadows and billowing silhouettes surrounded him. Those, combined with the ultra-bright light, reminded Zach of Bible school images of heaven. The pain surging through his body quickly dispelled that notion, immediately followed by the realization that the pillow-clouds were airbags, and the heavenly illumination was generated by the vehicle that had just rammed their car.

Alcorn!

Zach managed the door handle, rolling out of the undamaged passenger side of the cruiser. Barely overriding the ringing in his ears, he recognized what sounded like distant popping noises. The door glass erupted in a blizzard-like shower, the fragments reminiscent of a snowfall blurring the headlights as bullets tore through the patrol car. The ranger kept moving, his tortured intellect screaming commands to his body to move away from the incoming fire.

The soft, fresh grass of the roadside ditch soon replaced the hard, hot pavement. Zach stayed low, coaching his numb right arm to draw his weapon. The limb wouldn't respond.

It took superhuman effort to reach his .45 with his left hand. At the same moment that he finally managed to pull the weapon, he spotted the profile of someone moving by the T-boned sheriff's car. He recognized Alcorn's outline, the major creeping cautiously around the wreck, his pistol directed at the passenger compartment.

Zach chanced movement. He had to chamber a round into his pistol and was unable to use his free hand. For a split-second, the ranger's mind returned to his training, the instructors compelling the recruits to practice charging their weapons with only one working limb.

Rolling onto his back, Zach pinched the .45's slide between his boots and pushed, the pistol's action doing its job and loading the first round into the chamber. Alcorn saw it, too.

Both men fired at the same moment, both working their trigger fingers over and over. The firefight's thunder rolled through the pines, flashes of muzzle-lightning shattering the rural Texas night.

And then it was quiet.

Zach's automatic locked back empty, the eight rounds in his magazine expended in less than two seconds. His first thought was to reload, but that reaction was quickly overridden by the hot streaks of burning fire that seemed to be consuming his right shoulder.

Dropping the useless firearm, Zach reached with his good hand to soothe the agony. Warm, sticky thickness of blood oozed through his fingers. His blood. He was hit.

It required every bit of willpower to scramble to his feet. He had to get away – Alcorn would be coming. Straining against the protests of agony blaring from every nerve in his body, Zach started to stumble away. He glanced up, expecting to gaze into the muzzle of Alcorn's weapon pointed at his temple, but the major wasn't there.

Zach's head needed to clear before he spied the body lying beside the wrecked police car, the prone outline backlit by the still shining headlights. It wasn't moving.

Zach limped over, his worthless right arm making the short trip difficult and unbalanced. Alcorn moaned as his subordinate approached, as much from the dreaded anticipation of verbal confrontation as physical misery.

There was a crimson hole in the major's chest, another in his stomach. Zach knew the man at his feet claimed no hope of survival. The senior officer's eyes were open but unfocused, his chest heaving to draw in air.

Zach kicked away the empty pistol lying next to the immobile man.

The movement prompted Alcorn's attention, his stare boring into his adversary's face. "I guess I fucked this up royally," the dying man gasped.

"Why, Major? I just have to know why," Zach demanded, the question burning through his mind since he realized who had kidnapped Cheyenne.

Alcorn actually smiled, then his frame racked with a deep spasm of coughing. The red spots on his torso seemed to grow larger. "My first leave as a ranger... New Orleans... the French Quarter. There was a girl, Zach. A beautiful woman. I didn't know until a year later that I had a son."

Zach didn't understand. "Sir?"

"I couldn't do right by her. The department was so tight-assed about that sort of thing back then, and she didn't want to marry anyway. I had to watch him grow up from afar. I sent money... ran interference when I could."

The major paused, a painful hack so strong his whole body seemed to convulse. Zach took a knee, watching the dying man gather himself to finish his confession.

"He did well, Zach. I helped now and then... but he did it mostly on his own, despite not having a father around," the senior officer explained, his eyes searching for some sign of compassion from his charge. "You see, he always hated me... always thought I was some sort of Neanderthal completely out of place in his modern world. Now, I fear he was right. I've destroyed everything for him. I ruined it all."

"How so, Major?"

"You are going to release those documents, Zach. I know you are. They will ruin my son's life. I'd ask you not to, but I know you will."

Zach shook his head, still trying to clear the brain fog. "I don't understand, sir. I'm sorry, but I still don't get it."

The major hacked again, a thin line of spittle and blood now running down the man's cheek. "Aaron Miller... the president's chief of staff... is my son."

Zach was stunned. Despite the exhaustion and wound, his commander's statement sent the ranger's mind on a quest to fill in the missing pieces of the puzzle.

"The cartel money... in the NY Jets gym bag... the girl?"

"I kept that money for a rainy day," Alcorn coughed. "When Hendricks went nuts, I was desperate to get those sealed records to protect Aaron. I could just see some reporter getting a tip and making the connection that tied it all together," he explained, pausing to catch his breath and gather his thoughts. "I hired a con I knew to bribe the clerk in Baton Rouge and end this, but he fucked it up...."

He paused momentarily, deliberating whether his intense need for absolution outweighed his hedonistic desire to avoid facing how he screwed up so many lives. Realizing that he was at the confessional point of no return, he continued. "...Figured with that quick trigger finger of yours, you'd kill him... wrap up the loose ends. That's why I assigned that case to you."

Zach felt ignorant, like a puppet who just discovered he had strings. "When I brought Hendricks out, you couldn't let him talk. He'd expose your son."

Alcorn barely nodded. "I was there just to make sure the FBI teams didn't take him alive. I heard over the radio that you were going in. So I separated myself from the group of rangers I'd brought with me. I wandered off in the woods to take a piss and found a good place to take the shot."

Zach could connect the dots from there. Kara Hendricks's call and the documents in the lockbox had re-exposed the major's son.

As the young ranger's supervisor, Alcorn was uniquely positioned to know the inner workings of Zach's life – both professional and personal. No doubt the major had put Zach under surveillance, probably from the moment he'd left the bank branch. *Those papers were the key,* Zach realized, his neurons firing in rapid succession, assimilating his newfound information with the events of the past. Ross Garcia had died, not because of the damage he could do to Heidi Clifton, but due to the threat the court documents posed to Aaron Miller.

Zach's mind was compiling the facts far too quickly to acknowledge Alcorn's remark. The ranger suddenly stiffened, the dawning horror of his boss's level of corruption becoming subjective again. "You are the one who called Buffalo and warned him we were coming. I was supposed to have been the first one through that door," he muttered.

The major nodded, "You were damned lucky. Too lucky. I was running out of time and getting desperate. Taking your girl was the only way I knew for sure to get to you."

Zach's deepening scowl exposed his growing anger. Data assimilation and somewhat objective interpretation of events had begun to yield to a flurry of emotion. The man who he thought embraced and embodied the legacy of the Texas Rangers had taken innocent life... had ordered Zach's execution... had kidnapped Cheyenne.... had desecrated not only his pledge to "protect and serve," but also violated any sense of morality he might have ever claimed.

Sputtering again, Alcorn seemed to make one last ditch effort at defending his actions. "I know you don't have any children yet, but you'll understand when you do," he whispered in a voice growing weaker by the second.

Alcorn stopped talking, his chest's heaving struggle now slower, longer gaps between rise and fall. A few cycles later, it stopped.

Zach checked for a pulse, the act more from habit than any hope of the man beside him still having a heartbeat. Alcorn was dead.

For a few moments, the ranger just sat, staring at the man he'd esteemed and trusted for years. The betrayal stung, its ache enhanced even further by the fact that Zach had considered Alcorn a mentor.

He shook it off, the throbbing in his own body shortly overriding his mental torment. He needed help. Soon.

The ranger fought to stand. Reaching through the patrol car's open door, he felt for the deputy's pulse and found none. The odd angle of the man's head was something Zach had seen before. *A broken neck... at least he went quickly*, he mused.

Zach managed the radio's microphone. "This is Ranger Zachariah Bass," he broadcasted. "There's been a collision; shots fired. I need help, officer down. I repeat, officer down."

The dispatcher responded, but Zach couldn't make out the words. His legs wouldn't support weight any longer. Sliding slowly down to the pavement, his back against the cruiser, Zach stared at Alcorn's body, waiting for help to arrive.

Chapter 15 - Birth

Zach couldn't get accustomed to having only one workable limb, a small bead of hospital orange juice dribbling down his chin after his clumsy attempt to drink with the wrong hand. The doctors had predicted it would be another few weeks before he could start therapy on his right arm.

The appearance of two large men entering his room caused fleeting concern, but it passed quickly when he recognized both as fellow rangers. "Ah, how nice of you boys to pay a visit to an injured comrade. Are y'all on the clock?" Zach joked.

One of them smirked, the other shaking his head as they took up positions on either side of the threshold. Governor Simmons entered the room.

"How are you feeling, Ranger Bass?" the state's chief executive asked with a smile.

Before Zach could respond, Detective Temple joined the gathering.

"I'm recovering, sir," Zach answered, completely astonished by the politician's appearance. "I hope to return to duty soon."

Simmons waved off the statement. "There'll be plenty of time for that, son. Do you feel up to having a quick discussion?"

Perplexed, Zach glanced at Sam. Her soft smile and reassuring nod set the ranger at ease. "Of course, sir. How can I be of service?"

Simmons peered over his shoulder at the two bodyguards, a nod from his head sending both men out of the room. The door closed behind them.

"Go ahead, Detective, feel free to bring our wounded warrior up to speed," Simmons directed, moving to take a chair.

Sam moved to Zach's bedside. "While you've been in here slacking off, I've been working to fill in the gaps of Major Alcorn's story. With the pending secession referendum and highly charged political atmosphere, Governor Simmons requested that I handle the situation confidentially."

Zach acknowledged her words, signaling her to continue.

"Two of the men with Alcorn the night of the kidnapping survived. They're singing like birds in my lockup. They were cartel enforcers who owed the good major a favor."

"He dirtied his hands with the cartel, too?" Zach asked.

"Not until they tried to kill him. Alcorn was hurting the boys down in Mexico. They put out a contract on his life. You bumbled into the middle of it a long time ago."

Zach nodded, remembering the NY Jets gym bag.

"As far as we can tell, the major didn't completely cross over to the dark side until Abe Hendricks took a shot at Clifton's plane. Reading between the lines, Alcorn was driven to protect his son's political career regardless of cost. When it looked like Aaron Miller would be tied to Hendricks, I believe your boss lost touch with reality. He cut a deal with the Mexicans, exchanging who knows what for some of their muscle. That's who tried to kill you in Washington. That's who helped with the kidnapping.

It's pretty clear he was suffering from some deep-seated guilt complex over not being a good father."

Shaking his head, Zach kept the story going. "When it looked like his son was going to become one of the most powerful people in the world, the Major starting pulling out all the stops to make that happen. He hired that pervert in Houston to acquire the original court papers in Louisiana."

"And then Kara Hendricks found the lockbox key," Sam finished. "He knew you had copies of those documents and probably had a good idea what you were going to do with them. When he verified the journalist only had a recently-made copy, he had to come after you."

"He tried to kill me twice, and when that didn't work, he went after Cheyenne," Zach finished.

Simmons interjected, "But as far as we know, Aaron Miller was completely unaware of his father's activities. There's no evidence to indicate his involvement."

The ranger didn't buy that, but the governor's statement didn't leave much room for debate. "I know you didn't come all the way over here to fill me in, Governor. I have a feeling there's more," Zach said.

Flashing his now nationally recognized smile, Simmons responded, "Detective Temple has convinced me that you still hold these incriminating documents. I came to discuss your intentions going forward."

With a suspicious tone, Zach urged, "Go on."

"What you do with those papers is up to you," Simmons began. "But I would like to ask personally that you not drag the Texas Rangers into what is sure to be a firestorm of outrage. Major Alcorn was wrong, and the organization should have caught on long ago. I'll give you my word that I'll take steps to make sure something like this never happens again. But, our people are going to need the rangers, Zach. If we do secede, they'll need to have faith in an honorable organization. I only ask that you keep that in mind, whatever you choose to do."

Zach merely nodded, not quite sure what to say. With the purpose of his visit over, the governor glanced at his watch and announced, "I've got to be going, Ranger Bass. Good luck and heal quickly. I'll leave you two officers to talk things over."

And with that, Simmons was gone.

Zach remained silent, staring out the window to avoid Sam's inquisitive stare. Memories of Alcorn's speech about the importance of the rangers' community floated through his mind.

"The triangle of survival," he whispered, flashing Sam a knowing smile.

Two days later, one of the most important headlines in the country's history appeared across the *New York Times*.

"White House's Miller in Cover-up," ran the Grey Lady, complete with two columns on the front page and three supporting back-stories.

At first, President Clifton merely shrugged, her breakfast barely disturbed by the breaking news. As the day wore on, she began to reconsider.

Like starving dogs, the media sunk its teeth into the story and wouldn't let go. Every cable network played, what in Heidi's view was a molehill, into an Everest of dishonesty, flagrant disregard for the Second Amendment, and salacious political scandal.

Aaron appeared in front of her desk, head tilted forward as if he were a scolded child. "I want to offer my resignation," the chief of staff said. "I'm sorry I've brought this scandal down on your administration."

"What the hell are you talking about, Aaron?" Heidi replied, clearly upset by his attitude. "This is just politics as usual."

But Aaron wasn't reassured. "Ma'am, the right has latched onto this, and they're not going to let go. My actions almost 12 years ago are fueling their political fire, and the fact that I am your advisor is just like pouring gasoline on the blaze. Any nut case decrying the overreach of the federal government now has evidence to back his claims. The NRA is going crazy, ginning up their membership with the battle cry, 'The government will seize your firearms – just look at who's running the White House.'"

Heidi waved off his little speech, "Like everything else in this town, this will die down and go away. You and the people down in New Orleans were doing the best you could under impossible circumstances. I would have probably done the same thing in your shoes. The fact that the Republicans don't like it means nothing. You're overacting."

"No offense, ma'am, but I would advise you not to underestimate this situation. Even before this news broke, the events after Katrina were the most effective drivers of fear mongering in our history. Even more importantly, today's headlines are influencing the Texas referendum. The polls are showing the secession vote is nearly a dead heat."

The president shook her head, refusing to accept his logic. "Tell you what, Aaron; I'll go on national television and reiterate my position. I'll stand beside you, and let the people know how valuable I consider your advice and how sound I consider your judgment."

"Ma'am, if you do that, you're going to lose Texas."

Heidi took a deep breath, "We're not going to run from this. We're going to turn around and punch it in the nose so it will fade back into the obscure shadows where it belongs."

Her words had the desired effect, Aaron's posture straightening, his poise returned. "Thank you, ma'am. You don't know how much I appreciate your support."

President Clifton took the podium, briefly flashing a smile to the gathered White House press corps. "I have a brief statement," she began, "and then I'll take questions."

With the teleprompter in view, she focused on the point where she knew the cameras' capture would seem she was making eye contact with the people viewing the conference. She began, "My fellow Americans, recently, much attention has been pulled to the actions of my chief of staff, Aaron Miller. I wanted to come before you and the press and clarify my position concerning gun rights and the Second Amendment to our Constitution and reaffirm my staunch backing of Mr. Miller."

"At no time during my campaign or subsequent service as your president, did I detect even the smallest hint that Aaron was anti-Second Amendment. In fact, quite the opposite is true. At every opportunity, I have informed the American people that I believe in individual ownership of firearms, and Aaron shares these strong beliefs. Twelve years ago, this honorable man faced unfathomable circumstances and made a decision based solely on his desire to protect the people of New Orleans. It is a disservice to me - and all of you - for the far right to twist this ancient history into some sort of testament that the federal government is out to disarm the American public. Aaron Miller continues to have my full faith and confidence. I'll take a few questions now."

Heidi gestured to a reporter in the third row. "Madam President, when did you become aware of Mr. Miller's actions in New Orleans?"

"I read the story in the press yesterday morning. That was the first I had heard anything about it."

Again and again, Heidi deftly fielded the anticipated questions, never backing away or giving an inch of ground. Her self-assuredness running high, she pointed to what she was certain would be a hostile question from the *Washington Post*.

"According to the documents published in *The Times*, Mr. Miller was rewarded for what many are calling government intimidation by pursuing the settlement with Mr. Hendricks. Are you saying that you support and agree with the methods invoked by Mr. Miller at that time?"

"No, that's not what I'm saying at all," Heidi shot back. "The officials in New Orleans at that time were facing a disaster of Biblical proportions. For all of us to sit around 12 years later and Monday morning quarterback their decisions isn't productive."

Heidi broke eye contact with the reporter, trying to move on, but he wouldn't let her loose. "A follow-up, ma'am. The actions I was referring to were almost two years after the storm. It appears as if the government was mounting a campaign to downplay the consequences of the gun confiscation and using some heavy-handed tactics to do so. Is it your position that justice was served in Mr. Hendricks's case against the city?"

It was a critical moment, millions of viewers watching their Commander in Chief, and Heidi knew it. If she said no, then there would be calls for investigations that could only lead to strengthen the small-government right wingers. If she said, yes, she would be portrayed as aligned with the anti-gun fanatics on the far left.

In those brief milliseconds, under the pressure of national exposure, Heidi became angry. That one single question from a hostile news outlet served as a fulcrum for the entire debate – an argument that in her mind was outdated and ridiculous.

As the press paused for her response, her outrage mounted. How had this issue gathered so much momentum? What was it that the right didn't understand? What possible justification could reasonable people have for wanting unlimited firepower in their living rooms? Didn't the incident in Houston prove that? What about justice for her dead staffers and all of those law enforcement officers slaughtered by a mentally unstable individual who could legally purchase a weapon of terror?

With a voice dripping with frustration, she finally responded. "Given the man's later actions in Houston, it seems to me that justice was not served. If Aaron Miller is guilty of anything, it is having let Abraham Hendricks walk free."

The turnout was impressive, with 85% of the eligible voters waiting in long lines at Texas schools, courthouses, and municipal buildings. Some precincts were forced to remain open until the wee hours of the morning just to ensure every voter could exercise the right of choice.

The computers then began their work, struggling to tally more ballots than had been cast in the previous two presidential elections combined.

It was 9AM the following morning when the results were called. Fox News was the first to make the announcement. Texas had voted to secede from the United States by a margin of 52 to 48 percent.

All eyes turned to Washington, the president's signature now required to grant the state its independence.

President Clifton sat in the conference room, surrounded by the solemn faces of her cabinet.

"Be careful what you ask for," were her first words after the election results were posted.

Gauging his boss's mood, Aaron spoke up. "There are many experts who believe austerity can be a product of limited size. Without Texas and her conservative leanings, you can proceed with our agenda, ma'am. We can begin invoking an entire series of reforms and improvements for our citizens. My prediction is the new republic will fail, leading to talk of their return to the union within five years, just like the last time this happened."

"So you believe I should ratify the treaty? Is that what I'm hearing?"

"Yes, ma'am. I believe you have to sign it."

Heidi's head snapped up as if she'd been stung. "I don't *have* to sign anything."

Aaron shook his head, "I didn't mean that literally, Madam President. I was only speaking from a political perspective. The conservatives now feel empowered. Many will relocate to Texas; others will sense their side is now vastly outnumbered, and they will seek to compromise. The federal government of the United States can again begin to function and improve the lives of its citizens."

"And if I refuse to ratify the TOS?"

"Then your presidency will end with the next election. You will be attacked without mercy, from all sides, both for going back on your word and wasting all this time," Aaron replied in a low tone. "Be rid of them, ma'am. Accept this event as one of the most opportune in the history of our country. We have eliminated a political segment of the population that no longer shared the same values as the majority of the country, and we will have improved the overall standing of our nation in the process. It is a win-win for all involved. Embrace it. Ride the wave of success and start implementing your objectives and agenda."

Turning to her press secretary, Mrs. Clifton nodded. "In today's press briefing, go ahead and let the media know that I will sign the treaty."

Chapter 16 – Celebrations... Almost

On July 3, the coastal city of Corpus Christi, Texas awoke to an unusual sight. It wasn't uncommon to see hefty ships in the city's namesake bay. After all, the port was one of the busiest in the United States. Nor was it unusual to witness massive hulls plying the dredged channel, since the facility was one of a handful along the Gulf Coast capable of handling Panamax-sized vessels.

What the sleepy-eyed residents weren't accustomed to seeing was a line of warships approaching the city's skyline. A lot of warships.

Stretching into the sun-brightened, eastern horizon, the grey outline of a dozen naval vessels gradually appeared out of the early morning mist. First came the Arleigh Burke-class destroyers, their decks bristling with missile launchers to protect the fleet from airborne threats. Next, sped a larger Ticonderoga class cruiser, its arsenal of Tomahawk cruise missiles making it one of the most powerful offensive weapon systems in the world. And finally, dwarfing all others, streamed the USS Ronald Reagan, a Nimitz-class aircraft carrier.

As long as three football fields and displacing over 100,000 tons, *Gipper* was an ominous, nuclear-fueled symbol of power projection. With an air wing of 88 state-of-the-art warbirds, this single ship boasted more offensive capabilities than the entire air force of many countries.

Fortunately for the citizens of Corpus, the carrier strike group gliding toward their town had no hostile intent. In fact, quite the opposite was true. *Gipper* and her escorts were on their way to a new homeport where they would participate in a ceremony welcoming the fleet to the Republic of Texas. Before the festivities on the 4th of July were concluded, over 40 such ships would lower the U.S. Stars and Stripes and raise the flag of their new nation, an emblem sporting a single, solitary star.

Zach stood on duty at the base of the reviewing stand, a mere six feet in front of Governor Simmons, wishing he could watch the big boats instead of the immediate surroundings. The nautical spectacle might have salvaged the morning.

Not only had the day's ceremonies cut into what was a rare, 3-day weekend for the ranger, the president-in-waiting's itinerary had required leaving Austin no later than 3:30 AM. Way too damn early, even for a country boy.

But today was special, the first, and most visible handover of U.S. military assets to the new republic as part of the Treaty of Secession. Tomorrow, there would be two countries celebrating their independence.

When the official date of the TOS was announced, Zach thought the choice was in bad taste. Many Americans were already stinging mad over the country's split – to make it all official on a national holiday commanding such historical significance was just throwing salt in the wound.

He'd mentioned as much to Major Putnam, his new boss's response being a grunt, joined by sarcasm, "Why Ranger Bass, I'm impressed with your sensitivity toward your fellow man." The derision wasn't lost on Zach.

Besides the lost time off and the early hour, Zach couldn't ignore the hypocrisy of the entire event.

The ranger, having been assigned to the governor's security detail at the time, knew full well that Texas no more coveted an aircraft carrier than it sought a mile-wide sinkhole. While the delegation from Austin had negotiated for a significant number of ships as part of the 9% defense allotment, the defensive specialists could see no reason for the Lone Star republic to require force projection of such magnitude. Many believed that carriers were on their way out, soon to be the dinosaurs of the seas.

After a quick scan of the growing crowd indicated no threat to his protectorate, Zach's eyes then glanced at the USS Lexington, a decommissioned WWII carrier moored nearby and open to the public as a museum. *Maybe they'll dock this one over there beside her*, he mused.

The entire argument, one of the thousands of such disputes between the two parties, had been an interesting dichotomy.

Much of the mainstream media often portrayed the new republic as a future bastion of hawkish, conservative, gun-toting rednecks that would show little mercy for the unfortunate or anybody that disagreed with their philosophy.

One editorial in the *NY Times* even went so far as predicting that Texas would be the first country to use nuclear weapons in the modern era – such was the intolerant nature of her spirit.

Yet, throughout the seemingly endless TOS bartering, the representatives sitting under the Lone Star had shown a pronounced tendency to barter for fewer military assets and more public infrastructure.

"We don't want an aircraft carrier," Zach had heard repeatedly. "We don't need nuclear submarines or stealth bombers. We would prefer more water rights along the Rio Grande, co-occupation at some U.S. embassies overseas, and a higher percentage of existing trade agreements."

For a while, it seemed like the Pentagon was trying to pass off all of the high-dollar, marginally effective weapons programs onto the new government. But the men and women selected by Simmons were four-star generals and senior admirals, professionals who knew the game and wanted to change the rules.

Some of the bitterest haggling had been over the small, insignificant assets. The U.S. delegation had readily sacrificed a full, heavy, armored division, but didn't want to pay more than a dollar per year to acquire a 99-year lease on the Johnson Space Center outside of Houston.

Texas, at one point, had walked out of the talks over Washington's offered address for the new Texas Embassy in the nation's capital, the delegates claiming the new republic was being corralled into an undesirable location.

But they got it done, and the ships now rolling into Corpus Christi Bay were proof of that. Tomorrow, at high noon central standard time, the formal handoff would be finalized. At that same moment, broadcast all over the world, the Stars and Stripes would be lowered for the last time on every military base, federal courthouse, postal delivery building, and U.S. office in the Lone Star State.

Zach wished he could watch, but he would be busy packing up and heading back to Alpine. His tenure as a bodyguard was up, the ranger gladly accepting reassignment to the criminal investigation arm of the Texas Rangers.

David pulled into the club's parking lot, hustling his bag out of the trunk with more urgency than normal. He wanted to get in some distance work on the putting green, but it wasn't looking good. A late start, looming tee time, and busy holiday crowd were all working against him.

Rounding the corner of the locker room, he stopped mid-stride, a manifestation of surprise commanding his usually stoic expression. There wasn't a soul on the first tee or the practice facility. As a matter of fact, there wasn't anyone in sight.

"The course can't be closed today," he mumbled, turning to the main clubhouse. "No way they'd shut it down on a holiday."

His state of isolation ended soon enough. Opening the heavy glass door of the lounge's entrance, he was immediately assaulted by a wave of sound. He strode into a standing room only crowd inside.

He shouldered his way through, more than a little curious about what was going on and searching for familiar faces among the multitude. Within a few steps, it was clear everyone was focused on one of the many flat screen televisions scattered around the facility.

He spotted Andy, Jimmy, and Paul at a table, his friends pointing at the single empty chair. "We've been saving this for you," Paulie greeted.

"Thanks. What's going on?" David asked, taking a seat while still studying the mass.

"Where have you been?" Andy asked across the table. "Today's the transfer of the flag and the signing of the Texas treaty."

Craning his neck to see above the gathered throng, David finally found a clear view. He watched as the U.S. flag was lowered, the scene looking like it was being broadcast from a naval vessel. On the other side of the split screen, the president was signing some sort of heavy-bound document. He recognized the governor of Texas penning an identical copy.

The view of the ship changed, a more distant shot that panned over hundreds of sailors in their bright, white uniforms lining the deck of an aircraft carrier. When the Texas flag began climbing the pole, all of the military personnel saluted crisply.

"That shit just isn't right," someone said forcefully from the bar. "That really pisses me off. I've been taxed to death the last 20 years to pay for that fucking ship, and now Clifton just gives it away like it's last night's leftovers."

The television then changed, displaying an image of a scoreboard-like sign - the national debt clock. On cue, the number declined drastically, taking into account the amount of the obligation now the responsibility of Texas.

"See there," someone answered the big mouth at the bar, "The president didn't give away those ships; she sold them to pay down our debt. Our country is now 1.2 trillion to the better."

"Sold them, my ass," another responded. "Practically gave them away if you ask me."

"Who needs Texas, anyway?" someone else shouted from the crowd. "Good riddance."

A sequence of assorted buildings and other facilities flashed on the screen, the American flag being lowered all around. Some of the video images were clearly courthouses and office buildings, but many were of military installations.

"This is Dyess Air Force base," stated an announcer, "Until a few weeks ago it was the home to one of America's B1-Lancer bomber squadrons. While the Texas Department of Defense won't finalize its deployment strategy for some months, most analysts believe Dyess will become the home of one of the new nation's fighter wings. After the full transfer is complete, Texas will own over 1500 aircraft, including state of the art F-22 Raptors and other stealth planes."

David noted the gathering had grown quiet, the mostly male assembly staring at the images being broadcast all over the world.

"This is Fort Hood in central Texas," came another announcer's voice as a new scene streamed on the displays. "Home to the newly named Texas 7th Calvary, a heavy armored division, complete with hundreds of Abrams M1A2 tanks and Stryker armored vehicles."

Someone at a nearby table broke the room's trance, "I was stationed at Fort Hood," noted the calm voice. "I thought I'd never see the day when an American flag wasn't flying over that base."

On and on the pictures continued, some drawing comments from the subdued mass, others met with melancholy, silent expressions.

"I knew this was going to happen today," Andy said, never taking his eyes off the screen. "But it just seems so... so... so disheartening. I had no idea it would hit me this way."

"It's almost like we lost a war and are surrendering," Jimmy added.

"Nothing's going to change, guys," Paulie announced in a cheerful voice. "Your customers aren't going away; your taxes aren't going to change, and you'll still be paying me money at the end of 18 holes. No big deal."

David evaluated the mood of the room as mixed. About half of the members seemed upset, many lowering their heads and frowning. The other half seemed not to care. He had to admit, the greatest country on earth seemed a little smaller now.

Glancing at his watch, he stated, "We're up in five minutes. Are you guys going to play or sit in here and watch this crap?"

There wasn't an answer at first, another murmur rolling through the gathering and drawing all eyes back to the televisions. A formation of soldiers was now on camera, row after row of men in uniform. After a shouted order, in unison, each man reached to his shoulder and tore away the patch of the American flag. On another command, the Lone Star of Texas replaced the Stars and Stripes.

"I'm playing," Paul said, sliding back his chair. "Texas might decide to invade California next week, so I'd better get in all the golf I can. I'd suck at bull riding."

"Might as well," Andy added. "This is depressing as shit to sit and watch."

Ten minutes later the foursome was rolling down the first fairway.

The End

From *Secession* — Book Two
Anticipated early 2015

The first shot in the tariff wars was fired by the United States.

A huge spike in construction was underway in the Republic, the building-boom initiated by both private and government expansion.

Austin didn't have enough facilities to house its growing bureaucracy, many of the functions previously performed in Washington now required in the Texas capital. There seemed an almost endless list of needs.

The TOS had awarded the new nation eight submarines, but Texas didn't have the dock facilities to maintain her new fleet. The 43 surface ships included in the treaty faced the issue of being homeless as well. From Port Author to Brownsville, massive projects were initiated to correct the situation.

Texas A&M University was chosen to become the new West Point of the South, a logical selection given the Aggies' tradition and history. But there weren't any facilities to house the additional cadets, the already-packed schools barely handling the current student body. The other military academies all faced the same issue.

It seemed like infrastructure was in short supply all over the fledgling country. Austin, already struggling to keep up with the pre-secession population growth, was becoming a nightmare. The city had been experiencing a decade of expansion as a state capital, the roads, sewers, schools, and water supply barely keeping pace with the influx of new residences and businesses. When the role of "national seat of government" was thrust upon the city, the explosion of growth was unlike anything the town's planners had ever anticipated.

Construction cranes rose skyward all across the new country. Massive development projects required steel – a resource that Texas didn't produce in near the quantities she required.

Supply and demand worked their typical magic, and prices soared.

Washington was experiencing the opposite problem – contraction. While the reduction in the national debt and burden on existing infrastructure were ultimately viewed as a positive, the road to achieving efficiency was proving difficult.

Federal employees had been given the option of staying in Texas or transferring to other locations. Reductions to Washington's payroll would be by natural attrition, primarily retirement. Or so was the plan. But that was going to take a while.

President Clifton's treasury was faced with 9.4 percent less tax revenue but only 4% fewer federal employees. Social security and federal pension payments remained at pre-TOS levels, as all of the retirees living in Texas still received their benefits. It was a cash-flow drain that again focused the spotlight on the federal government's siphoning of employee contributions instead of letting those funds grow via earning interest.

"We'll need to raise the federal deficit level in another two months," reported the Treasury Secretary, adding to the bad news.

It was clear from President Clifton's reaction that the news was unwelcome. "I have initiatives that I'm trying to push through Congress. Despite our majorities, the right is still pulling every trick in the book to delay our agenda. This won't bode well in the press."

"The nation's gross domestic product is taking a severe hit right now, Madam President, and it's more than just the missing output from Texas that's causing the downturn. Several major corporations are delaying expansion here in order to beef up their infrastructure there. As an example, the increased price of steel is putting a damper on everything from automobile sales to new construction. As a matter of fact, steel production is one of the few positives in our economic forecast."

Aaron shook his head in disgust, "How wonderful. One of our dirtiest industries is booming. This doesn't fit well with your global warming agenda, ma'am."

Heidi sighed, "The treasury needs revenue. We need to keep the environmental left in our camp. Seems simple enough – put an export tariff on steel."

The Secretary of Commerce, silent until now, cleared his throat. "Ma'am, trade tariffs are always a dangerous move. Retributions can be damaging, and the unanticipated fallout has historically done more harm than good."

President Clifton shrugged, looking around the room. "Okay, fair enough. What could Texas possibly do to us? Tax the export of BBQ sauce?"

Everyone chuckled politely at the joke. The Secretary of Energy waited, hoping someone else would speak up first. When they didn't, he cleared his throat and said, "Oil, ma'am. More specifically, refined petroleum products. A huge percentage of our national pipelines start in Texas at their refineries. Fuel oil, natural gas, gasoline, diesel… it all starts along the Gulf Coast and heads north."

"So you believe our tariff on steel would be countered with one on oil? Would they do that?"

"Yes, ma'am, I believe they would. I've worked with those people down there for over 30 years, and I am reasonably sure they wouldn't take kindly to trade restrictions."

Again, Aaron spoke up from his seat next to the president. "And what would be the impact of their counter-tariff?"

The SecEng spread his hands, the gesture indicating the answer was obvious. "Prices would rise."

Heidi nodded, a sly smile forming at the edge of her mouth. "And if prices rise, then consumption decreases – am I correct?"

"Yes, ma'am, but…"

The president interrupted the response, "There are many benefits to reduced fossil fuel consumption, and we all know that. Our carbon footprint goes down; alternative energy sources get a boost, and we keep our politically active, green friends working with our party. If the treasury receives a revenue gain as well, I don't see the downside here."

The typical arguments were floated, but it was clear to all that the Chief Executive had made up her mind.

Four days later, the White House announced a still tariff on all steel being exported from the United States.

The following morning, Austin countered, placing its own surcharge on all refined petroleum products shipped to the United States.

The Houston Post ran the headline, "The Tariff Wars Have Begun."

45595823R00231

Made in the USA
Lexington, KY
03 October 2015